398

Curial and Guelfa

Curial and Guelfa

translated from Catalan

by PAMELA WALEY

London
GEORGE ALLEN & UNWIN
Boston   Sydney

George Allen & Unwin (Publishers) Ltd,
40 Museum Street, London WC1A 1LU, UK

George Allen & Unwin (Publishers) Ltd,
Park Lane, Hemel Hempstead, Herts HP2 4TE, UK

Allen & Unwin, Inc.,
9 Winchester Terrace, Winchester, Mass. 01890, USA

George Allen & Unwin Australia Pty Ltd,
8 Napier Street, North Sydney, NSW 2060, Australia

First published in 1982

UNESCO COLLECTION OF REPRESENTATIVE WORKS
European Series

This book has been accepted in the European Series of the
Translations Collection of the United Nations Educational,
Scientific and Cultural Organisation (UNESCO)

British Library Cataloguing in Publication Data

Warley, Pamela
  Curial and Guelfa.
1. Catalan fiction
I. Title
849'.93   PC3937
ISBN 0-04-823217-3

Set in 10 on 11 point Bembo by Nene Phototypesetters Ltd
and printed in Great Britain
by Biddles Ltd, Guildford, Surrey

CONTENTS

For Emma and Peter,
Selma and Safiya

INTRODUCTION

Curial and Guelfa was written between 1440 and 1460, and it survives in a single manuscript which was identified in the Biblioteca Nacional, Madrid, in 1876. It has no title page and we know neither the name of the author nor the name he would have given his story. There are blanks in the manuscript where there should be the name of his hero's father and of his birthplace, but he is clearly an Italian although the book is in Catalan. The unknown author seems more familiar with Italy and France, and in particular with Burgundy, than with Spain and Catalonia, and there are obvious influences of French and Italian language and literature in what he writes.

All chivalresque novels are to some extent historical, purporting to represent the deeds and customs of a past time, remote or imaginary. *Curial and Guelfa* is set in an historical period identified by the appearance in it of King Peter the Great of Aragon, the hero of one of the great thirteenth-century Catalan chronicles, and of Charles of Anjou. They were rival claimants to the kingdom of Sicily and Naples in the late thirteenth century, a rivalry that still continued between Aragon and Anjou in the author's own time. Other historical figures take prominent parts in the story, including the King of France, the Dukes of Burgundy and Orleans, the Count of Foix, the Marquis of Montferrat; but often the author seems to have in mind the holders of those titles in his own day rather than in the time of the story. For example, there was no Duke of Orleans in the thirteenth century, but when the novel was being written the Duke was the poet Charles d'Orléans, whose father had been assassinated at the instigation of John the Fearless, Duke of Burgundy. Charles was taken prisoner by the English at Agincourt in 1415 and remained imprisoned in the Tower of London until 1440. His release was in fact due to Philip the Good, who had succeeded as Duke of Burgundy, and who negotiated his ransom and helped raise the money for it, and then provided Charles with a wife in the person of one of his nieces. The changing relationship between the two dukes is reflected in the novel.

History is mixed with a certain amount of fantasy, and the novel is given an epic element by the personal interest taken in Curial's career by gods and saints. Bacchus upbraids him for neglecting his studies, Apollo gives him a laurel crown, St. George gives him a cross. The author's determined display of classical erudition is a sign of his times: the Renaissance was dawning, the appeal of antiquity widening, and he carefully ensures that Curial is not only a valiant warrior but also a learned man. He is thus an appropriate mortal to adjudicate between the rival claims of Homer and of the supposed historians Dictys and Dares to have given a true account of the siege of Troy, and to pronounce on the relative merits of Hector and Achilles. But it would not have done for a Christian to take the pagan gods too seriously, and the balance is redressed by the comic scene in which Fortune berates Neptune, Juno and Dione for their unwillingness to help her persecute Curial.

The chivalric material is more varied than is usual in Arthurian romances and their derivatives such as the contemporary *Morte d'Arthur* of Sir Thomas Malory, and each fight is deliberately different from the others. Tournaments and single combat were features of aristocratic social life when *Curial and Guelfa* was written, and the readers for whom the book was intended would have been ready to appreciate these scenes. But the author is far from implying unqualified approval of such activities, and perhaps the most striking passage in the novel is an eloquent and impassioned condemnation of frivolous combat such as Curial and the author's contemporaries indulged in. Christian knights should not fight each other but the Infidel: the highlight of Curial's military career is his victorious command of the Imperial forces against the invading Turks, a reminder that the novel was completed within a few years of the conquest of Constantinople by Mohammed II. To some extent *Curial and Guelfa* is propaganda for a crusade, a cause dear to the heart of Philip the Good of Burgundy and his knights of the Order of the Golden Fleece. There is naturally a strong but generally unobtrusive religious element in the story.

Unlike traditional heroes, Curial has no giants or monsters to contend with, but neither has he magicians or enchanted weapons to help him, and his successes in the field are due to his superior technique and tactics. Above all, Curial and Guelfa and their companions are essentially human, their behaviour is far more complex than is usual in medieval fiction, and their story is for that reason perhaps more convincing and more endearing.

The author at one point apologises for the uncouthness of his style, and this is not entirely due to mock modesty. The translation has attempted to preserve the flavour of the original in this respect, as it has to be faithful in all others.

Curial and Guelfa

BOOK ONE

How great is the danger, how many the anxieties and cares of those who strive in the toils of love! Even if some are favoured by Fortune and after innumerable mischances reach their desired haven, there are so many who rightly complain of her that one might well think that of a thousand unfortunates only one will bring his cause to a glorious end. If the case that follows is judiciously considered, although there may be many who will say that they would wish their own loves to take a similar course, yet, knowing the certainty of pain which this bitter sweetness brings and the uncertainty whether the outcome will be felicitous or adverse, one should take great care to avoid setting out on this amorous, or rather, dolorous, path. This is the reason why I wish to relate what it cost a gentle knight and a noble lady to love one another, and how, with great struggles and afflictions, persecuted by many misfortunes, after a long while they achieved the reward of their endeavours.

A long time ago now, as I have read, there lived in . . . a gentleman called . . ., better endowed with wisdom and the goodwill of his fellow men than with those goods which Fortune assigns to man, for he was master only of a lowly house. With his wife, a very beautiful lady named Honorada, he lived apart from worldly affairs, modestly and honourably; but always they strove to win grace of their merciful Redeemer, and applied more continual diligence to this than to any other matter. Although they had no children when they were young, in their old age God wished to console them for this and so gave them a son, whom they named Curial, a child who from his earliest years was fairer than any other. His father and mother were so happy with him, they had yearned for him for so long, that nothing else in the world could have given them greater pleasure. But within a few years of his birth his father died, and the little boy was left fatherless.

Because of the great love she had for her son, the good lady was unwilling to let him out of her sight and indeed hoped that he would be content with the poverty which his father had left them; and so she kept him beside her. But in many poor men there is a noble heart. and so it was with him, and even in his infancy he despised such a life. Seeing that his mother was unwilling to let him go, penniless and on foot he ran away. He made his way to the house of the Marquis of Montferrat, who at that time was a young man and had only recently succeeded to the lordship and government of his lands, on the death of his father. He had a sister, a young girl of tender years, called Guelfa.

So Curial came to the court of the Marquis, who was staying in a castle of his called Pontestura, and stood among the knights and noblemen, looking at them to see if any of them would speak to him. When the Marquis came out of mass and found himself faced by this boy, he said to him: 'Whose boy are you?' 'Sir, I am yours', he answered. The Marquis halted and scrutinised him, and saw that he was very young, saw also his flashing eyes and such beauty in his face that nature could not better, and so he replied: 'It pleases me that you are mine'. And turning to those who were in attendance on him, he said 'By my faith, I have never seen such a fine-looking child, nor one that I like so well.' To Curial he went on, 'And you shall be mine, since you have given yourself to me – and even if you had offered yourself to anyone else, you would still have been mine'; and he asked him what his name was, and he answered that he was called Curial. Then the Marquis ordered that he should be dressed and equipped, and appointed him to his personal service, in his private apartment, as a page of his chamber.

Curial grew in days and in intelligence and in personal beauty in such a singular fashion that it was usual in the court, when anyone wished to indicate a high degree of beauty, to refer to that of Curial. And as it happens that when God gives physical beauty to someone He gives at the same time the goodwill of all those whose eyes behold it, there was no one who saw Curial who did not love him.

The Lord of Milan at this time was a young and noble knight who had a fair sister called Andrea. Hearing the fame of Guelfa's beauty, which surpassed beyond comparison the beauty of every other young lady in Italy at that time, although she was a young girl and had scarcely reached her thirteenth year, he fell in love with her, and entered into negotiations with the Marquis of Montferrat to the effect that, if he was agreeable, he would willingly give him Andrea to be his wife, if the Marquis would give him Guelfa. After long discussion, this was accomplished, and the Lord of Milan, sending Andrea to Montferrat, received Guelfa, to his great delight. She seemed to him even more beautiful than he had been told, and he fell in love with her so ardently that he had eyes and ears only for her and had no pleasure or repose unless he was with Guelfa. She was very wise, and sweet, and gracious in all her actions, and because her husband loved her beyond all measure, she had such power and ascendancy over him that he never did or commanded anything without Guelfa's knowledge. She conducted herself with such discretion that she was loved hardly less by her vassals than by her husband.

The second year of their marriage was not yet passed, however, when a great fever fell upon the Lord of Milan, and overcame him with such power that all the doctors agreed that he would die. So, in the presence of all his barons, he made his will and testament decreeing that Guelfa, with or without a husband, should be the Lady of Milan, and that after her the city should pass to whomever she wished; and while he was still alive he made his vassals swear to observe his will. So he passed from this life, and Guelfa felt incalculable sorrow; but eventually her tears yielded to the passage of time, and she began to mourn less.

Her brother the Marquis, seeing her young, tender, rich, and desired by many, and fearing that something undesirable might come of this, entreated her by letter to come to Montferrat, giving all kinds of excuses and reasons for the move. Guelfa, who was obedient, and loved her brother above all things which gave her happiness, at once set off for Montferrat, and she joined her brother in a town called Alba. She was received with honour by her brother, who assigned to her the most beautiful part of his palace for her residence. Often he would send for her to dine with him, or he and Andrea would go to dine with her. Thus for several years they lived in fraternal harmony.

★

Although the Marquis was very fond of Curial and pleased to have him in his service, he became so enamoured of Andrea, his wife, that he took no notice of anyone else, indeed, he was oblivious of every other thing. So the boy who had made such a notable entry into the Marquis's service was forgotten by his infatuated lord, and no longer favoured, indulged and made much of as he had been before Andrea's coming. So judging himself fallen from favour and rejected, he no longer strove to excel as he used to, but rather stood aside, which gave great pleasure to some of the envious people of whom the households of great men are always full. But because he was not lacking in good sense, the boy learned grammar, logic, rhetoric and philosophy, so as not to waste his time while he was in disfavour, and became proficient in these sciences, and he was also a

3

good poet, so that as his learning became known he became famous in many places and he was held in high esteem.

Guelfa, who was young and tender and lacked nothing save only a husband, knew herself to be pretty and much praised and rich and favoured by Fortune, admired and courted by many, and idle. But she saw that her brother had no thought of finding a husband for her, and she did not think it was seemly to ask him for one herself. Nevertheless, she could not resist the natural instincts of the body, which continually troubled her and goaded her without ceasing. She thought to herself that if it so happened that she came to love secretly some excellent young man, as long as nobody was aware of it, this would not be a shameful thing, and that a thousand and more other ladies had done this before her; and that even if some people might guess from signs what they did not know in fact, they would not dare to gossip about so great a lady as she was. And so she allowed her eyes to consider carefully all the young men in her brother's household. Since she was not concerned with blood or wealth, Curial particularly pleased her, above all the rest; and seeing that he was very refined in his person and noble of heart, and very wise for his years, she thought that, if he had the means, he would become a very worthy man. So she decided to help him, and from that time on she began to look out for him in company, and often called him to her, and talked with him very willingly.

This noble lady had a procurator, who received and looked after all the revenues of Milan for her, and administered them. He was a very wise man, discreet and estimable, fifty years old; and his name was Melchior de Pando. Guelfa loved this Melchior dearly, and entrusted to him not only all her riches but also all her secrets. One day, when she was discussing with Melchior the various members of the Marquis's household, they came to Curial. Melchior praised him highly, regretting his poverty and the Marquis's neglect of him, saying that in his opinion, if the youth had a little money he would undoubtedly become a man of high esteem. Guelfa, pretending to pity him, undertook to help him and to make him a man of importance in spite of his poverty, and there and then she gave orders to Melchior to take Curial to his house and, without revealing the true identity of his benefactor, to set him up and give him as much money as Curial could or would spend.

Melchior, who had no children of his own and was hardly less fond of Curial than Guelfa was, took him by the hand and led him to his home, and spoke to him thus: 'I knew your father well, Curial, he was a gentleman and a very estimable person, and a great friend of mine. I witnessed your entry into the Marquis's household, which has not gone as well for you as it promised to at first; and

4

things do not seem likely to change yet, for the Marquis has forgotten not only you, but himself too, and everyone in his house. Because I have no son or daughter or any relative to help me spend what God has given me, I have therefore determined, in order that my fortune may be of use to someone while I am still here to see it, to pass some of my worldly goods to you, here and now; and if I see that my gifts are not wasted on you, I shall make you master of far more wealth after my days on earth are ended.' And without waiting for Curial to reply, he took him by the hand and led him to a chamber where, opening a great chest full of Guelfa's treasure, he said to him: 'My son, here is part of my riches; take of it as much as you think you need to equip yourself as a young gentleman, and do not think that because you cannot carry away as much as you want this chest will refuse you another visit. It will always be ready to your command, and you will never take from it on one day so much that it will not be full again on the next, and indeed it will never be empty. But, my son, be wise, and remember that ranks are steps, to be mounted and reached gradually.'

The young man, utterly astonished by this unexpected happening, could not bring himself to move forward, nor dare to take any of the money. But the good old man took up some coins and gave him as much as he could carry, and commending him to God, sent him away.

Curial was so confused that he could scarcely find the way back to his lodgings, but when he had returned there, he began to put into effect all that the old man had told him. He bought fine clothes, and a horse, and engaged some servants for his household. Although he was already very well mannered, as soon as he began to rise in the world he grew also in virtue; and he left his old way of life, though that was good, and became very skilled and prudent, for he soon became a fine singer, and learned to play musical instruments (for which he became renowned), and to ride, and to write verses, to dance and to joust, and to exercise himself in all the other accomplishments that a young, valiant nobleman must acquire. And as he was very handsome in his person, and dressed very well, he was so courtly that in all the Marquis's court no one else was so much talked of; and this pleased the Marquis, and he thought that Melchior de Pando must have adopted him as his son, and given him all that the young man was spending.

Seeing her Curial grow in beauty and virtue, Guelfa sought his company more and more and encouraged him to become better and greater yet, telling him stories of how men through divers accidents often come to be great men from a lowly estate, especially those to whom God gives grace so that they are not downtrodden by their

5

poverty. By Guelfa's orders, Melchior spoke with Curial every day, spurring him on to do good, and giving him money liberally. And such was Curial's progress that the court talked of little else.

★

While matters stood thus, two elderly knights of Guelfa's household, seeing that Curial was so often in conversation with Guelfa and that his fortune and manner of life so prospered, deduced that this was due to Guelfa; and, driven by envy, they discussed it together, saying one to another 'Indeed, this lady has greatly changed her way of life from what it was a little while ago, for she used to be one of the most virtuous ladies in the world, and now she is quite changed. She no longer cares for our advice or our company, but misuses her wealth, giving it to that sly Curial, who will cause her to lose not only her honour but also her reputation. If this malady is not checked in its early stages it will grow, and we, who have nothing to do with it, may suffer from it – as we shall indeed deserve to do if we do not inform the Marquis.' They deliberated much over this, and finally decided that before they told the Marquis of their suspicions they would keep a careful watch to see if they could observe any sign of dishonest behaviour, and that only then would they speak to the Marquis.

The Marquis now saw Curial often, and told him of all his plans and pleasures, and seeing that his sister also enjoyed his company and conversation, he often sent him to her, which gave her great joy. The more she saw him, the more her love was kindled and grew warm, and it distressed her that he was unaware of it; once she told Melchior that she was afraid that the young man must be a coward. This state of affairs lasted for some time because Curial, not knowing that it was Guelfa who was giving him all that he spent, had not the same thoughts in his mind as she had. He sought to please her rather with witty sayings and jests, and he never gave any signs that he loved her, nor showed any awareness that she loved him. This caused the enamoured lady intolerable torment.

One day it occurred to her that it was only modesty that was depriving her of all pleasure, and since there was no other impediment she decided to try to overcome this and achieve her desire. While she was thinking this over, seeking a way to overcome her own cruel and inconvenient modesty, the Marquis sent Curial to invite her to dinner with him. She arose without hesitation, and ordering all her companions to precede her, she lingered behind with Curial, who had offered her his arm, and spoke to him thus: 'Ah, how wretched I am, how my love is wasted on you! Unhappy

6

that I am, I have loved you a long while, and given you all that you have received from Melchior, and in my thoughts I have made you lord of myself and of all my worldly goods. And you, crueller than Herod, ungratefully despise the gifts offered to you by love, which is kinder to you than you are to yourself! Ah, how unfeeling you are! Will you never hear the poignant words that I have so often let fall from my mouth in your presence? Oh, Shame, come to me, help me to fly from this insensitive creature, who seems to have no knowledge of people!' And as she said these words she could scarcely contain her tears.

By now they had reached the chamber of the Marquis, who received her with joy, and they sat down at table and began dinner. But the lady, thinking over what she had said, and wondering how her words would be received, could hardly eat anything, and said that she had only just got out of bed and had as yet no appetite. Curial for his part was pondering the words he had heard, and knowing now that it was Guelfa who had provided for all his needs, and was still doing so he was very thoughtful. He longed to answer her, and dinner seemed to be lasting a year. Although he was placed a long way from her, he kept looking at the lady whenever he could catch sight of her between those who were serving at table and those who were seated there, and he cursed all those who came between them. Whenever there was a gap formed by the movement of a head, or in some other way, the eyes of both lovers at once rushed to it, and when the gap closed, they lost all pleasure. So the meal passed for both of them, she without eating, he without peace. And in his noble breast, where no other impression of amorous delight had yet entered, there flared up a burning flame which could not be extinguished until the arrival of death. The meal ended, the tables were removed, and both were pleased. The lady lingered a little while, and then took leave of her brother and returned to her apartments, accompanied by many notable persons. When they arrived there she said to Melchior: 'Tell Curial to give you his reply to what I said to him today'; and turning to Curial, she said 'Speak to Melchior just as you would to me.'

So Curial went to Melchior's house and told him word for word what Guelfa had said to him, adding that he had suspected this for some time, and had been waiting for an opportunity to tell her of his passion, and that, since God had brought them to this point, he was hers to command; and he begged him to expedite matters so that the affair could be conducted with discretion. While he had thought that she would not be willing to listen to him, he said, he had borne his suffering, but now that they were both aware of how things stood, it would be harder for him to bear it. The old man, who for some time had realised that there was no way out but this, warned the young man, begging him to be careful and secret, and that he would need more wisdom in this than in any other undertaking, because already everyone wished themselves in his shoes and he was much envied and would be more so.

Returning to his lady, Melchior told her that Curial was born only to serve her, that she should command and he would only obey. 'Melchior,' replied Guelfa, 'I have set my heart on making him a great man, because I think he deserves it. To my mind there are many men whom all the riches in the world could not make good, and yet love alone can suffice to raise them up in a single day. It is true that my intention is to make him a man, but I do not intend to give him my love but rather to work to make him worthy and valorous by giving him to understand that I love him. So bring him to me at vespers, because I want to speak to him in your presence, and to set him on the right path.'

When the hour of vespers came, Melchior took Curial to Guelfa's chamber, and when they stood before her she began to speak. 'Curial,' she said, 'I decided to make available to you all my treasure, and without saying anything to you I have set you on the road to honour. It is true that I love you, and just as I have granted you what you already have, I will give you other things when I see that you must have them. In return I beseech you to find a way to increase your honour. You need not worry that money will be lacking; but I wish you to observe this rule: that you never ask more of my love than I am ready to give you. Besides this, be cautious and remember that if you ever reveal that you are my servant in love, you will lose me for ever, and I shall deprive you of whatever good you hope to have of me. Henceforward you cannot plead ignorance.' And with her hands on his cheeks she kissed him, and ordered him to return to his home.

Curial, contented beyond bounds, went home, and could hardly sleep that night, so full of happiness was he. However, when morning came, he went to mass and then went to join the Marquis, and spent the morning in pleasures, jests and pastimes. And when he thought it time, he went to see Guelfa, who wished for him more than for her own well-being, and spent some time with her, then took his leave and returned home.

The envious old men were at a loss to know what to do, for they could see nothing that was reprehensible except the frequent coming and going, and also the prosperity of Curial, which they thought was due to her.

★

8

One day, while matters stood thus, it happened that Guelfa, on her way to dine with her brother, had sent her companions on ahead and was bringing up the rear with Curial, whose arm she had taken. Thinking that this was a good moment, when no one could see them, she moved her head a little closer to Curial and gave him a kiss. Unfortunately it so happened that at that moment the two old men looked back towards them, in time to see those two, in whom love had produced this kiss, almost unaware of what they were doing, just as their heads parted. Without speaking, but muttering to themselves, they went to the Marquis's apartment. As soon as they entered, however, they went out again, and deciding together that this was sufficient occasion to carry out what they had so long wished to do, they determined to denounce it to the Marquis. So, having briefly considered what to do, they went to dinner, and spending little time over dinner, they returned to the chamber and waited there until the tables had been cleared and Guelfa, with a numerous attendance, had returned to her apartments.

Then the two old men took the Marquis aside, and one of them, named Ansaldo, who was a great orator and a fine speaker, with the leave of the other one, said: 'My lord, before my tongue utters a word, I beg and beseech you to listen with a pacific ear, and that the things I am about to tell you, although grave, will not move you to act until you can do so with due deliberation and care for your honour, which must be dear to you. It is our misfortune, which would to God had not befallen us, to have been in the service of your sister Guelfa, who for some time, while such was her will, lived virtuously and to your honour. This was pleasing to us because we thought that we could give you a good account of her honour, and we believe that if she had not come to your house, her way of life would have gone from good to better. Thinking to act wisely, you bade her come here, and we advised her to do so because we thought that her beginnings would be succeeded by improvements; and this would surely have been the case had it not been hindered by a devil, whom it pleased God should be born. This much is true: that we have endured with difficulty the dishonest and continued intimacy of Curial with Guelfa, expecting that we should see what we have seen. Many times we have been on the point of telling you, but thinking that this was your pleasure, we have up to now kept silent. We are not troubled that Curial prodigally spends and wastes her wealth, especially as we thought that this was supplied by your generosity, but what we have seen today, assuming reasonably that there is more to it, has disturbed us profoundly. Even so, did we not fear that if we kept silent the evil would grow and so our own guilt would be greater, we would not have spoken out yet. But today, just now, when Guelfa was coming to dine with you, she sent on ahead all those who were with her, and even us, who usually give her our arm, and she remained alone with Curial; and, turning to look at them, we saw him kissing her. This grieves us intolerably, thinking that we have come here in our old age to be panders. Please God that we, who in our youth lived virtuously, may not be robbed of the glory of our honour and good name by a nobody. And so we beg, warn and request you to take the opportunity to remove Curial in whatever way seems best to you from this lady's house, or give us leave to depart, for truly while this situation continues, we cannot see our way to remain here.'

The Marquis, who was wise and a good knight, believing Ansaldo's words, shook from head to foot, and was on the verge of rushing off without further reflection to do something dreadful to the two lovers. However, the other old man, whose name was Ambrosio, held him back, saying: 'Sir, do not be too distressed by what you have been told. Remember that he is a young man and that sometimes, however wise you are, you too acted as a young man. If these young people, driven by the power of love, or rather of folly, have done or are doing what they should not do, they are not doing anything new, but something that has been done by many wiser than they. So pause, moderate your feelings and think carefully, not in order to forget it nor to let it pass unpunished, but, I beg you, in order to act after consideration and counsel, so that you can better and more effectively protect your honour. Do not let those who have forgotten honour make you forget what is due to the wisdom that God has abundantly bestowed upon you above all other young men in Italy.'

At this, the Marquis, unable to listen further to the two old men, left them, muttering and shaking his head, and he shut himself into his room to consider what had to be done. That day passed and he scarcely left his room, but disturbed and pensive mused within himself, thinking many different things. The next day, accompanied by two young knights, strong and valiant, and by Curial too, and no one else, he entered a church, and taking Curial aside, spoke to him thus: 'Curial, up to now I have loved you and favoured you more than anyone else in my household, thinking that my honour was your concern and that to defend it you would face all dangers. Now I have been told that you love your pleasure more than my honour, and this surprises me greatly. You must consider that Guelfa is my sister and so I must be affected by all that is done against my honour in her person. If I were to act as a man in this matter, here and now, before you leave me, I should give you cause to curse her mouth which, yesterday, when she was coming to dine with me, you

10

kissed. The more you have received favour, honour and profit from me, the more I should be severe with you; but remembering that you have been brought up in my house since you were a little child until your present age, I am not willing to unmake in a moment what I have made with my own hands. Nevertheless, preferring you to be at a distance rather than close at hand, I tell you that you must leave my territory at once, and never return, and seek elsewhere someone who will bring your youth into a better harbour than I have your childhood.'

Curial, who had not expected this, at once felt his heart full of sorrow, and many things rushed to his memory at the same time. He thought that now was the time to show himself a man, so with a serene and undisturbed face he at once replied 'Sir, since I do not know who has told you this, I hardly know how to reply to you, but I will give you my true and simple explanation, and then, if the rank of the accusers merits it, these two hands will acquit me of the charge which is so wrongly and falsely laid against me. You can, if you wish, judge truly whether those who have told you this were moved by envy, or by desire to ingratiate themselves with you, for I, not knowing who they are, cannot tell. Guelfa, who is your sister, I believe to be a worthy lady, and I have no intention of defending her to you, for there is no need. For myself I say that if they are knights or gentlemen or men suitable to receive this reply, they lie falsely in their throats, and I will fight them hand to hand, one after the other, until I am quit from henceforward of this charge in your sight. If you have given me advancement, I think that for as long as I have been aware of this I have served you well, and I intend to serve you even more henceforth. It grieves me not to leave your house, but to leave your person, whom I have loved and love with all my heart, for you have indeed given me cause. Be sure that wherever I may be you may call upon my service as you have done until now, and yet better.'

When he heard this, the Marquis realised that Ansaldo and Ambrosio might well be moved by envy, for he really could not believe that Curial would commit such an error. So he replied 'Well, Curial, the great love I have for you persuades me to let these words and other things pass, and do no more about it, so, whether false or true, I will hold it as not having happened. But I beg you that if you have been truly accused you will take care in future not to fall into such folly, and if by chance it is not true, you will all the same beware of giving cause for talk about yourself, so that I, in order to defend my honour and avoid shame, do not have to do things that would displease me. And whatever has been said, do not think that you have lost my love, but I shall continue to regard you and treat

11

you as I have always done. The comings and goings to my sister's chamber, however, must stop, unless you go there in my company.' And turning his back, he would hear no more, and they joined the others and left.

In order to conceal the affair, and so that the envious Ansaldo and Ambrosio might know that he cared little for what they had said to him, when the hour for dinner came the Marquis ordered Curial to sit at his table and to eat with him. The old men were very downcast and considered themselves rebuked, but as they were extremely cunning and had no other course to follow save that of silence, they dissembled, waiting to see what the outcome would be.

Guelfa heard all that had happened through Melchior, and came near to quarrelling with her brother and returning to Milan. In the end she decided to remain silent, thinking that the matter would die down and be forgotten. But she suffered terribly because Curial no longer came to her rooms as he had used to. He continued to joust, which he could do better than anyone else, and she always watched him. The more she lacked opportunity to see him, the more her love burned and blazed. The days there was no jousting, Curial played pelota outside the palace, and so she could continually watch and see him.

Not many days after this, when the Marquis, with his wife and sister, was in a town called Casale, a herald arrived from Germany in search of a knight who was making the pilgrimage to Santiago de Compostela. He found him at an inn, lying seriously ill, and gave him a letter from the Duchess of Austria. In it she told him that after he had left on pilgrimage she had been accused of having committed adultery with him, and for this her lord and husband the Duke had condemned her to death. At the prayers of the Queen of Hungary, who was her cousin, it had been conceded that if he with whom she had been accused wished to defend her, he and a companion could fight the two knights who were her accusers in personal combat. If he won, she would be acquitted, otherwise the sentence would be carried out and she would be burned to death, and so die greatly wronged. When he received the letter, the knight, a very valiant man, was gravely ill and in such a state that it was impossible for him to go to aid the Duchess, and he at once felt unspeakable grief in his heart. Almost out of his mind with sorrow, he began to utter great cries and give vent to the greatest anguish in the world.

News of this reached the ear of the Marquis, and accompanied by Curial and many others of his court he went to visit the knight,

12

whom they found very distressed and afflicted. When they had greeted him they asked how long he had been ill, and how he felt, and if he had need of anything. When he heard this, the sick knight began to moan most pitifully. 'The sickness I have is this that has come upon me today,' he replied, 'which because of my misfortune I cannot remedy.' And he had then read the letter the herald had brought. When he heard it, the Marquis tried to console him, but the consolation he could offer was nothing in comparison with the sorrow the other felt, and after a while the Marquis left, still talking of his case and regretting the fate of the Duchess, who was a most worthy lady.

As soon as the Marquis went, the knight asked some of those who had come to see him who the man was who had stood beside the Marquis, and he was told that he was a very valiant young gentleman named Curial; and they told him secretly that a few days earlier he had been accused of a similar deed, with all the details of what had happened. The knight was silent, cursing in his heart all those who interfere in these matters.

When Curial had accompanied the Marquis back to the court he returned in secret to the sick knight, and as they spoke of many things, the herald joined in. 'Alas!', he said, 'What a pity it is that so noble a lady should be made to die through the envy of two wicked men!' The knight began again to weep bitterly, so much so that Curial, moved by his tears, wept too. 'I do not know you, knight,' he said, 'nor do I know the lady whom you say is wrongfully accused, but if it is as you say, and if you will accept my company, I will willingly be your companion in such a combat.'

The knight thanked him again and again, accepting him as companion in arms, and swearing an oath that this infamy was laid upon him against God and justice and the truth, and God knew that neither he nor the lady were at fault. Then Curial replied 'Bear up, knight, and look to your health, for since this is the case I am ready to defend the lady's honour, and your own, either with you or without you, as circumstances dictate', and taking his leave he went to his lodgings and sent word to Guelfa by means of Melchior. She was very pleased and at once sent to Milan for armourers to come and make equipment for Curial and the knight.

The sick man made a great effort and before long he was restored to health. Curial had liveries made, and trappings and other things prepared for the encounter, and was ready to leave long before it was time. The Marquis exhorted him to do well, and gave him some money, which Curial took although he had no real need of it. When the last night came, Guelfa ordered Melchior to bring Curial to her secretly and in disguise, and at the appointed hour Melchior with

Curial went to her chamber where Guelfa received them with joy. She asked Curial what preparations he had made, and when he told her in detail she turned pale. 'You have no need, Curial,' she said to him, 'for a woman as weak and of so little courage as I am to give you advice. I want only to remind you to remember that you are mine, and that there is nothing in the world I want save only your advancement and the growth of your honour. Because of this, and because I can see no better way for you to advance than through feats of arms such as this to which God has brought you, I accepted with patience, but not without a heavy heart, that you have offered yourself freely for this fight. The greater the danger and the fear, the greater the honour that will accrue to you from it. You have undertaken a just cause, and Fortune has favoured you in this, that you go to do battle for one who, as I have heard, is among the most noble and worthy ladies in the world, and who, together with that knight, has been wrongfully accused. Put your heart into it, for if you win your cause, as I hope to God will be the case, from henceforth no one will dare to speak ill of you and me, since he who defends the honour of another will defend his own with twice the spirit. Remember that you will be appearing before many kings and princes and watched by the most noble ladies in the world. Write to me often, so that I may know everything as well as the men who stand guard there. Do not let me die of longing for news of you, nor fear that you will want for anything, for I doubt whether you will dare spend as much as Melchior will give you.' And she put a very rich diamond in his hand, kissed him with lips already wet with tears and, commending him to God, told him to go. Curial wanted to reply, and had his mouth already open to speak, when she added: 'Go now, say nothing: remember me.' Sighing, he turned away and left her, while she stood still, watching him go; but as he lingered, her heart failed her, and she fell in a swoon to the floor. All her ladies came to help her and with many remedies they brought her round, and almost carried her to her bed. Curial, sad and sorrowful, returned to his quarters in tears.

Let everyone imagine for himself what were the thoughts and the many different reflections that occupied the two lovers that sorrowful night. When it was over and day had come, the German knight, whose name was Jacob of Cleves, rose early, and as soon as all his men were ready, mounted his horse and went to Curial's lodging. He found him already mounted, awaiting only the Marquis, who had sent word that he wished to ride a little way with him, and he should wait for him. When he arrived, they set off.

Guelfa heard the sound of trumpets, and asked what the noise meant. She was told it was Curial leaving, accompanied by the

Marquis and by many notable men, and that they were already outside the town but still in sight, and could be seen from the windows. 'Ah, wretch that I am!' cried Guelfa, 'Who can see them without breaking apart?' And although she was a lady of great courage and could well conceal her emotions, this parting she could not bear, but gave vent to her feelings in incoherent words. Nevertheless she was wise enough to make everyone leave her chamber, and all alone she wept over her grief for a long time. But she had great hope in the virtue of her valiant Curial and in the justice of the Duchess's cause.

If I were to recite in detail everything about the sorrow of the two lovers, it would make the book a very long one, and for the sake of brevity I will omit it. Wishing to write for your solace and pleasure, I will write only as much as seems to me necessary.

When Curial thought that the Marquis had come far enough, he turned to him and said 'My lord, you have done us great honour and have come a long way; turn back now.' The Marquis replied 'Curial, I pray God that he will allow you to return with the honour you desire', and taking his leave, they went their separate ways.

The knights continued their journey until they reached the kingdom of Hungary. One day, after they had journeyed into it for some days, on entering a city they came to a square where there were many people gathered together. They inquired why there was such a crowd, and were told that an old knight was about to be executed, accused of wickedly and falsely slaying in the street a very valiant knight who was lying dead in the square. 'Can it be proved that it was he who killed him?' asked Curial. They answered that it could not, 'but it is proved that there was ill-feeling between them, and that the dead knight had no other enemies, and that the old man had often threatened him with death. And now the brother of the dead man, a very valiant knight, has accused him. It is true that the knight who is accused has two sons recently arrived from Bohemia, but they dare not challenge the accuser, who has said that he will prove his case in combat against any knight who presumes to enter the field with him: the sons are cowardly knights, and do not dare to reply.' Curial said to his companions: 'Let us go and see if by chance we can do something to save the life of this worthy man.' 'Why should we interfere in other people's affairs?' asked Jacob. 'Let us look to our own and prosper.' 'So God give me honour,' replied Curial, 'I am willing to intervene in this matter, to see if I can do some good in it, so that this old man will not be condemned as guilty in his old age because he is powerless to defend himself.' And making his way forward, he saluted the magistrate in charge of the execution, who was only waiting for the old man to finish making his confession to a priest.

Seeing the strangers, the magistrate was anxious to do them honour, and approached them to return their greeting. Without more ado, Curial said 'What has this old man done that you are putting him to death?' Before the magistrate could reply, the knight who had accused him said 'He has falsely slain that knight, my brother, who lies before you.' 'You lie in your throat,' retorted the old man, 'I did not kill him, I know nothing about his death, although he did indeed deserve it. If I were the man I once was, I would make you take back your words. Ah, Perrin and Hans, you are no sons of mine! If you were, I should not have to die wrongly accused of a treacherous murder.' The two young knights, his sons, stood by in silence, but not with dry eyes. They were afraid of the accuser, who was a strong man, very experienced and renowned as a fighter. Curial said 'For God's sake, knight, pity his old age. When you have caused this knight, who cannot defend himself, to be put to death, what will you have achieved? Even if he is guilty, which he says he is not, it is a better vengeance to pardon than to do what you propose, with his sons here before you who through fear of you do not dare to defend their father.' The knight replied that he need not hope that he would change his mind. 'So God help me,' said Curial, 'I think that God means little to you, and still less does the honour of chivalry, which instructs you that you should not permit a man who has offended you to be punished by justice, still less one who has done you no harm.' 'Knight,' the other man replied, 'I am very surprised at you, and by what you say, but since you are so scrupulous in matters that do not concern you, and you see here his sons, who know the truth and so are not willing to defend him, take it upon yourself. I will be delighted to give you time to prepare yourself with arms for combat, and then you will learn what it is to fight against a just cause. As to what you say about it not being honourable for me to settle this affair by judicial execution, I cannot help it. Certainly I should prefer it to be done in another way, but since that is denied me, and his sons will not fill his place, I take the vengeance that I can, not that which I should like. It is indeed a greater shame for a family to have one relative die by execution than a hundred in combat.'

The old knight was listening to all that was said, and called out 'Ah, valiant man, whoever you are, have mercy on my old age! In my youth I took part in many fights to the death, defending not my own cause but that of others. If you have any claim to the honour

16

of chivalry, I beg you to show it now, for as a knight I swear to you that I am not guilty of what I am accused of.' Curial was on the point of accepting the offer of battle when his companion, Jacob of Cleves, exclaimed 'What are you about, brother? Do you think you were brought into the world to set right everything to do with arms that seems to you not well done? Be convinced, and let justice be done. He who asks for justice wrongs no one, and the magistrate would not condemn him if he were not sure that he deserves it.' The old knight cried out 'Ah, Jacob, I know well who you are! Do you not understand that by robbing me of the help of this noble gentleman you take my life? God grant that he be as much help to you in the combat you intend to undertake as you are now in mine! If you were such a knight as you think yourself to be you would not wait for him to offer himself to defend my cause, for you have many obligations to do so yourself, which there is no time to mention now; but I pray God may punish you for your ingratitude. And you, noble sir, who have pity for my old age, I beg you that if you wish to return with honour to those who long to see you, show your virtue now, and with your valorous person, which as I can see is more apt for such an undertaking than any other that I have ever seen, defend the justice of my cause. As for him who is trying to hold you back, I trust to God that not many days will pass before he has need of the aid which I ask of you now, and that, craving the succour of which he seeks to deprive me, he will find himself in terrible distress!'

When he heard these words, the blood leapt in Curial's heart, and looking the accuser in the face, he said 'Knight, I pray you, by the good and honour that is within you, let this worthy man live, who, even if you do so, since he is eighty years old, cannot live for long.' The accuser said that he would not, so Curial, changing his entreaties for anger, said to him 'Tell us, then, what you require of him.' 'Satisfaction for the death of my brother, whom he treacherously caused to be slain in the street.' Then turning to the old man, Curial asked him, 'And what is your reply?' 'That he lies in his throat, and if I had good sons they would defend me. So I ask you, as the noble gentleman you are, to defend me against the great wrong that is being done me.' 'With the help of our Lord God and his precious Mother, I shall defend you' answered Curial. And he turned to the accuser and said, 'Since neither God nor the Virgin Mary has prevailed against you through prayer, my lance and my sword will pray to you, and we shall see if you obey them. Prepare your arms immediately, for I will defend the truth of this man.'

Hearing Curial undertake to fight, Jacob of Cleves said to him, 'Curial, why do you promise what you cannot perform? You know that in a little while you and I must face two knights in battle to the

17

death, and you have promised me this; and now I see that you want to fight here. I tell you, if you had a hundred bodies there would not be one too many for my combat, if you wish to perform as you have begun, so many are the accidents that might befall us on the way. I beg you, leave this and come with me, and when we have done what we have to do, then you can defend this man – whom I myself would defend if I had not previous obligations elsewhere.' 'Jacob,' replied Curial, 'I see clearly that if this man is not helped now he is a dead man; his business cannot be delayed. Now that I have undertaken to defend him I would rather die than fail the word that I have just given. It is true that the law of arms does not permit it, but the need of this worthy man, and his spirit, which does not yet wish to leave his body, require it. So I pray you, give me time to free him, and I shall follow you at once.' Then he said to the magistrate 'I ask you to grant this man the time that our battle will last, and if by chance our Lord and the rightness of his cause help him, to restore to him the honour and reputation of which this knight wishes to deprive him together with his life.' The magistrate answered that he would do so.

The accuser went off to arm, muttering that he would do better to continue on his way instead of undertaking to fight in a matter that was no concern of his. Curial, more excited than one can say, hurried to his lodging and quickly unpacked his equipment, got himself into his armour, and choosing a strong and very handsome horse, mounted to ride off to the appointed place. Although he was a stranger Curial was well escorted, not only by his own followers but also by the friends and relations of the old man. As I have said elsewhere, Curial was one of the most handsome gentlemen in the world. He unfurled his standard, which was grey and black party, with a lion argent rampant across both colours of the flag; and he wore a very rich and fine helmet surmounted by a lion holding a bird in its paws: some said it was an eagle, others a milan, or kite. The two young knights who were the old man's sons came forward to carry the banner and the helmet, but Jacob shouted to them 'Leave them alone, shameless knights! God give you a bad death, for your baseness and great cowardice have jeopardised my own business. It would be better for you yourselves to take up arms and fight to deliver your father!' The banner and helmet were entrusted to two knights of Curial's company, and with an escort of minstrels and trumpets and a show of great gaiety they went to the appointed place.

When the magistrate saw Curial arriving he was very surprised that he had come so soon, and he exclaimed 'Never have I seen a knight with such a good seat in the saddle. Ah God, why did you not make me like that?', and to the old knight he said 'So God give me honour, you should be thankful that He has sent you help such as this in your dire straits.'

The accusing knight, whose name was Harrich de Fonteynes, was already in the field, making a show of fury at the delay in settling the matter. When they were about to move off, Jacob of Cleves came forward and said 'Harrich, you know that this gentleman has God on his side because he offered you peace, which you disdained. I beg you for Christ's sake, who forgave His death, to forget this quarrel, especially as it is not certain that this man killed your brother. If you will not do it for Jesus Christ, you will have God as your enemy as well as the knight who stands before you.' Harrich appeared more furious than ever, because he thought that it was fear made him speak in these terms.

The heralds began to shout 'Laissez-les aller!' The magistrate commanded his trumpet to sound, and everyone withdrew from the field; and the two knights began to move towards one another.

This Harrich de Fonteynes was a very good horseman, very strong, and with great confidence in his ability as a knight. Spurring on his horse, he rushed at Curial, who approached likewise, kicking with his spurs as hard as he could. When Harrich struck Curial he hit the shield and his lance broke, without shifting Curial from his saddle; but Curial, who was far stronger and more skilful, had a thick and stalwart lance in his hand, and struck him so hard that he knocked him from his horse. Harrich fell to the ground so heavily that he was stunned, and since he moved neither hand nor foot everyone thought he must be dead. No one spoke, however, but waited to see what Curial would do. When he saw that the knight did not stir, he dismounted and removed the helmet from Harrich's head. Harrich lay like one dead, and Curial gazed at him for a long while, until the knight came to his senses, and found himself on the ground and at the mercy of his enemy. Although he did all he could to rise he strove in vain, for Curial stood over him sword in hand, and threatened to kill him whenever he tried to get up.

Then Curial said 'Harrich, God knows that I have no desire for your death, for you have not offended me in any way. Acquit this old man, I beseech you, who is now waiting in the executioner's hands, to the great shame of all knights and gentlemen, and especially, if you consider with right judgement, to your own shame. I beg you again, if the prayers of a man who can give you life or death deserve to be heard, to withdraw this charge, and re-member that no requirement of chivalry brought you to this pass, but your own lack of judgement.'

Harrich, who feared that he might indeed have misjudged the

19

case, and fearing Curial's sword which was aimed at his head, replied 'For your sake, knight, I will hold the old man quit and believe that he owes me nothing; for if right had been on my side neither you nor any man would have overcome me.'

The officials, who had been listening to all this, ran to the magistrate who at once came to raise the fallen knight, and released the old man. Then the knights left the field, Harrich de Fonteynes going first, then Curial and the magistrate. The magistrate did Curial great honour that day, but the pleasure of Jacob of Cleves was still greater, thinking that with such a companion to defend the Duchess the battle would end to his honour.

What can I say of the old knight, whose name was Auger Bellian? He went up to Curial and knelt at his feet to speak to him, but Curial would not let him remain like that, and raised him up at once. 'Sir, knight' he said, 'I pray God to bless the hour in which you came here, for had you not come my head surely would not now be on my shoulders. I have in this country a large and rich estate which I wish to be yours, now and for all time. This is a small thing in comparison with what you have done for me, and I pray that God will reward you, for I cannot do enough.' With a cheerful face, Curial replied 'Sir Auger, I do not want your estate; in God's name let it be yours and your sons'. I am more than content with the honour that your righteous cause has brought me in this day's battle. Go with God, for I do not want you to be obliged to me in any way for it.'

He ordered his equipment to be packed, and the next day he departed. The magistrate was no sluggard, but rose early in the morning and joined Curial. 'Noble sir,' he said to him, 'I pray you, by the goodness and honour that is in you, to agree to let me join your company in this journey you are making and, if circumstances require it, to permit me to be a partner in your honours, for I know for sure that any knight in your company cannot fail to win honour wherever he may go.' Sir Auger too begged to be accepted as a servant, for he would not leave him for anything in the world. Curial, very content, admitted them into his company, and many others who went with him to watch the combat, and to all he gave whatever they had need of. Thus, when they reached the place where the Emperor was, it was a large and goodly company.

★

So by stages they reached the Emperor, who had heard that Jacob of Cleves was coming to defend the Duchess, bringing with him the young gentleman who had recently been victorious in combat, and he was very pleased. Many dukes and princes went out to meet them to do them honour, but more than for any other reason it was because they had heard that he was the most handsome and best fighter in the world. There was much fêting that day, and the Emperor kept Curial beside him, and could not see enough of him. He asked about the combat, and the old knight told the whole story while Curial wore a bashful expression, and would not look anyone in the face.

Then Jacob of Cleves, in the presence of many gentlemen, said to the Emperor, 'Sir, I have learned from this herald that the Duchess of Austria has been accused of adultery by two wicked men, and the Duke, believing them too readily, has condemned her to death for this. With the help of God, and confident in the righteousness of the Duchess's cause, I am ready to defend her together with this companion whom you see here. We pray that you will preside over the battle, for it does not seem reasonable that the Duke should be both the judge and a party to the matter.' 'Jacob,' replied the Emperor, 'the combat shall take place in my presence, and I will have the Duchess brought here, and her accusers, and the Duke as well.' He at once wrote to the Duke to set off forthwith, bringing the Duchess and those who had accused her, ordering them to present themselves before him on the day of St Mark, the twenty-fifth of April, because there were two knights who wished to defend the honour of the Duchess in combat.

The Duke was willing, and on the day named he appeared before the Emperor accompanied by many barons and other important people. Meanwhile Curial made himself known by his rich apparel, and by banquets and other festivities in which he spent freely, as he did also in making many gifts and keeping up a large establishment, so that he was held in high esteem.

The Emperor had had prepared a place where the fight was to take place, very fair and wide, surrounded by stands for the spectators, for many had come to watch from Germany, France and Italy and many other places. On one side, but outside the lists, there was a scaffold, very high, surrounded by firewood, on which stood the accused Duchess; and close by was a lit fire.

The Duke of Bavaria watched his daughter mount the scaffold, and said to her, 'Daughter, if you are guiltless of this crime attributed to you, trust in our Lord God that he will bring you out of it with the honour you merit, and you will obtain cruel vengeance against your accusers.' Her mother the Duchess, overcome with grief, wept bitterly, and so did many other noble ladies who had come in her company, and so did the Empress, who was her cousin. When the Emperor gave the order, however, everyone took their

21

places, cursing the two evil men who had brought her to such great and shameful peril.

Meanwhile the two accusing knights had come into sight, bearing a banner azure with foxes semé, and their horses had caparisons to match; and with a large company they reached their tent and dismounted. Not long afterwards Jacob and Curial appeared on the scene, with a standard black and grey party and a lion rampant in the centre, surrounded by an infinite number of counts and barons on foot, and a loud noise of trumpets and minstrels. Everyone in the stands turned towards them as they dismounted at their tent. The accusers had heard that Curial was a very good fighter on horseback and so, thinking that they would have the better of him on foot, contrived that the combat should take place on foot; and the others were content that it should be so.

When they emerged from their tents and the Emperor gave the order, the accusers entered the field, one of whom was called Otho de Cribaut and the other Parrot de Sant Laydier, and bowing to the Emperor, they made their way to their pavilion, which was azure with foxes semé. Immediately and without delay came Curial and Jacob, and as soon as they had entered the field, Curial looked for the Emperor and then approached him, and kneeling on one knee, asked him to make him a knight. The Emperor descended one of the stairways that led to his box, and going to Curial, he knighted him. When he returned to his place he said to the princes and lords around him, 'I think that I have knighted the most handsome gentleman I have ever seen, and if he is as gallant as he is handsome, I should not like to be one of the accusers!' Many things were said in praise of Curial on that occasion. When he had made his reverence to the Emperor and to the dukes and duchesses present, a great noise of weeping arose from the scaffold on which stood the Duchess of Austria, which made all the ladies and almost all the men join in. Curial was then cooling himself at the entrance to his pavilion, and when he heard this, he gave a great cry and leapt up into the air so high that all those who saw it marvelled at it, and then he went inside and sat in his chair. The pavilion was of grey and black party with a lion rampant.

The Emperor ordered the Dukes of Holland and of Lorraine, who were old and very wise gentlemen, to try to bring about a settlement between these knights, and to see whether the matter might be settled and the Duchess freed without a battle. So they began negotiations, and went first to the accusers. They told them to remember that they were Christians and that God was just, and showed his justice in combats such as this one, and they suggested that they should withdraw the accusation, which did not concern

22

them, and desist from fighting; or if by chance they knew of a way by which the battle could be avoided, they should speak, and they would willingly make use of it. The knights replied that they knew of no way by which the fight could be avoided save that the other knights should renounce the defence of the Duchess. So the Dukes went their way, and came to the other pavilion, and entering it, they greeted the knights and told them that they had been to the other pavilion and that they had certain knowledge that the battle could be avoided if they wished. They asked them if they would agree to this and find a way by which the matter could be settled. 'Sirs,' replied Jacob, 'I know no way save one: that these two knights should retract what they have said, and then the battle would cease.'

The Dukes replied that they could not return to the others with this reply, it was an embassy that they would not bear, and so they should think again; for that course of action seemed to them a dishonourable one. Many words were exchanged over this. Finally Curial, who up to that moment had kept silent, said, 'I beg, sirs, that you remember that you are knights and the sons of ladies, and give due regard to this matter. Since it concerns the Duchess, in whose defence we have entered this field, this combat cannot be avoided, we cannot leave it, nor is it right that we should, without great dishonour. If only our own interests were at stake it would be an easy matter to find a way to end the fight. But as things are, how can we let it go now that we have come so far? Look, if you please, as I am looking, at that sad and unfortunate lady who gazes at us on the one side and at the fire on the other. Let us make an end of words and do what we have come here to do, for it seems to me that this matter can have no honourable end either for us or for the others, save in battle. For myself I assure you that unless my companion renounces, which I do not believe he will do, I shall not leave the lists without fighting, and you will find me here either dead or victorious.' And Jacob agreed.

The Dukes did not return to the other pavilion but went to the Emperor and when he had heard their account he ordered the trumpet to sound. At once the knights came out, they were given battle-axes, the pavilions were taken down and out of the lists, and the Emperor commanded that everyone should leave the field except for those knights who were to do battle and the judges. And this was done.

Then the king at arms, by order of the Emperor, proclaimed at the four corners of the field that no one should speak or make signs, on pain of death, and he made the knights swear that they had no magic writings, stones or charms, or any device that could assist them save only their arms, which were axes, swords and daggers. Now you can say that as they looked at each other their souls were parleying with their bodies; and the Duchess, sad, wretched and in utter anguish was praying God to help her champions. So indeed were all the ladies and most of the men in the stands.

Then the Emperor's trumpet sounded and the judges led the knights to the place where they had marked the ground; and when the trumpet sounded once more, the knights moved in to attack. As they started forward the Duchess on the scaffold fainted and fell, but no one noticed or looked in her direction.

Otho de Cribaut advanced towards Jacob of Cleves, and at first they struck each other mighty blows with their axes, and then they began to use more cunning, to try to deceive the other, and they fought very valorously, for they were strong, very skilful knights.

Parrot, who was at that time considered one of the best and fiercest fighters in Germany, and who had many times engaged in mortal combat in the lists and had always come out with honour, rushed at Curial with his axe held low intending to strike him in the face with the point. But Curial, stepping aside a little, let him go past, giving him such a mighty blow on the basinet with his axe that the handle broke. As Parrot turned, Curial put his hand to his sword and they struck each other fiercely. After many blows had been given and received, Curial came close enough to Parrot to grasp him by the skirt of his armour with his left hand, and began to strike him with the tip of his sword as he pulled him and shook him now this way, now that. Parrot saw that the axe was no use to him in these circumstances and let it go, and taking his sword, began to defend himself bravely.

While they were thus engaged, the other pair had already dropped their axes and were grappling with each other. Otho was much stronger than Jacob and overcame him and threw him to the ground and was trying to kill him when Curial, seeing what was happening, took his sword in both hands and lunged at Otho's side as he was bending over Jacob, knocking him over on to his back on the ground. Then turning back to Parrot, who was about to hit him, he said, 'Ah, false knight! Did you think the field would be left to you?' And he struck him so hard, with such fierce blows, that Parrot knew he had much to do to defend himself against Curial. Curial, realising that his opponent was tiring and out of breath and could do no more, rained blows on him ever faster and then, letting go his sword, seized him with his hands, lifted him a little and threw him bodily to the ground. When he had fallen he was so tired that he had neither wish nor power to rise.

Turning round, Curial saw that the other two knights were again on their feet and fighting fiercely, but he brought this to a swift end,

24

for he seized Otho by the shoulders and span him round so that he fell again. Then Jacob ran for his axe, and before Otho could get up again, he struck him several blows on the head, so that he could not get up, but gave himself for lost, and despaired of his life.

Curial had by now removed the visor of Parrot's basinet, and Parrot lay stretched out, his face bathed in sweat, so weary that he could hardly draw breath or, consequently, speak, and he showed no sign of rising. Curial said 'Tell me, Parrot, what moved you and your companion to accuse the Duchess of such a shameful crime?' 'Ask my companion if he is alive, knight,' replied Parrot, 'for he will tell you. I know nothing of it, save that I am his companion-in-arms, as you are yourself.'

Then Curial looked towards Jacob and saw that he was about to kill Otho by thrusting his dagger into his eye, and he shouted to him 'Stop, wait; that knight must have another end.' And he said to Otho 'Tell me, disloyal knight, what had the Duchess done to you? Why have you brought her to this point?' 'She has done nothing,' Otho replied, 'but Jacob offended my honour and lost me the favour of the Duke, and not knowing what to do to avenge myself I thought that this was a way I could defeat him. I undertook this battle trusting in the ability of Parrot, and not expecting that it would end like this.' 'So the Duchess did not commit the crime of which you accused her?' asked Curial. 'No, indeed' replied Otho. 'Ah wicked knight!' said Curial, 'how little you know of God and the honour of chivalry!' The judges were called, and Otho confessed to them without constraint that evilly and with great malice he had accused the Duchess, thinking that the Duke would send soldiers to kill Jacob on the highway, not expecting that he would behave so cruelly towards the Duchess.

Curial said to the judges 'Well, sirs, have Jacob and I more to do on this field?' They replied 'No, what you have done already is enough.' The fallen knights were lifted from the ground, the Emperor came down from his stand and coming to Curial, took his hand and said, 'Ah, valorous knight, would to God that I were such as you and that you were Emperor! Ah, honour and glory of the world's chivalry, how grateful must all true knights be to you! The Duke of Bavaria could not, with half his duchy, repay the great honour you have done him, nor the Duke of Austria, not to mention his wife, with all he has in the world!' And turning to the others he said, 'And you, wicked knights, what punishment is sufficient to repay you for your ill deeds? Let Curial say what should be done to you.' 'God forbid, Sir, that I should seek the death of any knight', replied Curial. 'Here they both are, there is the Duchess, whose concern it is. Do as you please, for I wish no further part in it!' It was the hour for vespers when the Emperor ordered the knights from the field, and as the defeated knights led the way, the Duchess of Bavaria stood waiting at the entrance to the lists for these evil men. When she saw them, she ran towards them, her fingernails stretched out towards their faces, crying out 'Traitors . . .' but the gentlemen around her held her back and took her away. And so with their heads hanging low, heavy with shame, they were taken from the field.

The Duchess was brought down from the scaffold, and the two false knights were taken up on to it, the fire was lit, and they died a cruel and shameful death.

★

The freed Duchess, beside herself with joy, came to the Emperor's palace and asked to see her champions, and they were pointed out to her. She ran at once to Curial and cast herself at his feet, trying to kiss them. Curial was embarrassed and moved his feet away, and raising her up, he knelt before her saying, 'Ah, lady, for God's sake you must not make so much of the little that Jacob of Cleves has done for you, for he was bound to it by the bond of chivalry, and I and all other knights were and are obliged to it by our rank. But I beg you to seek my help in any future thing in which I can serve you, and I will do all that is in my power.' The Duchess and her mother and many other ladies were weeping for joy, and Curial was very embarrassed indeed, and in order to free the knights from the crowd of people who were thronging about them the Emperor led them into a private room and shut himself in with them and a few others.

A great supper was prepared and the tables set, and the two knights, especially Curial, were given places of honour at the table, and there were many dishes, splendidly served. Then the Duke of Bavaria wished to demonstrate his magnificence before everyone. He had a very beautiful daughter, a young damsel about fifteen years old, and by reputation and in fact the most beautiful at that time in all the empire of Germany. Taking her by the hand, the Duke went to Curial and said 'Curial, my dear friend, I do not know how to repay you for the honour you have done me this day except by giving you this daughter of mine as your wife, and begging you to accept half my land, over all of which you shall be lord after my days are ended.'

Hearing these words, and seeing the girl, who was indeed of extreme beauty, Curial blushed red all over; but before he could reply, indeed just as he was opening his mouth to speak, Melchior de Pando, who had arrived from Montferrat and for a long while had been struggling to get near him, with great difficulty and effort made a way through the press of people and in the presence of all handed him a letter written in Guelfa's hand. At once Curial lost all the colour that had come over him, and he lost too his power of speech, for as he tried to reply he stammered and his lips trembled so that they could form no word, and he was powerless to reply. The Duke was a very wise man and perceived that the letter had upset him, so he went on with what he was saying, adding 'Do not be perturbed, Curial, by the offer I have made you. I am returning with my daughter to my house, but I hold her as yours whenever it pleases you to accept her.'

The noise of trumpets and minstrels was great, and what with that and the people who were shouting, talking and whispering, if Jupiter had thundered they would not have heard him. When supper was over and the tables had been cleared away, the Emperor took Curial by the hand and with a cheerful air began to make much of him. Ordering that dancing begin, he asked Curial to dance. When a space had been cleared in the great hall, Curial obeyed the command and prepared to dance a simple dance.

But the Duchess whom he had freed came up to him and said 'Sir knight, it is true that you have saved me from death, for which I am more indebted to you, after God, than to anyone else in the world. You have brought me down from the scaffold, but you have not restored me to my husband, nor won his grace for me and I beg you to do this.' Curial, ashamed that he had not done this already, took the Duchess by the hand and began to lead her towards the Duke, who, hearing that they were approaching him, moved forward to meet Curial, and saluted him in a very friendly way. Curial and the Duchess knelt to speak to him, and the Duke hastily raised both Curial and the Duchess. 'Sir,' said Curial, 'I do not need to explain to you what has become of those two knights who presumptuously attempted to stain the honour of the lady Duchess your wife, and how the truth has come to light, to their great shame and hurt. The victory that has been won over them must not be attributed to my companion nor to myself, but to the justice of the Duchess's cause, which would have made victorious on this occasion the weakest knights in the world. I pray therefore that you will take her back into the love and grace in which you formerly held her.' To these words the Duke replied: 'Curial, it is true that my wife has not offended me in any way, and even if she had, if such a knight as you pleaded to me for her I could not say no.' And taking her hand he said to her 'Wife, kiss Curial, as the best and most valiant knight in the world, to whom you and I are so beholden that we shall never be able to repay him for the honour he has done us.' The Duchess kissed Curial and then the Duke kissed her. Seeing this, the Duchess's mother, who was the Duchess of Bavaria, came over to Curial and embraced him and made much of him, as did many other princesses and ladies.

Then the Emperor came over to that part of the room and ordered that everyone should move away and dance, and this was done. On the Emperor's command, Curial took the freed Duchess by the hand and danced a simple dance, followed by many ladies and gentlemen, with such grace and elegance that it was marvellous to see. The Emperor stood watching Curial's demeanour, wondering at what he saw, and he said 'I have certainly never seen anyone as competent both in the field and in the chamber as he. By my faith, it is a great loss to all the world that he is not a great nobleman. Cursed be Fortune that she has not set this knight in a higher estate!'

The dancing had already gone on for a long time and the night was passing, when Melchior de Pando went to Curial and said to him 'Curial, it is time to go to your room.' Then Curial remembered Guelfa: and turning to the Emperor he took his leave and went to his lodging, not without a large company of people to escort him. There he dismounted, and offered a great collation of costly sweetmeats, sugar and precious wines. More than half the night had already passed, and in the monasteries they were rising for matins to the sound of bells, and still some people would not leave Curial. At last Melchior suggested that everyone should go home, and so taking their leave they returned to their dwellings, still talking about Curial.

No sooner had they left his chamber than Curial, taking out Guelfa's letter, kissed it many times, and knelt on the floor to open it. He looked first at the signature, which said 'Your own Guelfa', and his eyes filled with tears; and when he had read it, his heart, which was hanging by a thread, was filled with so great a longing to see her that his blood rushed from it, his pulses ceased to move, he turned pale and fell to the floor, just as if his soul had deserted him. When Melchior saw this, and Jacob of Cleves, who was still there, they lifted him up and put him on a bed. They pulled his hair and his nose, and called his name but to no avail, for his spirits were far away. Those who stood by, overcome with compassion, lamented loudly, and with cold water and other means tried to bring him back to his senses. Eventually they succeeded, and when he had recovered he gave a great sigh, and without daring to speak at all, he began to weep bitterly, looking at each person in the face without a word. All present were amazed, and with kind words attempted to console him.

When he felt better he requested everyone to leave the room, keeping back only Melchior. To him he said 'Ah, Melchior, my father, how is the goddess of the world? Does she remember me? Ah, Cupid, whose weapons are firmly fixed in my heart! I gaze often at the heavens, and in the third of them contemplate your mother, the shining rays of whose splendour illuminate this overcast heart, promising me good hope. Tell me, if anything in the future is sure to you, whether I shall ever see again her whose slave I am, without whom I should despise and hold as nothing the sovereignty of the world. Tell me if she wishes me well and holds me as hers, as she told me. Ah, woe is me! How and when shall I deserve the good things she has given me and the honours she has done me, and does me every day? What counsel has won for me, what fates have decreed for me, that this queen of nobleness should raise me up at her expense?' Melchior, who had heard all this said to Curial 'Why do you behave and talk like a woman? Wipe your tears, which you shed too readily, they are unbecoming in a knight. Do not let good do you ill. Read your letter and do not moan before you have cause.'

So Curial read the letter and found in it words full of consolation, and promises of sure and certain hope which lightened his heart. After he had read it once and many times, he folded it into a very thin strip and bound it with gold thread and grey and black silk, and hung it round his neck. Later he had a case made for it in the form of a golden lion, with many precious stones and large oriental pearls, and wore it always, hanging on his breast. Such was the reliquary of the first letter that Curial received from Guelfa.

Having spent the rest of the night in this way, Melchior took his leave, and they went to bed.

★

Almost at once the day came, and the clear shining sun banished darkness from the face of the earth. As he got up, Melchior heard a loud noise of trumpets and minstrels and of many notable people at the door of Curial's lodging, and he went to Curial and woke him, saying 'Wake up, Curial, and get out of bed: look at the street, and the house too, full of people come to do you honour!' As he got up, the Duke of Austria arrived, accompanied by many important people, and at the door of Curial's bedchamber he cried aloud 'Curial, how are you?' Curial came out of his room, bowed to the Duke, and with many pleasantries they chatted away the time until Curial was ready.

The Emperor, who had passed a sleepless night, sent Curial these presents: a wide belt of gold with many valuable pearls and precious stones, which was worth a great deal; a golden collar, with pearls so large that perhaps none like them had ever been seen, and many diamonds and rubies; and he sent him also a very rich golden sash, and two robes. One was of dark green satin embroidered as follows: around the hem of the robe were trees whose roots, trunk and branches were of pearls, the moving leaves of fine gold, and the fruits, which were mulberries, were of precious sapphires, garnets and emeralds; and these trees covered the whole robe in such a way that the cloth was barely visible. The other robe was of black velvet, and round the hem was the head of a dragon embroidered with such great skill that it seemed to be devouring whoever wore the robe; its eyes were two large shining rubies of inestimable value. And in addition he gave him all his gold plate, and four fine horses, and ten hackneys.

This gift from the Emperor arrived just as Curial, accompanied by dukes and gentlemen, was about to leave his chamber, and it was seen by all, who praised the Emperor for his munificence, saying that he had acted very impressively in this. Curial went back and put on one of the robes and such of the jewels as seemed fitting, and he gave to the messenger who had brought them all that he had worn as a squire, for which he was much praised.

The Duke and Duchess of Bavaria, and the other Duke, their son-in-law, had arrived, and they conducted Curial with all possible honour to the palace, where the Emperor was holding a reception for the kings, princes, dukes and counts who were there, and a great feast had been prepared.

No one should be surprised that we say nothing here about Jacob of Cleves. It is not relevant to our subject to speak of him further, for we are here only to recount the deeds of Curial. In any case, although Jacob of Cleves was fêted, honoured and favoured, in comparison with what was done for Curial this was a poor thing, and so we will pay no more attention to it.

Melchior de Pando was very much afraid that Curial would not be bold enough to speak to the Duke of Bavaria about the suggested marriage, since it was such an important matter and a match that no king in the world could refuse. He feared that if Curial yielded, seeing the honour that was done him, the news would reach Guelfa's ears, and she would not have long to live. So with great difficulty, because of the throng of people, he managed to get close to Curial as he stood among those lords, and said to him in a low voice 'Curial, if the Duke of Bavaria speaks to you again, remember her who has made you a man. Remember Guelfa who, if you give her cause, will soon die, or else live a life of sorrow.' At the name of Guelfa, Curial looked at Melchior, his expression changed and he turned pale, so that the Emperor, seeing this, said to him 'What is it, Curial? Has something happened?' 'Sir,' Curial answered, 'this gentleman is as a father to me, he has brought me up and tended me and made me a man of substance at his own expense, always giving me freely whatever I needed. And now he has come here to remind me of a matter of great importance to me, for which I must soon return to my own country.' The Emperor turned to Melchior and did him honour. 'Worthy sir,' he said, 'never regret what you have done for this knight. Your old age and your possessions could surely not be better spent than by nurturing such a knight, whom I should rather be than anyone else in the world. If I can help you in any way whatever, tell me, and for love of Curial I will not fail you.' The old man fell at the Emperor's feet, and Curial too, all embarrassment, and kissed his hands, thanking him very much for his offer.

After this the Emperor sat down at table with the kings, and only Curial and the Duchess besides. Opposite there was another table, a very long one, where sat princes, dukes and great lords, including Jacob of Cleves and Melchior de Pando, and then other tables for barons and knights. The feast was a very grand one, they were splendidly and copiously served with many dishes and precious wines. I will not, however, relate the order of the banquet, because there is not time.

When they had dined, the minstrels came and began to sound their instruments, and the Emperor and Empress laughingly began a simple dance, followed by many people, and they danced many other dances. It was a great and cheerful feast that the Emperor gave that day, and everyone was impressed, for if all the kings in the world had been present there could not have been more gaiety and animation.

The Duke of Bavaria had not forgotten what he had undertaken, and when the party was over and the Emperor had gone to rest, he took Curial by the hand and begged him to sup with him. Curial accepted very willingly, and so he led him to his palace determined to fête him well. He ordered that at the high table there should sit no one but himself, the Duchess his wife, and Curial, and that only ladies should serve them, among whom the freed Duchess, his elder daughter, whose name was Clotho, was to be the mistress of ceremonies, and his other daughter, who was called Lachesis, should serve the wine.

This Lachesis was a damsel scarcely fifteen years old, tall and wonderfully beautiful, and that day she had taken great care in adding artificial beauty to the natural beauty with which God had endowed her amply and copiously, more than any other damsel in the empire of Germany. I will not waste time in describing in detail all the circumstances of her beauty, but he who wishes to imagine it must read Guido delle Colonne where he describes the beauty of Helen, and be content with that. Lachesis was no less lovely, for Nature must have set her forth in the world with great care, to make people wonder at her. Chief among her beauties were her eyes, more beautiful, lustrous and gay than ever had been seen before, and when she looked at someone, straightaway he forgot everything else and wished for nothing but to gaze at her. Thus with her eyes alone she kept many beasts in the pasture who, were it not for her, would have sought liberty elsewhere. Nevertheless she was so cold that no man, however handsome and valiant, could ever warm her heart nor could anyone in the world discover whether she inclined more this way or that. And many ladies who, if she did not exist, would have had suitors in plenty were thus constrained to honesty because of her. Besides this, all she did and said was done and spoken with so much grace and charm that she was admired above everything.

As soon as Curial set eyes on this damsel, therefore, and contemplated one by one all her beauties, he stole back his heart from Guelfa, to whom he had first given it, and prepared to present it to Lachesis. She in turn kept her eyes fixed on Curial, and within herself, impressed by his handsomeness and his knightly prowess, anxiously sought some novel way by which she might please him.

While the two of them were thus preoccupied, a noble damsel called Tura, who was preparing the knives for Curial and who no less than Lachesis was captivated by him, noticed this. Seeing that Curial was not eating, and being herself both fair and very clever, she said 'Curial, is it because you are looking at me that you forget to eat, or is it because my service does not please you?' Curial came to himself again at this, and taking his eyes from the lady on whom they were fixed, he stretched out his idle hand to the dish and made a show of eating. The Duchess said 'Tura, you have done me a service, and inspired him!' Tura laughed and replied 'Lady, I would have done it earlier but I feared the custom of his country, for it is said that if anyone invites them they go away; so I said nothing.' The Duchess laughed long, and Curial, seeing that they were laughing at him, laughed a little too; but he could not answer. He ate a little and drank less because he dare not ask for more, for then Lachesis, in order to serve him with wine, would have to come behind him. The Duchess however ordered Lachesis to take drink to Curial.

Now that day she was wearing a dress of white damask lined with ermine and embroidered all over with eyes, from which came golden loops worked in various ways. And although the loops were empty, certainly many had been caught in them, Curial among

32

them, who was caught by a noose so fast that he was powerless to escape. Lachesis, escorted by many knights and ladies, went for the goblet and presented it to Curial. He realised that it was very significant for him to receive it from the hand of Lachesis, yet it seemed even more so to refuse it and leave her to hold it, so reaching out his hand, he took the goblet and drank. As Lachesis received back the goblet the Duchess, her mother, said to her 'Lachesis, drink the rest for love of Curial.' And she did so.

Then said the Duchess 'Curial, what do you think of my daughter?' 'Madam,' he replied, 'I think you have the most beautiful and most charming daughter in the world.' 'And what pleases you most about my daughter?' the Duchess went on. 'Madam, everything that I see in Lachesis is the most beautiful of its kind in the world,' replied Curial, 'but her eyes are so beautiful that I cannot believe that God could make others like them ever again, and her gown certainly suits her face.' So talking of this and of other things, the supper came to an end. I will not linger to describe the dishes nor to name the guests; be assured that nothing was lacking that might ennoble the banquet.

After the tables had been cleared away, the Duke ordered his daughter to sit beside Curial, which made him more happy than anything else that could happen to him. There were present besides many counts and great barons and their ladies, and numerous damsels, and they played cheerfully all manner of games such as are customary at such feasts in great courts. After much of the night had passed, everyone went away, but the Duke would not let Curial leave his palace that night and ordered that he should sleep in the chamber in which Lachesis usually slept, which was very richly furnished. Melchior de Pando had not yet been able to say a word to Curial, so surrounded was he by ladies and damsels who were escorting him to his chamber, and with some displeasure, but with a good escort, he returned to his lodging.

When Curial had gone to his room and taken some refreshment, the Duchess said to him 'Curial, here is Lachesis's bed: sleep well, and take care that you have no bad dreams.' 'Madam,' answered Curial, 'I am sure this bed is a comfortable one, but do not believe that I shall find sleep or rest in it.' Understanding Curial's words, the Duchess laughed, and taking her leave, went off with all the other ladies.

When Curial remained alone with his attendants, finally free of all the people who had been encumbering him, he looked around Lachesis's chamber, and saw that it was very richly furnished with all the things that were fitting for such a lady. Amongst other things there was on one side an altar, with an altar-piece of St Mark, very

33

finely worked. As soon as he saw St Mark, with his lion, he remembered Guelfa, and at once forgot Lachesis's eyes and found himself at fault. Kneeling before the altar, he said in a low voice 'Ah, wretch that I am! Where am I? What wind has carried me from one country to another? Oh unfortunate man, oh man of little wisdom! What have I done? What penance can suffice to purge so great a crime as this that I have committed? Ah, disloyal heart, what have you thought? Ah, false, treacherous eyes, why do I not tear you from my face so that you do not steal me again from her whose I truly am?' And mingling infinite sighs and tears with these words as he remembered the great offence he had committed against Guelfa in looking at Lachesis with longing eyes, he longed to cry out aloud, but fearing that those who were in the room might hear him, he dare not speak.

So rising from the altar, he went to the bed, which was very richly covered with a coverlet of white damask lined with ermine and embroidered with eyes and golden snares in the same way as Lachesis's gown had been. The curtains were of the same damask, with the same embroidery, and looking at the bed, Curial marvelled greatly not only at the beauty of Lachesis but also at her cleverness, so that he now thought that there was no more beautiful nor more clever damsel in the world.

And while he was musing thus, his sighs forgotten, he looked round and saw a closet, which he entered. This was where Lachesis usually coiffed herself and performed her toilet. It was well hung with satin, and in it there was another pretty and well-appointed bed on which he found all Lachesis's jewellery. There were ornaments of pearl for her forehead, earrings, necklaces, pendants, sashes, chains, belts, bracelets, brooches, rings and many other jewels of gold, with pearls and stones of inestimable value. Among the other things, one that he admired very much was a large brooch with big pearls and rich diamonds, in the centre of which was a lion whose eyes were two very fine rubies. Its breast had an open wound and from this there came a ribbon on which were engraved letters which read 'The heart that desires knows no rest'. The sight of this lion, however, did not have the same effect as that of the altar-piece, for it failed to remind him of Guelfa, but looking round him and examining all the jewels one by one, he said to himself 'Indeed, nothing less precious would become so noble and so fair a lady.'

While he was examining the jewellery the night passed without Curial being aware of it, until his attendants said to him 'Curial, before long it will be dawn.' Then Curial undressed and got into bed, and no sooner had he done so than he fell asleep as though he were in a coma. And in this sleep, as he dreamed, there came to him a vision.

There appeared to him a young boy, very poor and quite naked, without any protection, and as he went begging alms from house to house he found no one who would give to him or show him any pity, so that it seemed he must die of hunger. And as he was gasping for breath and at the point of death, he saw a lady, so fair that Venus herself would have been pleased to have such beauty as hers. This lady was dressed all in black, in widow's weeds; and before the boy had begged alms or even dared to speak to her, for so great was the reverence she inspired, she cried out to him 'What do you want, boy?' The boy answered 'Lady, I am dying of hunger and cold.' At once the lady took off her gown and wrapped him in it, and it seemed to Curial that this helped him. Then she raised her hand to her breast and tore out her heart, and said to him 'Eat this bread and be content, for it is enough to satisfy your hunger.' And the boy ate the heart and it seemed to Curial that there was no sweeter food in the whole world. And as he ate it, he saw him grow and become a handsome man of fine stature. Then the lady said 'Eat well and be satisfied on this condition: that if ever you see me dying of hunger, you must take pity on me.' The boy promised, and that done, he went away; and there remained Curial and the lady.

After this, it happened that he seemed to see this lady in a state of poverty, sad and deeply afflicted, her hair all dishevelled and loose, her face pale and sorrowful, and so thin that there was no flesh between skin and bone, as though she were dying of hunger; and he saw her asking for food from the man to whom she had given all he needed, and he would give her nothing, but turned his back on her and forgot her entirely. The lady, seeing such ingratitude, lost all her strength and, not knowing what she could do nor wanting to take anything offered to her by anyone else, she was at death's door, especially when she saw that wicked man giving to another lady the bread that should be hers to eat. Curial felt like killing him. After this, he saw the heavens open and Phoebus, who sees all things, telling Venus of this ingratitude. She at once sent her son Cupid to bring help to the lady, who stretched his bow and let fly two shafts, one of lead, the other of gold. With the leaden arrow he struck the lady in the middle of her heart, with that of gold the ungrateful man, and so deeply were they wounded that the lady fell asleep, while the man suffered in agony, in the greatest possible pain, and longed for death but could not attain it.

The dream lasted a long time, and meanwhile the day came and the sun, opening its eyes, gilded the face of the earth. Curial was still sleeping when Melchior de Pando came to his room, knocked and was admitted. He entered, and finding Curial asleep, woke him, saying 'You sleep too much, Curial.' At this, Curial sat up in bed, as confused as though he had just returned to life from death, and said 'Father, you have rescued me from great trouble, for I was about to kill the most ungrateful, inconsiderate man the world has ever seen.' And he told him the dream, word for word. Melchior, nodding his head, said only 'Ingratitude is a bad thing, indeed I think that it is so great a sin that a man can rarely or never atone for it.' Curial did not understand what Melchior had meant, but he rose very quickly from his bed. Just then the door of his room opened and in came one of Lachesis's attendants, accompanied by several other damsels, and presented to Curial the white gown that Lachesis had worn the previous day. 'Curial,' she said, 'Lachesis sends you her greetings, and says that at supper yesterday you praised her eyes. If they could serve you or give you any pleasure when removed from her, she would have torn them from her head without regard for her hurt, but since she knew that they would be no use to you and that she would miss them very much, she refrained from doing so. However, she sends you these from her gown, begging you, if you would have her live, to make from them doublets for yourself and to wear them when you see her.' Curial took the gown with great delight and rejoiced in the gift more than he could say. Uttering a thousand thanks, he replied that he would do as Lachesis commanded, and sent her his greetings.

At once he sent one of his servants to have the gown made into doublets, as he had been asked, which was done immediately. From that time on Curial wore only the doublets that had been made of that cloth. Melchior, observing this, remarked 'Curial, that damsel may have the name of Lachesis, but she is surely Atropos, and in time you will discover this.'

★

The honour with which Curial was treated, which increased from day to day, made him not only forget everything about Montferrat, as though he had drunk the whole river of Lethe, but even to despise it to the extent that although Melchior urged him to return there Curial did nothing about it, but lived so happy that he would have liked these festivities never to end.

The Duke had left his chamber and mass was about to be said when Curial came out. The Duchess and Lachesis advanced to meet him, and as soon as the damsel saw him a change came over her, she lost her usual composure and as though she could not control herself she stammered 'Curial, God give you good-day'. No less stirred by

36

the beauty of Lachesis, Curial embraced her and took her arm. The Duchess asked Curial 'Did you sleep well last night?' and Curial answered that he had. And so they went to mass. The Duke showed Curial great honour and continued to hope that Curial would ask him for Lachesis as his wife, since he had offered her to him, but Curial, in spite of all he saw, could not really believe that he would give her to him and moreover, remembering Guelfa, he did not dare put himself forward. And so he hung back and did not presume to utter a word on the subject. Perhaps if the Duke had asked him once more he would have seriously considered it, but the Duke thought it would be shameful to raise the matter again, and so it never came to pass.

They heard mass, and when the pax was passed round the Duke took it and called his daughter, and kissing it, gave it to her saying 'Fair daughter, go to Curial and give him the pax.' Lachesis did as her father bid her and gave it to him; and when Curial and Lachesis had kissed it, both were so full of emotion that it was clear to everyone that they were in love, for Lachesis turned crimson and trembled like one who had never loved before, and Curial was all confusion. As she returned, stumbling, to her place, her strength failed her and she seemed powerless to move. Perceiving this, Jacob of Cleves hurried to her and helped her to walk, with some difficulty, back to her place; and still, as she went, a girl newly in love and unable to conceal her emotions, twice she turned back to look at Curial. At last she reached her mother's side, and as the Duchess welcomed her she said 'You have grown very pale.' 'Madam,' said Lachesis, 'all this morning I have felt a weakness in my heart so that I am afraid I may faint, and just now I felt it more strongly than ever. If Jacob of Cleves had not come to my aid, I should have had to sit down before I reached you here.' The Duchess helped her to sit down, and laying her hand on her breast found that her heart was beating so fast that she was amazed, but her pulse-beats were very weak, for no matter how hard her arms were rubbed no movement could be felt in them.

When mass was over, everyone gathered round the Duke, and so escorted him to his apartments. When all had entered, there arrived a messenger from the Emperor to say that Curial was to go to him and was expected for dinner, and that he had some good news for him. So Curial took his leave of the Duke and Duchess and of Lachesis too, and made his way to the Emperor's residence.

As Curial set off, Lachesis gazed after him, and as soon as he had disappeared from her sight, her spirits left her, and with a trembling voice she turned to her mother and said 'Madam, I am dying.' Then, losing all her colour, her lips going quite white, and covered with a cold sweat, she fell. Her mother the Duchess cried out, and with cold water and other remedies tried to bring her back to her normal state, but as this had no effect, her mother, who was an experienced lady and knew well what was the cause of this sickness, called to her 'Lachesis, see, here is Curial!' No less than Thisbe at the name of Pyramus, Lachesis opened her eyes at the name of Curial, and stretched out her arms and raised her head. Her mother kissed her many times, but when Lachesis realised she had been deceived she asked, unable to conceal her passion, 'Where is he?' Her mother answered 'Daughter, he is here, and says that you must exert your-self to recover, or he will die.' Then they lifted her up and put her to bed.

Curial had not yet reached the Emperor's palace when there came a messenger from the Duchess for him. Melchior recognised him and asked him 'What do you want?' 'Sir,' said the messenger, 'no sooner had Curial left than some misfortune, I do not know what, befell Lachesis, and she fell seeming dead, and if they had not brought her round again by uttering Curial's name, she would certainly have died. So the Duchess begs him to return so that Lachesis will not die through not seeing him.' 'Go back to the Duchess, friend,' replied Melchior, 'and tell her that Curial knows, and would willingly return were it not for the urgency with which the Emperor requires his presence. As soon as he learns what the Emperor wishes, he will do as the Duchess commands.' And so the messenger returned without Curial knowing what had happened to Lachesis.

When he reached the Emperor's chamber, the Emperor greeted him with great warmth and said to him 'Curial, listen to what this herald has to say.' When Curial asked him, the herald replied 'Sir knight, I have come here to proclaim that the King of France has ordered a tourney to be held at Melun, to take place in six months' time, in which the King in person will participate. It will be divided into four parties, that is to say, the knights who come to the tourna-ment, if they are in love with widows, shall have ornaments of grey and black; if they love married ladies, of purple; if damsels, of green and white; and if they love nuns, of green and grey. So it will be known of each what manner of lady they love. Know, moreover, that the Duke of Brittany and the Duke of Orleans, who are young and very valiant knights, will ride out on the first day of June, with the King's leave, each with two hundred knights of his household, and in the manner of travelling knights, or knights errant, will go out into the countryside to fight any knight who is travelling to the tourney whom they may meet on the road. Any knight who does not travel as a knight errant will not be admitted to the tournament, nor will any honour be shown him, nor will he be held to be a knight. I assure you that many dukes and counts and other great lords, knowing of this, are making preparations for the first day of June, as I have said, to ride forth and increase their honour.'

When Curial heard this, his blood bubbled within him, and the Emperor embraced him warmly and said to him 'I do not think that you will be absent on that occasion.' 'I am not my own master, sir,' replied Curial, 'and so I do not know what I shall be ordered to do.' And turning to the herald, he said 'Tell me, friend, if the knight who goes to the tourney has never had a beloved, what should he wear?' 'White.' 'And if he has had one,' Curial went on, 'and now has no longer, what should he do?' The herald answered 'Let him have all black ornament'. The Emperor laughed and said 'I do not think, Curial, that either of these styles of ornament will do for you. But now we shall see how those who make it clear to all will declare themselves.'

Dinner was ready, and they took their places at table. When they had eaten, the Emperor retired and Curial went to his own lodging and found prepared for him in his room Lachesis's bed, in which he had slept the previous night, with all its hangings as he had seen it. He was delighted with this, but Melchior certainly was not and indeed felt as though a flame had struck him in the face. However, knowing that Curial was afire with love for Lachesis, he thought that if he tried to draw him away from her suddenly, he might break with him and he would have achieved nothing. So he determined to bring him to realise the situation gradually.

Accordingly he said 'Ah, what pleasure Guelfa will have, and how happy she will be in her heart when she hears of the honours you have won, not only in the battle but after it. I believe that there will be no happier lady in the whole world. So, Curial, I beg you to leave this country and as soon as you can get away from here, in the name of God, let us go. It is the act of a wise man to leave while the welcome is still warm and not wait for it to cool and disfavour befall him. Besides, you know that this tournament has been proclaimed, so let us go and see what Guelfa commands you to do. I take it as certain that although the Emperor himself is going he will be hard put to it to go as well and richly equipped as you will be, even if he may have more people in his company.'

Curial gave every appearance of having great pleasure in what Melchior was saying, and replied 'Alas! when shall I see her? Shall I live long enough, and will God give me grace, to make her honoured above all ladies in the world as she above all others deserves?' Melchior replied 'Curial, take leave today of the Emperor alone, and go from here: for guests and fish stink after three days.

When people see you staying on here, idling and wasting time, your honour will suffer. In God's name, return to the place you came from. If you go now, you leave behind you the reputation of the most noble knight in the world, which you could lose in a moment by some accident against which a man cannot protect himself.' 'All you say is true,' answered Curial, 'but to take leave in such haste would be a discreditable thing to do. But I beg you, prepare all my people so that I can soon go back to Montferrat, and meanwhile I will take my leave.'

While they were thus engaged a messenger came from the Duchess. He saluted Curial and said 'Lachesis is now much better, sir.' 'But what has been the matter with Lachesis?' asked Curial. 'Sir,' answered the messenger, 'after you left the Duke's residence, she fell into such a deep swoon that until just now she was thought to be dying; but now, thanks to God, she is in good health.' 'By my faith,' replied Curial, 'until this moment I knew nothing of it.'

He mounted his horse at once, and rode to the Duke's residence where he was received with great honour. He was conducted to the chamber where Lachesis lay, and as he entered, she saw him and at once losing all her strength, she fainted. The Duchess cried out 'Ah, Lachesis, my daughter! My daughter, Lachesis!' And she asked Curial to give her a kiss, which he did, and after he had kissed her many times, she regained her senses. 'Ah, Curial,' she said, 'I was afraid that I was dying, and I sent for you, and you would not do me the kindness of letting me see you.' Curial set about excusing himself, saying that he had known nothing about it. The Duchess then called the messenger whom she had sent, and he explained that he had told Melchior de Pando. Curial insisted, with an oath, that he had not told him and that he had heard nothing at all about it. And his heart grew extremely angry, and were it not for the great love he had for the old man, Curial would certainly have shown how annoyed he was by this incident. However, as Lachesis was already better and quite well, Curial took his leave graciously, and told Melchior that another time he should not vex him so.

The livery was made as Curial wished, but he always wore doublets made from Lachesis's gown. He began to send off his baggage, and he had made for himself a gown of black Flemish cloth on which was embroidered a hooded falcon mewing, or changing its feathers, so nothing remained save for him to exchange farewells.

Going to the Emperor he took leave of him, upon which the Emperor showed him great favour, asking him to pay him a visit and to write to him if there was anything he could do for him, saying that he would rather do a favour for him than for anyone else in the world. He also took leave of the Empress; and the Duke of Austria, knowing that Curial was leaving, came to give him valuable presents, begging him to make use of his services in whatever way he pleased, and he also gave him a sword whose ornamentation could not be easily valued. And so he took leave of him and of the Duchess, and went next to the residence of the Duke of Bavaria to make his farewells.

As soon as he arrived there, Lachesis, who knew that Curial had come to say good-bye to her mother and herself, went forward to meet him, and begged him to listen to what she had to say. Accordingly they went apart from everyone else, and Lachesis began thus: 'Curial, the necessity in which I find myself has banished shame from me so that I am forced to say what I would willingly have concealed. But because I think that any lady or damsel who loves or wishes to love needs no excuse if she chooses a noble and valorous man who befits her own nobility, I am emboldened to speak, and whatever may come of it, such is my condition that if I tried to behave in any other way, I could not. This much is true: that I have never loved any man in the world, nor has my heart ever inclined to love anyone. But now it is completely changed and beyond my own control, and in your power. I beg you that, since my heart is yours to command, you will treat it well so that it does not perish and I with it. We have deserved as much, I think, by wishing you so well.' And so saying, she was unable to hold back her tears, and she wept bitterly.

'Lady,' Curial replied, 'there is nothing that I would not do more readily in your service for any damsel in the world; when the occasion arises you will find me as you desire, and so I shall treat your heart well. I beseech you, treat me well too, who suffer no less pain on your account than you say you suffer on mine.' Having said this, he took leave of them, receiving gifts of inestimable value. So he bade farewell to the other lords and ladies, mounted his horse, and rode away on the beginning of his journey.

When she saw Curial go, Lachesis began to be very sad, and her mother said to her 'Daughter, do not let this knight's departure grieve you. For your sake I will make sure that the Duke and I go to the tourney, and we shall see him there.' 'Madam,' answered Lachesis, 'it is true that it would be some consolation to be sure of going there and of meeting Curial again, but by what God can I be sure of having sufficient strength not to die for him before then?' 'There is no need for you to do so', said her mother. 'Be cheerful, and remember that all the most beautiful damsels in the world are certain to be there and you must do your best to be ready to appear among them. Make sure that sorrow does not have the power to rob you of your beauty so that, through your own fault, nobody will

41

talk about you, and he who now has you in great esteem will prize you little. Love does not care for a sad or morose heart. Cheer up, and send him something to wear for your sake in the tournament so that you will be able to recognise him.' Lachesis dried her eyes and thought about the tournament, and from that time on did all she could to increase her beauty, as her mother had advised.

★

We have said a great deal about Curial and Lachesis and have ignored Guelfa, who was suffering not a little from her longing to see Curial, praying and fasting continually for his safety, and hearing three masses every single day. When the first letter reached her with news of the combat he had won to free the old man, she was very pleased and rejoiced in her heart. The Marquis too celebrated this event in his house, and said many things in Curial's favour which also gave Guelfa great joy, though she did not show this openly, saying that, as experience showed every day, it was not surprising that a valiant and strong knight whose cause was bad should be vanquished by another less valiant. All the same, as much but as discreetly as she could, she made sure that the feat was talked about, and found great solace in this, and had no other pleasure save to hear people discussing Curial.

However, since one piece of news makes others forgotten, more news arrived concerning the festivities the Emperor had ordered on his coming, the great banquets there had been, how no one else was so talked about, and what rivalry there was to do him honour. You may well think how pleasing all this was to Guelfa, so much that she could scarcely hide it, but all the time she kept saying that she well believed that they would make a great fuss of him, as much for what he had done as for what it was hoped he would do, and that it was only to be expected that reports magnified the deed, and that often it happens that what men see and hear they repeat with interest. But still Curial's name was on everyone's tongue, for every day there came letters from those who had gone in his company, both those who were in his service and others as well, and the Marquis knew all these things and passed them on at once to his sister, who knew them already, long before. But she kept them secret, and the Marquis said them aloud.

Thus when Guelfa knew that St Mark's day would be the day of the combat, which was now close at hand, she began to grow sad and feel great pain in her heart, and lost the power of eating and sleeping, turning grey and pale. The doctors tried to cure her with purges and blood-lettings, and she did all they prescribed in order to conceal her malady, which they had no idea of. But as each day she grew worse, she told her brother that she would like to go to a convent of nuns of great sanctity, and that if it so happened that she were to die of this sickness, she would like to be buried there. The Marquis praised her for this, and she was taken there at once, beseeching her brother to ensure that no one visited her.

Meanwhile Guelfa had ordered a statue of St Mark to be made for her, very finely worked, and also an altar in the room where she lay, where she had masses said continually, and in all the hospitals and other places where poor people could be found she gave great sums in alms; and ceaselessly she prayed to our Lord Jesus Christ and His glorious Mother to help Curial and give him the victory. And what of St Mark? Naturally she vowed to fast on bread and water alone every year on the eve of his feast and to found a church in his honour and endow it richly. Thus the loving lady, full of care, awaited the news that would give her life or death. When the feast of St Mark arrived, she invited all the poor she could find, and she herself, barefoot, served them, and the nuns with her, and all marvelled at this. After the beggars had been served, she went to bed without eating or drinking, and all the nuns thought that this must be the last day of her life, and so they sent for the Marquis.

When he arrived, he said to her 'Fair sister, what is this sickness of yours that no one in the world can diagnose? Try, I beg you, to think of something you would like that can be obtained and may prevent you from dying.' 'My lord brother,' she replied, 'I do not know what my sickness is, nor have I ever met such inept doctors, for with all their science they have not yet managed to find any remedy. May it please God, who can cure me and who knows my sickness, to provide for it and bring it to a good end, for I must warn you that if He does not do so within a week I am sure that I shall no longer be in this world.' And as the hour of vespers was approaching, the Marquis said to her 'Alas, what danger must Curial be in at this hour! May God help him.' Saying these words, he took his leave of her, turned away and left.

When she heard this, Guelfa asked the Abbess to stay with her and the other nuns to leave, and she said to her 'Madam, I am dying.' And with her eyes clouded over and all colour fled from her face, she fell forward with her head on the Abbess's shoulder. The Abbess cried out, and the nuns who had just left came running back, and they tried all manner of ways to revive her spirits. They worked in vain, for Guelfa was now indeed more dead than alive. But after a long while she came to for a little, and sighed, and all the ladies cried 'Ah, Madam, for God's sake make an effort! Ah, St Mark, on this your feast day help her!'

43

Since Guelfa was in a very weak state both because of her anxiety and through fasting, she fell asleep for a while. No sooner was she asleep than she saw in a dream two foxes which, with many people looking on, were intent upon killing a naked lady, and the people were all untroubled and gave her no help. But when the lady had quite given herself up for lost, there came two lions, strong and fierce, especially one of them, and they drove away the foxes so that the lady was saved, and they gave her her clothes and dressed her. Thereupon St Mark appeared to her and said 'Be of good hope, Curial has justice on his side and has had the best of the battle, and has now left the battlefield.' And so the vision and the dream ended.

When she awoke, Guelfa's face had a better colour, and she said she would like something to eat. With the best will in the world the nuns gave her some food and asked her how she felt. 'Much better than before,' she said, 'and in faith I believe that I am cured.' Just then the Marquis arrived, because the nuns had sent for him, and he was very pleased to find his sister eating, for he loved her dearly. The Abbess said 'Sir, no sooner had you left than she felt that she was dying, but now she is well, thank God, and talking about many things.' The Marquis said 'By now the knights' combat will be over.' Guelfa made no reply and said nothing. 'I would give a great deal to know now how that battle has turned out,' the Marquis went on, 'for I am very worried about the outcome. I have heard that the other knights are strong and very valiant, and although Curial too is very valiant and strong, he has not been in the lists as often as the others.' The Abbess, who was incapable of silence, said 'Sir, I have heard that Curial has a lion as part of his arms. Last night I dreamed that two lions killed two foxes, and remembering this dream it seems to me that Curial and his companion are the lions and the others the foxes, because of their deceit, and so they are dead; and that is the news you must expect.'

Guelfa turned towards the Abbess, and seeing that her dream coincided with the one she herself had had, was convinced that Curial had won. 'My lord and brother,' she said, 'there are so many men today who through envy or some other cause accuse women of infamous conduct that they cannot be counted, and if such as these have accused that lady unjustly, you should only expect good news. God is just, and will not allow the rod of the sinner to fall for long on the righteous, for the righteous man does not sully his hands with unlawful things. So let them be: my concern is for my own recovery, and let the lions of the Abbess's dream win if they will.' The Abbess said 'I swear to God that the lions have triumphed.' 'That is because you wish it to be so,' replied Guelfa, 'and indeed I believe there is no one here who does not wish it, for Curial's sake, but much more for the sake of the Duchess, who would be burned if it happened otherwise.' 'In God's name, then,' said the Abbess, 'she will not burn, for the lions have won!' Guelfa laughed a little at the Abbess's persistence, and so did the others who were present. When they had talked for a while, the Marquis left and returned to his palace.

Guelfa was now far happier, and said to the Abbess 'In faith, I was pleased by your dream, for I too had the same dream while I slept.' And she told her all about the naked lady, whom she took to be the accused Duchess, and what St Mark had said. The Abbess said 'Come, lady, get up from your bed, and let all the nuns come and we will have a procession and sing the Te Deum, for Curial is ours, and is surely the victor and St Mark, who is a lion, has helped him.' Guelfa arose as though she had never been ill, and walked with such ease that she had no need of support. When they had made their procession and given thanks to God, everyone returned to their places.

Guelfa was dying to talk about Curial, so when they had sent all the other nuns away and she and the Abbess were left alone together, she began to talk about the news. Although she could do many things, she could not conceal her love for Curial and the Abbess realised she had a deep affection for him. So she said, 'Madam, I beg you by that God who can send you good news of the things you most love in the world, tell me the truth about a thing I am going to ask you.' Guelfa said that she would, whereupon the Abbess said 'Madam, from all that you have said I know that you are somewhat in love with Curial, and I beg you to tell me whether this is so.'

Guelfa replied 'Madam Abbess, my friend, I would not wish, nor can I, conceal from you anything that I could reveal to anyone, and I will speak to you openly. I realise that if I cannot hide my feelings you, or any other person to whom I may confide them, will also find it hard to conceal them, since they are of less importance to you. Nevertheless, the desire I have to talk about this matter, and the opportunity which you offer me, forces me to tell you what, if I were wise, I should conceal. But if the words which I say to you ever fall from your lips, this punishment you will have from me: that the tongue with which you have spoken them will be torn out. From henceforward I shall answer you that I do not know what love is, nor ever saw it, as far as I remember, nor know who it is. I have indeed heard that love is something, but I cannot see that it is anything more than burning madness and delightful suffering. It is true that I wish Curial well, and if this is what love means, then let it be love, for I do not know. I only know that I like to hear good of him, and wish him to be the best and greatest in the world, and would

45

like him to be near me and never go away. Now you know the whole truth of the matter.'

The Abbess answered 'Madam, nuns are indeed apart from the world, but sometimes they are wooed by men who have little to do, and in my youth I have heard this lesson four times and more. It is true that love is no more than a great, abundant affection that one has for something one finds pleasing, which engenders a desire to give pleasure in everything, and this love lasts as long as the person or thing continues to please, and after that there is no kind of love. But I assure you that you have greatly erred in keeping this a secret from me for so long, for it is a great relief to pain to have someone to tell one's sufferings to.'

And from that time on, each communicated all her concerns to the other, and read all the letters the other had received, and spoke of little else, and they became such friends that the Abbess spoke to her without any reverence. This continued for some days, until God willed that Guelfa should receive a letter from Melchior describing the battle that had taken place and relating in detail everything that had happened, as far as he knew. Guelfa and the Abbess had much pleasure from this, though they told no one of it.

Not many days passed before there came a gentleman whom the Marquis had sent in Curial's company and who had seen everything up to the time of the Emperor's gift to Curial, and he told the Marquis all that had happened since the day they had left Montferrat till the day he had left Curial. The Marquis was very content, and at once set off for the convent, where he found Guelfa, quite re-covered and in good health, and Andrea, his wife, who was visiting her. Straightaway the Marquis had his gentleman recount every-thing in detail, as he himself had already heard it. This made Guelfa very happy, although she made no comment, but the Abbess could not conceal her joy, and showed it to such an extent that everyone was surprised.

The gentleman had told everything, but when he came to how the Duke of Bavaria had offered Curial his daughter and his land, every-one was astonished, and fell silent and thoughtful. Guelfa was certainly not overjoyed, and looked round at the Abbess and turned a little pale. The Abbess came to her rescue, saying 'And what did he answer? Did he accept?' 'No, not then,' replied the gentleman, 'for just at that moment Melchior de Pando arrived and gave him a letter. Curial took the letter and made no answer to the Duke.' And then he went on to describe what the Duke had said, and all that had happened until the next day, when the Emperor sent him his presents. Everyone enjoyed hearing this and looked forward to knowing from other messengers what had happened later. After much talk on this subject, the Marquis and his wife went off to supper, still discussing Curial, a subject of which they never tired.

When the Abbess and Guelfa had dismissed the nuns and were left alone, Guelfa began 'Ah, mother, I am dead! I am sure that I shall not see tomorrow. Ah, wicked man, for whom have I set you up in the world? Lachesis can surely not deserve that I should prepare this knight for her to carry off? Ah, life, why do you remain to me? Leave me, I beg you, and preserve me from the great sorrow that I expect after what I have heard today! Ah, Lachesis, my sister, why do you love what is mine, and from so far away rob me of my life? I, wretch that I am, sent aid to your sister when she expected to be burned to death, and as my reward you have slain me! Alas, to do good I did ill! Ah, Clotho, why do you not return to me what I lent you, my Curial? I had no treasure more precious to send you, it served you against the fire that was to consume you, and you have stolen it from me and given it to your sister. You have made a good deal of what cost you nothing. Ah, Medea, noble and valorous lady! Now I wish you well, who knew how to remove false Creusa, kindling the fire that burned her; but I, in order to extinguish another fire, have kindled my own, in which I shall surely die! But why should I wish harm to Lachesis? What damsel with any feeling would not fall in love with Curial, seeing him in the state to which I have raised him?'

All the time Guelfa was saying this she was weeping, and the Abbess, overcome with pity, grieved for her. 'Lady, you must not lament like this,' she said, 'for as I heard, the Duke indeed offered him his daughter, but Curial would not accept her.' 'Mother,' replied Guelfa, 'Lachesis has eyes, and will see in Curial what I have seen. And on the other hand what fool would refuse so noble and advantageous a proposition as to have Lachesis for his wife, who brings her father's whole duchy with her? Ah, wretch that I am,' continued Guelfa, 'I wish that Lachesis had given him the start in life that I have, and that he was hers!' 'Madam,' said the Abbess, 'on my word, I cannot believe that Curial would do such a thing, and even though Curial is a good knight someone is bound to tell the Duke that he is not a suitable match for his daughter, and I doubt whether he will really give her to him. So be cheerful, soon we will have more news. And even if it is true, which it cannot be, you should expect that Curial will remember the benefits he has received from you and will be incapable of such ingratitude. So, madam, let us have supper, for on my word I swear that there is no truth in it.'

Unwillingly Guelfa sat down to table, and even more unwillingly had supper, wondering all the time what would happen. When they had finished, the Abbess led all the nuns into a delightful garden,

47

and in Guelfa's presence they played many kinds of games. But Guelfa paid no attention, she was thinking so much about Curial that she was unaware whether it was day or night. When the Abbess thought they had been there long enough, she rose to her feet and went away with Guelfa, and everyone set about their usual tasks. But Guelfa only thought and thought, and there was no way of making her thoughts more pleasant.

Not many days passed before other messengers arrived, one after another, through whom Guelfa learnt that the marriage had not taken place, although everyone predicted that it would, in view of the honours paid to Curial by the Duke of Bavaria. There were some who said that Curial had Lachesis's bed in his lodging and slept in it every night, and that he had had doublets made from her dress, all of which grieved Guelfa very much. And although she wished she might die, yet she hoped to see him again if he ever came, and to give him to understand that she cared very little about him.

★

While matters stood thus, there arrived Melchior de Pando, who had left Curial on the road, and after he had paid his respects to the Marquis he went to see Guelfa. She greeted him with much gladness, and asked him about many things to which he replied, and naturally she did not forget to ask about Lachesis. Melchior told her that she was a very beautiful, very gracious damsel. 'Is she married to Curial?' asked Guelfa. Melchior replied that she was not, that it was true her father had offered her to him but Curial never considered accepting her; and no one in the world would take it for granted that the Duke would really give her to him, since many great lords were striving to prevent this happening; and it had never been mentioned again. When she asked about the honour that was being paid to Curial, he replied that this was true, and that no one who had not seen it would believe it, and even one who had seen it could not well explain it. And this was right and proper, seeing how Curial had saved their honour, and if they had not done so they would have been in the wrong, and indeed they could not fête him as well as he deserved of them. 'Tell me, madam, was it so small a task, was there so little danger, for Curial to fight Parrot de Sant Laydier, a knight of five-and-twenty years, as tall as a giant, stronger and sturdier than any other in the whole empire, fiercer and more daring than a lion so that wherever he went everyone gave way to him and no one dared to take up his challenge? He had already killed three knights in the lists in mortal combat, and cared as much for a fighting man as you do for that dwarf-woman. Moreover he had to fight and overthrow Otho de Cribaut twice, who was also a very valiant knight and had already thrown Jacob of Cleves to the ground and was about to kill him. What Lancelot or Tristan ever did such a deed? These are miracles, not the work of any mortal, human man!'

Guelfa made some reply, but naturally she was displeased about the doublets that Curial wore. 'Well,' said Guelfa, 'I suppose it will not be long before he is here, unless Lachesis with her snares catches him again and makes him turn back from his journey. Tell me, Melchior, had he travelled far from Lachesis when you left him?' 'Madam,' replied Melchior, 'his body was more than eighty leagues from her, but his heart was never nearer to her than a thousand.' 'That remains to be seen' said Guelfa.

So, as you have heard, Guelfa fretted, unable to find respite in anything. Meanwhile Melchior wrote to Curial, asking him not to wear the doublets made from Lachesis's gown nor to sleep in the bed she had given him, otherwise Guelfa would be very offended. So Curial gave away his doublets; and day by day he came nearer to Montferrat.

When he knew that Curial was approaching, the Marquis ordered tents and pavilions to be erected in a large meadow outside the city, and prepared a splendid tourney, which he had been contemplating for a long time, in which he intended to take part himself. On the day that Curial was due to arrive he summoned Andrea and Guelfa and many other noble ladies, and they entered the stands that had been erected, suitably high, to await Curial. When he came he was received with great honour by the Marquis and other gentlemen, and he was given a place high up in the stands, between Andrea and Guelfa, who received him graciously and fêted him with great rejoicing.

The Marquis was an extremely fine horseman, very valiant, and feeling pleased with himself and in fine fettle, he dared to express himself – thinking he was speaking unheard – in words which were not as prudent as might be expected of such a gentleman on such a day and in such a place. This is what he said: 'I wish that Curial were on the opposing side, for I swear by the lady I love that I should show him in this tourney, man to man, that he does not love so fair a lady as I do, nor is he as faithful to her as I am to mine.' Then the trumpets sounded with a loud noise and he rode out into the mêlée with silk trappings embroidered all over with mallow leaves, and a standard of the same.

From the other side there approached a Neapolitan knight named Boca di Far, well mounted and richly apparelled and with a worthy company. He had come to the tournament rather for love of Guelfa than for the entertainment, for he hoped to win her as his wife,

49

with the help of Ansaldo and Ambrosio, the two envious old men.

So now both sides were in the field. The Marquis spurred his horse, and with a strong, thick lance in his hand struck the first knight he came to with such force that he knocked him from his horse, and then did the same to two more. But since he had by this time broken his lance, he put hand to sword and began to strike blows left and right with such vigour that people fell away from him wherever he went. Curial was watching without ever taking his eyes from him, and said aloud so that all around could hear 'The Marquis is a very valorous knight, but what he is doing now looks more fitting for a mortal combat than for a tourney.' Thereupon a gentleman came up to Curial and told him what the Marquis had said of him before entering the tourney. Curial was filled with anger, but made no reply, so as not to give cause for a quarrel; but he thought to himself that the Marquis, although he did him honour, must hate him if he could say such a thing.

Coming towards the stands, the Marquis performed many impressive feats, and wielded his sword with such effect that wherever he went the way was opened to him. As he approached the place where Curial sat, he said 'Curial, we who have not been in Germany know nothing of the use of weapons, nor can we strike with lance or sword, so be patient with us if we do not perform as well as you and those others who are more used to them.'

Just at this moment Boca di Far came up to the stands on his horse, named Saladin. He was the most outstanding knight in the tournament, stronger and better than any other, and he had been seeking the Marquis for a long time without finding him. Now he saw that, having just finished speaking, he was spurring his horse, lance in hand, to strike another combatant. So Boca di Far placed himself between them and struck the Marquis so firmly in the middle of his shield that he lifted him from the saddle and sent him flying from his horse the length of a lance, in full sight of Andrea his wife, Guelfa his sister, and Curial and the rest of the people in the stands, and many more. At this a great cry and noise arose from the stands. With some difficulty and the help of his men, the Marquis remounted, and entering the mêlée again, took a strong lance and sought up and down until he found Boca di Far who was striving to defend himself against the knights of the Marquis's household, who wanted to take him prisoner. The Marquis, incensed with wrathful indignation, struck him with his lance in the middle of the shield, but without shifting him from the saddle, and shattering the lance into pieces. Recognising the Marquis, Boca di Far spurred his horse towards him and there, surrounded by his knights, gave him such a blow on the head that the Marquis swayed in the saddle and clung to the neck of his horse, fearing he would fall again.

Some other knights came to the aid of Boca di Far and, making a way with their swords, seized the Marquis and indeed would have carried him off had it not been for a Catalan knight, a very strong man, mounted on a sturdy and brave horse, who came up and charged into Boca di Far with the chest of his horse so that both knights fell to the ground in a heap. The Catalan was the first to rise, and he held out his hand and said 'Up with you, Boca di Far!' With the help of his adversary, Boca di Far emerged from beneath his horse, which was lying on top of him, but when Boca di Far found himself free and was about to remount, the Catalan said to him 'Knight, leave the mare's son, for he is yours no more.' And although he had helped him to rise, he struck him with his sword so hard that Boca di Far felt this was going to be a fierce assault. Nevertheless he began to fight against him with great determination. While these two were thus engaged the Marquis paid no heed to their battle but seized Boca di Far's horse by the reins and led it to the stands, where he presented it to Curial. Curial accepted it gladly, and everyone recognised it as the horse of the knight who had unseated the Marquis.

The tourney had now continued for a long time, and harsh feelings were being aroused on both sides, so Curial asked the Marquis to put an end to it for that day. The Marquis at once ordered the trumpets to sound the retreat and everyone broke off their engagement save Boca di Far and the Catalan, who continued to fight so that no one could shift them from the spot. Then the Marquis ordered that the standards should be lowered, and finally some knights intervened between the two combatants and with some difficulty succeeded in separating them.

When the tourney was over the Marquis climbed up into the stands, where Curial and the ladies helped him to disarm. He summoned Boca di Far to him and did him great honour, saying that he was the best knight in the field and had achieved most success. Boca di Far said to him 'Marquis, you could well say that if I had taken your horse as you have taken mine.' The Marquis laughed and embraced him, and he fêted him well. Then the great supper was ready and everyone went to take his place. But Curial was full of anger; he looked all round and asked after a knight who in the tourney had borne a green shield crossed by a gold bar. When he was pointed out to him, Curial approached him and asked his name and where he came from, to which he replied that he was called Dalmau d'Oluge and that he came from Catalonia. Curial made much of him because he had seen many good things performed by him in the tourney and especially how he had struck Boca di Far a blow and then with great courtesy helped him to rise, and after that had fought him valiantly. In his heart Curial held this knight to be the best and most valorous, and taking the Marquis aside he asked him to honour the knight for he well deserved it and some time he might be of service to him. The Marquis did so, and when the Catalan came to him, he honoured him.

So they all sat down to supper, and the Marquis arranged that Curial should sit between Guelfa and Andrea, the Catalan knight on the other side of Andrea and Boca di Far beside Guelfa, and the Marquis sat opposite them all on a chair of state, and all the rest in due order.

There was a noble damsel named Arta who was considered a great beauty at that time, and she was serving as mistress of ceremonies in the hall, accompanied by many knights and gentlewomen. She was attracting a great deal of attention but the chief service she performed was to gaze at Curial, whose beauty outshone all others present, both men and women, and she could not conceal what had happened within her heart, and could not take her eyes from Curial. Noticing this, Guelfa, either through annoyance or through jealousy, said 'Arta, I thought that only in the tournament were there any wounded; but now I see that I was wrong, and I think that prisoners have been taken here too.' Arta made no reply.

When supper was over and the tables removed, Arta brought a very fine basinet and on behalf of the Marquis presented it to Boca di Far as the best and most valorous knight in the tourney. The Catalan knight took offence at this and said 'Bad luck to the foreigners whose merits are not recognised!' Curial heard this. He thought too that the Marquis had not awarded the prize justly, and also he had observed that Boca di Far never took his eyes from Guelfa and was saying things to her from which everyone could tell that he was in love with her. So he sent at once for one of his swords, the one that had been given to him by the Duke of Austria with ornaments of considerable value, and he gave it to the Catalan saying 'Take this sword, for you have struck better and more powerfully than any knight I have seen in the tournament today.' Moved by envy, Boca di Far said 'By my faith, I am sure that the knight has struck well with his sword, but in my opinion others have done as well as he.' The Marquis ordered that this subject should be dropped, and accordingly the Catalan, although very annoyed, obeyed his command for a long while, and talked of other things. But he had not forgotten what Boca di Far had said to Curial, and at last he said to him 'Knight, I do not speak through envy of your basinet nor do I wish to rob you of the little honour you have won today, but your great pride, which I cannot tolerate, makes me speak: and so I say that the Marquis has not judged well in awarding you the basinet as a prize, for there are others who have deserved it better than you. Although I do not include myself in this regard, since I am a knight of little worth, nevertheless I would be ready, if you agree, to return to the field and to prove to you in combat, man to man, that you do not merit the prize that has been accorded you.'

Now Boca di Far was a great lord and had come well-accompanied to the tourney, and he was in love with Guelfa, even if she would not look at him, and he took it as a great insult that a poor knight should say such things to him in her presence. So he replied 'Friend, at the moment I have no desire to fight, especially in a cause such as this, because I know that the Marquis has given me the prize more through his graciousness than through my merits. Undoubtedly he deserves it more than I do, but he adjudged it to me because it did not seem to him proper to pronounce himself to be the best; and I consider myself more shamed than honoured because of this.' 'The Marquis was not the best knight of the day,' replied the Catalan, 'nor should the prize be his.' At this Boca di Far was silent for a while, and then he answered 'Knight, I have already told you that I do not wish to fight, but if you persist in what you have said, I will give you a knight of my company to fight with you in this matter.' 'And I will give that knight another of my lineage and my name and bearing my arms,' replied the Catalan, 'and I will fight with you, for the other whom you offer to me has no quarrel with me.'

The Marquis knew that the Catalan was a powerful fighter, and he was annoyed that he considered himself the equal of Boca di Far, and he said to him 'Knight, I do not like what you have said, because you are forcing one of the knights who has done me most honour in coming to this gathering to do battle against his will.' 'Marquis, he has not honoured you but you him,' replied the Catalan. 'You made way for his lance in front of these stands, and then bowed before his sword. Perhaps you would have honoured him further if I had not intervened and answered for you better than you have done now for me; and you continue to honour him. It seems that you can never sufficiently honour those who bring shame on you.'

At this Curial intervened. 'My lord,' he said, 'let what has been said suffice, for this knight deserves more honour than you have shown him.' Boca di Far heard Curial's words and knowing that they both burned with flames kindled at the same fire he said 'Curial, if you say what that knight has said I will answer you.' 'Boca di Far,' replied Curial, 'I will not speak for the Marquis, but for myself I judge that the Catalan knight was today better than you by far, and is more deserving of the prize.' Boca di Far answered that he lied in his throat, and that he and a companion would meet him and the Catalan knight in combat over this matter. 'Boca di Far,' Curial answered, 'I speak the truth, and you have lied, lie now, and will lie as often as you say those words. I am content to meet you in battle, man to man, in this cause, and if this Catalan knight here present pleases to fight with your companion I shall be glad; if not, I will find other company.' The Catalan came forward, sweating all over with rage, and said 'Boca di Far, you have said a great deal and now we shall see if you are a man who lives up to what he has said. I shall fight beside Curial as long as my body contains my soul.' And thus the matter was confirmed by all.

The Marquis was very displeased by this and began to try to appease them, but the Catalan was more fierce and determined than I can say, and said to the Marquis 'Sir, are you trying to reconcile us?' 'Yes' he answered. 'You are rather doing the opposite,' said the Catalan, 'for we are in agreement and you wish to make us disagree. Leave us be, for I swear to God that I will accept no alternative to combat.'

Two knights of Boca di Far's company approached and asked the Catalan to produce the knight of his lineage he had mentioned, for they wished to have a share in Boca di Far's honour. At once two other Catalan knights came forward, one called Roger d'Oluge, the other Pons d'Orcau, and they said that in the name of St George they wished to take part in the battle against those two; and all gave their word one to another, so that they were four against four. Boca di Far requested the Marquis to preside over the encounter, and although the Marquis wished to be excused from this, he finally gave way, hoping that in the interval he could settle the quarrel without coming to battle, and with the consent of both sides he designated the feast of St John, which was close at hand.

In the few days that intervened he worked hard to achieve a settle-ment but without success, for each of the knights was already pre-paring as best he could for the day of battle. Boca di Far said to him, 'Marquis, remember that you have undertaken to arrange the battle for us, for I intend the fight to be conclusive. If you do not allow it to be a mortal combat, you may be sure that I will make the knights meet elsewhere before a judge who will allow us to fight to the death.' The Marquis assented, for he could see that all were agreed upon it.

Everyone was discussing the quarrel, and the festivities were disturbed. Seeing that they were all set on it, and that there was nothing he could do, the Marquis asked whether they intended to fight mounted or on foot. Boca di Far answered that he was a knight and so would fight mounted, for he had no desire to be a foot-soldier, and the others agreed, for their only concern was that the combat should take place. So when they had agreed also on the arms of attack and defence the Marquis left the stands and accompanied Curial to his lodging, and then went on to his own palace. Guelfa returned to the convent, thinking that it would be easier for her to speak to Curial if she were there. So everyone went off to rest.

That night the Marquis set guards round the convent, to see whether Curial would go to see Guelfa; but Curial did not stir from his lodging, and stayed safely indoors. When morning came he arose and went to join the Marquis and together they attended mass in the convent where Guelfa was. There they found Boca di Far, who had already heard mass and was trying to see Guelfa. When she heard that the Marquis was there and was asking for her, she would not leave her room so that Boca di Far would not have the pleasure of seeing her.

★

Knowing that Boca di Far was in love with Guelfa, Curial became very jealous and so incensed with fury and anger that he would willingly have killed him anywhere, had it not been for the thought that within a few days the combat was to take place, and that this would settle the question since one of them would die and then Guelfa would be left, if she wished, for the other.

The hour for dinner arrived, and the Marquis invited Curial and took him to his palace and fêted him, but not as much as the Emperor and the Dukes had done. Thereafter he gave orders that Boca di Far should go to the palace one day and Curial the next, and so they should share the time between them. At Boca di Far's request the Marquis went to the convent and brought Guelfa to the palace, almost by force, saying that while there were guests from afar he wished her to be there to do them honour.

Meanwhile the two envious old men set about arranging a marriage between Guelfa and Boca di Far. The idea pleased the Marquis very much, and he discussed it with her. Guelfa enjoyed seeing Boca di Far, who was a handsome man, a good knight, of a great family and extremely rich, and such a good talker that he could not be improved upon, so that everyone had pleasure in his company. But she loved Curial beyond all measure, and she was a wise lady, so she answered her brother 'My lord, in truth I have at present no desire for a husband, and I have no intention of accepting either him or any other. If I had set my heart on it, you can be sure I

55

would beware of taking as husband a man who faces the perils of mortal combat, as Boca di Far does, for I have no idea what the end of that will be, and I have no wish to find myself with the sorrow I have already experienced, of losing a husband and of seeing him die before my eyes without being able to help him. It is not purges and restoratives that are exchanged with lances and swords. I beg you not to mention the matter, for although Boca di Far is a good knight, he has too much on his mind at present.'

The Marquis praised this answer, and told Ansaldo and Ambrosio how Guelfa had replied, and that they should wait for the fight to be over and then speak of it. They passed the answer on to Boca di Far who was very satisfied with it, and was all eager and ready for the battle.

Curial, on the other hand, who heard about all these things, was dying of jealousy and envy, the first because he took it for granted that Guelfa loved Boca di Far, and the second because the Marquis held him in higher esteem than he did Curial, and showed him greater favour, and also because he was unable to speak to Guelfa and was eating his heart out. Guelfa, no less jealous of Lachesis, sent word to Curial that he should let her have the bed and draperies of Lachesis as she had given them to him, for she wanted them herself, and also that he should send her the gowns and other jewels that he had been given in Germany, of which there were many besides those we have mentioned. Curial did so, sending everything by Melchior de Pando. When Guelfa saw them, she kept everything because she wanted to make trial of Curial, and cause him to suffer as much and more than he had made her suffer about Lachesis. Secretly she set to work and made a pavilion from the curtains and hangings, and sent it to Boca di Far, asking him to keep it a secret until the day of the battle and then to set it up in the lists for his use.

Curial was dying to speak with Guelfa, who could well arrange a meeting if she wished although she was closely watched. When he saw that he was unable to speak to her, he sent her letters by Melchior, but as long as Melchior was with her she never read them or paid them any attention, so that Melchior came to believe that Curial's cause was well nigh lost. But as soon as Melchior had left, Guelfa would read the letters once and many times, kissing them and cherishing them as much as anyone ever could, and with the Abbess, who was always with her, she spent much time talking of Curial, for she had no joy, no recreation, other than speaking about him, and looking at all the precious things she had received from him. But although the Abbess warned her not to be so extremely harsh to Curial, she said 'Indeed I shall do worse, for the days Boca di Far comes to court I shall go and do him honour, and the days

56

that ungrateful wretch comes I shall not go out or take any notice. I shall make him suffer about Boca di Far as he has made me suffer about Lachesis.' And that is what she did. Curial grew so sad that everyone thought he was afraid about the battle, and considered him as already dead; and on the other hand Boca di Far was so happy that everyone took it for granted that he would be the victor.

The Catalans went to Curial and asked what their trappings should be on the day of the combat, and what their coats of arms. Curial, who was in despair and had given no thought to these matters, answered 'Sirs, I have other things on my mind and cannot think of such things at present, so I pray you to see to this, and I shall be content.' He told Melchior to give them all the money they might need, which he said he would do, but the Catalans said 'Curial, there is no need to spend much money, for pomp is worth nothing in such matters. But do not sit on your hands, for it is they that will do you honour; the rest is all smoke. We have agreed amongst ourselves that if you are willing we will have white trappings with the cross of St George, under whose protection the order of our knighthood is founded. Please give your mind to this and let us know now.' Curial answered that he was content, and willing to fight with those arms. So they left him, and had the trappings prepared, and everything needful for the day of battle. But they were displeased to find Curial so dejected, and considered him already dead.

Curial sent word to Guelfa, to ask her if she would send him something of hers that he might wear for her sake in the fight. She answered that he had enough of Lachesis's doublets and should be satisfied with those; that he must not suppose her ignorant of all that had passed, and so he must do without, she would send him nothing. Curial thought that he would die, and Melchior, who wanted to comfort him, could not do so, believing that Guelfa was really angry with him. Seeing this, Curial said time and again 'I should have done better to have stayed in Germany.' 'This is what happens,' replied Melchior, 'to those who have only one heart yet wish to bestow it in many places. But do not be downcast, for women are like this; they want to make trial many times of the men they love. If Guelfa, knowing what you have done, wishes to avenge herself on you, you should not be surprised but realise that this is nothing, and those who love drink draughts more bitter than this. It often happens that what they think is far off is really close at hand.' Curial was a little comforted, realising that what Melchior said was true. But he said to him 'Shall I not see her once before I enter the lists? Indeed, if I do not, I shall win no honour but surely die there.'

'Curial,' said Melchior, 'if Guelfa did not love you she would have ordered me not to give you anything that was hers; but indeed she has ordered me to give you, more freely now than before, whatever you want. So be reassured that Guelfa is yours whatever happens. I can see that because she wants to test you she is making you suffer in the same way as you made her suffer, and I am not surprised because well you deserve it. So, Curial, I beg you to trim your sails to the wind. A man would not know what is good if it were not accompanied by vexations, so think that conditions can hardly be worse for you than they are today, that if they change, it will probably be for the better. Some sing who will soon weep, that is the way of the world.' Curial made no reply and was silent.

He sent for his Catalan companions and, putting a good face on things, showed some cheerfulness, pretending, because he felt very little. When they had come, he invited them to dine with him and made much of them. He took up a harp and played wonderfully, as one who was a great master of the instrument, and sang so sweetly that his voice seemed that of an angel, its sweetness that of paradise. The Catalans were delighted to see him so gay. Then they were called to take their places at table, for dinner was ready. They ate, and Curial ate better than he had done for days past. After they had dined they kept company for a while, and then took some refreshment and went to rest.

After they had rested a while, Curial had his accoutrements set out and armed himself. When the Catalans saw him in armour they were very pleased, and they too sent for their armour and putting it on, they practised for some time. Although they were strong and fierce fighters to a wonderful degree, they recognised that Curial was no less strong than themselves, and held him in great esteem, and were convinced that Boca di Far had arrived on an unlucky day.

Curial told them that if they needed money they should tell him and he would give them plenty. 'We have no need of your silver, knight,' answered Dalmau d'Oluge, 'for by God's grace we have a king who provides for us in such a way that we can go round the world without taking money from anyone. We would not dare, nor could we spend all that he has given us, and gives us constantly every day. But God grant me the opportunity to help and serve you on some occasion like this we have at present on our hands, to which you have committed yourself in order to increase my honour, and then you will know that, as long as my body contains a soul, I have heart enough to do, not once but many times, what you are now doing for me.'

This Dalmau d'Oluge was a very energetic man, broad-shouldered and sturdy in all his limbs, and he was so strong that any knight who fought against him could by no means consider himself safe. He was not high-born, but he was as lofty in his heart as would have befitted a king. The other knight of Oluge was like him, but Pons d'Orcau was a man of noble lineage, tall and slender, very young, with red hair, and so refined in appearance that he seemed to have been painted, very temperate and strong, and so bold as to surpass description, cheerful, a good singer, a ready lover, and in short, everyone who knew him liked him well.

These Catalans, confident in their ability, were going about the world to take part in combats, and no important feat of arms could take place without them being present and carrying off great honour. So they were held in high esteem in the many countries they had visited in search of that honour which cannot be had without working hard for it.

★

Although she was pretending to be angry, Guelfa was suffering much anguish and longed to see Curial. Sometimes she was on the point of sending for him, and then at once repented of the idea, in order to avenge herself for all he had done to her, and she really did not know what to do with herself. So one day before the battle took place she sent for Melchior. 'What is that wicked man doing?' she asked him. 'Madam,' answered Melchior, 'he is preparing for battle.' 'And what kind of trappings has he had made?' asked Guelfa. 'White, with the cross of St George, like his companions' he replied. 'Well, tell him that he must not be displeased at what he sees,' said Guelfa, 'for I have given Lachesis's draperies to Boca di Far, because I want my enemy to have the things that belonged to my other enemy. Give him this leather bracelet to wear on the day of battle, and come back soon, because I need you.'

Melchior went off to Curial and gave him the bracelet, and he was as happy to have it as if he had won a kingdom, and indeed it seemed to him that he had won one. Then he told him all that Guelfa had said, and although he was displeased about Lachesis's draperies, still he was so delighted in his heart with the bracelet that all the rest was as nothing. So he said to Melchior 'Go back to my lady, since she has commanded you to do so.' And he did.

As soon as Melchior had left her presence, Guelfa took the Abbess by the hand and led her into a little room where she undressed herself completely. She took off the linen shift that she was wearing and gave it to the Abbess, and taking another one, she dressed again. Then she and the Abbess together, as quickly as they could, put St George's crosses on the shift, on the front and back, from top to bottom, and on the sleeves as well. When it was done she summoned Melchior, who entered at once. 'Give this shift to that fool as a present from the Abbess,' she said to him, 'and tell him to wear it tomorrow as his coat-of-arms.' Melchior took it with great joy, and just as he was leaving, the Abbess said 'Melchior, tell him that it is not I who gives it, but Guelfa. In faith, as soon as you went away she took it off, and she has been wearing it today. I helped her with the crosses, true enough.' Melchior turned away and went quickly to Curial, and when he had received the shift and heard what had been said he was beside himself with joy. He put on his armour at once and tried on the shift, and by opening the seams a little here and there it was adjusted to fit him well, although it covered him only a little way both back and front; but this did not trouble him at all. He was convinced that with this shift he would overcome not only Boca di Far but Tristan of Lyonesse, if he were to come to do battle.

The Catalans came to visit Curial and found him as cheerful as could be, and were pleased that he was in such good humour. The following night they all went to the convent where Guelfa often stayed, and had their accoutrements brought there, and all they needed for the battle. When the Abbess heard of this, she took leave of Guelfa to return home. 'Alas, woe is me!' said Guelfa, 'for until now I have found solace in your company. Ah, mother, what shall I do tonight? I shall surely die of anxiety. Ah, Curial, shall I see you? You will be where I wish to be!' The Abbess said to her 'Madam, I would not leave you if the occasion did not make it necessary, but these knights will be in my house and I must be there to do them honour. Think what message you wish me to take to Curial, and I shall deliver it to him without fail.' 'Ah, mother,' said Guelfa, 'will you be more faithful than Lachesis?' 'Jesus!' replied the Abbess, 'How can you think that, however mad I might want to be, Curial would fall in love with me? By my faith, now you make me speak more boldly than I would have done. If you yourself, madam, deprive yourself of all pleasure, I know not why, whose fault is it? I tell you for sure, no one in the world should weep for you.'

'Ah, what bitterness is mine! Let Curial live, and if he wishes he need not be mine: let him be whose he will, so long as he is victor. Alas, when he and Boca di Far fell out I was glad, and now I would give my life that the words were still unuttered! Ah, wretch, what have I done, for surely Curial would not have undertaken Boca di Far if he had not had reason to be jealous of him and me, and if Curial dies, I am dead! Alas, unfortunate woman, why did I wish to have vengeance of Curial because Lachesis did him honour? Honouring him, she honoured me, and men are obliged to receive the honours that women offer them, that is the custom; and if Curial accepted, he did well, and all the time he was mine in his heart and despised all other ladies! Alas, he has done much for me, for he scorned that marriage remembering my name, for when he saw my letter he turned silent, sitting at the table where Lachesis was being offered to him, a German damsel, born of pure blood and radiant with inestimable beauty! And with her there before him, a little piece of paper from me prevented him from holding out his hand to take hers! Ah, how grieved he will be when he sees the presents that Lachesis gave him and thinks that I have done it to avenge myself on him! But surely not – he will believe, and with more reason, that I love and honour Boca di Far and have favoured him like this, hoping that he will win honour. But, wretch that I am, why do I accuse myself? What good do words do me, for the truth is that he has caused me vexation, but far greater is that which I have brought upon myself. Ah, mother, when I see lances and swords aimed at Curial that would not be there if I had kept better counsel, what can I do? I would go down into the field and await them with bared breast if I could keep Curial safe from them! I cannot believe that Curial, suppose he is the victor, will love me any more, nor is it reasonable to expect that he would, for a woman who contrives death and dishonour for him whom she loves cannot want to be loved for long: sugar every day grows bitter. But if Curial will forgive me this, let him do as he pleases, even if he never comes here again.'

All the time she was saying these words Guelfa was weeping very pitifully. And she continued 'Oh Melchior, you have so often re-proved and reproached him for me, speak sweetly to him just once, and let me not lose him if you can keep him for me!' Melchior and the Abbess comforted her as best they could, and Melchior said 'Madam, be consoled, for your shift has made Curial forget all the sorrows he has suffered, and he is yours. But I beseech you, when he enters the lists and stands before you, make the sign of the cross for him, and at least open your mouth to say may God help him, so that he understands that you still wish him well. And do all you can to enable him to keep you in sight all the time.'

Guelfa, weeping, said that she would look at him and let him see her and pray God to help him; but how could she be sure to continue to live for as long as the battle lasted. 'Madam,' replied Melchior, 'be of good cheer, for tomorrow Curial will win more honour than any knight has for a long while.' 'Tell me,' said Guelfa, 'are they good knights, the Catalans who are his companions?' 'Yes,' Melchior answered, 'the best I have seen, and they will show this without fail tomorrow, if God wills.' 'Please God they will,' said Guelfa, 'for I am very afraid.' 'You may give away all the fear you have for a penny,' said Melchior, 'for I promise you on my word that you have no reason for it. Now I beg you to let us go, for it is already vespers, the knights will be at the convent and the Abbess should have been there before now.' As they took leave of her, Guelfa said 'Mother, console him for me, and if he is angry, tell him to forgive me.'

Melchior and the Abbess went off to the convent, where the knights had not yet arrived, and Melchior made ready refreshments of sugar comfits and precious wines, and by the time he had done so the knights had come. All the nuns welcomed them in a procession and went with them to the church, singing devout hymns, and afterwards they retired to the chamber where Guelfa used to stay. When Curial saw the altar to St Mark before which Guelfa used to kneel to pray, he too at once knelt, and when he had prayed he went to the bed that was Guelfa's, and as he looked at it, he sighed. 'Do not sigh, Curial,' said Melchior, 'for on my word you have no cause to do so. I think no knight in the world is more loved by a lady than you are by Guelfa.' 'Who should sigh more than one who is well loved?' replied Curial. Then the Abbess told him all Guelfa's lamentations, but when Curial had heard them he was silent and made no reply. Melchior said 'Have you no reply?' 'No,' said Curial, 'because I have leave to speak only to you.' Then the other knights came to join them and they partook cheerfully of the refreshments and went to sleep.

★

If Guelfa had a good night, may God give such a one to him who wishes me ill, for indeed she had neither rest nor comfort, but walked about her room like a mad woman, not knowing what she was doing. When day came, the knights rose early in the morning and heard three masses, and then put on their armour. Curial asked them not to put their basinets on their heads, and so they did not; and getting on their horses, which were strong and brave, they set forth under a white standard with a red cross, with trappings to match. But everyone looked at Curial's coat of arms, for they could see that it was a woman's shift.

The Abbess too mounted her horse and made haste to join Guelfa, who was riding to the stands with Andrea. She made an obeisance, and Guelfa asked her 'What news of the light of my eyes?' 'He slept in your bed last night,' answered the Abbess, 'and said that he had never been so comfortable. He talked with Melchior for a long time, but would not say anything of his feelings to me.' 'Alas,' said Guelfa, 'I did not remember to send word to him to speak as freely to you as to Melchior, for otherwise he would not dare to do so. Ah, wretched lady, how fearful I am! See what sorrow is mine! A man

62

who does not fear all the knights in the world fears me, a frail woman who can do him no harm!'

Then Andrea and Guelfa, accompanied by many notable persons, set off for the place of battle, and on the way they met the four knights who had slept at the convent. First of all went Pons d'Orcau, next Roger d'Oluge and after him Dalmau d'Oluge, and lastly Curial. When he saw Guelfa, he made a deep bow to her and to Andrea, and said 'Ladies, cross us, for now we can do no more than show our worth.' And so Guelfa made the sign of the cross, and raising her arm she laid it on Curial's shoulder, and said, weeping, 'I pray God will help you, and in praying for your life I pray for my own, which without you would matter very little to me', saying these last words in a low voice so that no one but Curial could hear them.

The knights rode on and the ladies, all of whom wished well to Curial, were lamenting grievously but at the same time laughing about the shift. Knowing what was making them laugh, Curial said 'Now I can be called the Knight of a Cote Male Taile!' So they came to the lists and dismounted at their tent, which was of white damask with a red cross.

Not long afterwards came Boca di Far with his companions, I cannot tell you how arrogantly. Before them came twelve horses on leading reins, richly caparisoned with green trappings embroidered with gold, with a great noise of minstrels and trumpets which was marvellous to hear. When Boca di Far approached the lists to bow to the ladies in the stands, Guelfa covered her head with her mantle and, cursing him, would not look at him. This however pleased Boca di Far who thought that she had hidden her face to conceal her tears and could not look at him for sadness. So they continued on to their tent, which was made from the draperies that Lachesis had given Curial. When Curial saw the tent, he said to himself 'Now I must be truly a knight and we shall see which of the two shall be Guelfa's.'

Soon they came out of the tents, and mounting their strong horses entered the field. The Marquis did not care for ceremony but set one party at one end, the others at the other end, according to how the ground had been divided, and then they were given lances and the Marquis ordered that no one should move until the trumpet sounded. Then everyone left the lists and no one remained save the eight knights.

Boca di Far moved a little away from his companions and signed to Curial that he should do likewise, and so Curial, making as if to draw apart, clasped his lance, spurred his horse, and shouting 'St George!' charged Boca di Far. He for his part charged too, and they

63

struck each other such a mighty blow that their shields were not strong enough and were pierced. The knights, being very powerful and valiant fighters, thus broke their lances without being shifted from the saddle and then, incensed with furious rage, set hand to sword and began to strike each other such heavy blows that it was obvious to all that they had no love one for the other. Meanwhile Dalmau d'Oluge, setting spurs to his horse, charged his adversary, whose name was Gerardo da Perugia, and struck him with such force that he knocked him from his horse and yet rode on in such a way that no one would have thought he had touched him. This Gerardo da Perugia was a very clever knight, very bold and aggressive and a very determined man, but he was not at all strong although on a horse he thought he was worth any other knight whatever advantages he might seem to have.

The same thing did not happen to Roger d'Oluge, for when he attacked the other Italian, whose name was Federico da Venosa, and tried to strike him with his lance, Federico hit Roger's horse in the middle of its forehead so that the horse fell dead and Roger fell without his lance making a blow. But he came out from beneath his horse and rose very quickly, and taking his sword in hand rushed at Gerardo, who like him was on foot, and they struck each other many great blows with the sword which was wonderful to watch.

What can I tell you of the Catalan, Pons d'Orcau? He was a man of nobler ancestry and purer blood than any of his companions, and he was opposed by a valiant knight, also of a great family, called Salones da Verona, who had so high an opinion of himself that he could not imagine that any knight in the world could withstand him. So, lowering their lances, they struck each other in the centre of the shield. The lances were sturdy, the knights brave and the horses very powerful, and the blows they struck were such that, since the lances could not break, both horsemen flew to the ground. Salones came off worse in the fall because he was unable to free one of his feet from the stirrup and he was left dangling while his horse dragged him along. Although the horse went only a little way and not very fast, Salones was in great difficulty and danger. Seeing his opponent in such dire straits, Pons d'Orcau took hold of the horse by its reins and brought it to a halt, and taking the knight's foot from the stirrup helped him to rise, although he might have killed him had he wished. Finding himself out of that danger, and realising that his adversary had helped him, Salones said 'Knight, if the cause of our battle were mine rather than that of Boca di Far, I should fight no more but retire in your favour, not for any fear of you but knowing the good I have received from you. However, the cause in which we meet is Boca di Far's, and you know why we are fighting. I am with him, and it would be base on my part to make peace with those with whom he is at war, and who wish to take from him life and honour.' When he heard what the knight said, Pons d'Orcau replied 'Knight, do not suppose that I have helped you for your good, but for my honour; do not spare me where you could serve me, for be sure that as I helped you to rise so I shall help you to die, if I can.' Salones realised that this was a very staunch and noble knight. Thus the battle was split up, half mounted and half on foot.

Dalmau d'Oluge, seeing that Federico da Venosa was still mounted and was already advancing upon him, put his hands to his sword, which was a very heavy one because he was of gigantic stature and extremely strong, and he struck Federico so hard on the head that, unable to withstand the blows that rained down thick and fast, he was forced to cling to his horse's neck or else he would have fallen to the ground. Dalmau d'Oluge perceived this and, taking hold of him round the body, pulled him hard, dragged him from the saddle and then draped him across the neck of his own horse, and so took him before the Marquis's stand and there let him fall. The Marquis crossed himself and said that he had never before heard of any knight doing such a thing to another. Then Dalmau dismounted, because Federico had got up, and he took hold of him again and held him up as safely as if he had been dead, and finally dropped him to the ground again, and taking off his helmet told him not to rise again or he would cut off his head.

Then he went towards Pons d'Orcau, and found him fiercely engaged with Salones. Salones was rapidly weakening and was already so tired that he could do no more. So Dalmau watched them for a time and saw that his companion was having the better of it. So too was Roger, who was fighting the other Italian with great fury but seemed to be much fresher than his adversary, and his strength was lasting better so that everyone could see that he had the advantage.

What can I tell you of Curial? He and Boca di Far were fiercely locked in combat, and if Boca di Far was far stronger and fiercer than any of his companions, yet it availed him little, for Curial was still stronger and fiercer and more valiant than he, and if they had been on foot the battle would have been over. But Boca di Far had the better horse, and with his horse's help was acquitting himself well. Moreover he was a good horseman and so was holding his own although Curial struck him great blows. What alarmed Boca di Far most was to see that Curial was getting better, giving stronger, heavier blows, striking with more vigour than before, whereas he himself was continually weakening, and now his care was only to strike blows from time to time and to keep as far as possible out of range of Curial's sword.

Much of the day had now passed and the heat was increasing all the time. Boca di Far had been wounded in the armpit by a blow and this was weakening him, and even if no worse were to befall him, he could not escape. The blood was flowing internally which was doing him great harm because his heart was failing. Thus on the one hand through his growing weakness, and on the other because of the blows he was receiving, he could not control his horse. Everyone who was watching, seeing the strokes that Curial was delivering, was amazed and said that Curial was not so much a knight as a tempest and a destroyer of knights.

What more can I say? Curial knew that Boca di Far was exhausted, and cried to him 'Boca di Far, who deserves the prize, you or the Catalan?' Boca di Far made no reply, for Curial struck him so hard on his helmet that he fainted and fell forward on to his horse's neck. Then Curial with more blows stunned him with such force that Boca di Far, abandoning his horse, fell and could not rise. Curial also dismounted and went up to him, and taking off his helmet saw that his face was all bloody, and looking at his eyes saw that they did not move, and he seemed already dead. Curial was very displeased at this, because he did indeed wish to defeat him, but not to kill him.

So Boca di Far was slain, and his companions were very sad and considered themselves lost, and although they continued to defend themselves, though feebly, they soon retreated. Then the judges came on to the field, picked up Boca di Far and put him on a death-bed covered with rich cloth of gold, and led out the knights thus: the two knights who had retired went out first, as having been vanquished, after these came Federico da Venosa, and lastly they bore out Boca di Far with great honour, as befitting one who had been not vanquished but overcome by arms. After these four the Marquis led the other four equally out through the gate of the lists, and then, when they had mounted, the Marquis accompanied them as far as Curial's house. There they had supper accompanied by many notable people, who showed great joy at their victory. The judges disarmed the dead knight, and the others too, and sent their accoutrements and their horses to the victors.

The next day the Catalans went to take leave of the Marquis, and then set off on their journey back to Catalonia. Curial accompanied them for a part of the way, and after making many offers of service to them, and they to him, he gave them some presents and returned home, while they continued on their way.

★

There was at this time in Aragon a very noble and valorous King named Don Pedro, a robust, strong and valiant knight, and while he lived he did many deeds in battle worthy to be recorded with veneration, against Saracens as well as against others. When he learned that those knights, his vassals, were nearing Barcelona on their way back from this combat, he showed his magnanimity by sending his three sons to welcome them and do them honour, accompanied by many notable people. (The eldest of the three was Don Alfonso, who died before his father, and the others were Don Jaime and Don Frederic.) When they reached the royal palace he welcomed them with great happiness and fêted them as though they were kings, for this King held good knights in wonderfully high esteem. The knights of his realm, seeing that the King loved and honoured all knights, and especially good ones, tried hard to become good ones, so that in his day there were few knights in his kingdom who did not make great efforts in feats of arms, even to death.

So the King went with these knights and made much of them. He made them sit down to supper with him, and made the Prince, Don Alfonso, serve as master of ceremonies. His other two sons, Don Jaime and Don Frederic, stood at the ends of the tables holding torches for as long as the supper lasted; and when they grew weary of this, some of the distinguished knights who were near them took their places for a while; but when food was brought in, or the King approached, they took back the torches. The other knights who saw this were envious, not of the honour that these knights had won, but because they wished similar honour for themselves.

When supper was over, the King, mindful of the virtue of his remarkable generosity, gave them precious gifts and large estates on which they could live so that thenceforward wherever they went no one could call them poor knights. Everyone commented on the singularity of the King's action in so honouring these knights, and when the King heard this, he called together all those who could be assembled in one place and said to them 'I do not honour my knights for their own sakes, but I honour the chivalry that is within them and has shown itself so valorously in their persons. This same honour, and more, shall I pay to any of you when it shows itself in your persons.'

All praised the King for his great generosity, and realised as truth that while this King lived, chivalry would be upheld, and when he died, chivalry would feel his loss.

BOOK TWO

This second book is for the most part concerned with chivalry, considered in different ways, and it is assigned to Mars who, according to ancient belief and poetic fiction, was the god of battles. This Mars is a hot planet and to him is attributed the quality that everything that might harm him he rejects. Mars of his own nature causes wars, battles and disturbances, deceit and secret thefts: he imparts greatness and valour of spirit and causes dreadful things to be undertaken in battles. He gives liberality, and strength to endure wounds, he gives vigour, might and agility, generosity and chivalry; he brings a wife. He completes his course in two years and spends sixty days in each sign of the zodiac. His house is in the sign of Leo, below him is the sign of Aries and he rules in the sign of Scorpio. His temperament is hot and dry, his colour a shining red with a little black. Jupiter and Venus temper his malign influences, his effects are hot and his nature produces lust, in which he is encouraged by the sign Leo. According to Macrobius his complexion is fiery and his whole nature proud and pugnacious.

So Curial in this second book, which begins in the twentieth year of his life and ends when he is twenty-one, was somewhat proud, to which the influence of Mars inclined him. However courteous and humble a young warrior may be, since he is accustomed to war and battles it is hardly to be expected that the lion which Dante saw in the first canto of his book should not appear before him with its head held high, or that Capaneus should not bear him company. No one should wonder, therefore, if Curial, contrary to his true nature, becomes a little arrogant, for the office he seeks to exercise both requires and demands it. In many, and indeed in most, things he observes decent moderation, as you may see below as you read this book.

In this book mention is made of 'knights errant', although 'errant' is used wrongly, because one should say 'travelling': 'erre' is a French word and means 'way', and 'errer' means 'to travel'. But I intend to follow the usage of those Catalans who translated books about Tristan and Lancelot and turned them from French into the Catalan language. They always said 'knights errant', for they were never willing to alter this word 'errant', meaning 'travelling', and so they left it, for what reason I cannot tell. So I shall say 'errant' for 'travelling' also, following the old usage, although I shall be speaking incorrectly and be rather deserving of reproach.

Curial had left the Catalan knights on the road and returned to his lodging. He learnt that news was coming in every day from many different parts of the wonderful feats that were being performed by knights errant in many encounters, and he felt ashamed that he had not already set off. 'Father,' he said to Melchior, 'you have heard the wonderful accounts that are given of these knights every day. I feel that I am at fault in remaining here without doing anything, for perhaps I shall never again have such an opportunity to exercise my person in similar noble deeds against such a variety of opponents. Go to my lady, I beg you, and beseech her on my behalf to command me what to do, for I dare not leave the house for shame.'

Melchior went to Guelfa and explained to her what Curial had said. Remembering the Lachesis affair, for she knew all about it, Guelfa became incensed with rage, and in some confusion, as though she lacked judgment, she replied 'Tell him he did not ask my advice when he went to Lachesis, so he must not ask me now but do as he pleases, for I am not interested in what he does'. The worthy man said nothing and remained in thought. After he had reflected for a while he said 'Madam, I am very surprised at you. Why do you take his request in this way? Now you are giving yourself cause to be angry with yourself, you are wounding yourself with your own hands! It is true that a noble and beautiful damsel, very rich, and favoured above all others in Germany, fell in love with Curial; but if he, remembering you, let all this go, why do you blame him? Doubtless everyone who knew about it thought it foolish of him to have acted as he did, but his love for you is so great that without you he would consider the whole world as nothing. So grant me this favour and speak to him, I beg you, and order him to do whatever you please, for his only wish is to obey you.'

'I do not want to plead with you, Melchior, nor with him,' replied Guelfa, 'nor is it my wish to speak to him at present. However, since you are so anxious that I should, come back to me presently and I will consider meanwhile, and let you know what I want him to do.'

Melchior busied himself with other matters until it seemed to him time to return to his lady. When he arrived he found her alone with the Abbess, and they began to discuss the latest news together and soon found themselves talking about the tournament in France. 'Tell Curial, Melchior,' said Guelfa, 'that he should leave here in God's

70

name as soon as he pleases, and you are to give him as much as he needs. He is to write to me often about everything he does, whether it turns out adversely or prosperously for him, so that I know everything. He is to have green and white trappings, which you have, so give them to him; and a shield entirely black. I should like him to conceal his name as far as possible, if he wishes to please me, so that if he does anything good it is sufficient to know that the knight of the black shield has done it. Bring him here with you this evening and I shall speak to him, although I had not intended to do so for the present.'

When the hour for vespers came, Curial went in disguise to Guelfa, who received him honourably and, in the presence of Melchior and the Abbess, said to him 'Curial, it is true that I have wished you well and shall continue to do so as long as you wish it. But as you value my life, spare me, I beg you, the vexations you caused me when you were in Germany. Remember the condition in which you were before I began to work for your advancement. I assure you that when I thought of that and remembered your ingratitude I was reduced to such an extremity that I thought I should die. I have told Melchior the conditions I wish you to observe on this journey you intend to make, but you may treat them as you will. Moreover, I have decided that you should take Arta with you so that she can observe everything that happens. I did not tell you this before because I thought that you would find it irksome and expect to find yourself in many dangers on her account. Tell me what you think of this; and please do not trouble to make excuses for what has passed, for you would only re-open my wounds.'

'Madam,' replied Curial, 'I do not want to excuse myself, nor would God have me do so, for I have not sinned nor do I intend to sin in any way that warrants excuse. God who watches us from above and sees into every heart, caring equally for all, holds me quit, and so should you. From now on I shall obey your command in all things; if you wish Arta to come with me, rest assured that I shall do my best as long as I live to be able to give you a good account of her. So that you may see that I fear no peril when I think of you, I beseech you to give her to me, and I shall do her all the honour I can.'

Guelfa said that she was content and, stretching out her arms and almost weeping, she embraced and kissed him, and then told him to return to his lodging. When he had returned home, and before he went to bed, he and Melchior decided upon all that would be necessary for the journey, and then they went to rest.

Curial was very well supplied with horses which, on his way back from Germany, he had sent forward to the various places through which he would have to pass on his way to the tourney. He had also a good stock of excellent weapons and of servants and, in short, of all things befitting a notable and great knight, or indeed a great lord. As for Guelfa, she gave Arta many jewels and lent her many more and valuable ones, and did all she could to prepare and equip her well.

The next day when the hour for vespers approached and Arta was all prepared to set out, Guelfa said to her 'Arta, you are going in the company of one whom I would dearly love to be with, and I am sending you for this reason: I have learned that Lachesis, the daughter of the Duke of Bavaria, will be there, and it is said that she is the most beautiful damsel in the world. I want you to make a careful study of her beauty and find out if it is as great as it is said to be. I also want you to see how she and Curial behave towards one another, and how pleased they are to see each other. Write to me often and tell me everything you think is important, and I shall write to you too. Do your best to ensure that Curial does not stir a step without you until you get to the tournament. If you can, become friendly with Lachesis and see if she is intelligent and how she conducts herself. She will be hard put to it, I think, to be better dressed and adorned than you. So go with God; and throughout the journey call yourself Festa, that is the name I should like you to have.' So Arta took her leave and after exchanging many kisses she left Guelfa and the Abbess.

Curial went to the Marquis and took leave of him, telling him that he wanted to travel to exercise his calling. Before day broke, leaving behind all his men save for the few he had sent on ahead, and taking only two untried squires, he set off with Arta.

Arta knew that Curial and Guelfa were in love, but throughout the journey, however long it lasted, she never heard a word about it from Curial's lips, although she tried as hard as she could to do so.

So they travelled day after day until between noon and vespers one day they arrived at the house of a vavasour. While Curial was talking to him there came a damsel in great distress, mounted on a palfrey, her hair all dishevelled, tearing at her face and weeping, and crying out 'Alas, I am dead!' The vavasour who had been talking with Curial got up and asked her 'What is the matter?' 'Oh sir,' she answered, 'two base knights tried to take me by force from my brother, a good knight, who was taking me to the tourney, and they have attacked my brother and I think they have killed him. Defend me, sir, do not let them kill me as well as him!' The vavasour, who was a worthy man but old in years, looked at Curial. 'Well, knight,' he said, 'you have a damsel in your company, get up and prepare to defend this one. It is these two knights, or devils rather, I am sure, who have seized more than eight of them in the last twenty days, and they capture and disarm the knights and humiliate them most shamefully. Let us see what you can do, for you may be sure that whatever may be the fate of this damsel will be that of your own.' As fast as he could, Curial rose and put on his armour and, choosing a good strong horse, prepared to go. But Arta cried 'Do not leave me!' He was mounted and ready to leave the house and the two knights who were in pursuit of the damsel, expecting to find her in that house, were already in sight. When they saw Curial with a damsel they thought she must be the one they were seeking, and made towards her. Curial shouted 'Leave her alone, shameless knights, that damsel has someone to protect and defend her!' 'Indeed?' they asked, 'Will you defend her?' 'Yes, certainly' said Curial, and taking a strong, thick lance in his hand he aimed at one of the knights and struck him so fiercely as he charged that he knocked him from his horse. The knight fell with such a thud that he was stunned and unable to think about getting up. Then Curial turned and charged the other one who, full of anger and ill-will, was already advancing on him, and as they met they gave each other such blows that the knight broke his lance on Curial's shield, although he did not shift him in the saddle. He did not prosper, however, for Curial struck him so powerfully in the middle of his shield that the lance pierced it and the knight also, so that the blade came out between his shoulders. The knight fell dying to the ground, his eyes clouded over and his senses left him, and he passed from this life without regaining consciousness.

Curial immediately dismounted and went to the first knight, who was now trying to get up. He put his foot on his chest and said to him 'Ah, base knight! Are you and your companion trying to bring back the evil customs of Breus Saunce Pité? Get up, and let me have the damsels you have seized and the horses and armour of the knights you have shamed, and swear to abandon this dastardly practice, or your head will be forfeit.' 'Sir knight,' he answered, 'It is true that my brother and I swore to perform these deeds in order to test our persons against knights errant, but we have never attacked a knight treacherously nor have we fought other than man to man. However, I will give you all that we have taken, with pleasure, for our vow was only to last until we encountered a knight who could overcome us and then we would give him all that we had taken from the others.' 'Up, then' said Curial; and he gave his hand to the knight and helped him to rise.

But when the knight saw his brother lying motionless on the ground and the shaft of the lance in his chest and the steel blade protruding from his back, he cried 'Ah, my brother, what has become of you?' And turning back to Curial he took his sword in his hand and advanced on him, saying 'Now that he is dead I have no wish to live. Either I avenge my brother or I die'; and at once he began to strike great blows with his sword. For a long time Curial did no more than protect himself, receiving all the blows on his shield. This emboldened the knight, and he struck again and again, as hard as he could, while Curial continued to cover himself with his shield and forbore to make any attack, for he was reluctant to lay hands on this knight so as not to kill him as well as his brother. The knight strove with all his might and hit Curial's shield until he was exhausted, without Curial striking a blow. When he was tired out, he drew back to recover his breath and his strength, while Curial stood his ground, quite safe and unharmed.

When the knight felt that he had rested enough and was about to set on Curial again he said to him 'Knight, I am returning to the fight to conquer or die. Tell me your name, please, so that if I die I shall know who it is that has sent my brother and myself out of this world.' 'What sent your brother out of this world,' answered Curial, 'were the grievous and intolerable wrongs you have committed against knights errant, and the base and foolish practice you have embarked upon, which could hardly have continued much longer even if I had not come this way. You cannot know my name, for I do not wish to tell you and I do not think that you are likely to be able to force me to do so. So please take more care for your life than you are doing, otherwise I shall be forced against my will to take from you that which you want to take from me.'

When he heard Curial speak like this the knight looked at him with fear. But in spite of this he moved again into the attack and struck him great blows as hard as he could, but they all fell on the shield with which Curial was defending himself wonderfully. Curial thought to himself that the knight was very strong but even so his body did not match his valorous heart. He realised that the blows of his opponent were not such as to be able to do him much harm because they were delivered by an arm that was already weary and weakened; but he still would not hit him, and this troubled the other knight.

All those who were watching were amazed and could not think why Curial was not fighting. When the combat had been going on for a long time and the knight could do no more, forced by weariness he drew back and struck his shield into the ground and loosed the aventail from his helmet to breathe better and to cool off a little. All this time Curial did not move but still stood his ground, and so Arta came forward and said to him 'Are you enchanted, knight? What are you doing? Can you not see that that knight is continuing to fight you with all his might, and if he can he will fight you to the death? If your life is of no account to you, at least have pity on this damsel and myself. If that cruel knight does manage to overcome you, which God forbid, we shall have to suffer bitter death or live wretchedly in long servitude. I was not entrusted to you for that, nor did you promise any such thing but undertook to keep me safe from all adversity as far as was in your power. I see no sign of you using your power at present to defend either yourself or me. Please wake up, and remember the lady who gave me into your care.'

Inside his helmet Curial laughed, and said to her as a joke, 'Damsel, in God's name go back to your place. You can be sure of one thing at least, that even if you are taken captive they will not kill you. Have no fear for my life, for I can only live as long as God has ordained. You may suppose that I can do no more than I am doing, otherwise I should have done it.' Thinking that Curial could do no more, Arta was terrified, but she kept silent, wondering what the outcome would be.

While matters stood thus there arrived two squires, each on a good nag, and a page leading by the reins a fine horse with a knight's armour piled up on the saddle. As they arrived they saluted the company; but when they saw the knight, who was their lord, with his sword in his hand, and his brother lying dead on the ground, they were grief-stricken and began to lament loudly. Soon after came a man on foot wearing only a shirt. When he reached the spot where the fight was taking place and saw the dead knight, he knelt before Curial and said 'Sir knight, God bless the hour in which you came here, for you have rid the world of the most vile practice that has ever existed in this kingdom. You see here before you a knight from Germany. As fate would have it I was going to the tournament at Melun with a damsel, my sister. These knights here assailed me, one after the other, and as soon as one was wearied by fighting the other, coming fresh to the battle, would attack me, and in this way they overcame me, captured and stripped me, leaving me as you see. About this one whom I see lying here, dead, I think, I shall say nothing; but the one who still lives is the worst and most discourteous knight that has ever been seen. Rid yourself of him, I beg you, so that this vile practice will be ended in this part of the country.'

The damsel who was this knight's sister ran towards the squires, crying 'Leave the horse and armour alone, you bad men, and give me this knight's clothes. Today will bring to an end the wicked practice that these knights have instituted.' The knight took his belongings, and dressed and armed himself, and taking his horse's reins he stood waiting to see what would happen.

When Curial had seen all this, he said to the knight 'What do you

75

mean to do about this battle? Shall we leave it, on condition that you surrender to me all the damsels you have captured and all the arms and horses of the knights you have attacked, and swear to give up this custom; or will you fight to the end? It seems to me that even if I do not touch you with my sword you will have defeated yourself before nightfall. If it so happens that night still finds us here, you may rest assured that you will not win this combat but that your dastardly custom will be brought to an end with greater hurt to yourself.'

'Tell me your name, knight,' replied the other, 'and on that condition I shall do all that you command.' 'You cannot know my name,' Curial said, 'neither you nor anyone else at present, so look to your life. You would be wise, while there is still time, to make a virtue of necessity.' The knight was on the one hand prepared to die, seeing that his brother lay dead before him, but on the other hand he considered that if Curial vanquished him without striking a blow he would be utterly humiliated, and most of all he saw that fighting could do nothing to help him. He did not know what to do.

The vavasour, who was an old and very wise knight, went up to Curial and said 'Have mercy, knight! After all the harm that has been brought about by the folly of this knight and his brother, spare him the shame of what you want him to say. You see what I am; I will answer for him, and let no more be done in this matter.' Then he went to the other knight and asked him to return his sword to its sheath and fight no more, which the knight did. Then he took them both to his house, and showed them into separate rooms, where they disarmed, and he gave them clean clothes and had supper sent to them separately. Meanwhile he sent for the damsels and arms and horses of the knights who had been stripped. The dead knight he had taken from the battlefield and disarmed, and he gave him into the charge of the two squires. They took him away and he was buried very honourably in the chapel of a castle that belonged to him, to the general sorrow of all his vassals.

In the morning the captured damsels and the arms and horses of the knights who had been humiliated arrived. The knights heard mass, and the defeated knight made a solemn vow to desist thenceforth from his base practice and never again to attack any knight errant who passed that way.

Curial requested the old vavasour to accompany the damsels to the tournament and to take the horses and arms of the disgraced knights, saying that it was very likely that they would find escorts there, friends or relations who would take them back to their homes, and that if all else failed the king would doubtless make excellent arrangements for them. The vavasour agreed, and the vanquished knight of his own accord offered to accompany them. So they parted, and the vanquished knight went off to his own castle.

Curial too mounted, and in spite of the vavasour's entreaties would not spend another day there. 'But from now on,' he said, 'it will be necessary to go along the roads armed, for we are already in the territory where we must expect to meet knights errant.' So he dismounted again, armed himself well and, giving his lance and shield to his squires, he remounted and took leave of the vavasour. This worthy man mounted a palfrey, and came a little way along their road with them. 'Sir knight,' he said, 'I have not served or honoured you as I should have done and as your valour deserves, but I beg you to be patient with me, and if you are free to tell your name to any knight, let it be to me. Let me also commend to you two of my sons, young knights who left here five-and-twenty days ago to ride to the tournament as knights errant.' When he heard this, Curial halted. 'Fair host,' he answered, 'if I could tell anyone my name I would willingly tell it to you for the goodness and honour which are yours. But I may tell no one at all, and I beg you to pardon me. If I can be of any help to your sons, you may be sure that as soon as I know who they are I shall not fail them. God grant that if there is anything I can do that may serve your pleasure and your honour I will repay you for what you have done for me in your house, for in faith I hold myself deeply obliged to you.' 'Then you will not tell me your name, sir knight?' asked the old man. 'No indeed, not now' replied Curial. 'Certainly you are not one of those knights,' said the old man, 'who whenever they go on a pilgrimage or even depart from one place in order to go to another, leave written tablets or painted inscriptions on the doors of the places where they have lodged, with their names and coats of arms painted and helmets, which perhaps they never put on their heads, never using the weapons they carry except for a table knife when they sit down to eat. Yet you, who are such a knight as you have proved yourself to be, hide your name? Go in God's name, and may He be your guide, for I know that chivalry itself is dearer to you than a reputation for chivalry, and you will not lack honour wherever you go.' So Curial said goodbye to the knight, and went on his way.

As they passed the castle which had belonged to the dead knight the bells began to ring the alarm, and his men were eager to come out and attack Curial. The other knight, however, who had survived the battle, kept them in check and would let no one go out from the castle, ordering them expressly not to sally and so break the promise he had made. Curial was unaware that that was the knight's castle and had stopped to see what all the noise was about. A worthy man from the castle came to him and said 'Knight, keep on your

77

way. This castle belonged to a knight who was killed yesterday evening in an encounter with lances, and it is said that you killed him, so everyone within the castle is debating whether they should attack you. Go away, I beg, before worse befall you, for it would be a great pity if a knight as valorous as they say you are were to die or be worsted, as you would be if you linger here.'

When Arta heard this she gave no time to Curial to reply but said 'Let us go, knight, and keep on our way. Now you know that this is the castle where they imprison damsels and dishonour knights, please let us go on and take the good advice that this worthy man has given you. Perhaps the knight who swore today to give up his wicked practice will want to come and take revenge on you for causing his downfall, now that he can have the help of his people.'

Curial saw that Arta was frightened and laughed a little, and without answering her he took his lance and shield. Then he said 'Good sir, truly we are travelling this road as other knights errant are, neither doing nor seeking harm to anyone. But if the people of the castle come out now, perhaps not all of them will return.' 'Ah knight!' replied the worthy man, 'you are only one knight alone, what can you do against the eight knights who are here, with many others who would help them?' 'So God give me counsel,' said Curial, 'I wish they would come out and fight as knights errant, and then perhaps they would let knights errant go by in peace.'

While they were talking, a knight errant came into sight along the road, with a lance in his hand and a shield on his arm, and when he reached Curial he said 'Knight, do not deny me a joust, according to the present custom of the land!' When Curial heard this he turned, and they rushed on one another very boldly. The knight struck Curial in the middle of his shield, and his lance flew into pieces. Curial, who was far stronger, hit him sharply in the middle of his shield as he approached so that he was lifted out of the saddle and sent flying lightly to the ground and fortunately for him came off with no other hurt than the bump he received when he landed.

Curial did not give him another look, and Arta said 'Knight, we have done enough here. In God's name let us go, for the people in the castle cannot say now that we fled in fear of them.' Curial looked round towards the castle, and seeing that no one was coming he took leave of the worthy man and slowly rode on. The worthy man helped catch the horse of the knight who had been unseated and gave it back to him.

No sooner was the knight back in the saddle and preparing to follow Curial than, in spite of their lord, the eight knights came out of the castle. Curial had not gone very far, and he could see them as they charged on the knight, and attacked him, and although he was a brave and valiant fighter there were so many of them together that they struck him, knocked him to the ground, disarmed him and took away his horse. Then they started to lead him in great humiliation to the castle. Curial, seeing this grievous wrong, turned his horse and as fast as it was humanly possible he rode at them crying 'Ah wicked men, certainly you have no sense of the honour of chivalry!'

As he galloped towards them he met one with his lance and immediately unseated him, and he fell to the ground; then Curial rushed on another and knocked him off his horse in the same way. What can I say? He struck down four knights with the lance, and when it broke on the fourth charge he took out his sword and began to strike the base knights with such force that he felled them all one after the other, leaving three gravely injured. All the people in the castle were watching and they were calling to their lord to go out and help his knights. But he replied 'God forbid that I should go against the promise I have made. I have told you already, it makes no difference that there are eight of them, for if there had been a hundred he would do the same to them one after another, as he has done to these.' They were amazed at this, and admired Curial so that everyone would have liked him as his lord.

Curial recovered the arms and the horse and freed the knight, and made him re-arm and mount his horse. Then he sent for the knight who had sworn to give up his evil ways, and in the presence of the commanders of the castle, whom he summoned to him, he said to him 'Knight, have you not sworn to me this very morning to abandon this vile and felonious practice? By the beauty of this damsel who is in my charge, I vow and promise that I am about to do to you what I was unwilling to do yesterday evening, and I do not know what God holds me back from removing your head from your shoulders. This wickedness must last no longer!' The knight excused himself with reason, saying that they had sallied against his will, and proved it by the testimony of his commanders. 'Ah, King of France!' exclaimed Curial, 'this should not be allowed in your kingdom!' and turning to the commanders of the castle he said 'See here: I promise and vow to you that if you follow this practice any more you will all come to a bad end, and that soon.' They all said that they would not continue it, and begged Curial to enter to take some refreshment. But Arta replied swiftly 'God preserve me from such refreshment! Let us leave here, I beg you.' So Curial and the other knight turned their backs and rode away.

They had gone only a little way when they met a knight, fully armed and alone, without any companion, and as soon as he saw the knights and Arta he stopped in the road and said 'Damsel, I take you, according to the custom which is newly established in this kingdom.' Curial halted and waited to see what Arta would do and say. 'What have I done to you, knight,' she said, 'that you should take me?'

'You have done nothing,' answered the knight, 'but the custom is that if a knight errant meets a lady or a damsel in the company of another knight errant he may take her unless someone defends her by force of arms.' 'And when he has taken her,' said Arta, 'what happens then?' The knight answered 'He keeps her in his company until another knight takes her from him.' 'And if no one takes her from him,' she asked, 'what will he do?' 'Come along with me,' he said, 'and I will show you. Do not waste so much time in words.' 'Go with God,' said Arta, 'you have no need of me. You must have had some strange dream last night.' At this the knight became angry and said 'By my faith, you are coming, whether willingly or by force' and stretching out his hand he took hold of her reins and began to pull her along. 'Leave me alone,' cried Arta, 'for you do not know the knight who is accompanying me. Did you forget to cross yourself this morning when you got out of bed?' Then the knight said 'This time you are coming with me, and we shall see what devil I should cross myself for.'

Curial said nothing. Arta slid off her palfrey and said 'I am certainly not going with you before you have defeated these two knights here.' 'In God's name,' said the knight, 'they care nothing for you otherwise they would have said that I should not take you away. They have little regard for you, I think, or they are not fit knights to escort a damsel along the road; and so get on your horse, or I promise you on my word that I will use violence on you.' At this Curial, seeing that they were both getting angry, laughed aloud.

So the knight who was travelling with Curial said 'Knight, I would have gone forward to defend your damsel, save that I did not want to annoy you. Please allow me to defend her, in return for the honour which you have done us today.' Curial replied that he was willing, and the knight moved forward and said 'Knight, leave the damsel alone and consider what great presumption it is on your part to take her from two knights such as you see here.' 'I should take her from a thousand such if they did not defend her,' replied the knight, 'but I think I have as much right to her as you have. Let us see whose she will be.'

Thereupon the two knights began to advance upon one another, and they struck each other so violently when they met that the defender broke his lance upon the encounter and it availed him little because the other gave him such a blow on the shield that it knocked him very shamefully from his horse. Then he went back to Arta and said 'Come with me, for these knights certainly do not deserve to escort a damsel.' As she still refused his company, the knight reached out and took her by the hair and said 'You will come whether you like it or not.' At this, Curial, who had taken all that had happened as a jest, called out 'Vile knight, for that piece of villainy I have half a mind to cut off your hand!' And he rushed at him, and the other knight rushed at Curial. Curial struck him with such force that he made him fly from his horse on to the ground and then, as he struggled to rise, dismounted and ran towards him. He took him by the helmet and spun him round violently so that he fell to the ground again. Tearing the helmet from his head, Curial took hold of his hair and said 'Vile knight, so you seize damsels by the hair? What more could Breus Saunce Pité do? Surely there could be no more discourteous knight in all the world than you, if you had the strength. I know no reason why I should not take your life for the great discourtesy you have shown.'

The knight was so astounded that he did not know what to say; but he answered 'Knight, I have done nothing that a knight errant should not do, for to take a damsel who is travelling in the company of knights errant is the custom of knights, and if I took her by the hair it was her fault because she would not come with me. So do not blame me for something for which I believe I am quit.' So Curial left him, but in such a fury that he came very near to cutting off the hand which had pulled Arta's hair. He mounted his horse and Arta mounted her palfrey, and they rode on without caring any more about the knight. But Curial was so angry that he did not speak or say anything at all, and the others dare not speak to him.

While they rode along like this the other knight went along beside Arta and asked her 'Damsel, I beg you, tell me who is this knight who is escorting you, for by my faith I do not believe any damsel today is accompanied by a better knight than the one who rides with you, and you may truly consider yourself safe since you are in his charge.' 'I cannot tell you any more than that he is a knight' Arta replied. 'He is most surely a knight,' said the other, 'and I know that better than you, but please tell me something to give me some idea of who he is.' 'I can only tell you that if he continues as he has begun he will be known everywhere as a knight' answered Arta. 'But please tell me who you are, and may God give you good news of your love.' At this the knight sighed and said, 'Alas, unhappy that I am! What have you said? I come from Savoy, and I am the Lord of Salenove.' 'Ah, in God's name!' said the damsel, 'I have heard of you and of the lady Raimonde de Gout, daughter of the Lord of Saut.' 'Alas!' he said, 'and does this knight know of me too?' 'I do not know' said Arta. 'And what is your name, lady?' he asked. Arta answered 'I am a damsel of little importance, and it would serve you nothing to know my name; and I should not dare tell you it without leave of the knight, who I know would be very displeased.' 'Heaven forbid that I should displease him!' he said, 'but at least tell me where you both come from.' 'Please do not ask,' answered the damsel, 'because I cannot tell you any more now.' So he was silent.

They came to a point where the road divided, where Curial stopped and, turning to the knight, said 'Knight, we must part, since the road parts us. Choose whichever of these you please.' 'Sir knight,' replied the knight, 'I have no wish for roads that part us, for I should like to go in your company, and I should prefer not to leave you if you will let me stay.' 'Truly, knight,' replied Curial, 'if I were to have the company of any knight I should not leave yours. But I have determined to travel on my own at present, so choose your path and I shall be content to take the other.' So the Lord of Salenove took his leave, chose the right-hand path, and so left Curial.

Then Arta said to Curial 'Do you know who that knight is who has just left you?' Curial said that he did not. 'Then know that he is Lord of Salenove, your great friend.' 'In God's name,' said Curial, 'I am glad he is here. Did you tell him who I am?' 'Certainly not', said Arta. 'I beg you, Arta, that you will not tell anyone who you are for anything in the world,' Curial said, 'for through you they would know who I am, and that would be a more serious matter to me than you can imagine.' Then Arta told him how Guelfa had ordered her always to call herself Festa, and that was what she intended to do if he agreed. Curial laughed, and bid her always do what her lady had ordered her.

★

They continued their journey until they came to a convent of nuns, where they were very warmly welcomed, and many of the nuns were very taken with the beauty and grace of the damsel, who was so pretty that in few places would her equal be found. But they all fell in love with Curial, and could never tire of looking at him.

After they had given them a meal, they asked Festa if she were the knight's wife, to which she answered that she was not. The nuns looked at each other and began to laugh, and they said to her 'How is it, then, that you are travelling with him?' 'What!' she exclaimed. 'Is it so strange that a knight errant should escort a damsel?' 'It is not strange,' they said, 'but although they are called damsels, they are women.' 'In God's name,' said Festa, 'it is not true of them all, nor will it be true of me and him, please God.' 'Not all men are ill-bred' said the Prioress. Another nun began to laugh, and speaking very softly, thinking that Festa would not hear, she said 'You may say what you like, but I shall not believe either today or tomorrow that he does not do more jousting with you than with knights errant.' 'I should not be surprised,' replied another, 'for there is less danger in it!' And so all, some here and some there, began to tease Festa who, finding herself nettled on all sides, said 'I think you would all like to have him here as your sacristan!' They all laughed most heartily at this; and so jesting together they passed the day.

When evening came and they had had supper, Curial was taken to a splendid chamber in which to sleep, and they asked Festa if she wanted to sleep in that room with her escort. 'I have often slept in the same room as he,' she answered, 'and so I should not mind it now. But whenever I can find somewhere else to sleep I always do so.' 'In God's name,' said the Prioress, who was a young and very pretty lady, 'sleep as you usually do and pay no attention to these jests. I promise you on my word there is not a single one you see here, however holy she is, or thinks she is, who would not like to go to the tourney with him as you are doing. You suit each other well, for, on my word, although you should be very grateful to God for the great beauty He has given you, you should be no less grateful to Him for the handsome knight He has given you as escort. Only a little while ago I returned from the court of my lord, the King of France, where I had been on convent business, and there I saw many knights, but I assure you I do not remember seeing one anywhere near as handsome as he is.' 'Then what is your name, madam?' asked Festa. 'I am Yolande Le Meingre,' answered the Prioress, 'and I have two brothers. One is Jean Le Meingre, who is also called Boucicaut, and the other is Robin Le Meingre, and both are knights of good renown.' Festa had already heard of this lady and knew that she was a great lady of excellent family, and so held her in higher esteem than previously.

When the evening refreshments came they all gathered around Curial and played many games together, but the Prioress talked to Curial the whole time and gave him no opportunity to join in the games or to answer the questions that were asked him. So one of the nuns, who knew much of the world and was very free of speech, said to her 'Madam, I think that if this damsel had known that you were going to keep her here and go yourself in company with this knight she would have come very unwillingly.' 'Hold your tongue' said the Prioress, 'it is not the practice of nuns to waylay and imprison knights.' 'That is true,' replied the other nun, 'but I do not know whether he considers himself to be in safety or in prison, since you keep him here in your power. But I am sure that you would

83

be able to lay about you as well or better than any knight errant who is going to the tourney.' The Prioress laughed heartily at this, and so did they all. Curial laughed too, but Festa thought she would die of vexation. She asked the Prioress who was the nun who had been speaking and the Prioress answered 'Jeanne de Bourbon'. When Festa heard this name, she turned towards her and made a deep curtsey, but Jeanne said 'You have no call to be polite to us, damsel, because I do not think you will be able to get your knight away from the convent this time, and if by God's grace you ever regain him, be careful never to let him into a convent again!' All the nuns made much of Curial and Festa, and there was such laughter and gaiety that it was wonderful to see.

When Festa heard the jest, however, she wanted to make a joke against those who were teasing her, and so she said 'Let him be your knight, then, in God's name, and I will quit my part of him to you. By my faith, I promise you that you will not have him long before you regret it.' 'How so?' they asked, 'What have you done to him?' 'I have done nothing to him,' answered Festa, 'but I can see you are in a state to come to blows tonight as to which of you should have him.' There was an old nun who sat a little apart from the rest, and she said to Festa 'Friend, you are quite capable of that, and you would take part in the combat if it came to one. I do not know what kind of a state you see us in, but I can see you are in such a one that you will not let him out of your sight if you can help it!'

The talk lasted a long while, and then a young and gentle lady called Gilette de Berry, who had not yet spoken, went up to Festa and said, 'Sister, pay no attention to their jests. I invite you to sleep with me tonight.' 'Had you not rather invite the knight?' asked Jeanne. 'No, it would be no use' replied Gilette. 'Let the Prioress have him, in God's name, for I know she will not share him with anyone, but at least she will not compete with me in this.' Festa accepted her invitation.

Then the Prioress put an end to the recreation and rose to her feet, as did all the others. 'Sir knight,' she said to Curial, 'on my word I do not remember ever having such pleasure since I entered the convent as we have had this evening on account of you and this damsel. God bless you both for coming here. By the goodness and honour that is yours, I beg you, tell us your name so that we may inquire and know how you fare in the tournament.' 'Lady, I promise you truly,' said Curial, 'that if I had leave to tell my name to anyone I should most willingly tell it to you.' 'Then at least,' said the Prioress, 'I beg you by the lady you most love in the world, tell me what manner of shield you will carry in the tournament.' 'A black shield' Curial replied. 'In God's name,' said the Prioress, 'there will be many black shields there, but what device will you wear so that you may be better identified?' Curial replied 'I will tell you more than I meant to: I shall wear on my shield a hooded falcon with an armlet of leather round its neck.' 'I pray that God will let you return with all the honour you desire,' said the Prioress, 'and I beseech you to visit us on your way back from the tournament, if it is at all possible.' And Curial said that he would.

Then they all took leave of Curial and went to rest. Gilette de Berry took Festa by the hand and led her to her chamber, but she was not allowed to have her to herself, for Jeanne de Bourbon, Yolande de la Sparre, Isabel de Bar, Blanche de Bretagne, Catherine d'Orleans, Mathe d'Armagnac and Beatrice de Foix all entered the room, and there they entertained each other with indescribable delight and mirth.

They asked Festa all about the knight, and Festa told them everything that had happened since he had begun to ride as a knight errant. They enjoyed this very much and said that it would have been very unsuitable if God had made so handsome a knight other than valiant and daring, and they esteemed him even more highly than they had before. Jeanne de Bourbon, wanting to make merry with Festa further, said 'Damsel, do me a favour, I beg you, which is well within your power and will cost you nothing.' Festa replied that if she could she would, gladly. 'Certainly you can, if you will' said Jeanne. 'What I want you to do is to put on this habit of mine and be a nun here in this convent, and I will go with the knight and see how these knights errant treat damsels they meet on the road.' 'Perhaps even if I agree the Prioress will not give her consent' said Festa. 'We can easily deceive her over that' replied Jeanne. 'I will get them to say that I am ill, so that you can stay in bed all the time, taking syrups and purges, and making out that your eyes hurt so that you need not go outside the room or let any light be brought into it, and thus you can manage very well. And if she happens to find out, the deed will have been done, or perhaps the tourney will be over and I shall be back.' All of them laughed merrily at this and said 'Indeed, you are a born trickster'. 'This damsel is the one who knows all the tricks,' said Jeanne, 'who goes through the world seeing all the fine things there are, and we can only learn of them by hearsay.'

They did their best to entertain Festa that night, and made a huge bed on the floor on which they all lay together, with all their clothes on, so that no one slept but all spent the night in frolic and jests.

When morning came all arose, and Curial armed and mounted his horse and took his leave of them. When Festa had also mounted her palfrey Jeanne said to her 'Tell me, damsel, will you not do as I asked?'. 'Lady,' answered Festa, 'I told you that if it were in my power I should do so, but first you would have to deal with the knight.' 'Go then,' said Mathe, 'here at least you are safe from anyone catching hold of you by the hair!' And so they parted laughing.

They rode all that morning without encountering any adventures worth mentioning, but when they had done about half the day's journey and the animals were tired both by the labour of travelling and by the great heat, a herald, who had been following them for a long time, caught up with them. When he was level with them he said 'I have followed you for more than two leagues to speak to you on behalf of a knight who is coming behind and will soon be with you. He begs you to wait so that he need no longer pursue you.' 'What does the knight want?' asked Curial. 'Have you ridden far in this kingdom?' asked the herald. Curial said that he had not. 'So it would seem,' replied the herald, 'or you would know what he wants.' 'Even if I had travelled a great deal in this kingdom,' said Curial, 'I cannot know until I have been told.'

'Knight,' said the herald, 'early this morning we passed a convent of nuns where you slept last night, and when the knight inquired for news, if they knew any, all the news they could tell was of you and this damsel, of whom all said she was the fairest in the world. So the knight, wishing to have this damsel to take to the tournament rode very fast to overtake you. When he saw that he could not do so he ordered me to hurry on until I could catch you up, to ask you on his behalf to send the damsel to him by me, and you would give him great pleasure and could continue on your way freely. Otherwise please wait for him, for he will soon be here to take her according to the custom of knights errant.'

When Curial heard the news, before replying he looked at Festa's face and began to laugh. Festa, very annoyed, said to him 'What are you laughing at? Let us go, keep on our way, and enter some town, for there must be one somewhere, and I am sure I shall not be taken by force there because they only take damsels they meet on the road.' Curial made no reply to Festa but said to the herald 'Tell me, friend, is the knight close at hand?' 'I do not know how fast he has been travelling, but I think he should be about half a league away, more or less' answered the herald. 'Let us go now, as fast as we can,' said Festa, 'for to my mind it would be stupid to wait for him until he comes, whenever that may be. If you will take my advice we will stay here no longer; and if you will not, put me in a safe place, for I do not want to follow you any more, and you can go where you please.' 'Friend,' said Curial to her, 'I cannot make you safer than by keeping you with me and setting myself at risk to defend you. So do not worry, let the knight come in God's name, and perhaps he will not care for you.' 'Sir,' she said, 'I beg you to take me away from here and put me somewhere safe.' 'Very well,' said Curial, 'Let us go back to the convent and I will leave you there, since you wish it so much.' 'Woe is me!' she said, 'what if the knight is coming that way?' Curial began to laugh.

The herald came forward and said 'Damsel, do not be unwilling to wait for the knight, for on my word I swear that there is not likely to be a better nor more valiant knight in this realm today. I am sure that when you see him you will be pleased to ride with him. Even if the knight who is escorting you is a good knight, you should not mind having a better one if you can, for I swear again, on my word, that of all the knights I know this one is the best and most valiant.' The herald thought that this information would please Festa, and so he was trying to say as much as he could in his favour. But she thought that she would burst, and with her eyes full of tears she slid from her palfrey and fell on her knees before Curial, begging him, in the name of the lady who had entrusted her to him, to stay no longer in that place and not to wait for the knight.

When Curial heard his lady named he was troubled, and did not know what to do; as he stood there, the herald gave a loud shout, 'Here is the knight!' So Curial took his shield and lance and told Festa to get on her horse, which she did. The herald went to his master and told him that the knight had waited, and had not stirred a foot from the spot where he had overtaken him, and added that the damsel was the fairest he had ever seen. Then the knight said 'Will he give her to me peacefully or will he defend her in combat?' 'I think he will defend her,' replied the herald, 'because if he did not mean to do so he would have kept on his way. But as I see he has waited for you I do not think that he is afraid of you.' 'Let us see' said the knight. 'Tell him that he must give her to me or prepare to defend her.' The herald went to Curial and delivered the message. 'Tell the knight that flesh such as that of this damsel is sold at the price of blood, and he can have her in no other way' replied Curial, and before the herald could deliver his answer Curial was preparing to joust.

When the knight heard the herald's reply he too clapped spurs to his horse and rode against Curial, and struck him so hard as he advanced that his lance flew to pieces. Just as Curial made to strike him through his shield the knight's horse raised its head so high that the lance struck it in the forehead and it fell dead to the ground. The knight, leaving the saddle, shouted aloud 'You have not fought as a knight, for the mare's son had not hit you nor asked you to deliver the damsel. You have killed my horse like a coward, to avoid battle. I did not think that it was for the price of a horse's blood that you

87

wished to sell her. I call you to fight on foot, and I swear to God and the Virgin Mary that to avenge my horse either I shall lose my life or I shall take yours, if you will dismount. If you avoid me you will have behaved twice as a base knight, and even if I have to follow you like a pilgrim to the end of the world you will not escape me.'

Curial looked at him, and before replying he dismounted. Then he said 'Knight, you speak very discourteously, for I did not wish to strike your horse. Just as I reached you to make my thrust it raised its head so that against my will the blow fell where I did not wish it to fall, and so it happened that the horse was the cause of your safety and bore the punishment for your insulting demand. However, according to what you say, you wish to avenge your horse and fight me to the death. Here is my horse; since you intend that one of us should die here, one horse is sufficient for the other. Either you will not need a horse or you can take this one, which will carry you until you find a better.'

The knight hardly allowed Curial to finish speaking before, with shield on arm and sword in hand, he rushed at him and struck him a mighty blow on the shield. Curial too hit as hard as he could, and as they doubled their blows you could see fragments of shield falling in every direction, sparks flying from helmets struck by the swords, the knights' hands moving furiously and each striving to vanquish the other. And if each of them thought himself a good and valiant fighter, he now found someone to surprise him as they fought in that encounter with all their might and without restraint, for they cared for nothing but to strike tremendous blows. The first on-slaught lasted so long that both would willingly have taken a rest if the other had allowed it, but shame prevented them and made them continue to fight against their will.

Now the shields were reduced to such a condition that if the battle had lasted any longer they would have served little purpose, and their hauberks were slashed and had lost many pieces of mail. They were already wounded with many minor injuries and were bleeding continuously, which made them lose some strength; the great heat, which was increasing all the time, caused them much discomfort, and they had not eaten or drunk that day, so that they were exhausted and hardly able to continue. Eventually the challenger took a few paces backwards and struck his ill-used shield, or what was left of it, into the ground; Curial, however, seeing him move away, did not follow him nor did he move from where he was although he had as much need of rest as the other, for he had never encountered anyone who so nearly matched him.

The herald, who had been watching the battle up to that moment, went to Festa, who was on her knees with her hands and eyes raised to heaven, her tears flowing freely, and said to her 'Damsel, do not weep, for if I know anything about it you will stay with your knight this time.' 'Ah, bitter is my lot!' said the damsel, 'Who can be sure of that?' 'Your knight's sword will ensure it,' replied the herald, 'for by my faith I do not think there can be a better knight in the world. Up to now he is by far the better of the two and if he continues as valiantly as this the battle will end to his honour. Until now I have not met a knight, except yours, who could defend himself against my master, and we have found and tried many. But now I see that he is very tired and can do no more, otherwise he would have already started to fight again.'

The knights had been resting for some time when Curial noticed a great cloud of dust raised by people coming along the road at a fast pace. 'Knight,' he said, 'I see a great cloud of dust and I think that it means that people are approaching. If you do not avenge your horse before they reach us I think you will have lost the opportunity and that they will intervene between us.' So the knight raised the wretched, broken piece of shield that remained to him, and clasped his sword and began to move towards Curial. But Curial gave a leap as lightly as if he had not fought at all that day and smote him with his sword, and the knight hit him fiercely and each added strength to strength. Curial, longing to win the honour of this encounter before anyone arrived, summoned all his might and rained down many prodigiously hard and heavy blows, and fought him vigorously and with such power and fierceness that the knight no longer knew where his hands and feet were, for he was not given a chance either to strike or to defend himself. He no longer had any trust in his knightly virtue, while Curial continued to strike him, better and more strongly than ever.

Seeing his master in such dire straits the herald spurred his horse and galloped towards the people who were coming along the road. He found that they were the Prioress of the convent they had left that morning, with a large party of nuns. 'Hurry, ladies, or my lord will die!' he cried to them. The nuns hurried as fast as they could, but however fast they went, the knight, who through weariness and loss of blood could do no more, had already fallen on to his back and Curial stood over him not knowing whether to kill him or let him live. Meanwhile the ladies arrived and, dismounting, they ran to Curial, begging him not to fight any more until they had spoken to him. He drew back, therefore, and he had good need to, for he was so tired that if the other had been able to fight he could not have lasted long.

The Prioress went first to the knight who was lying motionless, and the herald unfastened the aventail of his helmet, and when they looked at him he appeared to be dead. He was still alive, however, but so overcome with exhaustion that he could hardly breathe and could not speak, and moreover he was stunned by the head-blows he had received and lay so spent that he could hardly open his eyes. The Prioress and her nuns threw rose-water on his face, and wiped the sweat from it so that he recovered consciousness, and making a bed of their cloaks, they laid him on it and began to ask him how he felt. He answered, as best he could, that he was well and wished to continue the fight, at which the nuns and everyone laughed, seeing him in such dire straits and yet still in search of more suffering.

'Sir knight,' the Prioress said to him, 'I beg you by your goodness and honour to grant me a favour I shall ask of you.' The knight said that he would. 'The favour you have granted me,' said the Prioress, 'is peace between this knight and yourself, that you shall hold him quit of this battle and that he may go away freely.' 'For your sake, lady,' said the knight, 'I am content to do so, on condition that he gives me the damsel for whom I have fought him.' At this the Prioress began to laugh again, and all the others too. 'Do not worry about the damsel, you have no need of her. When you are better perhaps you will be able to find another one, for there will be many going to the tournament' she said. 'Let this one go, for she does not want you.' 'Well, lady,' replied the knight, 'for your sake I will let her go today. But she may rest assured that if I meet her another day I shall take her without fail.' 'Very well' said the Prioress.

Then she went to Curial, who was talking to Festa, and in the sweetest way possible she spoke to him thus 'Oh valorous and most noble knight and our sweet guest! I have cursed my life a thousand times today because the nuns and I have been the cause of this strife that has befallen you. This knight, who is called Bertrand du Chastel, would not have known that you had a damsel with you if we had not told him. As soon as he heard, especially as he heard us praise her great beauty, he went off in a frenzy and raced after you, and I swear to God that I should not have come here now if I did not know that he is the strongest and most valiant knight in the kingdom. All those of the lineage of du Chastel are very strong and valiant knights, and fearing for you I rode as fast as I could. Praise be to God that the event has turned out other than I feared, which gives me unspeakable joy. So with these ladies who have come with me I beg you to pardon that knight, who seems likely to die, and to forget about the combat, for he appears to me to be in such a condition that even if you wish to fight on he will surely be unable to do so.'

Curial, who was anxious to please the Prioress in every way, answered that he would on no account go against her command, but was very grateful to her for all she was doing. He said that if the question had not been settled in this way he had no idea of what the outcome would have been, for the knight was so insulting that only death would have brought them peace, and he thanked God for bringing her to that place. All the nuns gathered round Curial and, with Festa, bound up his wounds, and they did the same for the other knight. He was so badly injured that he could not rise from the bed on which they had laid him. So Curial went to him and said 'Knight, you sent me word by this herald that I should wait for you here, and I waited and am still waiting for you, and I shall wait as long as you please. If you wish me to wait longer, tell me and I shall satisfy you; or if you give me licence to leave, I shall do as you command.' 'At the insistence of these ladies, knight,' he replied, 'from whom I cannot and should not defend myself, I hold you quit for the time being. But if it happens that I meet you another day you will give me either the damsel or death. If these ladies had not come, it would have been a different matter.'

Angered by his reply, Curial said 'Knight, I shall speak as I do not usually speak and say what I should prefer not to say and what is unfitting to say to a knight but for your impertinence, which forces me to say what I should gladly keep back if your discourtesy did not overwhelm me. I could have despatched you from this world had I wished, and if you love your life please put this folly out of your mind. I did not find you so strong or so fierce that I should esteem your menaces or yourself. Heal yourself, and then you may threaten; and so that you may know and seek me, my name is Curial, and throughout this journey and in the tournament that is to follow I shall carry a black shield with a hooded falcon on it, and thus you may know me. If it so happens that we do not meet either on the road or at the tourney, you will find me at the King's court, if I live, and then you may find lists for us where I shall willingly follow you. If you are as good a knight as you think you are, you should not forget the words you have said and those you have heard.'

Then he turned to the Prioress and the nuns and took his leave of them. They embraced him and made much of him and his damsel, who then mounted their horses and rode away. They travelled on until they came to the house of a knight, who was rather old in years and very worthy, and dismounting there they were received very honourably and well served. Here Curial stayed for some days until his wounds were healed, and then he armed himself well and with a good horse he prepared to leave and continue on his way.

The nuns took the wounded knight with much difficulty to the convent, and put him to bed and tended his wounds. All this time nothing was said that would cause him distress, although they had learned from the herald all about the quarrel between him and Curial. When he had provided himself with arms and a horse and wished to depart, he said 'Ladies, God be with you. I promise you on my word that if I encounter that knight you know of, I shall take his damsel from him however unwilling he may be, and I shall do to him what he wished to have done to me, had he been able.' The Prioress, who loved Curial well, replied 'Knight, have you not yet recovered your wits? Are you not ashamed to say such things? Why not ask your herald what condition you were in when we reached you, for I see that you do not know. I beg you, do not pursue him any further nor think about his damsel, for from what I have heard you will win nothing from him, and you may be sure that you will not find prioresses to save you from death everywhere you go.' 'What is this, madam?' asked the knight. 'What condition was I in, then, when you arrived?' 'You tell him, herald,' said the Prioress.

Then the herald told him. 'You were indeed in such dire straits, sir,' he said 'that you were not a hair's breadth from death. You had fallen on your back and showed no sign of being able to get up, and if the other knight had wished he could have sent you to the next world. He could certainly have done so, and I was very much afraid that he would, because of the outrageous thing you had demanded of him and the insulting words you had used to him when you wanted vengeance. I swear to you on my word that from the true things I have heard of him the knight could have fought another knight after he had dealt with you, as valiant as you are, and been successful against him as he was against you. I saw him come to the second onslaught so fresh that he was striking as strongly as when the battle began. Consider to what a point he must have brought you if you cannot remember anything about it. I assure you I have never seen a knight in such dire straits as you were. I beseech you, take the good advice the lady Prioress is giving you, and do not follow that knight for I cannot think you will add to your days or your honour by doing so.'

The knight lowered his head and struck his horse with his spurs and, without speaking, full of anger, he rode away.

★

When Curial had left the worthy man's house he travelled on that morning until he encountered a knight with a damsel whom he had recently taken from another knight, whom he had overthrown. The damsel was lamenting most pitifully and when Curial drew near them she rode towards him in tears, slid off her hackney and with

92

bitter tears mingling with her words she said to him 'Sir knight, I beseech you to help a knight from whom this knight took me a little while ago, leaving him wounded on the road. If he is not helped he will soon die.' 'Damsel,' said Curial, 'who is the wounded knight?' 'He is the Lord of Montlesu, sir' she answered. When Curial heard the name his blood left his heart, because this Lord of Montlesu was a great friend of his and it was not long since he had parted from him in Germany, where he had performed feats of arms and acquitted himself very honourably.

So he went to the knight and said to him 'Knight, I beg you to let this damsel return to the knight who was escorting her, for she says he is wounded and may die if he does not receive help.' 'I shall willingly let the damsel go,' said the knight, 'if you will give me yours.' 'You cannot have mine,' said Curial, 'nor do I want yours, but if you will please me in this I shall be most grateful. Otherwise I shall do something else which may please you equally.'

The knight, seeing how politely Curial was asking for the damsel, thought that he was not the sort of knight who would demand her by combat and so he said 'Knight, let us settle it thus: you must joust with me and have either the two damsels or none, otherwise you will not leave this place.' So saying he spurred his horse, and going first some distance away, turned to charge at Curial. On his approach he struck him with such might that his lance shattered to pieces, but Curial, who was far better and stronger and more skilful, struck him full centre, so hard that he sent him flying a lance's length from his horse. The knight, who was agile and very strong and had received no other hurt save that of the fall, got up quickly, and taking his sword in his hand he said boldly 'Down, knight, down! Dismount and let us fight on foot with swords, and for the moment I will grant you the advantage with the lance.' Curial answered 'Knight, the custom of knights errant is to joust, and whichever comes off best takes the damsel.' The knight replied 'Even so, you will not have her unless you fight me first on foot.' Curial replied that he did not wish to fight, nor would he in such circumstances, and going up to the damsel he told her to mount her horse.

One of Curial's squires had jumped down to help her on to her hackney, but the knight, with raised sword, rushed between them to prevent him from lifting her. Curial was by now angry, and he came forward and said 'By my faith, she will mount whether you will or no' and he called to the squire 'Go, help her to mount.' Although the knight shouted 'He will not', the squire went forward and took hold of the damsel to lift her up, but the knight, maddened and incensed with furious rage, struck the squire with his sword, thrusting it into his stomach. The squire cried out 'Sir, I die for you', and the knight, still not satisfied, turned on the damsel, who was trying with all her might to climb on to her horse, and struck her also with his sword, so that she fell to the ground dead.

Seeing the squire and the damsel killed in this way, Curial thought that he would go out of his mind, and, still mounted on his horse, was on the point of running the knight down and trampling on him with the horse, for he deserved no other death. But finally he decided to dismount to fight him, and as he did so the knight not waiting for Curial to come to him, started forward and with incredible boldness rushed at him with his sword. Curial, overcome with anger, ran at him, and they struck each other hard and terrible blows with their swords. The knight, who was powerful and bold, made great efforts, but his strength was not equal to the arrogance of his heart. When the combat had lasted for a long while and the knight was so tired that he could not raise his arm for weariness or get his breath at all, thinking that Curial would allow him to retreat to take a little rest according to the custom of knights errant, he drew back; but Curial took no notice and followed after him, smiting him again and again even more fiercely than before, so that he could not collect his senses. The knight gave himself up for lost, and without trying to attack, since he was not capable of doing so, he tried for a while to defend himself. But it availed him nothing, for Curial was determined to put him to death, and rained blows upon him so terribly that the knight could not continue. 'Knight,' he said to Curial, 'do you know with whom you are fighting?' 'No,' answered Curial, 'nor do I want to know.' 'Know then that this battle has been the death of me, and you have killed the Lord of Montbrun.' And as he spoke, he fell. 'If you are dead,' said Curial, 'I say it is Breus Saunce Pité and no other who is dead, and whether you be the Lord of Montbrun or Montnoir you have deserved all you have suffered and worse.' And he ordered his other squire to take the helmet off his head. When the helmet was removed, he saw that the knight was still alive, but he ordered the squire to cut off his head and throw it away as far as he could, and this was done.

When the Lord of Montbrun had been killed, as you have heard, Curial ordered his squire not to move from the spot until he had sent for the bodies of the other squire and his damsel, and he rode swiftly along the road by which the knight and the damsel had come, until he reached the Lord of Montlesu, who lay on the ground, his leg having been broken in his encounter with the Lord of Montbrun. Curial quickly dismounted and said to him 'Knight, what is wrong with you that you have not risen?' 'Sir knight,' the knight answered, 'some while ago I was coming along this road with a damsel whom I was taking to the tournament, and I met a knight on his own, with no company. He wished to take the damsel from me, according to the custom of the kingdom, and so I had to joust with him. He struck me so hard that he knocked over both me and my horse, and the horse fell on my leg and broke it in two so that I cannot move from here; and all he cared about was to take away my damsel, along that road by which you have come. I am surprised that you did not meet them.' 'Yes, I did meet them,' said Curial, 'unfortunately.' He went to catch the knight's horse and then, with Festa's help, he lifted the knight into the saddle as best he could, and asked him if there was any place at hand where they could find shelter. 'Yes, there is an abbey close by,' answered the knight, 'which I left only this morning.'

They at once set out in that direction and reached the abbey, where they were received and served with great civility, and the sick man was put to bed and tended. Curial immediately sent for the dead squire and damsel and had them buried in the monastery with an inscription describing how the knight and the others had died. He also sent to have the Lord of Montbrun disarmed and buried in the middle of the road with a stake on which the dead man's accoutrements were hung, with a tablet nailed to the stake relating the cause of the death of the cruel Lord of Montbrun. Then Curial rode away with Festa, without making himself known to the injured knight, and they continued their journey towards Melun, talking of these events as they went. Curial sent his squire on in advance as a herald, giving him the name Vengeance, and gave him his arms and device, on which were words reading 'Do not climb so high that you hurt yourself nor descend so low that you demean yourself'.

★

Curial was very displeased by these shocking happenings, for although he liked to test his physical prowess he preferred to do so without it leading to death and offence to God, and so he was sad. But Fortune was not yet satisfied and every day sought new ways in which to bring misfortune upon him.

Accordingly, after they had left the monastery, in which they rested for several days, they had not been travelling long before they met a dwarf who, as soon as he saw them, said 'Knight, I pray you, stop a little while I speak to you.' Curial halted and said 'Tell me what you want, friend, and I will wait and listen willingly as long as you please.' 'Sir knight,' said the dwarf, 'tell me, please, if you have come from the monastery that is close by.' 'Yes, we have' said Curial. 'We have been there for several days.' 'Was there another knight there besides yourself?' asked the dwarf. 'Yes, there was', replied Curial. Then the dwarf said 'Sir knight, I will tell you why I ask. I have been sent by two knights who are seeking a knight who, it is said, killed the Lord of Montbrun a few days ago, and I am sure that if they meet him he will surely die. I want someone to warn him of this so he may avoid so great a danger.' 'Who are these knights who send you?' asked Curial. 'One is called Charles de Montbrun, a valiant and skilful knight who is the dead man's brother, and the other is Jacques de Montbrun, his uncle.' 'Are they coming this way?' asked Curial. 'Yes, they are,' replied the dwarf, 'and you will meet them before long.' Then Curial said 'Friend, go with God, and when you get to the monastery you will have news of the knight whom you seek and will learn all about the matter and how it happened.' 'Then, sir, please change your route,' said the dwarf, 'for the two knights who are coming are so angry that they will not leave you without a fight for anything in the world.' 'Thank you, friend, for your good advice' said Curial. 'They will not bother with me, and I shall not bother with them.' 'What if they will not let you pass without doing battle?' asked the dwarf, 'what will you do then?' 'I do not know now' said Curial, 'When it happens, then I shall know what to do.'

After this the dwarf left them and went to the monastery where he found the Lord of Montlesu, who was not yet cured and knew nothing of what had happened, because Curial had given orders that he was not to be told. The dwarf asked the Abbot about the matter, and the Abbot showed him the tablet on which the story of the deed was written. The dwarf asked him 'Is this the knight I met on the road, with a damsel and carrying a black shield?' 'The very same' said the Abbot. 'Well then, by now he will be a dead man,' said the dwarf, 'for he was taking a route which would certainly bring him to those who are looking for him to kill him.'

So at once he hastened to his horse and went back along the way he had come, so fast that he caught up with Curial. 'Knight,' he said to him, 'how can you have so little sense as to continue along this road, knowing what you have done and having heard what I have told you?' 'I have not yet seen any other road save this one today,' replied Curial, 'and I cannot leave it until I find another.' 'You will repent of it,' said the dwarf, 'when repentance is no longer any good to you.' And striking his horse with his spurs he hurried on towards the approaching knights.

He had not gone very far before he met them, and he told them everything that had happened, his first conversation with the knight, his journey to the monastery, the death of the Lord of Montbrun, who had been slain through his own fault by a knight, who was close at hand; and how he had spoken to him again and he had been unwilling to change his route although he had advised him to do so, telling him that the two knights were coming in search of him.

The two knights stopped then, and the dead man's brother said 'Sir uncle, I beg you not to lay a hand on the knight, for I shall fight him and avenge my brother. If we both fight him we should be committing a vile act, and we should both be considered villainous.' The uncle answered that he agreed. So Charles de Montbrun prepared to do battle, and sent the dwarf to the knight with the message that he must be ready for a fight to the death. Curial took his lance and shield and had his horse's harness tightened, and rode onwards calmly and slowly. The other two knights advanced at such a speed that it seemed they could not reach their own undoing fast enough. When they were near Curial, Charles de Montbrun called to him 'Knight, you have killed my brother wrongfully.' 'You lie in your throat,' replied Curial, 'I did not kill him wrongfully. If I was indeed the cause of his death, I am not to blame, and to prove my case I will fight you.' 'Before you leave here you will pay for it' replied Charles. 'It often happens,' Curial answered, 'that those who think to avenge the shame of others increase their own.'

Charles de Montbrun set spurs to his horse, and with as much speed as he could rushed on Curial and hit him with such force that his lance was shattered into firewood. Curial saw that he must use all his strength, and struck him in return with such skill that the lance pierced the shield and the whole blade entered his breast. From this encounter Charles de Montbrun fell dead to the ground, and Curial, his lance broken, rode beyond him. His squire at once came up to him and gave him another very strong lance, which he had been carrying. Curial took the lance and turned towards the other knight, waiting to see what he would do; but he was waiting for Charles to rise. Seeing that one knight was not getting up and the other not moving, Curial said to the squire and Festa 'Let us go, in God's name' and they set off.

But Jacques de Montbrun, seeing that his nephew did not rise and that Curial was moving off, shouted 'Wait, knight, you will not leave this place' and spurring on his horse he rode at him and struck him in the middle of the shield hard enough to break the lance. The blow he received was different, however, for Curial struck him with such skill that he sent him flying ignominiously from his horse, and he fell with such force that he lost all inclination to fight. Curial drew up and, giving his lance to his squire, waited motionless to see what he would do. With great difficulty he picked himself up off the ground and limping, for he could move in no other way, he said to Curial 'Knight, I beg you to dismount, for I wish to speak with you.'

97

Curial dismounted at once and went to the knight, who asked him to tell him how the Lord of Montbrun had died. Curial told him everything, without lying at all, and then the knight said to him 'Friend, go with God. I hold you quit wherever you go, for you have done what a good knight should do, and if you had done otherwise you would have failed in true chivalry.' Then Curial mounted and rode away.

Jacques de Montbrun had the dead knight taken to the monastery and buried without honour, and where all could see it he had written up the cause and manner of his death. He also spoke to the Lord Montlesu, who was a kinsman of his, who was not yet cured and knew nothing of what had happened. When he heard of the death of his damsel he thought he would go mad, and when he heard the rest of the events that had followed he wished he had known the knight who had so fully avenged him. But it was too late, and he never knew who he was.

★

Curial continued along that road all morning, looking for somewhere they could rest. 'Ride no more as a knight errant, I beg you', Festa said to him. 'So many dangerous things happen as a result of your doing so, and one day you are bound to suffer some serious harm.' Curial answered that he would not cease to do so for anything in the world, and that he would continue in that way until he came to the tournament because it would be a great disgrace if he were to travel in any other fashion. So, parched with thirst and with weary animals, they rode on for a long while through the heat of midday, when the sun is at its strongest, without finding anywhere they could take a rest. And Festa, watching Curial, remembered all his feats of arms.

As they travelled on, far in the distance they saw a grove of trees, and so they turned their steps in that direction. When they reached it they found a plentiful stream of water flowing from a beautiful clear spring close at hand, and they dismounted at once and sat down to rest in the shade of the trees and the coolness provided by the stream, fetching bread and other refreshments they had brought with them to eat. They unharnessed the horses too, and let them wander to crop the grass, which was very good and tender.

While they were reposing in this verdant spot, a fine white horse approached Curial's horse, and they began to snap at each other. The noise they made attracted the attention of Curial and his party, and they were very surprised. 'That horse must have run away from some knight', said Curial. 'Go and catch it, and look after it for its owner.' The squires ran towards the horse, but as they neared it four other squires arrived and took the horse, and led it away, and Curial's squires returned to their resting-place. 'Who were they who took the horse?' asked Curial. 'We do not know,' they replied, 'but they say it is theirs, and so they took it away.'

Just then one of the squires who had taken the horse came up to Curial and when he had greeted the company he said 'Sir, I am sent here by four knights who are encamped on the far side of these trees. They ask you to do them the honour of joining them in their tents, since you have none of your own, and you will be more comfortable than you are here, and your enjoyment will be the greater.' 'Who are the knights who sent you here, friend?' asked Curial. 'They are from Aragon' replied the squire. 'There are many good knights in Aragon' said Curial. 'If you will tell me their names you will do me a great favour.' 'Certainly' said the squire. 'One of them, who is my master, is don Juan Martines de Luna, another is don Pero Cornell, another don Blasc d'Alagó and the fourth is don Juan Ximenes d'Urrea. And you, sir, what is your name?' 'I, friend, am from a foreign land,' answered Curial, 'and I am a poor knight, unknown and of little renown, and it would serve them nothing to know my name. But tell your masters that I send them infinite thanks for their great courtesy, of which I should avail myself very willingly if I were stopping here. However, I must leave and so have no need to accept their most kind offer. Please tell them this on my behalf.'

The squire looked long at Festa, and thought her the most beautiful damsel he had ever seen, and he turned to address her saying 'And you, lady, will you come?' The damsel replied that the knight had answered for all, all were his to command. Thereupon the squire took his leave and returned to the knights. When he told them what he had seen and heard, and when they learned that there was a damsel, and such a pretty one, they said 'Let us take her, according to the custom that prevails in this kingdom!' Pero Cornell, rising to his feet, said 'This adventure belongs to me, for you have all fought today and I have done nothing. So leave it to me, I beg you.' And they all agreed.

But there was a very intelligent herald travelling with them, who had heard all that had passed, and he said to them 'Sirs, what do you mean to do?' 'Go and take the damsel, according to the custom of knights errant.' 'You will commit a serious wrong if you try to do that,' the herald said, 'for two reasons. First, because they are at rest and the custom concerns only those damsels who are met when travelling, with a knight who is armed; secondly, because you have offered them shelter and your company, and to attack them now, where they are resting, would not be right, as you well know.'

'Yes, but he has learned our names and will not tell us his.' 'Tell me, squire,' said the herald, 'did the knight use force to make you tell him the names of these knights?' The squire replied that he had not, but had requested him to do so, and he had answered his request. Then the herald said 'What do you wish to do, sir knight? Sit down again, for it will add nothing to your honour if you attack the knight today. Perhaps you will meet him tomorrow, and then you can demand the damsel from him. Perhaps you will have her, or maybe you will wish you had kept silent, for such is the way of the world. But if you wish I will go to see the knight, and speak to him, and perhaps you will learn something about his condition.'

He went off, and as soon as Curial saw the herald he recognised him, because he had seen him before in the company of Jacob of Cleves. The herald recognised Curial too, and went up to him and made a deep bow, which the knights could see through the trees. Curial said to him 'Bonne Pensée, you are welcome.' 'Sir' he said, 'and you are well met. By my faith, I am more pleased to come across you than any other knight in the world.' 'Where are you going?' asked Curial. 'I am going to the tournament with four knights from Aragon' replied the herald. 'They have never been in this country before and so I am guiding them through the regions where they can find the most exacting and arduous adventures, and we have come this far. Up to the present time I assure you they have performed such feats with their persons that if they continue in the same way they will return to their country with great honour.' 'Do they always ride together?' asked Curial. 'Yes,' said the herald, 'for the King, their lord, has ordered them to do so, and nothing in the world will part them save injuries and illness and so they are always together. I do not think any four better knights are going to the tournament, for they are strong and very valorous and of great vigour, and moreover they are so lofty-hearted that each one of them considers himself equal to a king, and you will see how they demonstrate this on the day of the tourney.' Curial was delighted to hear this news and said 'Now we shall see what will become of the pride of the Bretons and the English, who believe that there are no other knights in the world beside themselves.' 'And what of the Normans?' said the herald. 'I promise you, these four knights are sufficient for any other four, and those of the best.'

Curial enjoyed talking to the herald, and said to him 'Bonne Pensée, please do not tell my name to those knights or to any other, for this time I do not want to be known.' The herald looked at Festa, and saw that she was so pretty that he was certain he had never seen anyone to equal her. 'You have a beautiful damsel, sir' he said. 'I do not know if I am beautiful,' said Festa, 'but I think I am a great

100

nuisance to him, and shall be more so if we continue together for long!' The herald laughed and then took his leave, and Curial asked him to commend him to the knights.

The herald returned to his masters and gave them Curial's greetings. They asked him if he knew the knight, and he said that he did, but that he could not tell them his name as the knight had forbidden him to do so. They could be certain, however, that he was one of the most noble and valiant and courteous knights in the world, and they would soon see this for themselves. 'He has already proved a good companion in arms to knights of your nation, and is very well-disposed towards all your compatriots.' The knights were pleased to hear this, but it made them still more eager to know who he was, and so they sent back the herald to say that the knights would like to visit Curial and his damsel.

Curial sent back word that he would be grateful if they would not come to see him, but that they could certainly see the damsel. And he told Festa to make herself ready to go to them, and ordered the herald not to return to the knights until the damsel was ready. And so it happened. Festa took great pains to prepare herself, and meanwhile Curial armed and mounted his horse. When Festa was ready she was helped on to her palfrey, and escorted by the herald and the squires he sent her to the knights, who received her very honourably and entertained her as well as they could.

Festa said to them 'Sirs, the knight in whose company I am begs you to excuse him for not showing himself to you and for not revealing his name. He is yours in whatever serves your honour, and if it ever happens that his company may benefit you you will surely have it, for he is devoted to all of your nation.' The knights thanked her very much for his offer and in turn offered their service both to Curial and to her; and they all said she was one of the most beautiful damsels they had ever seen.

While they were talking, don Juan Martines de Luna went to Festa and gave her a rich gold chain saying 'Damsel, I do not remember having ever seen a damsel as pretty as you, nor one whom I liked so much, and so I beg you, for the honour of the knight who is your escort, and for my own sake, to wear this chain'; and he put it round her neck. Festa accepted the present, thanking him with all her heart. 'Sir knight, you are certainly kinder to me than the knight who took me by the hair' she said, and she told them about him. They laughed, but at the same time they were angered by the villainous thing the knight had done. But they also said that he must have been a good knight because even if he had failed in courtesy he had not failed in chivalry.

When they heard that Curial was already armed and mounted

101

they accompanied Festa back to him, on foot, and he thanked them for it. They looked at the knight and saw that he was big and strong and in good fettle, and they made many offers of service, and he to them, so that nothing more could be said. 'Sirs,' said Curial, 'I know that you are subjects of the King of Aragon, who is the best knight in the world with the lance, as I have heard, and I am so devoted to all his subjects so that I would willingly serve them in every way possible. It was for this reason I sent my damsel to you, which I swear I should not have done for any knight who was not of your nation.' They thanked him many times, and then Curial took his leave and departed.

As they journeyed that day Festa talked about the knights, saying 'On my word I do not believe there are more courteous knights in the world.' 'Indeed, I think so too,' said Curial, 'and they look to me to be good knights, strong and valiant.'

They came to a town where they found good and suitable lodgings for that night, and early next morning they left. Fearing that he would be recognised, Curial disguised himself as much as he could, and would have covered his shield if he had not promised Bertrand du Chastel to carry a black shield with a hooded falcon on it throughout the journey and during the tournament. He made Festa wear a veil so that her face could not be seen, and then they set off. They had not gone very far before they met the four knights, who had spent the night in another town close by. When they saw Curial the knights sent the herald to bid him halt and break a lance with them, according to the custom of knights errant. Curial at once stopped, and taking a lance in his hand he turned towards them. First don Pero Cornell came at him, and they struck each other so hard that the lances flew into pieces, but otherwise it seemed as though the knights had done nothing. Curial took another lance from one of his squires and faced another of the knights, and again they struck each other vigorously and again the lances broke, leaving the knights still in their saddles. Then another of the knights advanced ready to joust, but the herald intervened and said 'What are you trying to do? Can you not see that the knight has no lance and there is no other one for him here?' 'Since he has no lance,' said the knight, 'I will fight him with the sword.' 'You will do wrong if you do so,' said the herald, 'for the practice of knights errant is only to break lances, unless there is some cause which leads to a fight. Moreover, I think in spite of his disguise, that this is the knight who left us yesterday.' The knight who had put hand to sword stopped and said to the herald, 'Indeed, Bonne Pensée, I think you are right.' Curial stood still without moving, waiting to see what he would do, but the herald went up to him and said 'Sir knight, you have done

102

wrong to joust with these friends of yours. You were not recognised by them because of your disguise, otherwise they would not have engaged with you; but you, knowing who they were, should have avoided the encounter.' 'Bonne Pensée,' Curial answered, 'the breaking of lances, as you well know, is the salutation of knights errant, even if they are brothers. I should not have invited them to do so because I know them, but if they had invited me and I had refused it seems to me that I should have shown them discourtesy, and it might have been accounted cowardice on my part. Give them my greetings.' And he turned away and went on his way.

The herald returned and gave the knights Curial's greetings, and they realised that he was indeed the knight to whom they had spoken the previous day. They said to one another that he was indeed a valiant knight and that they had not yet seen one who could wield a lance so well. Then they went along the same road, following behind Curial until they could find another that they could take in another direction. Thus they continued until they came to a town. Curial went to an inn, where he found good lodging, and when the four knights arrived they also stopped at the same inn. Although Curial did his utmost to conceal himself from them it happened that he was seen by a squire in their company. This squire had been present at the combat at Montferrat in the company of Pons d'Orcau and recognised him at once, and running to the knights and the herald who was with them, he said 'In faith, sirs, I know the knight with whom you jousted.' 'How do you know him?' they asked. 'Because he is lodging here.' 'That is true,' they said, 'but how do you know who he is?' 'This is the knight who killed Boca di Far,' the squire said, 'with Pons d'Orcau, whose squire I was, and with the other Catalans.' They looked at one another, and asked the herald 'Is he speaking the truth?' 'He says so' said the herald. 'I say nothing.'

So they told the herald that, since they now knew who the knight was, he should go and tell him not to hide himself from them any more. The herald went straight to Curial and said 'Sir knight, in spite of all your care you have been recognised by one of the squires with these four knights, who in my presence told them that you are the man who killed Boca di Far with the Catalan knights.'

Curial was displeased to find that he was known, and said to the herald 'I am indeed sorry, Bonne Pensée, to hear what you have told me, but since I had to be recognised I would rather they knew me than anyone else, and I am glad of that. If God had willed, however, I should have preferred to have remained unknown to them and to everyone.' 'Sir,' said the herald, 'that is due to no fault of yours but to the workings of Fortune. Since that is how it is, they beg you to conceal yourself from them no longer, for they would not and do not hide themselves from you.' 'You see how it is, Curial' said Festa. 'It seems to me that these knights are noble and good, and you never know what your needs will be. After all you have done on this journey you must expect to have many enemies and people who envy you, who will seek to do you great harm. You have taken honour from many families and diminished their prestige and reputation, so that many will owe you a grudge and will seek to bring you down if they can. Since these know who you are, and they seek your friendship, be willing to accept theirs, for it will be to your advantage.' So without further thought Curial said to the herald 'Tell them that this damsel and I will be pleased to come to their room and have dinner with them.'

The herald was very pleased and at once returned with this message to the knights. When they heard it they were delighted and prepared to honour them as much as was possible. Curial dressed himself well, with many jewels, and so did Festa, in readiness to visit the knights. When the hour for dinner arrived the herald returned and said they might come to dinner whenever they pleased, and so Curial gave Festa his arm and they left their room and went to that of the knights, where they were very honourably received, and with great merriment. They were such a handsome and well-dressed couple that the knights were full of admiration, and especially when they saw the beauty of Festa they said 'May he who tries to part you be parted from the one he loves!' Don Pero Cornell said 'Lady, as soon as I heard that this knight was escorting a damsel I wanted to demand you from him according to the custom of the kingdom; but now I think that I should have striven in vain and should have returned with my nose out of joint. And if by chance Fortune had ordained that I should win you, on my word you would have suffered a great loss and made a change for the worse, I think!' And everyone laughed.

Then they all washed their hands and took their seats at table and were splendidly served.

By now they were near Melun, where the tourney was to be held, and people were assembling there from many parts of the world, and the captains had already set their flags at the four corners of the field.

They were still at table when a herald arrived at the inn and asked for lodging. He was told that there was room and so he dismounted. Bonne Pensée knew him and went to ask him for news, and they talked for a long time. When Bonne Pensée returned he said to the knights 'Sirs, here is Bonté, the herald of the Count of Foix, and he has come from Melun and has much news to tell, if you wish to hear him.' Curial said nothing, but the others said 'Come, knight, tell him to enter if you will, for he will not heed us.' Curial said that he might enter, and the herald then came in and saluted all the company, who returned his greeting. 'Sirs,' said the herald, 'I beg you to tell me if you know any news of a knight who carries a black shield and has a damsel with him.' 'Many knights carry black shields,' answered Curial, 'and have damsels with them, and we cannot tell which of them you are seeking.' 'I am seeking a knight who, a few days ago, vanquished eight knights and so rid the world of the evil practice of confiscation' replied the herald. 'If you know anything of him, please tell me for I have some news which he will be glad to hear.' 'I cannot tell you anything about the knight now,' said Curial, 'but I think he will be at the tournament and you will be able to find him there. However, tell us what we can tell him, if you will, and we shall gladly do so if we meet him.'

The herald answered 'Sirs, the truth is that I am seeking a knight who is by renown and, I believe, by his deeds the best knight in the world. Knowing what is told about this knight of the black shield who is performing such marvels, I believe that no other knight would do them save the one I seek, and so I assume that this must be he. A noble damsel is seeking news of him throughout the countryside, and if I could take her some reliable information I should be a fortunate man, and the knight too would for sure be content.' 'Who is the damsel who is seeking him?' asked Festa. 'She is called Lachesis,' answered the herald, 'and she is the daughter of the Duke of Bavaria, and the most beautiful damsel in the world.' 'Mind what you are saying' said the four knights. 'I know well what I am saying,' answered the herald, 'and it is certainly true.'

Bonne Pensée said to Bonté 'Come and dine, and afterwards we will tell you what we know about the knight.' So the heralds went off to dinner and the knights and Festa were left on their own. 'That herald is looking for you, Curial' said Festa at once. 'Lachesis is impatient, I think, if she is doing so much to find you. Please say to the herald that he is to tell Lachesis that the knight is certain to be at the tourney and will ensure that she recognises him whatever may happen, but that she must keep it secret and let no one else know.' 'I will not tell him,' said Curial, 'because to speak like that would be as much as to say "I am he": but I will get Bonne Pensée to tell him.' And they all agreed.

So Bonne Pensée was summoned and told what reply to give Bonté; and it was done. But after dinner the herald returned to the knights and said 'Sirs, which of you makes me this reply?' 'Bonne Pensée makes it,' said Festa, 'and so do not doubt it. Go with God.' 'Tell me, friend,' Curial asked him, 'who are the captains in this tournament?' 'For the Germans and Italians,' answered the herald, 'the Duke of Burgundy; for the English and Scots, the Earl of Derby; for the nations of the Langue d'oc and all those of the Spanish language, whom I think will be few, the Count of Foix; and for all the rest, the French and other nations, the Duke of Orleans. But although this order has been instituted I do not think that either this will be observed or the other order concerning the colours of the different classes of lovers. It is true that there are four flags raised at the four corners of the field, and every day, morning and evening, lances are broken and there are great celebrations, but the King and Queen have not yet arrived. Even if countless tents have been erected and there are already many people and more arriving each day, everyone is keeping their trappings and other ornaments for when the King has come and all the court is assembled.'

'Tell me, friend,' said Curial, 'are there many knights from Spain?' 'No, only two,' replied the herald, 'one Pinós, the other of the Barges family. It is said that a dozen or so notable knights are riding through the kingdom and have performed many wonders, and perform more every day, but they are not expected at the tourney.' 'Do you know their names?' asked Curial. 'Only don Blasc d'Alagó, don Pero Maça and one of the Urrea family. Some say that the King of Aragon is coming, but this is not known for sure. I think that the Count of Foix, who is his vassal, must know. But I have heard wonderful accounts of other knights from Aragon who are travelling as knights errant, so much so that one must believe that Tristan and Lancelot, who in time gone by were famous as the best knights in the world, never tested themselves against knights of that nation, unless the authors who wrote of their deeds bridled their pens; or perhaps one might think that they were moved more by will than by reason to write what is read every day in their books.'

'How good a knight is the King of Aragon, that he should be coming to the tournament?' asked Curial. 'Certainly the best in the world, so I have heard' said the herald. 'He bears much ill-will towards the Duke of Anjou and all his house because he killed his father-in-law, King Manfred. He would have been pleased if the Duke of Anjou had ridden as a knight errant and then perhaps he would have made him repent of what he did.' 'Ah, how I should like to meet him!' said Curial. 'Are you not going to the tourney, then?' said the herald. 'Indeed I am' said Curial. 'Then, in God's name,' said the herald, 'you will have no need to ask who he is, for if he is there his lance and his sword will point him out to you at once.' The four knights laughed heartily at this.

Then Festa asked 'Are there any damsels?' 'Yes,' replied the herald, 'and so many that there would be enough to conquer the

106

world, if modesty did not prevent them.' 'Where will Lachesis be?' asked Festa. 'I do not know,' replied the herald, 'but I suppose she will be near wherever her knight is, if she can see him.' 'Tell me, friend, has she brought fine clothes with her?' 'Yes indeed' said the herald. 'She is better dressed than any that have been seen so far, but there are many damsels who are keeping themselves in reserve for when all the court is assembled.'

After this he took his leave and departed.

★

The herald had given the knights much to discuss and ponder. When he returned to Melun he told Lachesis what he had seen and heard, and because of the details that the herald had described Lachesis thought that the knight must be Curial. So she sent one of her damsels, Tura, to ride back with the herald and a good escort to the place where he had left the knights.

Meanwhile, when that day was over the knights began to make ready to leave for the tournament. But Festa said to them 'Sirs, this tournament, I have heard, is to last a week. If you are agreeable, you could prepare here all the things that you will need when you get there, so that nothing will be lacking.' All agreed that this was well said, and so they remained where they were. Curial had his pavilion brought to him, which was the largest and most richly decorated at the tournament. It was all in green and white, of soft velvet with gold embroidery, and the ropes were green and white silk and gold thread. High up on the top was a golden ball on which was a lion holding a bird, which some said was a falcon, others a milan, or kite. And he also had brought to him all the horses he had for the contests, with their harnesses, and all his own equipment, especially many black shields. When the Aragonese knights saw all these things they were full of admiration. They too had their tents brought to them, not the ones they always carried with them on the journey but other decorated ones, and their equipment, and they made all possible preparations.

When everything was ready, Tura arrived at the inn. She saw Curial before he could hide himself, and made him a deep curtsey, and seeing that there was nothing he could do, Curial advanced and took her arm, and made much of her. The herald went off to find Festa and said to her 'One of Lachesis's damsels is here.' Festa at once sent word to Curial that he was not to say that she was with him, but with the Aragonese knights, and she asked their permission for this. 'Why do you want to do this?' they asked. 'So that this damsel pays

107

no attention to me' she replied. And they said they were happy to do so.

Curial led Tura to their room and there Festa made her welcome. Tura asked her where she came from and she said from Aragon, and what her name was and she said Festa. 'In faith,' said Tura, 'you have a good name, and without you the affairs of the world are of little worth.' Tura was very pretty and a good talker and wonderfully lively and cheerful. Curial said to her 'Tura, I beg you not to mention my name, because I do not want these knights to know it.' 'Is the damsel theirs?' asked Tura; and Curial said that she was. 'She is very pretty,' said Tura, 'but she will be nothing beside Lachesis.' Curial made no reply.

Then Tura gave Curial a letter from Lachesis, and a gold chaplet with many precious stones and large pearls, and the gold lion brooch which he had seen before. She gave him a very fine tent too, with four divisions inside, made of crimson satin embroidered with loops of gold and with eyes. On the door was a white greyhound, so well worked that it seemed alive, with a collar of pearls and sapphires, and round the edges of the door were letters worked in pearls and precious stones which read 'How can my poor heart bear the great sorrow it must suffer?'

Tura gave all these things to Curial on Lachesis's behalf, and Curial accepted them with a cheerful face, and praised them very highly, both because they deserved it for their own worth and because of her who sent them. Refreshments were brought and they had an enjoyable time; but Festa went close to Curial and said in his ear 'Do not read the letter without me'. Curial said nothing.

Then a pleasant room in the inn was provided for Tura to stay in, and she went to rest because she was tired by her journey. She told Curial to write a letter while she slept for a little, because she wanted to leave soon, and Curial replied he would do so with pleasure. So Curial and the other knights escorted her to her room and then returned to their own, where they found Festa deep in thought. Without more ado she said to Curial that they should return to their own room, so they took leave of the knights. When they were alone Festa said to him 'Curial, Curial, I do not say that you should not show that you are glad to see Lachesis, but I beg you to remember my lady. If she learns that you go a hair's breadth beyond what she would wish in your dealings with Lachesis, I promise you you can expect to bury her that very day; so be careful what you do.' 'Festa,' replied Curial, 'it will be just as you command and no more. But how can I prevent Lachesis from doing me honour and making much of me, or from wishing me well? How can I refuse the honour she wishes to do me, for there is not a king in the world who would

108

not accept the courtesies and the compliments of such a lady, nor is there any knight in the world, however much in love he be, who, while remaining loyal to his lady, would not serve Lachesis to the best of his ability? To my mind, it must suffice my lady to know that I am hers whatever may happen, and no other lady's. I do not know what else I can do, and I regret having come here, for in truth I do not think I shall be able to conduct myself as I need to, and those who are absent are too ready to believe too much. So write only the truth, I beg you, and I shall be content. I cannot say how sorry I am that that damsel met me here. So let us see what I should write to Lachesis. 'Let us read her letter' said Festa. And they did so.

In the letter they saw that Lachesis complained that he had not written to her nor spoken of her, and she commended herself to him, and sent the jewels and the pavilion, and asked him to use it so that she could see it and so would know where he was. 'This is a good letter,' said Festa, 'and I will send it to my lady to exonerate you. But please do not write to Lachesis, but send a message by her damsel, that you have vowed not to say your name nor write to anyone in the world throughout this journey; that you will use her pavilion with pleasure but beg her not to come to it because many people will then realise who you are; and that you will go to her before the tourney is over.' Curial was satisfied with this reply.

So when Tura had finished sleeping Curial was ready, and he went to her and they spoke for a long time, and he told her what they had decided he should say. Tura said it was well, but that she would be grateful if he would write if he could; but Curial said that he could not. Curial was wearing on his left arm a gold bracelet set with many stones and pearls and an inscription around it which read 'A lover without a beloved'. Seeing this bracelet, Tura told Curial that since he was not sending a letter he should send Lachesis the bracelet, and Curial gave it to her. When she read the inscription she said 'The opposite is true'. 'I do not mean to join issue with you over that' replied Curial. Then she took leave of all the knights and Festa, and so departed; but Festa did not know that Tura was taking away the bracelet, nor did she notice.

The time for the tournament arrived, and the knights sent their pavilions and all their equipment to the field and there on the Saturday morning they set up their tents near a spring among broad groves of trees, a long way from the field, and all their things were laid out in order so that those who came to see them would know that they were knights of some consideration and estate. The tents that were Curial's were certainly the most richly ornate and remarkable that had ever been seen in such a gathering.

★

At this same time the King of Aragon had been riding continuously for three months or more as a knight errant and without being recognised had performed feats of arms worthy to be recalled with veneration. Now he sent his tents before him to the camp – not rich ones, so that his identity would not be revealed by them – ordering that they should be placed in the most out-of-the-way position there was. And this was done. (If our concern were not solely with the deeds of Curial I should write here some of the notable actions that have come to my knowledge which were accomplished by his valorous arms to his honour, no less admirable or less dangerous than those you have read.)

Those who erected his tents, thinking to be away from the main encampment, chose a place near those of Curial and the Aragonese knights. When the King arrived at his tent and dismounted he was recognised by a squire of the Aragonese knights, who went to his master and told him he had seen the King. His master then went to the King, made his obeisance, and asked him how it was that he had come all alone. 'I am not alone,' said the King, 'my sword kept me company. Tell me, are there others with you?' 'Yes, sir, the knight from Montferrat who fought against Boca di Far with Pons d'Orcau and the others.' 'Bring him to me,' said the King, 'but do not tell him who I am.'

The knight went and told his companions that the King was encamped near them and that he wished to see Curial, but they were not to tell him who he was. And this was done. They said to Curial 'Close at hand is a knight who is a kinsman of ours, strong and very valiant. Because he is all alone we should like to honour him and include him in our company.' Curial replied that he was happy to do so. At once they went to the knight and saluted him, and he returned their greetings. The King looked at Curial and saw that he was a fine man, well proportioned in all his limbs, and he was much taken with him. Curial looked at the King and saw that he was very robust of person and tall in proportion, with an awe-inspiring gaze, his eyes flashing and seeming to arouse reverence wherever he looked. He spoke little; but he should have been more moderate in his actions, for he was very energetic and so confident in his physical strength and in the loyalty of his vassals that he undertook many redoubtable and dangerous exploits and feared nothing. Curial said to the other knights 'This must be a valorous knight indeed; and if he is not, one should never trust appearances.'

Meanwhile the King's servants had prepared dinner, and the King said 'Come, take your seats at table.' 'Sir knight,' said Curial, 'I beg you to do these knights and myself the honour of dining with us in our tents, which are close by.' 'There will be time for everything' answered the King. They sat down to dinner without paying any heed to rank and precedence, except that Curial was perhaps shown more honour than the others; but from the style in which he was served Curial realised that this knight was of more consequence than the other Aragonese, and he noticed all the plate was of gold and everything, except the tent, was very sumptuous, and all the knights who were the King's subjects came to dinner looking much grander than Curial had ever seen them before. Curial wondered at this, and he observed also that when the other knights were talking apart with the King they bowed to him, through habit, not because the King wished it. On account of these things, and of what he had heard from the herald and others, he believed that this must be the King of Aragon, but as yet he said nothing.

★

So the hour came when they were to attend the eve of tourney, and the King said to the knights, almost as though he were giving an order, 'Come, knights, let us go to the eve of tourney.' So they all armed as well as they could and they took black shields, each knight with his own device on it. The King had two crossed swords on his shield. Festa made ready and then they all set off towards the stands. Festa was helped to a seat in the stands, where she was received very honourably because she was richly apparelled, enough to equal the greatest lady there, and because it was seen that she had come accompanied by six well-mounted knights. So she was honoured more perhaps than some who were of greater consequence, and moreover her beauty was such that it attracted many people to keep her company.

When they saw that Festa was in her place, they saluted her and left her, turning towards where the jousting was taking place. The King, who had no love for the French because of the Duke of Anjou who had killed his father-in-law, saw where the English were breaking lances with the French, and setting spurs to his horse Pompey, he rode towards the Duke of Orleans, who was riding with his lance couched looking for someone to strike. The King met him with a blow on the shield so mighty that it sent him flying as far from the horse as the lance was long. The French hurried to help their captain to his feet while the King next struck the Count of Poitiers hard enough to send him to the ground. He did not stop there for he made another thrust, against one called Jacques de Brabant, powerful enough to unseat him, and this time the King broke his lance. Thus in the first charge he cleared the way for the knights who were coming behind him so that they could pass without hindrance.

Seeing the King so wonderfully successful with the lance the five knights who accompanied him were full of admiration, and they too began to charge, and whoever came against them was sent flying to the ground, and in a short time they had made their presence felt.

There happened to be on the field a very valiant Norman named Guillaume de Rouen who had made some marvellous charges with the lance during that eve of tourney. Seeing what these knights of the black shields were doing, he left the mêlée and took a new horse and refreshed himself. Then taking a stout lance in his hand he went to that part of the field where the six knights were, and observing the knight of the hooded falcon, he thought he would like to attack him but saw that he had no lance, and feared that this might be acting against his honour. However, he noticed that evening was falling and the sun was low and soon he would be prevented from performing feats of arms, and so he decided to charge him. As he charged he hit him so hard that the lance pierced the shield and the saddle-bow, without touching his flesh, however. This was the most serious thrust that Curial had ever received. Seizing his sword, the knight of the falcon hit Guillaume on the head not once but many times, and continued to strike him, giving him no respite nor any opportunity to turn away, so close did he keep to him, and the knight had to cling to his horse's neck. But as is the custom in tourneys, other knights came and separated them and parted them by force, and each went his way, seeking other opponents. Soon the Norman returned, however, and advanced on Curial sword in hand, and Curial closed with him and they exchanged mighty blows, fighting with such ferocity that if it had lasted long they would without doubt have been badly wounded. But it happened that don Juan Martines de Luna came by and saw the Norman, who had troubled him some time before, and when he recognised him he struck him with his lance through the middle of the shield, giving him a large and dangerous wound and sending him flying ingloriously to the ground. They took no further notice of him and passed on.

As the sun had already set, the King of France ordered the retreat to be sounded, and everyone left the field. The squires went to fetch Festa, and when she had mounted her palfrey they returned to their tents by another secluded path, not that by which they had come; and they all praised the King for what he had done. When Curial saw the respect that all gave the King he said 'Sir, I entreat you to tell me who you are.' The King said 'I am the King of Aragon, your friend.' 'Ah, sir!' said Curial, and he fell to his knees and kissed his hand. 'I certainly did not expect that I should have so noble and valorous a knight to be my master and lord here.' The King raised him and put his arms on his shoulders with great geniality. When Festa realised that he was the King she said 'Sir, if all Christian kings were such knights as you and had such vassals there would not be a Moor left in the world.' Then they sat down to supper.

The rest of the knights who were subjects of the King of Aragon were searching for their King throughout the encampment, and could not find news of him. But when they were told that six knights with black shields had done wonders in the eve of tourney they asked 'Did those knights have devices on their shields?' and they were told 'Yes, one has two crossed swords, another a hooded falcon.' And thus the knights realised that they were those they sought. They asked if it was known where they had their quarters, and were told that no one knew, but they were shown the way they had come; and they were also told that if those knights came to the tourney next day they would fare ill, for the Duke of Orleans had vowed he would concern himself with them only.

So these knights left and continued to search up and down from camp to camp until they saw a bright light of torches among the trees. As they made their way towards it they sent a squire on ahead to discover if it were they, and the squire, going forward, saw from the servants that the King was there. He accosted one and asked if the King were there, because nine knights from Aragon were seeking him. The servant went inside to tell the King, and when he heard this he commanded that they should come to him.

They came at once, and made their reverence to the King and greeted all the company; and they had their tents pitched, and encamped there. They told the King what they had heard that the Duke of Orleans had said about the knights of the black shields, and this pleased the King greatly. Turning to Curial he said 'If he has much to do with us he is not likely to leave with a sound head, I think.' 'Sir,' said one of the knights, 'I beseech you not to fight in the tournament tomorrow, let us see what happens: there is plenty of time for you to bear arms whenever you please.' 'You should have said that before they had told me about the intentions of the Duke of Orleans,' said the King, 'and perhaps I should have paid heed to what you say, or perhaps not. But now you must forgive me; I shall not fail to go, and you will see if my hide is as tough as yours and the others'.' 'Sir,' said Curial, 'if I were such a knight as you, so strong and valiant, I should fear no knight in the world.'

Talking thus, they sat down to supper. The King looked around and saw there were fifteen knights. 'I think they will be in a fine sweat before they have beaten us!' he said. 'And there should be more coming, so that we will be thirty knights when we are all together. But even if we are no more than we are at present, I am

113

sure that with the help of the beauty of our damsel they will not easily vanquish us.'

At this point Bonne Pensée arrived from the King's stands and was given a warm welcome. He told them that the King of France and all the knights and ladies had praised the knights of the black shields for their chivalry, and their damsel for her beauty. He said that the King himself was going to enter the tourney the next day, and that the Duke of Orleans had taken it into his head that he would defeat the knights of the black shields, and the King had said that he was undertaking a great enterprise but that he would keep him company.

When the King of Aragon heard this he was content and said 'Knights, things promise well and will turn out better, please God. If anyone says that a fairer damsel than our own has come to the tournament he will not know what he is talking about and will be hard put to it to uphold what he has said. So, damsel, be of good cheer!' 'Sir,' said Festa, 'since your majesty wishes it, in spite of them all I shall have to be the most beautiful this time!' And she and all the others laughed merrily.

The beds were made, and they went to rest.

★

The knights of the black shields were already asleep, but neither the Duke of Orleans, who was head over heels in love with Lachesis, nor the Count of Poitiers slept so early that night, remembering that they had to vanquish the knights of the black shields or be humiliated for ever. So they went through the camps asking knights not to carry black shields. And it was done. The Duke of Orleans had thirty very good knights, with green shields with gold gerfalcons on them, who would not leave his side, and there was also the Count of Poitiers who had green shields with fringes painted on them, with letters saying 'They are fringes'. They agreed that they would ride side by side and that wherever they found a black shield they would charge it.

By morning this resolution was widely known, and Bonne Pensée, who had risen very early to go to the stands, heard of it because no one was talking about anything else. He ran back to the King and told him and all his company. The King was glad of it, and the knights too, but Curial especially welcomed it, more than one can say. The King had a standard, black with two crossed swords, raised and placed outside his tent so that the other knights who were looking for him could find him. Thus they all came together so that

114

soon after sunrise there were twenty-eight knights, well-mounted, all with black shields.

The Count of Foix came to that part, alone and in disguise, and making obeisance to the King begged him to grant him the favour of admitting him to his company. The King replied that he would on no account do so that day, but that perhaps another day he would do as he requested. He said moreover that since he was captain over a fourth part of the tourney it was not fitting that he should join another company. 'Sir, those orders have been discontinued,' the Count said, 'and no battle order will be observed, but he who acquits himself best will carry off the honours of the field. You, sir, have a small company for what you will need to do, and if you knew the undertakings that have been entered upon against you, you would not refuse any knight's offer.' 'Count,' replied the King, 'my greatest desire in the world is to test and learn by experience how much confidence I can have in my person, and whether I am good for fighting another knight in the lists, or for going into battle among many people, or for enduring great fatigue. That is what has brought me here, and I assure you the only thing that displeases me is that a certain knight I know of is not here, otherwise I should prove to him, man to man, that many things he has taken in hand he has not done well. However, if heaven ordains it and God grants me long enough life, he will be put to the test.' The Count said 'The King of France will take part in the tourney today, and many good knights with him.' 'It is a long time since I had such good news' said the King. 'So, Count, keep on your way and do not interfere with us. But whatever happens be careful not to tell anyone who we are.' The Count went away unwillingly, for he would have liked to remain in their company.

The King sent for Curial and asked him to see that his damsel was arrayed as grandly and as richly as possible. So Curial went to Festa and told her to do her utmost to dress herself splendidly, and better than she had ever yet done. And she did so, and embellished herself in every way so that there was no equal to her in the whole gathering. Meanwhile other knights arrived, and the King's master of ceremonies ordered them all to take their places at table.

When they had had dinner the King commanded Bonne Pensée to go to the stands to see how things were progressing. He was gone only a short while before he returned to say that most people were already in the field but that nothing was as yet happening as the Queen and other great ladies had not appeared. He had heard from a herald of the Duke of Burgundy and from another of the King of England that if the knights of the black shields needed help they could have it, if they wished, otherwise each would look to their own affairs.

The King ordered that everyone should arm, saying that what they did here was to their honour, so they should strive to their utmost. Everyone armed; and the King took his standard, which was black with crossed swords, and looking round him he saw a young nobleman, young but valiant and of good physique, from the mountains of Aragon, called Aznar d'Atrosillo, whom the King had brought up in his own chamber. He knighted him then and there and said to him 'I entrust to you this standard and my honour.' The newly-created knight mounted a strong horse and took the standard. The King, looking round, saw that they were thirty-five knights.

They had some refreshments, and then, when all had taken black shields, each with his own device (which in some cases was badly painted due to shortage of time), and had laced their helmets on their heads, and when Festa had mounted a very fine hackney, the King said 'I do not think that any knight would be well advised to take Festa by the hair now, nor would he prize his life very dearly if he did so!' Everybody laughed; then, setting off at a slow pace, they rode to the battle-ground.

Lachesis had not been present at the eve of tourney, but now she came to the stands with her mother. She had spared no pains to make her appearance as splendid as possible, and won high praise for her inestimable beauty. She had put a good deal of study into making as much of her beauty as she could, for there was no master of medicine, expert in such matters, that she did not make use of, to prescribe and prepare material for improving her skin and making it pale, and blanching her face, bosom and hands. I think that she believed there was no other paradise save to be beautiful and to delight oneself with earthly desires. Besides this she was so covered in rich jewels that all who saw her were full of admiration, and on her left arm she wore Curial's bracelet, which she treasured not a little and would not have readily given to anyone who asked for it. Everyone gazed at her and many were afire for her love, for besides her beauty she was so graceful that no one who saw her could fail to love her.

As soon as the Duke of Orleans heard that Lachesis was on her way, he set off, armed as he was, to meet her on the road, and to escort her to the stands; but she refused his company, saying as a pretext that she would not like to be the cause of any other knights fighting him to take her from him in accordance with the custom of the kingdom. So she went up into the stands; and although the Queen made much of her because

116

she was a great lady and a foreigner, she did not like her very much.

Now came Festa, escorted by the knights of the black shields, who was received very honourably and placed close to Lachesis, everyone thinking that since she was so richly dressed and so nobly accompanied she must be a great lady of high degree. All gazed at her, men and women, and because she was so incredibly beautiful everyone was eager to be near her. The Queen welcomed her with great warmth, not only for her great and excellent beauty but also to spite Lachesis. So the beauty of these two was continually debated, and one could not vanquish the other. Both blushed to hear the opinions expressed about them. Some said 'Ah, Holy Mother, what eyes!' Others were saying 'Oh God, what a mouth, what teeth!' So they were picked to pieces: they were looked at together and looked at separately; no one knew what to say of them, nor did they find anything worthy of reproach.

Oh celestial beauty! Oh angelic faces! What pleasure the Lord and Creator of humankind took in creating these two damsels, according to worldly opinion! And if Lachesis had worked hard to increase her beauty I promise you that Festa was not negligent or remiss or backward, but with much skill and knowledge acquired by long and arduous study she busied her hands, and with those long, slender, delicate fingers, those nails of ivory, she added beauty to beauties, for of her face, head, bosom or hands there was nothing omitted that could be improved by cosmetics or artificial beauty aids. Ah, how well the great philosopher called Plato knew them when he said that women's wisdom consisted in their beauty and men's beauty consisted in their wisdom!

So it might be said that the beauty of these two was in contest, and one could not vanquish the other. All that those who observed them could decide was that the German had the longer neck and the Italian had the smaller mouth: in all the rest they were equal. Festa saw that Lachesis was wearing Curial's bracelet, recognising it by the words 'A lover without a beloved'. When she asked who she was, she was told that she was Lachesis, daughter of the Duke of Bavaria, and Festa was worried and said to herself 'Perhaps that bracelet will be an unlucky one for the giver.'

When the standard with the swords was seen, and the knights of the black shields around it, everyone moved towards it to see them. By order of the knight of the crossed swords, Bonne Pensée proclaimed at the four corners of the field with a great flourish of trumpets that any knight who wished to maintain that the damsel of the black shield was not the most beautiful in all the stands should come forward, and there would be someone to prove it to him by force of arms. That day Festa was wearing a gold chain with a little

117

black shield hanging from it which fell over her left breast, set around with valuable diamonds and huge pearls. The people moved aside saying 'Now there will be a great fight, for the Duke of Orleans and the Count of Poitiers will give them such sport that they will remember it all their lives!'

The Duke of Orleans sent for the herald and said to him 'Tell me, who ordered you to make that proclamation?' 'The knight of the swords' answered the herald. 'Tell him,' said the Duke, 'that Orleans says that Lachesis, daughter of the Duke of Bavaria, is incomparably more beautiful, not only than her of the black shield but also than all the ladies in the world, and he will prove it on this field.' So the Duke of Orleans came forward with a green standard bearing a gerfalcon of gold, and everyone guessed that it was because Lachesis was a German. The Duke was newly enamoured of Lachesis, and so deeply aflame with love that he could think only of her. He was a worthy man and a very good knight, and bold; and the Count of Poitiers, who came with him, was also a good strong knight.

The King, high up in the stands, was observing the bearing of the knights as they arrived, and when he saw all the knights of the black shields together with their standard he said aloud, so that many heard it, 'I am certain that the honours of the day will go to those of the black shields, for there are many of them who look splendid knights.' Don Juan Martines de Luna had golden scourges on his shield, and each of the others had his own device according to his own fancy and all were very well mounted, better than any others in the tourney.

The Duke of Orleans looked attentively towards the part of the field where the black standard was raised. 'There are many of those knights, it seems' he said; and he was told that there were a good thirty-five of them and that the Burgundians and the English were saying that if they needed help they would provide it when asked. 'In God's name,' said the Duke, 'whoever vanquishes those of the black shields will vanquish all the rest.' The King of France had the field surveyed and it was reported to him that everyone was present. Then the King's trumpeter sounded a call and each of the knights took a lance in his hand and made ready to move. But the King of England sent word to the Duke of Burgundy to watch what became of the knights of the black shields, and sent a similar message to the Duke of Brittany, so that they would not be endangered. At the second trumpet call the knights all began to draw near one to the other; and the herald was telling the knight of the swords what the Duke of Orleans had said about Lachesis's beauty, and as he uttered the last words, the King's trumpeter sounded another call.

The standards moved forward and the knights began to strike

blows that were marvellous to behold. Those of the black shields, all close together, engaged with those of the Duke of Orleans and the Count of Poitiers, of whom there were many, and particularly with the fifty under the banner of the gerfalcon. So fierce was this attack that at the first encounter they struck down a large number of their adversaries, breaking them up into two separate groups, and the standard of the gerfalcon was knocked to the ground. In spite of the efforts of the knights of the black shields, the standard was raised again at once by force of numbers, but there were many loud cries from those who lay on the ground among the horses' hooves. Thus the tourney began, seeming more like mortal combat. The Count of Armagnac came to the aid of the Orleanists, and the Duke of Holland rode against him in a valiant encounter in which many knights were unhorsed.

The King of Aragon saw that the Duke of Orleans and the Count of Poitiers were fighting side by side and endeavouring wherever they went to cause harm to the knights of the black shields, so he called to Curial and together they rode to encounter them. First the King, with a strong lance in his hand, took aim to strike the Duke of Orleans, but the Count of Poitiers intervened and received the blow on his shield. This did him little good, for he was struck full centre with such force that he fell from his horse gravely wounded. Then the King put hand to sword and galloped towards the Duke of Orleans, to strike him, while Curial espied a knight, named Jacques d'Agraville, approaching to strike the King, and met him with his lance with such force that he knocked him from his horse. The King came up with the Duke of Orleans and rained down such heavy blows on his head that the Duke was stunned, and swayed in the saddle not knowing where he was, while the King continued to smite him with his sword, asking him which damsel was the most beautiful.

The Duke's followers came in haste to help him, and those of the black shields strove to keep them away, and fought among them with such energy that everyone was kept occupied. The King lay hold of the Duke of Orleans and setting spurs to his horse pulled him so hard that he dragged him willy nilly from the saddle and draped him over the neck of his horse and carried him to the stands, where he presented him to the damsel of the black shield, the fairest of them all.

The Duke was welcomed, consoled and fêted, but when they tried to disarm him he would not allow it and sent a messenger to the knight of the swords to ask what he must do to be released from captivity. The knight's reply was that all he need do was to say publicly that the damsel of the black shield was the most beautiful

119

damsel in the world. When the Duke heard that if he wished to return to the tourney this was what he had to say, he secretly had a black shield brought to him and then begged Lachesis to put her hand on it; then he said 'I declare that the damsel who has the black shield is the most beautiful in the world.' And immediately he laced his helmet on his head, mounted his horse and returned to the tourney. Thus the knight of the swords was deceived, for he was not aware of the trick; but it may be that before the tourney was over he who had read the text had provided the gloss, and had told him about it.

Next the Duke of Bourbon and the Duke of Bar entered the tourney together, and the King of England and all his followers joined battle with them, and they engaged each other in a way marvellous to behold. There you could see unhorsed knights and riderless horses in great numbers. The knights of the black shields gathered together again and began to strike right and left, and there you could see helmets wrenched from heads and shields from necks in a way marvellous to behold, and wherever they went they lay about them and passed on leaving the way open behind them, and everyone went aside for them. Then the Duke of Brittany entered the tourney, and against him came the Dukes of Berry and Brabant, and they met in a sharp clash of arms which left many on the ground.

The King of France watched the knights of the black shields from the stands, and they were fighting in a way so marvellous to behold that there was no saying which was the best of them. 'Either I am not the knight I was,' he said, 'or the Duke of Orleans will be avenged today for the violence that was done him.' The Count of Foix, who had not yet taken the field, was standing near the King and when he heard him say this he laughed aloud and said to the King, still laughing 'You yourself may yet be the prisoner of the damsel of the black shield!' The King laughed too and said 'I shall not take leave of her, for it may well be so!'

The Count called Phoebus, his son, and said to him 'Phoebus, go to the tents and arm yourself, and take a black shield, and four other knights, no more, and see that they have black shields. Then go into the field and wherever you find the knight of the crossed swords tell him that the King of France is now entering the tourney against him to avenge the Duke of Orleans. Ask him to make you a knight, and then do not leave him.' Phoebus did what his father told him, and not knowing who the knight of the swords was, went in search of him. He looked until he found him, and told him what the Count had said, and entreated him to make him a knight. The King raised

120

his sword and tapped him on the head with it, saying 'God make you a good knight.'

Then the knight of the swords called all his followers to him in one place and leaving the tourney they went to a certain place where they took some refreshment and good fresh horses. The King asked Phoebus who he was, and he answered that he was Phoebus, son of the Count of Foix, and this pleased the King greatly. When they were rested they took stout, strong lances and rode slowly back to the tourney. On the way they met Bonne Pensée, and he said to them 'The King is already mounted and any minute will be in the tourney.' So the knight of the swords took Curial's hands and said 'Now we shall see what happens. Perhaps he who thinks to avenge the shame of others will increase his own!'

The King of France was already in the mêlée and performing excellent feats of arms with many knights who had entered with him. Although the Duke of Burgundy and many others approached him, the King rode all over the field in search of the knights of the black shields, without finding them. However, just then they arrived, and when the French saw them they started to shout 'Here they are! Have at them!' But they can never have said anything of which they so soon repented, for those of the black shields, with their standard in their midst, bore down on them with such force that each one of them unhorsed his adversary. Then they went in among them and broke them up, divided and scattered them, giving them no opportunity to form together again. When they had broken their lances they took their swords and fell to among the French, and what with their assaults and the French defending themselves, the noise of the fighting was such that it sounded as though many smiths were striking great blows on as many anvils.

When he saw this the Count of Foix was afraid that something disastrous might happen, and he hurried to the King of France, who had already done much fighting, and said to him 'Ah Sir, what are you doing? Is it not time for you to have done with this labour? Grant me a favour, I beg you.' The King said that he would and so the Count said 'Leave the field now, for that is what you have granted me, and fight no more.' The King said that he would but that first he must break a lance on the shield of the crossed swords. Then the King, who was a very notable and good knight, took a lance in his hand and charged the knight of the swords, striking him on the shield so that the lance flew into pieces. The knight of the swords saw from the trappings, which were all white, that it was the King of France who had hit him with his lance, and he went up to him and struck him on the helmet with his sword such a blow that it made him fall forward. He was about to strike him again when

121

the Count of Foix intervened and received the blow on his shield, and it took a great piece from it.

So the King of France left the tourney and went to the stands and was disarmed; and he said that he had broken a lance on the shield of the best knight in the world, which made him very content. So great was his joy that in all that day no favour was asked of him that he did not grant.

Curial was incensed with furious rage by an Englishman who had struck him treacherously with a lance and disappeared so swiftly that he was unable to get to him. But looking around he saw another Englishman, named Lord Gloucester, who had already given the knights of the black shields no little trouble. He drove his horse towards him and chased after him with a lance in his hand, catching him up in front of the stands. The Englishman heard a shout 'Look out, here is the knight of the falcon!' and turned at once, and with lance in hand charged Curial, striking him in the middle of the shield so that his whole lance shattered to pieces. Curial, who was furiously angry, met the knight with such force that his lance pierced the shield and entered the raw flesh, and knocked him shamefully from his horse, so that he did not know if it was day or night. Curial dismounted, and holding his horse by the reins he took the shield, which was all white with a gold crown, from the fallen knight and sent it to the stands, saying 'Give it to the most beautiful damsel.' The man who took the shield carried it to Lachesis, and she was delighted, sure that it was Curial who sent it although in the tournament he was known only as the knight of the hooded falcon. In the stands, Lachesis took the shield joyfully and hung it round her neck. Many were watching, and they said 'Lachesis is surely the most beautiful damsel of all, since the knight of the falcon has said so.' Festa thought she would die of envy, and, overcome with fury, she swore that she would cause Curial some vexation greater than that he had caused her. Indeed, I believe that most women are incapable of dominating the feelings that come upon them and their hearts soon discharge the hatred which they have perhaps unjustly conceived; and so it happens that usually they avoid the need for vengeance.

Curial returned boldly to the tourney and began again to fight as vigorously as if he were just starting and had done nothing all day. But there was an English earl called Lord Salisbury, large of stature and a valorous and famous knight, who had seen what Curial had done. First he helped raise Lord Gloucester, and had him taken half-dead to his tent, and then he summoned all the knights who had come in Lord Gloucester's company, together with those of his own, and told them that the knight of the falcon must be vanquished that day. Then without attacking anyone he rode about the field looking high and low until he saw the knight of the falcon giving battle in front of the stands and outshining all the other knights in the strength of his efforts. Then Lord Salisbury charged him, with more than fifty knights altogether behind him. Curial's horse received such a blow in the middle of its chest that, brave and powerful though it might be, it could but fall. Finding himself on foot amid so many adversaries, Curial performed such wonders in his own defence that there was no one who did not fear his sword. But however much he did, by force of numbers they laid hold of his horse and were endeavouring to take it away and make it captive. They could indeed have succeeded if someone had not cried out to the knight of the swords 'Come quickly to the knight of the falcon! He is fighting on foot in front of the stands and they are trying to take him captive!'

The knight of the swords gave a great shout, calling together as many of his followers as he could, and advanced his standard with as much speed as he could, incensed with furious rage like a ravening lion. He broke into the throng of knights, making them give way, and with great difficulty reached the spot where Curial was fighting and performing in defence of his honour deeds worthy to be remembered. One of the knights of the black shield called Pere de Moncada, seeing Lord Salisbury on a fine large horse, charged at him with a thick strong lance in his hand and struck him a severe blow which knocked him from the saddle with his legs in the air, and he fell on the ground close to Curial. When he saw him at his feet, Curial gave him his hand and helped him to rise. 'Do not think I have helped you for your good' he said to him. 'You must defend yourself or you may lose what all the kings in the world cannot restore to you.' Then he rained terrible blows upon his head so that however good his helmet was it had never had such a trial, and sparks of fire flew from it. Curial used such violence on him that Salisbury could not withstand the hard and heavy blows that Curial was inflicting on him and he was forced to his knees. Indeed it was the general opinion that he would have killed him had it not been for the King of England, who came shouting great cries to that part of the field and made his way through the throng with a crowd of knights to attack the knights of the black shields. Although they were all there together they were unable to prevent the rescue of Lord Salisbury, but he left his horse behind, which Pere de Moncada gave to Curial.

When he had mounted, Curial looked for the King of England and recognising him by the golden lance he wore above his helmet, he rode at him and struck him so fiercely on the head that the King

123

was unable to remain upright and had to embrace the neck of his horse. Spending no more time on him, Curial struck another Englishman hard enough to send him from his horse. The knight of the swords loved the English with all his heart, as much as he hated the French, and he ordered the knights of the black shields to leave that part of the field. When the King of England heard this he was delighted, and longed to know who the knight was.

So they moved away with their standard towards the company of the Duke of Burgundy, among whom were two very valiant knights, one of whom was called the Lord of St George and the other the Lord of Vergues. But when the knight of the swords saw that the Lord of Vergues was wearing a coat of arms of red and gold bars, which are the arms of the kings of Aragon, he ordered his knights that no one should fight against him. The same thing happened when he saw the Lord of St George wore white trappings with a red cross. 'How I should have liked to engage with these Burgundians and Flemings,' he said, 'if it were not for the arms they are wearing! Leave them alone, for my sake. Let us attack the French!'

Bonne Pensée went to the Lords of Vergues and of St George, who were companions in arms, and told them what the knight of the swords had said. When they heard it they sheathed their swords and withdrew from the tourney, and said to Bonne Pensée 'Say to the pride of the chivalry of the world, that is, to the knight of the swords, and to his noble company, that when we heard what he had commanded we left the tourney for today, and we will not strike a blow against them.' So they turned back and watched what happened, sending word to the Count of Flanders, who was lying ill in his tent and had entrusted his knights to the Duke of Burgundy, that they would on no account fight any more that day.

The French, however, were by no means so safe. The knights of the black shields closed with them, striking strongly right and left, and whatever knight they met had no choice but to fall from his horse or cling to its neck; and in a short time they had made themselves known and avoided.

The Burgundians, who had striven hard against the French that day, went to their Duke and said to him 'Sir, the knights of the black shields have through courtesy refrained from fighting against your knights, but they are causing great havoc among the French. It is true that we too have caused much trouble today, but we should not allow others to molest them as well. Tell us what you would have us do.' The Duke went to that part of the field and saw how they were all performing feats never before heard of or seen, and he said 'In faith, it would not be very courteous to try to take from these men

124

the honour they have won today by force of arms.' He went to the knight of the swords and said 'Sir knight, I beg you to do no more battle with these today.' Curial went close to the King, who had not heard very well, and told him what the Duke had said; and then the King led them away.

When the standard of the crossed swords, and those who fought beneath it, arrived in front of the stands, the hour for vespers was long passed and all the standards had withdrawn, and almost no one still wished to fight. The Lords of Vergues and St George approached them and greeted all the company. 'Sirs,' they said, 'we have not been able to determine which of you has proved the best knight today, but we have observed that you, sir knight of the swords, have been captain of your company in this day's battle. If it is not disagreeable to you, we entreat you to yield to our first request, which is that when the tourney is over you should all come together to supper and to rest in our tents.' The knight of the swords replied that there was no senior or greater among them, for they were all companions and friends, and that they would willingly accept their invitation if it were possible, but at present they could not do so, and he begged them to excuse them. Then the Flemings said that if they were unable to accept to go to their tents, they would like to have supper with them, if they pleased. The knight of the swords agreed with pleasure; and thus they rested, while nothing was happening in the field.

The King of France decided to close the tournament for that day, and when he heard this the knight of the swords moved his standard forward and they galloped up and down the length of the field, shouting their cries. But nobody moved against them because everyone was tired and weary, and when the King of France saw this he ordered that the tournament be ended for that day, and everyone returned to their quarters.

The King of France returned to the city and everyone reclaimed their damsels except Curial, for the Queen entreated the damsel of the black shield to remain with her for as long as the tournament lasted. Festa agreed, provided that her escort, the knight of the falcon, were willing. The Queen quickly sent a messenger to him, asking him to allow this, and he at once replied granting her request, and so the Queen took her away with her. In front of Festa was borne a golden cup with a lid, and on the lid were many large pearls and fine stones. This had been offered as the prize to the best knight, and although there was nothing to choose between the knights of the black

125

shields it was awarded to the knight of the swords because he had fought well and had been captain that day. Since he had already left, the prize was brought to his damsel, and she led the way and all the rest followed after, however great ladies they might be; and Lachesis, to her disgust, had to follow in her train, feeling she could die of envy.

Ah, how brief a time lasts the smoke of this vainglory! That day the damsel of the black shield would not for sure have changed places with St Catherine, so favoured and fêted was she! The Queen never tired of lauding and honouring her and speaking well of her, so that there was no end to the praising of her beauty, grace, charm and other virtues above all others ever before seen. I believe she was as fervent as the friars minor who on St Francis's feast day, when they preach, do not know where to begin! Lachesis went off with her mother, ill-satisfied but well-escorted and favoured.

The Queen began to interrogate the damsel of the black shield, asking her from what country she came. 'Madam, I cannot tell you,' she replied, 'I am forbidden to do so.' 'Then at least tell me your name' said the Queen. And she told her that her name was Festa. The Queen laughed and said 'On my word, you have the most noble and pleasing name I have ever heard, and to be sure, you are a feast to all those who see you, and it has been a feast to me today to have your company. He who gave the shield to Lachesis took the wrong turning in doing so, for it was due a thousand times more to you than to her, and as God has made you beautiful, so he has given you the best and most valiant knight in the world as your escort. God be praised for bringing you together!' The Queen was very ill-disposed towards Lachesis because she was so beautiful and had spoken contemptuously of the Queen's beauty.

Festa was surrounded on all sides by ladies and demoiselles, and when the King heard that Festa had remained with the Queen he was pleased, and he sent for her and did her much honour. He asked her where she came from, and she replied that she could not tell him for anything in the world, so the King only learned that her name was Festa. He laughed at this and said 'You are indeed a feast to the eyes that behold you, except to Lachesis's eyes: for I am sure she is jealous, although she has no need to be because Our Lord has made her very beautiful.' The King knew that she was accompanied by the knight of the falcon, and he asked her to tell him who the knight was. 'Monseigneur,' replied Festa, 'the Queen asked someone to ask me that, and then she asked me herself and I, because I had not leave, dared not tell her. But since it pleases you to ask I will tell you, on condition that you will both promise me not to tell anyone on earth.' They promised, and Festa said 'The knight's name is Curial.' 'Ah,

Holy Mary!' said the King, 'What names! Upon my word, the name befits such a knight as that one. Tell me, Festa, and who is the knight of the swords?' 'Sir,' she said, 'I saw him yesterday for the first time, together with the other knights of the black shields, for they all arrived yesterday or today; but he came all alone, and I can tell that he is Lord over all the others, for this can be seen in everything they do; and Curial knelt to him!' 'Ah, Blessed Virgin!' said the King. 'Who can this knight be?' 'I do not know,' said Festa, 'but I think he is the best knight in the world.' 'He has shown that in many ways,' replied the King, 'and so God give me honour, I do not believe there is a more noble company of knights in the world, for there is nothing to choose between them. One of them may be greater than the rest, but not better, for all together are such that any knight who thought he could undertake anything these could not do would be mad indeed!'

As they talked thus of many things, the knights who had taken part in the tourney came to the King when they had disarmed, to make their obeisance, and there they saw the damsel of the black shield. When they learned that her name was Festa they all began to laugh saying 'It is indeed more festive and enjoyable to be with you than with your knights, for on my word one fares ill if one goes anywhere near them in the tourney!' 'They are knights who do as well in the chamber as in the lists,' said Festa, 'and I promise you that if they were here you would be as delighted with their company as with that of anyone.' During all that evening nothing was talked of save the knights with the black shields, and there was no one who would venture to say which of them was the best, so valiant were they all.

As the King saw that everyone was weary he did not think there should be any more tourneying that week until the following Sunday, when everyone would be sufficiently rested, and the Kings-at-arms and all the heralds were ordered to proclaim this everywhere. So they had supper and enjoyed themselves.

After supper the King sent word to the Queen asking her to come and to bring Festa with her. The Queen came, and the King took Festa's hand. 'Wherever you are present there can be no lack of festivity' he said. There was dancing and singing and much merriment, and Festa sang well and better than any damsel in the world.

When they had amused themselves for a long while, Festa looking round at the people present saw Melchior de Pando, who had been watching the tourney all day without knowing which knight was Curial. Festa made a sign to him not to speak, and to stay where he was, and after she had let some time pass she rose and went to him. She told him that Curial was with the knights of the black shields,

127

described to him where they were quartered, and told him to go there; so he departed. Since much of the night had now passed the King and Queen and all the lords and ladies took leave of each other and went to bed.

★

You have heard how the knights of the black shields left the tournament and made their way back to their tents. The Lord of Vergues and the Lord of St George followed them, and were housed in Curial's sumptuous tents. Supper was ready as soon as they had entered, and when they had disarmed they had an agreeable meal, discussing endlessly the wondrous feats that had been done that day in the field.

When the Lords of Vergues and St George saw Curial they said that he was certainly the most handsome knight they had ever seen, and they were so impressed by him that they could hardly take their eyes from him. But Curial showed all possible reverence to the King of Aragon, and the Lord of Vergues, seeing the honour in which the knight of the swords was held and not knowing who he was, longed to know his identity. So he went to Curial and asked him with great earnestness to do him the favour of telling him who the knight was. Curial answered that since he was present himself the Lord of Vergues should ask him, and he would certainly be told.

As they both turned to look at him Curial laughed, and the King said 'What is the matter?' 'Sir,' he replied, 'this knight is aggrieved with you, not unreasonably, for he says that in his opinion much honour and reverence is paid to you but as he does not know who you are he cannot know how he should behave towards you; and this is indeed true. He says also that only he and his companion are ignorant in this respect, since everyone else knows you and they cannot think who you are; and so he begs you with all fervour, because he has come to join you, and also so that he may be beholden to you for the rest of his days, not to conceal your identity from him. And I know, sir, that if he knew your name he would serve you willingly and wholeheartedly.' Having spoken thus he said no more. When he heard what Curial said, the knight added 'Sir knight, I entreat you not to withhold your name from me, and I shall be your servant in whatever you please to command.' Then the King said 'I am the King of Aragon.' At once the Lord of Vergues fell to his knees, and the King raised him up and laid his arms on his shoulders; and the Lord of St George did likewise. 'Sir,' said the Lord of Vergues, 'this is a matter in which it has pleased God to show me grace, and today the greatest desire I had in the world has

128

been realised. I am of your lineage, Sir, and bear your arms, and consequently I am your servant against everyone in the world. There was nothing I desired more than to meet my lord, and you are he. Therefore I entreat and beseech you that henceforward you hold me as your servant and command me in all that I can do that will be of service to you, and I shall not fail you.' In a like manner the Lord of St George offered his service to the King, and the King answered that he was pleased to know them and that henceforward they could live confident that he would be a true kinsman to the one and a friend to them both.

Great was the mirth in those tents that evening, and everyone was as merry as they could be. The Lord of Vergues asked as a favour of the King that he and his companion might carry black shields and be admitted to their company on the day of the great tourney, and this the King granted. Then they all went to bed. The King gave the company leave to retire and kept only Curial with him, ordering that everyone should go his own way until the following Saturday. He did not wish to remain in that place any longer for fear of being recognised, as he had no desire that anyone else should know who he was. Everyone understood that they should leave as secretly as possible.

So the next day the King arose before day break, and the other knights likewise, and they all went their separate ways, leaving their tents behind without anyone to guard them. The King commanded the Lord of Vergues to go to court, however, and if his damsel had need of anything, to be ready to supply it as best he might. The Lord of Vergues was very content that the King should make use of him, and he replied 'God knows my desire to serve you, sir, rather than any other lord in the world, and I shall do your command whatever befalls.' So saying, he went to his quarters with the Lord of St George, his inseparable companion. The Count of Flanders asked them where they had been and they replied that they had been invited by some knights and had supped and slept with them.

The Count of Foix also asked his son what had become of the knights in whose company he had been, and he replied that they had all gone away, leaving their tents unguarded; and the Count was very surprised.

When the night was over the day dawned bright and clear. The King had been wondering who the knights of the black shield could be, especially the knight of the swords; but his imaginings had strayed far from the truth, for although he could not think who they were he took it for granted that all the knights would come to see him and then he would be able to find out.

The previous night Melchior de Pando had not been able to find the tents of the knights of the black shield, but in the morning he sought until he found them, and recognising Curial's tent he entered it. He found no one there, nor in any of the others, and he was very surprised. So he decided to remain in those tents, expecting that they would return and then he would see them. After a while he wondered what he could do there all on his own, thinking that perhaps someone would come to rob them, or would say that he had gone in to thieve and would kill him, and that it would be wiser to go back to Festa in case she knew something which would give him assurance. And so he went away.

He was unable to speak to Festa that day, however, as the King held a very grand and formal reception. Among other things he had had a great table prepared for all the knights of the black shield in the most honourable part of the hall; but when the hour for dinner came and everyone had assembled, there was no sign of the unknown knights. They waited for them to come and dinner was very late.

The King called Festa to him. 'Festa,' he said to her, 'I do not know either the knight of the swords or the knight of the falcon, and I should like you to point them out to me if they are here, so that I can honour and make much of them, as they have well deserved.' Festa searched everywhere and then returned to the King and told him that they were not there, nor was any other knight of that company. The King was displeased, but continued to wait for them, and so the day grew older and dinner still waited.

The Count of Foix went to the King and asked what they were waiting for, why they were not dining; and the King answered that he was waiting for the knights of the black shield. 'Do not wait for them, sir,' he said, 'for they have gone away.' The King was disappointed and very sorry, and he blamed himself for not having made better arrangements. So then all took their places, but the King allowed no one to sit at the table he had intended for them, and it remained empty. All through dinner the King remained pensive and did not eat or enjoy himself.

When they had dined the King said to Festa 'I do not know whether you or I have lost most, for your knights have gone away and left you here. But as long as I keep such a pledge as you I am not afraid of losing them.' 'Sir,' said the Count of Foix, 'they have left their tents with no one to guard them; give orders that they should be guarded.' The King said he would like to go to their tents in their absence, to see at least if he could not absorb some of their good qualities; and the Count laughed at this.

When the siesta was over the King went to have his supper in the tents. When he saw Curial's two richly decorated tents he assigned them to the Queen, and he himself took over the King of Aragon's, not knowing whose it was, although taking everything into account it was not nearly as fine as the others. Everyone was talking about the knights and wondering why they had departed without saying anything to the King of France. The King however thought that since they had left the tents they would return and then he would meet them, saying to himself that they could not avoid him in that way. Festa did not mind their having gone away for she knew they would not leave her but without fail would come back for her, and so she was of good heart. When Melchior de Pando came to her and asked if she knew anything about them she said that she did not, but that she took it as certain that they would return at least to fetch her, even if they did not care about the tents.

While the King was taking his pleasure in the tents and all the knights were examining them, the Duchess of Bavaria and her daughter arrived, well escorted by notable persons. Lachesis was wearing a gown of crimson satin embroidered with gold eyes and loops, and wore on her sleeve the same greyhound and motto that was on the tent she had given Curial. When she came into sight, everyone said 'That gown and this tent are exactly the same.' The King called Lachesis to him and said to her 'Lachesis, your gown makes me believe that you must know the knight whose tent this is; pray tell me his name and all that you know about him.' Lachesis replied that the knight was called Curial and that he had defeated the German knights who had accused Clotho, her sister. And she told him what he had done to free the old knight, and how he had killed Boca di Far, and all the feats he had accomplished on the way to the tournament, explaining that he was also the knight of the black shield who had done such notable deeds on the highways; and she said many other things in praise of the knight. The King was very glad to hear all this, and it so strengthened his desire to see him and to have him in his house that he could think of nothing else. He asked her how it happened that she was wearing a gown like the knight's tent.

'Sir,' said Lachesis, 'I had this tent made in Germany and sent it to him so that I should recognise him here at the tournament. I will tell you, sir, that there is nothing in the world I love more than I do him, and I am compelled to this by what I have told you he did to save my sister, for which I am and shall ever be obliged to do whatever I can for him.' Lachesis said so much in praise of Curial that it was clear to the King that she was in love with him, and was unable to conceal it. The King asked her if she knew anything about the other knights in his company, and she answered that she did not. 'Ah!' said the King, 'when shall I see them? I am impatient to know them, and if I knew where to find them I should go to them.' However, he took it for granted that he would see them in any case at the tournament the following Sunday and then would do all he could to meet them.

The King of France decided to stay that week in the tents, always hoping to see the knights, and holding great feasts. The Queen was displeased because he fêted Lachesis and would hardly let her leave his side. On the other hand the Queen made much of Festa, and showed her as much favour as she possibly could, giving her jewels and gowns, although she was already well supplied with them, and praising her continually for her beauty and cleverness above all other damsels she had ever known. The King too did her much honour, and these two damsels were the favourites at court.

Hardly anything but the tournament was ever talked about at this time, and much fault was found with Lord Salisbury for his attack on the knight of the falcon. The knight who had unseated Lord Gloucester and had taken his shield had acted throughout as a true knight, fighting man to man, and since Lord Salisbury was present at that combat, if he had wished to help or had helped Lord Gloucester then he could have done so without incurring blame. But to leave them when he saw them fighting, and to go and collect knights together and then all of them together to attack a single knight, that was ill done and was not to be expected of a knight such as he thought himself to be. If by chance the knight of the falcon had killed Lord Gloucester while he was looking for other knights, Lord Salisbury would have been left without his cousin german, and perhaps would have lost an opportunity for revenge. Moreover the obligations of chivalry did not permit attacks of that kind to be made in such circumstances nor in such a manner.

Many have said that Achilles killed Hector falsely and not as a knight should, in which perhaps they are wrong: but he killed Troilus falsely like a weak and cowardly knight. When Troilus was molesting the Myrmidons he was fighting as a worthy, bold and valiant knight, and if Achilles had killed him with his own hand in defence and aid of his own men, he would have done well. But it is clear to see that he feared to face him in combat on his own, and instead he exhorted and drove all his men to attack Troilus alone, ordering them to surround, encircle and kill him. What was worse and brought him into greater disrepute, he had the valiant knight, whom as you have heard he killed so falsely, tied to the tail of his horse and dragged over the ground. To use cruelty to those who cannot defend themselves is the work of a Jew. There are others who say that Achilles did well to kill Troilus whatever the circumstances, for victory is sought in many ways, and he is held a wise knight or captain who most wisely and cautiously seeks and achieves coveted and uncertain victory with least harm and danger and greatest safety.

132

Because many words, and some almost angry ones, were uttered on this question, the King, who was a very wise lord, ordered them to be silent, and put an end to the debate.

★

At this time a son of the King of France fell gravely ill, and this interrupted the festivities because the Queen begged the King that tourneying should cease. So he gave the order, dismissed the tournament and then returned to Melun, and the Lord of Vergues installed himself in the tents. It was feared that hostility would arise from this between him and the Count of Foix, who also wished to guard the tents, and sent his son there, as having the right to do so. The other knight also wanted to guard them, as a kinsman and new servant of the King of Aragon, to whom the damsel he highly honoured had been entrusted; yet neither of them dared say to whom the tents belonged. Many people criticised them, saying that they were only doing it in order to keep the tents for themselves if the knights did not return; and many opinions were expressed about this matter.

The King was perturbed and did not know what to do about it, so he called Festa to him and asked her who should take charge of the tents. She said that she would send him a worthy man to look after two of them, but about the rest she did not know what to say. 'Ah, Festa!' said the King, 'I think you only care about Curial's tents!' 'Sir, I should care for them all if I could,' she replied, 'and if they had been entrusted to me; but there is nothing else I can do.' 'Then I beg a favour of you,' said the King, 'which will satisfy the greatest wish I have in the world without it costing you anything or harming you in any way.' Festa granted it. 'Tell me, then,' said the King, 'who is the knight of the swords?' 'You do me great violence, sir,' said Festa, 'in making me tell you his name against his wish. However, since you so desire it, I will tell you, on condition that you tell it to no one.' The King promised, and then she said 'He is the King of Aragon, the best knight with the lance in the world today.' 'Alas!' said the King, 'why have I dismissed the tournament? He will not come back again, and I shall never meet him. Unhappy that I am, I did not know such a knight was in my kingdom.' 'Is it true that he is a good knight?' asked Festa. 'Yes indeed,' said the King, 'the best in the world, and all others are nothing beside him.'

Many matters were discussed in the court. In a few days the King's son had recovered, which brought the King happiness, and he regretted having dismissed the tournament, and considered re-opening it. But there was nothing to be done, for the foreign knights had all gone home.

When the King of Aragon heard that the tournament had broken up he was very disappointed and said to Curial 'Curial, since the tournament is over I shall go away, and you must leave me now for I do not intend to remain here any longer nor to travel in company with any knight in the world. So go with God; but I beg that you will visit me, and I assure you that I shall be as pleased to see you as any knight in the world.' Curial entreated him to let him accompany him at least until he had reached his own kingdom or had found another of his knights to serve him and keep him company. The King refused, and asked him instead to go back to his damsel and to take her many greetings from him. And so the King returned to his kingdom.

Curial made his way towards Melun, and when he reached his tents he found Melchior de Pando there, who gave him news of Guelfa, but brought him no letter. He told Curial that she had ordered him to follow Curial's route and to learn as much as he could of what had befallen him and what he had done; and that she had been pleased with the letters he had sent her. Then he told him that the lady's intention was that he should stay for some time in the court of the King of France but should do his best to ensure that nothing was known about the feats he had performed, so that they were not as yet accredited to him.

Curial was very pleased that Guelfa ordered him to remain in France, and he said to Melchior 'And what is to become of Festa?' 'I shall take her back with me' said Melchior.

The King of France returned to Paris and had the King of Aragon's tents taken to the church of St Denis, saying that he did not know to whom they belonged but they would stay there, well guarded, until their owner claimed them.

Curial met the Lords of Vergues and St George secretly and informed them that the King of Aragon had gone away, and sent them his greetings, and he asked the Lord of Vergues to send his damsel to Melun. So they wrote to Festa to come to Melun with the escort that the Lord of Vergues would send her. Festa took her leave of the King and Queen, from whom she received precious gifts, and departed, bearing many greetings for the knights of the black shields. The Lord of Vergues accompanied her much of the way and then gave her an honourable escort, and so she came to Melun, where she was warmly welcomed by Melchior and Curial, and everyone made much of her. Then Melchior told her that Guelfa's commands were that she should return to Montferrat and that Curial should remain in Paris, and so she should make ready for the journey.

134

Curial asked Festa whether she had told anyone his name and she replied that she had told the King and Queen under some duress. Curial was displeased, for he did not want to be known at all; however, he said that since his lady ordered that he should stay in Paris he would carry out her command. And he commended himself to his lady and asked them to tell her.

They were all together in Paris for four days and then Melchior and Festa prepared to leave. Festa was weeping bitterly and could not be comforted, and Curial, seeing that they had come to the parting of the ways, became sad and could not speak for sorrow. 'Do not weep,' said Melchior to him, 'that is no work for a knight. In every way you are a better knight than any other, but in weeping you are a woman, and that fault detracts much from your virtue and honour.' 'On the contrary,' said Curial, 'it is a virtue to rejoice with those who are joyful and to weep with those who are weeping. But if it were as you say, I could not help myself, for when I remember that I am far from my lady I fear to lose my life; and now that I have to part with you, it is as if my soul were leaving me.' 'Well, however that may be,' said the worthy man, 'I think that your sojourn here will be to your honour and profit, which Guelfa has well understood; for it is written that no prophet is welcome in his own country. If you consider carefully, Montferrat is too narrow a field for you to achieve what Guelfa means you to; so remain with God. But I beg you to behave with discretion and not to give the lady cause to be angry with you through your own fault. I shall send all your servants and your chattels, and do not hesitate to take out bills of exchange in my name, which I shall acknowledge without fail.' 'Sir and father,' answered Curial, 'God knows that all my desire is to be near my lady so that I may serve her in everything that pleases her. But since she wishes this, I can do nothing else: I will remain wherever she commands. But I beg you both to ask her not to believe false news and that, by her mercy, she will not try me in my absence but that if by chance something is said to her that makes her angry with me she will hear me before condemning me.'

Turning to Festa he said 'So, Festa, my sister, Fate does not permit me to take you back as I brought you, to present you to the lady who entrusted you to me. If I have not honoured you as your merit deserves or as I should have done, I beg your forgiveness, because I have not failed through my will, but you must attribute it to my clumsiness, for I have done all I could. I am always at your command, for there is no one in the world I desire to please more than you.' And he embraced her like a brother, turning quite pale, and commended her to God.

Then he said to Melchior 'Father, I entreat you to write to me

135

often, for I shall have no repose or joy save when I read your letters; and if my lady will write to me, that will give me life.' 'Be of good cheer, Curial' replied Melchior. 'Soon, please God, you will have news that will give you joy.'

So Melchior and Festa went away to Montferrat and Curial remained in Melun, full of care and so sad that he could not be cheered. But it is the nature of tears to yield to the passage of time, and Curial forgot his weeping, since it was fruitless, and cheered up, and forgetting his cares gave himself to arranging how he was to live. He went to Paris and bought a fine house there, which he hung with Arras and many other notable tapestries, and furnished his rooms with such taste, superfluous things being excluded and those that were necessary copiously and abundantly supplied, that whoever came to his home judged that his surroundings befitted his fame and renown.

I cannot believe that the skill I possess in writing will be sufficient to set down appropriately what is to follow, nor can my fingers control my pen, which turns red and becomes abashed when I think that in the chapter I have to describe the happiness of Guelfa when her damsel returned to her. Blushing, she crossed herself, and her face took on a new expression; and when Festa fell on her knees before her and kissed her hands, she became covered in confusion. 'With what affection, oh most notable and great lady, does the valorous Curial kiss your hands!' said Festa. 'There is no hour of the day in which he does not remember you, and never is your name mentioned without him bowing his head and bending his knee. I tell you for sure, oh excellent lady, that there is not in the whole world a more fortunate lady than you.' 'Tell me everything you have seen since you left here, my Festa and my joy, my comfort and my solace' said Guelfa. 'Tell me no lies, friend. But wait a moment, say nothing yet – give me time to call the Abbess, who has been the sharer in my longings and my sufferings . . . See how she comes, with hurrying steps and open mouth, panting for breath so that she cannot speak. Tell her what greetings you bring her, if you have any. Speak for she cannot ask you.'

'I was not yet out of the house in which I left the sorrowing Curial when I heard a great noise of feet running after me, and turning round I saw the wretched Curial hastening to me. Bending towards me, unable to utter a word, he put to his eyes a handkerchief already half soaked in tears, and when he had stood there for a moment in silence, and his anguish allowed him to speak again, he said "Sweet

136

Festa, commend me to the Abbess, my very dear angel." And I looked at him for some little time, turned to a marble statue, my mouth incapable of speech. But then Pando, who was with me all this time, revived my half-dead spirits saying "Answer and let us be gone." I had only time to say "I will." Then I turned away, wishing to start my journey to come here, drawn by my longing to see your ladyship, but drawn back too by the sight of Curial, with such force that I could not move from the spot until Pando said "Let us go." Then, weeping, I left that sorrowful knight who, I do believe, remained on that very spot all that accursed day.'

Neither Guelfa nor the Abbess could restrain their tears but wept tenderly. When they had cried a great deal, Guelfa said 'Sweet Festa, tell me now in detail all that you have seen since you left here. See, my ears are open and ready to receive your words, my heart sharpens its pens and prepares to write in my memory what they dictate so that I may continually read them there and remember them; and I shall be a miser in guarding this treasure, which I should like to spend prodigally.'

Then the astute girl began to relate the journey as far as the house of the vavasour and, not forgetting the bad supper, told them of Curial's fight with the two brothers, and all the other deeds one after another in the order in which they had happened. Many times the Abbess and Guelfa were afraid for Curial and listened to the events with great fear; at others they laughed, such as the sojourn in the convent, and the knight who seized Festa's hair. In short, Guelfa and the Abbess spent the rest of that day, and many others, in listening intently to news of Curial. That day they could hardly eat, nor sleep that night, recalling those feats of his.

But Guelfa still feared Lachesis and thought she must be lacking in shame, and her honesty of little worth; and she said that it was quite true that the god of love had no eyes. They never had enough of talk concerning Curial, although Guelfa always returned to Lachesis, whom she could not put out of her mind, so fearful was she lest, being so shameless, she would rob her of Curial.

When they had talked of this a great deal, the verdict and conclusion of the discussion was settled: that Guelfa would continue to give and to send to Curial not only those things that were necessary for his expenses but also the things he might like to have, so that there should be no need for him to deny himself them through poverty. This was put into action at once, and Melchior was ordered to give Curial everything he wanted, without any question, and all his servants and chattels were to be sent to him, with many other things that Guelfa gave him on this occasion. When Curial received all this he was very happy.

★

137

Curial did not wish to be the subject of talk while he was in Paris, nor that any of his feats of arms should be discussed, and if any of them did become known, that they should not be considered worthy of esteem. However, the Lord of Vergues and the Lord of St George pointed him out to the King, and the King approached him, and fêted him and made him many offers; and he was shown much favour, which pleased some and greatly displeased others. Lachesis made much of him in public, and had no joy or peace save when she was with Curial. The Duke of Brittany, the Duke of Orleans and Charles of Bourbon were not so tranquil, nor were they pleased, for they were young knights, each of them was in love with Lachesis, and they strove all they could to please her. She did look kindly upon them but when Curial was present her attention and favours were all for him, while the others were dying of envy and jealousy. This was a disadvantage to Curial because those lords would certainly have shown him favour for all his innate virtues and graces had it not been for Lachesis, and instead they all strove to bring disfavour and humiliation upon him. On the other hand, Curial was looked on with favour by the King and many others, the Count of Foix and the Lords of St George and of Vergues were often in his company, and if they had not been there perhaps many would have tried to do him some mischief. It was also owing to them that the Duke of Burgundy frequently invited him to his residence and favoured him and sought his company, and he tried hard to persuade Curial to enter his service and be his follower, but Curial would never consent.

This was how matters stood for several months, during which there were many tournaments and jousts in Paris. Whenever the time for one of these approached Curial would make preparations as though he were going away, so that no one was aware of where he was; and then he would come to the jousting-ground in disguise, and every time he carried off the prize. No one knew or could find out who he was, and the King and all the course were puzzled, but Curial contrived so that no one should know of his doings save only Lachesis.

One day there was a great entertainment, and when she had wearied of dancing and was talking with the King, who was praising Curial, in order to win favour with him, the shameless girl said 'I will tell you a secret, sir, which I am sure you have longed to know and will be pleased to hear.' 'Tell me, then I pray you' said the King. 'I would have told you before,' she said, 'but I feared that others would learn it and that I should suffer, so I entreat you to keep it secret when I have told you.' The King said that he would. 'Well, sir' said she, 'would you like to know who is the knight who carries

138

off the prize every time there is a tourney or jousting? It is Curial: and he does it so secretly that no one knows who the victor is save I, to whom he sends the jewels that he wins as prizes.' 'I always thought that it was he, for two reasons;' replied the King, 'firstly, because he is the most valiant knight in all the land at the present time, and secondly, because when these festivities happen no one ever sees him.'

Lachesis was very worried at this time by the pressure that was being put on her by many people in the matter of marriage. Her mother was being urged by the King to give her as wife to the Duke of Orleans, and her mother was willing and wished to force her into this marriage. But Lachesis, laying aside all fear, answered that she could give her death if she wished, but not a husband. On the other hand Lachesis did not want to return to Germany, although her mother wanted to leave and was making preparations for the journey every day.

While matters stood thus at court there arrived from the Holy Land a Breton knight named Bachier de Vilahir, otherwise known as the Boar of Vilahir, because he had very large teeth and also because it was said that when he was angry or when he was fighting he foamed at the mouth like a wild boar.

The knight was a huge man, very fierce of aspect, intemperate in his actions, very proud and arrogant, and this added to his dominating manner. He was of such great bodily strength that he feared nothing he ever set eyes on; furthermore, up to that time things had always gone well for him and he had the reputation of being the most valiant knight in the world, the boldest and the fiercest. Knowing that this was how he was regarded, and finding that as a result he was favoured, praised and feared, he despised all other knights and would say publicly that the deeds of Tristram and Lancelot were nothing remarkable, for in those times knights lacked good weapons, warriors were very feeble both in body and in spirit and if by chance anyone showed a little daring the rest would take to flight and fear him. And if they had been alive now, and Hector, Hercules and Achilles in addition, of whose deeds so much had been written, they would easily find knights who would make them be on their guard.

Thus this Boar of Vilahir was held in high esteem, and the greatest lords paid him honour, and he was so fêted on his arrival that he was beside himself with joy. When he was asked what had happened on the voyage he had made, he would relate many marvels, which seemed indeed miracles to his listeners, about battles with Moors, in which he had always been victorious, and similarly against other peoples, on land and on sea, claiming the glory of victory for himself, asserting that if he had not been present those who were in his company would have been utterly lost. Everyone stared at him and, almost stupefied by such vigour, believed him to be the most outstanding knight in the world; and many said 'Of course, if he had been at Melun the knights of the black shields would not have won the renown they carried off that day!'

The deeds of this knight were so often discussed that you could not go anywhere without hearing about him, and people marvelled how Nature could have produced such a frightening and terrifying monster. This topic was discussed so much that men of intelligence grew weary of it, and Curial especially would go away from any place where there was talk of the Boar. One day some people were tediously praising the deeds of the Boar in Curial's presence, and without saying a word he was beginning to move away from them when a noble squire, who was a great friend of the Boar, said 'You do not like anyone to speak well of anyone but yourself, Curial. Since you are a knight you should not be displeased to hear about other good knights, especially this one, who, upon my word, is the greatest and chief of them all.' 'I am not displeased by the good I hear spoken of the Boar,' said Curial, 'on the contrary, God knows, I like to hear it. But to hear the same thing many times is tedious.' 'In truth, it is the black envy it arouses in you that makes you find tedious what others enjoy' answered the other. Curial, already a little angry at what the nobleman had said, answered 'I have not yet seen anything about the Boar that could move me or anyone to envy him!' 'And you are not such a knight that the Boar or any other should care much for your words' retorted the other. Curial was by now furious and unable to restrain himself, so great was his anger. He stretched out his arm and caught hold of the other by the front of his clothes and said 'I care little for your words, and if it were the Boar himself who said them I should prove to him that he had spoken ill-advisedly.'

Those who were standing by intervened to separate them, and had some difficulty in restraining the nobleman, who was enraged beyond belief. Curial needed no holding, and went away to his house thinking of many other things.

Rumour of the words that had been exchanged spread its wings, and in a busybody made its way to the dwelling of the Duke of Brittany. He and the Boar and other knights were trying, like those who make bricks without straw, to find a way to discredit Curial while concealing their own hand in the affair. When they heard this story the Boar said 'What more do we need? Now there must be combat between him and me.' They sent for the nobleman, whose name was Guillaume de la Tour, and at the Duke's request he told them all that had passed between him and Curial. The Boar was so irate that he thought he would die of anger. That day the Duke of Orleans, Charles of Bourbon and many others met in the house of the Duke of Brittany, and taking counsel together they decided that the Boar should fight Curial man to man, and so it was resolved; and the Boar undertook to bring this about.

On the other side, the Duke of Burgundy went to Curial's house, and so did the Count of Foix, the Lord of Vergues, the Lord of St George and a large number of other great barons, and taking counsel together, the Duke of Burgundy maintained that Curial should write to the Boar whereas the Count of Foix and all the others disagreed, because the Boar had not offended Curial but rather Curial the Boar, not of his own will but as a result of the words of Guillaume de la Tour, who had spoken foolishly. Curial had satisfied him in word and deed but thereby had incidentally offended the Boar, who had not merited it. Thus it was better to wait to see what the Boar would do, since he was not a knight to suffer the loss of one hair of his honour, and would be receiving advice accordingly. So each one departed to have dinner in his own house, except the Lords of St George and of Vergues, who remained with Curial.

When the hour came for going to court, the Duke of Burgundy, the Count of Foix and many other great lords fetched Curial, and they all went together. The others had already been there for some time, waiting for Curial to arrive. When the King heard that Curial had come with his companions, he was worried that there might be a great deal of disturbance, and he sent for the Boar and told him that he had gathered that he wished to speak to Curial concerning some foolish things that had been said to him. The King asked him not to do so, but to let these things pass, since Curial was a foreign knight and a very courteous one, and had been commended to him; and he did not wish any other knight to provoke him or seek to harm him. The Duke of Brittany, who hated Curial on account of Lachesis, replied to the King 'A fine thing it would be if a foreign knight of whom we know nothing may live among us and we are forced to honour him while he dishonours us.'

Just at that moment Curial approached and at once the Boar said to him 'Curial, your name does not accord with your deeds. I wished to speak to you, but the King my lord has forbidden it. I shall only say that I wish to challenge you to fight and that you should choose the weapons and find a judge and a place, on this condition: that if the judge you choose does not permit the battle to be a fight to the death, you will be vanquished, and be held a liar and a traitor; or else I will undertake to find a judge who will accept this

141

charge; that if he will not permit the battle to be a fight to the death I shall be vanquished, and be held a liar and a traitor.'

When Curial heard this he did not reply at once but stood awhile in thought. Then with soothing and soft words he replied 'I accept your challenge, Boar, and although the laws of arms, or at least the custom of knights who bear arms or fight duels, lays down that I should choose the weapons and name a battle-ground, nevertheless I should prefer, if it seems fit to you and you are willing to undertake the charge, that you should choose the weapons and name the battle-ground with this charge, that the choice is yours, and if you wish we will enter the lists today or tomorrow and you will find me ready to do with my hands what you have dared to say with your mouth.' The Boar answered that he was willing and so it was agreed between the two parties.

The Dukes of Orleans and of Brittany were pleased and more than pleased that a combat had been agreed upon, and they begged the King to be the judge and to let the combat be taken to a decisive end. In truth the King was unhappy that the battle was to take place and he would rather anything in the world than that he should preside over it, but the Dukes were united in their eagerness and the King could hardly avoid agreeing to preside. But he said that nothing in the world would induce him to swear that he would let it have a decisive end but that it must be understood, seeing the anger of both knights, in which he had a share, that on the day of battle he would see what each was capable of and that perhaps they would wish that they had not done and said such a foolish thing; and that when all were agreed he would give them to understand that it would be better for them to have peace. And he named St George's day for the combat.

The next day the Boar sent Curial a letter by a herald in which he named the weapons thus: firstly, that each should arm as he wished and saw fit, with the usual arms of war, and that they should bring no knives, poisons, spells, stones or other such things, and that they should have similar axes, swords and daggers, naming the length of each of these weapons. He sent him also the letter from the King, in which he ordered them to be in Paris on St George's day, ready to enter the lists to do battle.

Curial was very pleased to receive the letters, and he welcomed the herald but said that he thought the day appointed by the King was very distant; and he gave the herald a very sumptuous robe of his and a large sum in gold, which delighted the herald, who returned to the Boar full of praise for Curial.

The Duke of Burgundy, the Count of Foix and many barons and knights showed much honour to Curial, some because they considered he merited it, others to spite the other side; and they used to go to his house and accompany him to court and escort him back, and this they did every day, so that Curial had plenty of good company, and many supported him.

Guillaume de la Tour was longing to take the field, and he sent a message to Curial by the same herald, with the consent and approval of the Boar, saying that he well knew that the words on account of which Curial and the Boar were to fight had been exchanged between the two of them and that it would be more appropriate if they were the two to do battle; but since this could not be, he entreated Curial to find a companion in arms against whom Guillaume could fight so that the combat should be two against two. Curial's answer was that the friendship which was between them was not such that he needed to gratify the desire that had been expressed; but that since he saw that Guillaume was eager for his own hurt he would gratify him more generously that he could entreat; and so, with the King's permission, he would find someone to kill him. Then Guillaume de la Tour made supplication to the King that he would grant him the favour of permitting the battle to be of two against two. The King granted this with pleasure, for this affair had brought a black humour on him and for this reason he was glad that there were to be more people seeking their own ruin; for the greater harm done the sooner his anger would pass. So the herald returned to Curial and told him the King had given his permission. Curial was pleased, and began to think who to have as his companion in arms on the day. After some thought he decided he would not have anyone from France at all, although many offered themselves, but wrote to the King of Aragon, explaining the situation and asking if he would send him a companion for the fight.

The King of Aragon was not pleased to receive the news, but he passed it on to all those of his household, and when it became known you could have seen the knights rejoice and each one show himself to be eager to go to France to do battle. When he saw the eagerness of his knights, each one of whom begged to go and sought people to plead for him, the King rejoiced; but that day he did not make up his mind. But when Aznar of Atrosillo heard the tidings, without saying anything to anyone he left Barcelona at once, and went as far as La Boca before he slept. From there he wrote a letter to the King his lord, telling him that he had already left to go to join Curial and do battle at his side; and he begged and entreated him not to be angry with him but to write to Curial and say that he was sending him. At midnight he rose and continued on his way in rapid stages, afraid that the King might send messengers after him to call him back. So he reached Paris and made himself known to Curial, who was very pleased to see him, for he recognised him as the standard-bearer at the tournament and knew him to be valiant and valorous, strong and bold, so that any knight who had him for a companion would have good reason to be content.

When the King of Aragon received Aznar's letter he laughed and read it aloud to all those who were present. 'So God help me,' he said, 'I always knew that Aznar had more need of a bridle than of spurs, and he is indeed a wonderfully good knight and, God willing, will be yet better.' Many were discontented, because all of them would have liked to have a part in Curial's honour.

The King quickly had splendid trappings made and sent them to Aznar together with a large sum of silver, and he wrote to Curial, to the Count of Foix, and to the Lords of Vergues and St George, commending Aznar to them. When Curial received the King's letters he was well pleased, and he handed on the others to the lords to whom they were addressed, who at once came to offer their services to Aznar and took him to the King of France, to pay his respects and be presented to him. Curial had been unwilling to accept him as his companion, thinking it would be foolish, after he had written to the King, to take a companion without his leave; but once he had received the King's letter he accepted Aznar as his companion with indescribable joy.

This Aznar was a young man, twenty years old, excellent at wrestling and at tossing the caber, a great master of all kinds of weapons – sword, axe and dagger – and so light-footed that when he jumped or vaulted he seemed to fly. He was so strong that in his native land there had never before been anyone like him. He had a great mane of thick, wiry hair, a dark complexion, and large hands; he was broad of shoulder and chest, very swift in his movements, and as bold as a lion.

When he had made his obeisance to the King of France, the Duke of Burgundy said 'This, sir, is Curial's companion in arms.' The King looked at him, and then he looked at Guillaume de la Tour, who was present, and as Aznar was being led away to make his bow to the Queen the King said to Guillaume, loud enough to be overheard by many people, 'You must be very eager to suffer, and I think that God will provide for you in this, for here, it seems to me, is someone who will scratch your itching sores for you!' It was said that this Guillaume had had ringworm, and that the King used to be fond of him but now disliked him because the whole affair had come about through his fault, and he had been the cause of it all.

Everyone stared at Aznar and judged him to be a very valiant knight, and very strong although he was still young and tender;

144

and it was the general opinion that four of them would have plenty of work to do.

★

Curial was more dear to Lachesis than her own happiness, and so when she learned of the combat that was to take place between him and the Boar she felt great sorrow in her heart and she anxiously begged her mother to do her best to prevent the fight taking place. She knew for sure that although Curial was a valiant and strong knight, the Boar, by reputation and by the swaggering account he gave of himself, surpassed and outdid all knights however good; and even if Curial was as good as he and better, she did not want to expose herself to fear of the outcome of the battle, which was most uncertain. 'Madam,' she said, 'I have heard that they have no good reason to fight, nor is there any real cause why they should, and so it is fitting that you, who are a lady of ripe years, should endeavour to bring about peace and to prevent this affair. For you must know that if things turn out ill for Curial, which God forbid, you may expect my death to ensue; God will not let me live to hear bad news of Curial nor to see him die a violent death nor be in danger of it. Besides, it is all due to the jealousy and envy that is borne him on my account, and everyone will say 'this is all because of Lachesis': think what kind of honour that is for me. Would to God I had never seen him, or at least that I had not come here!'

'My dear daughter, I understand all that you have told me, and I think you err in three ways. First, you love a man who is not suitable for your nobility; secondly, Curial loves another, as I have heard and do believe; thirdly, on his account you may let slip one of the best matches in the world. If I were to intervene to bring peace between them it will be said that I am moved by interest and not by humane reasons, and it seems to me hard to increase my honour by acquiring a reputation as a go-between in my old age. So let them be: Curial is a very good knight, and it is no easy thing to defeat such a knight, as many knights have shown and discovered. Furthermore, the King is a wise lord and you may with reason expect that he can see what you see, that the battle has no good cause, and he will not do anything that will lie heavily upon his conscience. Even if I were to decide to intervene in this matter, it is not yet time to do so, for the incident is so recent that neither would accept advice.'

When Lachesis had heard what the Duchess, her mother, had said, she stood a while in thought and then blushing a little, she spoke thus: 'You should not be surprised, oh illustrious lady, at the reply you are going to hear nor should you attribute it to lack of shame

145

on my part, for the necessity in which I find myself breaks and severs the laws not only of shame but also of reason; and even if I should feel shame, before you it has no place since you are my mother and know all my concerns and my needs. Therefore I have determined to overcome and conquer my shame rather than suffer a pain that I might avoid. You have said many things to answer which, if I were to do it fully, would take long. I will remember only those which are essential, and they are two: first, that Curial does not correspond to my nobility, and secondly that he does not care for me and that you know whom he does love. Although it is very difficult for me to try to warm blood that is already cold and icy and a heart in which no impulse of natural heat lives or holds sway, since love forsakes and shuns age, the passage of time and the multitude of days enforcing and necessitating this, and although I take it for granted that all I say will be vain and fruitless, nevertheless I will not be silent but will remind you of what you have often preached to me, and in doing so will satisfy these two arguments of yours. As to the first, do you remember, madam, the words of Ghismonda to Tancredi her father concerning Guiscardo, and her description of nobility? You have often praised that reply, commending the lady for her wisdom and virtue. Guiscardo was a young man, a page, and he had never performed knightly deeds but passed his time in courtly delights, play and pleasures; yet Ghismonda, seeing that the young man had begun well, divined that he could conclude better and chose to love him, and loving him, gave him her love; Guiscardo's worth was not a thousandth part of Curial's. She was the daughter of the Prince of Salerno, she had married into the lineage of the kings of Sicily, the eldest son of the Duke of Capua, and so her honour must have been very dear to her. But Love, who is merciful, and benign Fortune brought them together and in order that one should not mourn the other for long, provided that their deaths should be almost simultaneous, or immediate, and Fortune was so favourable to them that both were buried in the same tomb. It is obvious to all that Curial is the son of a gentleman and of noble lineage as you and I are, and if the stones could speak they would say the same. In the first place, we see him in high and indeed in noble estate; we know him to be favoured by the Emperor and held in great esteem by kings and dukes. That he is a knight I need not say, for you know it as well as I, or perhaps not so well, since I, because it concerns me most, have taken care to inform myself of it as far and as fully as I can – but you know sufficient about it if you remember how much honour his chivalry has brought us. Ah, wretch that I am, I tremble now, seeming to see the fire ready to consume Clotho, my elder sister! But with the water of his chivalry he extinguished it.

And you know well that the lord my father, the Duke, presented me to him with all his duchy, and when Curial was momentarily disconcerted and did not reply, my lord the Duke said "Curial, I take her away with me as yours: I shall return her to you whenever you wish!" Am I to make my father a liar, and to break his decree and ordinance? God forbid. Moreover, in spite of all the fervour of love which burns within me, I have not behaved dishonestly but have safeguarded your honour and mine, as I shall do as long as I live. Do not have so little trust in the good that God has implanted in Curial that you should ask me or wring from me, even with my own consent, anything that would bring dishonour upon me. Let us love him at least, for the benefits we have received from him, and if we are so ungrateful as to deny him his reward, do not let us forget them and if we forget them, let us not return evil for good, which would be a devilish thing to do. As for your second point, if Curial is loved by Guelfa I am glad, and I am grateful to her, for Guelfa caused him to rise and has made him a man, and has placed him and maintains him in the position and estate he enjoys. So who can reproach Curial if he loves Guelfa? Indeed, let who will blame him, I do not, especially as I know Guelfa to be one of the most honourable ladies in the world. Humanity and virtue have moved her to give him advancement on account of his merits. I have never heard anyone, wise or foolish, speak dishonourably of them, and even if I had it is no concern of mine, nor have I so little sense as to inquire into it. At least he is not her husband. Marriages are in the hand of God, and He will give him to whomever He pleases. I think there is just one objection you would make to me, and that is that he was a poor nobleman. I never saw him poor but very rich, and always living in almost royal state. Even if it were true, I do not care; he has nobility, what does it matter if he lacks an inheritance? My father has offered one to him, and when he has given it, Curial will be worth as much as him and more. If my father had no inheritance, would he be worth as much as Curial? No indeed, for Curial is very worthy without an inheritance, and when he has one he will be worth more than any other; and on my word, he is so already. As to the other things you have said, I leave them unanswered. Now do as you wish about it, for I do not mean to trouble you further.'

This answer greatly perturbed the Duchess, and she replied 'My very dear daughter, your words convince me of your state of mind, and I know that you are right in many of the things you have said. But to cite Ghismonda to strengthen your case is wrong. I will not deny that Ghismonda was all you say: very valorous, wise and of great virtue, and the words she said I know were said very wisely. But it is obvious to all that she was less honourable and discreet in her dealings with Guiscardo, and for that reason they came to the end that you know well. A woman needs other things besides the ability to speak well: it would have been better for her not to have been so able, or at least not to have trusted so much in her own ability, because if women know how to colour their errors with words they take liberty to do things which, if they had not that confidence, they would refrain from doing. No more of this: I shall always try to content you in what you have asked me. The request is honourable, but even if everyone knows that he has done us much and great honour and pleasure I must have some pretext for interfering in this matter. When time provides the opportunity I shall not let it pass in vain.'

★

Guelfa had already heard something of the battle that Curial had undertaken, and as she waited in extreme anxiety for further knowledge, one of Curial's gentlemen came to her and told her all about it. Guelfa felt great sorrow and was very unhappy that she had ordered Curial to remain in Paris.

'Alas, how sad I am!' said Guelfa. 'Will there be no end to my grief? Ah, Curial! Why has God made you so noble and valorous? It would be better for you to be less strong, then so many misfortunes would not dog you and at least you would be preserved from danger and I from fear! Ah, how safe it is to follow the middle path, for the extremes bring no repose! I have taken great delight in contemplating your knightly virtues, but I am sure that the fears I have had to bear, and this one, which is greater than all the others, will bring my days to an end. But why do I lament, wretch that I am? What help can it be to Curial, what profit can come to him from it? It would be better, I think, to dry my tears and do something to help him, if I can. One thing alone comforts me, that I know Curial to be a good knight: but where there is one good knight, there is another as good, or better. Here and now there is no more I can do but help him with money and with tears, for I am good for nothing else. As far as I can see, the right is with Curial, for his opponent was determined to fight him on any pretext, and Curial had no choice but to defend himself. So, Paulino, go back at once to Curial and tell him to exert himself for my sake, and to give orders for whatever he needs to be done, and it shall be done at once.' And she wrote letters to Curial, the best and most encouraging she could, and sent him money and jewels: but the pain remained in her heart. She had a statue of St George made, and every day she heard three masses, all said in honour of the saint. Paulino returned to Paris, where he gave

Guelfa's letters and jewels to Curial, his master. Curial was so pleased he was beside himself with joy, and made his preparations for the battle as splendid as he could.

Many attempts were made meanwhile to prevent this fight from taking place, but the Boar took no steps, nor did he wish to, that did not lead to the combat, nor did the Dukes of Brittany and Orleans advise him to renounce it, considering Curial as good as dead, and each thinking that when he was dead, Lachesis would be his, regardless of whether she would be pleased or not.

Those who were trying to conciliate them would go to Curial, asking him to give up thought of battle, and he always replied that the matter was not in his power but was the Boar's business, and he was concerned only to defend himself; and that if the Boar did not attack him, even if they were already in the lists, he would make no move. He answered with such mildness and with such soft words that everyone was quite sure that he was greatly afraid and would be well pleased if the matter were dropped. The Boar did not behave like this, but spoke with such ferocity and fiery words as if he believed he would terrify them all; and at last, when they continued to press him, he told them to go away, whether they wished or not, for he would listen to them no more.

So each of them made preparations for the battle, as splendid as he could manage. As the day approached, the Boar went to the King, escorted by the Dukes of Orleans and Brittany, and made this supplication:

'Oh most excellent and high King, you well know that the principal condition agreed upon concerning the battle that is to take place between Curial and myself is that if the judge chosen by me does not allow the battle to be a fight to the death I must be the vanquished and held to be a liar and traitor, and for this reason Curial laid the charge upon me. Seeing you, sir, to be the greatest king among Christians and consequently in the world, and since I am your vassal and have served you not only in your presence but also in many foreign lands on both sides of the sea, spreading afar the greatness of your majesty, it was my wish to choose you as judge, in order to show my worth before you as I have shown it many times in many places, so that you may know what sort of man I am, what I can do and of what I am capable, so that you may see in my actions what you have heard of me by repute.'

The King had already replied that he would do in this matter as God guided him, but that he would not commit himself on this point, when Curial received tidings of the supplication that the Boar was making. Then he ran, or rather he flew to the King, and kneeling before him, begged him to be pleased to grant what the Boar

149

had asked. 'He has not yet told me what he wants,' said the King, 'and since he has not said it, I answered at once to what I thought he wished to say.' 'I do not ask you to give me land, money or jewels,' said the Boar, 'I only ask that you will give your word that you will let the battle be a fight to the death, for otherwise, even without a fight, I should be vanquished and held to be a liar and a traitor.' Curial said again 'Ah, sir, you are used to do great favours to those who entreat you! Will you not grant this little one to this knight who says he has served you so well? Grant it, at the entreaty of all those here present who, as I see, will take it as a great boon.' Then all besought him, again.

The King saw that he was urged by each of the combatants and by the dukes, who were very insistent, and, unable to refuse but against his own will, said 'Since you desire it so much, I will grant it, and so I promised.' Without waiting for him to finish uttering the words, Curial seized his hand and kissed it.

Everyone said 'On my word, Curial is very clever, and there is no one in the world who can get the better of him, for it is he who wins the honours of this supplication.' So they each went their own ways, preparing for the day of battle, which was close at hand.

★

During this time the two old knights of Guelfa's household had been insistently persuading the Marquis to make attempts to find a husband for his sister, reproaching him for negligence and delay. As soon as the Marquis said that he was willing if a suitable match could be arranged, befitting the honour of his sister, they replied that they had heard there were many great and notable matches to be made in France and that if he wished they would try to arrange one, so that the noble and worthy lady would not spend her time vainly; and they added many things that it would take long to record. But they thought only of separating Curial and Guelfa.

Moreover, they said to him that, as he well knew, Anthony, monseigneur, the uncle of the Duke of Burgundy, had a claim to his marquisate and had often requested him by letter to acknowledge this of his own free will or else he would be forced to seek some means of recovering it for sure; and since Curial was in those parts and enjoyed such favour, it would be well to settle this difficulty and that at no time as at the present had the Marquis had such a good opportunity. And they offered, if the Marquis so wished, to go themselves to arrange these matters so that his interests might be served and his affairs and his honour would not suffer through the deficiencies of his servants.

The Marquis was pleased with this, and entrusted these things to them, ordering them to tell Curial all that had to do with the matter of monseigneur Anthony; but they were not to tell him anything at all about the marriage they were to negotiate. The decision was made, and they continued to discuss these matters on other days in other places; and when the letters and documents were ready, they took leave of Guelfa, left Montferrat, and made their way until they reached Paris.

Curial was informed of the departure of Ansaldo and Ambrosio by Melchior de Pando, and on the day they were due to arrive in Paris he went out to meet them with an honourable company, and brought them to his home to rest, and there he fêted them and did them honour. And as long as they were there he provided them with all that they needed, so that they had no need to spend money. They told Curial the purpose of their coming, revealing only the matter of monseigneur Anthony, in which Curial offered his help, to be of service to the Marquis. He asked them, however, if they would wait until his duel was over, because it was to take place so soon that he could not undertake anything else. They answered that they were content, and that they would not say a word until he told them to. They kept to this, and it turned out well for them, for many reasons which will be told in their time and place.

Leaving these matters, the old men questioned Curial about the battle he was to do, and he told them everything, to which they replied 'Sir Curial, there is no call for advice, for the affair has reached a point where nothing can be changed. We would have you remember only that you are a knight, and the honour that chivalry has brought you, which we trust that our Lord God will now increase so that no knight in the world will be more honoured: as indeed you are now, and shall be more so hereafter, God willing.'

'Dear friends,' answered Curial, 'I owe to God but one day, and that I shall pay Him whenever He chooses. My resolve was never to challenge another knight to battle, however weak he was, nor to refuse any knight who challenged me, however strong he may be. I have been challenged, and I believe that justice is on my side. God will judge between us, and to Him I commend my cause. Let Him do His will in this as in my other affairs.'

When they had finished talking, they went to supper and were splendidly served with a great provision of food and many different precious wines. The old knights were amazed, and looked at one another as they observed the large house, richly furnished, full of well-behaved servants distinguished by many different insignia; they saw the abundance of gilded plates, and the manner of service; they saw the men, each intent on his office, serving noiselessly; and

151

they thought this was not like the house of a knight but rather of a duke or great lord. They saw the meats brought on accompanied by minstrels, they saw knights and barons arrive during supper to honour and fête Curial joyfully, and he them. Yet Curial continued to honour the old men, to present them to the others so that all did them honour and offered them their services, for his sake.

After supper the Duke of Burgundy, the Count of Foix, and the Lords of Vergues and St George came to Curial's dwelling, and finding the minstrels playing, they began to dance and make merry. Thus passed much of the night until each went away happy to his home, leaving Curial with Ansaldo and Ambrosio. As it was time to sleep, the old men were shown to their apartment and taking leave of Curial, they went to bed.

Truth to tell, the old men were tired by the exertions of their journey and had need of rest, but the welcome that Curial had provided for them left them no room for sleep. As soon as they were alone, each vied with the other in relating all they had seen, as though each had not seen it all for himself. One said to the other 'Did you notice such and such a thing?' and the other asked 'And did you see such and such another?' 'I should never have believed it, for sure' said one, 'even if I had been told, without seeing for myself.' 'It is hardly credible even so' replied the other. 'On my word, this is very wonderful. However it may be, I think we shall now see what we have hoped for happen to Curial, for it is said that the Boar is the strongest and most valiant knight in the world, and even if Curial is a good and valiant knight, he is not as strong nor such a one as they say the other man is, and so he will die in this encounter and be dishonoured for all time. And if by chance the opposite happens, we shall part him from Guelfa by the marriage we are going to negotiate; and if the marriage does not come about, perhaps there will be other ways to prevent him from returning to Montferrat; and if none of this comes about, we are now such friends of his that we can profit by him. And so our journey cannot be fruitless.'

They went to bed, and if they had not been given two beds in which to sleep and thus been separated, I do not think they could have slept all that night: for Envy, of which they were full, would not have allowed it, nor do I think they would have taken much rest for thinking of ways in which to harm Curial.

Ah, mean and hapless Envy! Ah, false, worthless hag! How do you come, with your lean and wrinkled face, your watery eyes and trembling head, to penetrate to the very bones of these two old men? What has that valiant knight done to you, what reason have you for harming him? In what way can it profit your accursed and abhorrent condition? Do you not know that even if Curial were to fall from his present state it would not do you a farthing's worth of good, for his virtues would not transfer themselves to you, you would not inherit his fortune nor his victories. If you envied only the things that are fitting to you, and if when the other lost them you could acquire them and were sure of this, although it is a great sin it would not be abominable; but to bear envy and be eaten up within for something which you could not have whatever befall is unprofitable torment. If Guelfa loses Curial she will not welcome you in his place nor give you what she gives him, but rather she would withdraw into a more humble state and cast you out of her household, not needing so many to serve her.

What a mean and wretched condition is yours, that profits neither you nor anyone, so that you strive fruitlessly! Can you say that you rejoice and are pleased to have harmed him? Do you not think that perhaps his successor will be yet more hateful to you, so that you will not recover from this abominable malady but will continue to go from bad to worse? Answer me – what good did it do you to cause the angels to be driven from heaven, to make the first father sin, and all the many other ills that have come about because of you? The Jews who accused our Saviour did not know you well, indeed, let them consider what they have acquired through you; and if everyone knew you as well as I do you would not find a resting-place wherever you went. False and evil Envy, let each one work to make his own choice, and depart from mankind, for your currish ways are hateful to God and to man.

★

The long and troublesome night was over, and when the day came, clear and bright, Ansaldo and Ambrosio, to show themselves as other than they really were, went to Curial's chamber. When he saw them he greeted them with a cheerful face and received them courteously, asking them how they had slept.

One of them answered 'Indeed sir, I have not slept well, thinking about this business of yours; I pray God will bring you through with honour. Truly, if victory was in my hand you should have it without asking.' 'Thank you very much' said Curial. 'I expect as much and more from you. But I beg you to lose no sleep over this, for it hurts you and does me no good, and to spend time vainly is not wisdom. Enjoy yourselves as I do, on my word, and do not think about the battle, for two reasons: first, it is I who am challenged, and I have only to defend myself, not to overcome the other, and indeed if he does not overcome, he is held the vanquished; secondly, right is on my side. So for these two reasons, if God is neutral between us,

153

although I continually pray Him to help me, I have some certainty of victory, which the Boar cannot have as things stand. So enjoy yourselves, for the matter lies in these hands of mine, not in your thoughts.' And they ceased to speak of it.

The Duke of Burgundy came with numerous other lords, and when they had heard mass they mounted and went to court. The King commanded that as soon as they had dined the four combatants should send him their arms, both offensive and defensive, because he wished to see them. He went in person to the battlefield and gave orders as to where the tents of the combatants should be placed. On the same day, accordingly, Curial had a tent erected outside the lists, and the Boar did likewise, opposite it, and raised a standard before it, all black with large gold letters which read 'Good luck'. The King returned to his residence and took his seat at table, and everyone went off to have dinner.

As soon as the knights had finished dinner they sent their weapons to the King, who looked at them and had them examined, and then ordered that they should be returned.

An infinite number of people had come to see the fight, and many stands had been erected round the lists, which were suitably commodious.

It was the eve of St George, and the King sent for Curial and his companion, and when they had come he said for all to hear 'Curial, do not think that because you are foreigners you will lack support or that the others will receive, either in word or deed, a fraction more honour or favour than is due to them, for I intend to preside in this affair with as much impartiality as I possibly can: so do not have any such fear. And if there is anything you lack which you find you are in need of, tell me and I will see that it is given you, if it is within my power.' 'Monseigneur,' replied Curial, 'I have never thought, nor would it ever cross my mind to do so, that your excellency would conduct yourself in this affair save in the way you have indicated. You are a great king and a valiant knight, and I am sure that you will give such an account of yourself that no one in the world could reproach you for it.'

'And have you need of anything?' he asked Aznar. 'Tell me and I shall not fail you.' 'There is one thing I want,' replied Aznar, 'and that I ask of you – that you should hasten matters, for a lady whom I love will give me no rest at night, indeed I swear that at night I seem to see her and hear her say "Hurry up and come to me". So I beseech you again to hasten, and let her not be frustrated in her desires.' 'Tell me, Aznar,' said the King, 'is she pretty?' 'I take for granted that she is the most beautiful in the world, for no one sees her without falling in love with her.' The King laughingly asked him again 'Tell me,

154

does she love you?' 'In truth, sire, I believe she does, and tomorrow, God willing, you will see proof in my deeds, for I hold that when I remember her, he who comes to fight me does so to his harm, and that is certain!' The King laughed heartily, and everyone murmured that this man must be a very valiant warrior and one who would give a good account of his honour.

Then they left the King and returned to their lodging, very well accompanied. The King remained with many dukes, counts and barons, and everyone said openly that they had never seen such a gallant pair of companions-in-arms for the lists as were Curial and Aznar; and that it was indeed true that the Boar was a very valiant and strong knight, brave and daring and enterprising, but that Curial was no less a knight than he, even if he did not talk so much. Between the other two it was easy to see where the advantage lay: Guillaume de la Tour was a knight of small physique and not very strong, but yet he was as lively and bold as a lion, and so insulting that it seemed a devil was in him. He was very dextrous too, and well-practised in the use of all the weapons that pertain to a knight, and for this reason there was some hope for him, because otherwise there was no comparison between him and Aznar.

The day of battle arrived. Everyone rose early in the morning and went to take the best places for viewing, and not only the stands but all the grounds around were full of people. The King and Queen came, and I cannot describe the number of lords who came from places far away, and the multitude of knights and barons. I do not think that there had ever been such a throng gathered together for such an encounter before, for it depopulated the towns, robbed villages of their inhabitants and left castles with no one to guard them, because the fame of these knights was such and so widespread that everyone wanted to see them, especially in these circumstances.

The dukes and great lords vied with one another in supporting their favourite, and with much pomp and display escorted them to the battlefield. Curial and Aznar went straight to the King's box and made their reverence to him, and then to the Queen and to the other lords and ladies, and then with a great clamour of trumpets and minstrels they went to their pavilion, which was extremely magnificent. Their coats of arms were white with the cross of St George. From the other side approached the Boar and Guillaume de la Tour, with no less pomp and clamour, and their coats of arms were of red with white crosses. Guillaume de la Tour entreated the Duke of Brittany to make him a knight, but the Duke refused to knight him in the presence of the King, until the King sent word to command

155

him to do so, and thus Guillaume was created a knight. So the four knights entered severally their own tents.

The King then opened the ceremonies which are customary in such battles, sending mediators to try to make peace between the combatants. They went first to the Boar, but he foamed at the mouth and said that only death could give them peace; and in short none of them wished anything but to come to blows, and they returned to the King with this answer. Next the King made them swear on the Cross and the Gospels that they had no charms or spells or any other aids save only the arms that have already been named.

While all this was going on, a friar minor, of whom it was said that he was a man of a very holy life and a member of the royal house of France who had heard about the battle when he was in Angers, came to Paris as fast as he could, arriving just as the knights were due to emerge from their tents to do battle. With an impatient heart and a loud voice he cried to the King 'Are you a heathen that you do this? Why do you turn yourself into an enemy of God, acting against His law which forbids such folly? Tell me, sir, are these knights fighting against Moors, to uphold the law of Christ, will they kill Herod, His enemy, or what are they doing?'

The dukes and lords told the friar to be silent, that this was a matter that concerned knights, not friars; and although the friar continued to shout louder and would not be silent, such was the tumult made by the lords that the friar was not heard, but was pushed away and thrown out because of the interference he was causing to what they were anxious should take place. Otherwise they would have shown him much honour, for he well deserved it.

The day was advancing; and lo and behold, another interference – a damsel arriving with a fine escort, who sent a request to the King that she might see Curial before the battle. The King asked who she was, and was told that it was Festa, at which news he was pleased, and he sent for Curial to come out of his tent. Curial went to a corner of the lists and when he saw Festa had come he was very happy; but she, when she had given him all the messages of goodwill from Montferrat, said to him, almost weeping, 'I would rather have found you wearing other clothes, and in different circumstances.' 'My sweet Festa,' replied Curial, 'I have never been, and you have never seen me, dressed better than I am at present. Go to the Queen, who will be glad to see you. As for me, there are not two people in the world who give me such cheer as you have done: blessed be God who has brought you here and gives much honour to her who has sent you.' The Queen received Festa with much festivity, and sat her close beside her, saying 'What do you think of your knight, Festa?'

'Woe is me! I would I had found him otherwise!' the damsel answered.

The heralds proclaimed at the four corners of the field that no one should speak or make signs, and all the other things which are customary on such occasions. Then the tents were struck and removed from the lists, the knights lowered the visors of their basinets, their friends and kinsmen left them, and only the officials remained with the combatants, who took up their axes and started forward.

The Boar had many times won honour on many battlefields where he had been engaged in fights to the death, from all of which he had emerged with glory, and his chivalry was held in high esteem in many parts of the world, so much so that many people had begun to write books about his victories, with letters of gold even if the deeds were of silver, as is the custom of authors. If the Boar had been content with this his earthly glory would have been assured, because it was proclaimed and magnified by the tongues of kings, dukes and great lords and he had no need to display it for inspection so often and in so many places. But he believed that nothing was due to Fortune and thought that only his boldness and his strength were responsible for his valorous acts. It did not occur to him that the envious dogs had drawn him out of the forest, not for the Boar's own good, but for their own purposes, spurring him on with barks and yelps and plenty of bites, and he had come into the field which he could leave only by vanquishing and overthrowing the wise huntsman who awaited him at the gate. And so I saw him (and I still seem to see him), with his back and neck bristling, his head lowered, his teeth gnashing and sharpening themselves one against the other, and foaming at the mouth as he flung himself, without restraint or moderation, at Curial.

Curial approached the Boar with calm and deliberate step, and when they met, they struck many mighty blows at each other with their axes. The Boar thought that this attack would cause Curial to fall back, but no such thing happened, for Curial held his axe across his body, stood firm and steady facing the Boar, and, giving him a great push, moved him a good distance away from him. This action made it clear to the knights, and also to all those who were watching, which of the two was the stronger. The faces of the observers turned pale as death, and a great variety of opinions passed through their minds.

The two knights struck each other even harder, and the Boar exerted himself more boldly than wisely, swinging his axe with all his might. Curial defended himself but only struck when he could be sure of doing harm to his enemy. The Boar strove more than I can

157

say, with all manner of strokes and a great deal of effort, endeavouring with incredible rashness to gain the advantage over Curial. But the strain of his efforts and on the other hand the rough treatment he was receiving, were making him very tired because of the extreme ferocity of his onslaught, whereas Curial was avoiding his blows by turning them aside, or striking his arm, and besides whenever he saw an opportunity he struck the Boar such strong blows that the Boar was hard put to it to withstand them. So the fight continued a long time, both knights wielding their arms as great masters of the art.

The other two, however, were fighting a very different battle, for Guillaume de la Tour knew that Aznar was much stronger than he, and after the first blows he put himself on the defensive, thinking not only to defend himself with craft and skill but to overcome his opponent that way. But craft is of little avail against greater craft combined with great strength, and it is wrong to trust one's knowledge, for it is worth little against knowledge and might united.

So when Aznar realised Guillaume de la Tour's lack of strength, after he had borne with him a little to sound him out, he let himself go without restraint, and struck him such blows that it was fruitless for him to counterpass, parry or even to move away, for however much he wheeled and counterpassed, the other followed and pressed him, landing countless blows. He so harassed Guillaume that he did not know what to do, because no method of defence was of any avail against that thunderbolt of chivalry – for he struck more like a tempest than a knight. So many blows landed on his head that Guillaume began to lose consciousness.

When Aznar realised this he drew back and was unwilling to continue fighting, but turned towards the others. He saw that they were engaged in mortal combat and giving each other terrible blows, and that the Boar was less strong than Curial. Curial, who had been the defender, was now challenging, while the Boar sought to defend himself, and if the King had seen fit, matters were such as to decide the question, for there were certainly some who repented of having said so much. The Boar was giving ground to keep out of Curial's reach, but he followed and fought him with might and main; the Boar was growing weary and short of breath, so that he could only gasp. In spite of this it seemed to Aznar that the combat would continue a long time, and he approached to help Curial, raising his axe to strike the Boar. But Curial shouted to him 'Leave him to me. I assure you that on account of this battle he will not be the first to take a seat at the table of Paresse.' Then Curial smote even harder and showed what he could do, for all that day he had been holding back. The Boar wheeled round and came back at him, but could hardly lift his arms to parry the axe because he had been hit so often and so hard that he was no longer capable of striking a blow. Gradually retreating step by step, he came to a corner of the field, hoping that he might find some way of helping himself. As soon as he did so he nearly fell on to his back, and would certainly have done so if the fence had not supported him from behind.

Seeing that Curial had no need of help, Aznar turned back to his own opponent, who was resting on his axe, and made towards him. Guillaume, although tired and weary, faced up to strike him, and like a rabid dog eager for death, began to attack Aznar. But it availed him little, for after a few strokes had been exchanged, Aznar seized hold of his arm, and rained down a terrible storm of blows which laid Guillaume on the ground. He lay there, stretched out, making no attempt to defend himself and barely able to breathe, in fact he was stifling for lack of air. Aznar stood over him, removed his visor and said to him 'Guillaume, do you want to go on fighting?' 'Yes' he answered, but he did not move hand or foot. Then Aznar said 'Do you surrender to me'. 'I will not' he replied. 'Can you not see that I can kill you?' asked Aznar. 'Do what you can,' answered Guillaume, 'the victory is yours, but I shall never surrender.'

The King ordered the officials to go between the knights and not let them fight any more, and he descended from his stand in haste, and went to Aznar and forbade him to continue the fight. Then he went to the others, who were come to the end of their battle, and said to Curial 'I entreat you, on my honour to desist from this battle.' Curial drew back and stopped fighting. But the Boar, like all Frenchmen, who become brave as soon as the officials intervene and show great displeasure at the intervention, just at that moment came out of his corner, and cried loudly to the King 'Sir, this is not what you promised me. Why do you seek such dishonour to me? Death is worth more to me than life now. Will you kill me, since my opponent cannot?' And as he said this he hurled himself at Curial like a madman, trying to strike him with his sword, for he had dropped his axe. But Curial went for him and seized hold of him, and everyone thought that he would have thrown him to the ground if the King had not been there to ask him to let go. So Curial began to make away from him but the Boar tried again to attack him, and again he would have fallen if Curial had not held him up. Curial said to the King 'I beseech you to move away, Sir, and let me punish this fool, who would already be safely dealt with if you were not here.' It was all the officials could do to restrain the Boar, for Curial did not move, and the King, angry with his foolish actions, said 'Indeed, Boar, you have little sense, and your behaviour is not worthy of a knight'; and he gave orders that the Boar and his companion in arms should be taken from the field. Then the King called the other two knights to him, and with one on either side of him he led them from the field in the greatest possible honour. They had to wait some time, however, before they could leave the field because the Boar and his companion could hardly stir for weariness, and they had to be disarmed before they could move.

As the King was leading out the two foreign knights, the Duke of Burgundy and the Count of Foix and many other great barons gathered around Curial and Aznar, and singing merrily went with them to the King's palace. There the King dismounted and gave the knights leave to return to their quarters. Then you should have heard the shouting of knights and gentlemen, the clamour of trumpets and minstrels, great rejoicings and much festivity. 'Would to God I were one of these two!' everyone was saying. They went to Curial's house, where they found supper prepared. Many lords and great barons were guests there, and a copious multitude of knights, and the festivities were such that I cannot describe them; but I can assure you that it was long since such a supper had been held in that city.

For some days nothing but the combat was talked of in Paris. In truth, it was thought that it might have many unpleasant and unseemly consequences, for although everyone generally considered that the foreign knights had had the best of the encounter, some friends and kinsmen of the Boar, resentful of this, were saying and declaring not absolutely the contrary but claiming that the Boar was still undefeated and could have defended himself had not the King intervened.

The Boar realised that Curial was a far more valiant knight than he, and coming across him in the midst of all the great lords of the court, who were talking of this and that in the King's presence, he seized the opportunity to address him thus: 'Sir Curial, it is true that, encouraged by bad advice, I undertook to fight you of my own free will: some people, unaware of the condition in which I was when the King intervened on the day of battle, speak and judge now of what they knew nothing of, and say what is not nor ever was true. Accordingly I, who know the truth of the matter better than any other, in order that there shall be no possible grounds for doubt, will declare the condition in which I was. The truth is that I was so tired and weary that I could not continue, whereas you were striking at me again and again, better and stronger than ever; and when I took up my place in the corner of the field I hoped to find some relief, which your arm denied me. It would have been of little avail, as I realised at once, and you might have slain me then if the King had not prevented it (for which I am in no way grateful to him). Because of this, I grappled with you like a man out of his mind longing for death, since escape was not to be hoped for. And would to God that it had come to me, for when I caught hold of you I could only keep myself upright; otherwise I should have fallen from fatigue. But the King, whom I could not resist, drew me away from death, which I was seeking with all my might at your hands: and I could indeed see it visibly, but through fear of the King it fled away and disappeared. So, as lesser than you, and of little strength in comparison with you, I surrender to you here in this place, which on the day of battle I would not have done for anything in the world. Do your will with me, and neither I nor any other will prevent you.'

All who stood around and heard these words were amazed, and looked at Curial's face, to see what he would do. As soon as the Boar had finished speaking, Curial took his cap from his head and said to him 'Sir Boar, I wonder what has counselled you to say these words. It would be a more reasonable thing for me to say them to you, and I beg that they should stand for me; because indeed I have never been so hard pressed as I was that day. So I am very grateful to our lord the King, who was unwilling to let one of us, or indeed both of us, to be lost for so trivial a cause. For God alone knows the end of what is to come, and those who make judgement on it, so please them, would do better to be silent, for neither they nor anyone in the world can know what the outcome will be. So, Boar, here I stand, and if you will, I am quit of your hands; if not, send me where you will and I shall remain there at your orders until such time as it may please you to hold me quits and restore my liberty to me.'

When those standing by heard what the two knights had said they were amazed and did not know what to say. But Aznar came forward and approached Guillaume de la Tour and said 'Indeed, Guillaume, I will be no less courteous than those two: I am your prisoner, I swear to God that I shall not leave you until you have received from me the ransom you required from me and I can pay.' 'Sir Aznar,' answered Guillaume, 'I am content to have such a prisoner as you, and I ask you to come with me and keep your word.'

All were pleased at this new concord, and the Boar kissed Curial and Aznar, and similarly Curial kissed Guillaume, but Guillaume did not kiss Aznar but with a fierce and angry face, taking leave of them all, he took him away to his house. There he had a splendid dinner prepared, and sat Aznar next to a very pretty damsel named Yolande, who was his sister, and they ate very well. When they had dined, all three went into a chamber, and Guillaume said 'You are my prisoner of your own free will, Aznar, and you have sworn not

161

to leave me unless I take ransom for you, and I told you that I agreed. The ransom I ask of you is that you should give my sister a kiss, and then you are quit.' So Aznar kissed the damsel, and Guillaume put round his neck a rich golden sash that the Duke of Brittany had given him; and he said 'Aznar, you have paid the ransom, but I have not paid the debt I owe you, for you had me on the ground and could have killed me had you wished. But you were more merciful to me than I was to myself, and gave me life, which I was seeking with all my might to lose. So do of me and with me whatever you please, and you, Yolande, do without protest all that Aznar wishes, for he has given you such a brother as I am, whom you would have lost if he had had as little wisdom as I.'

When he had taken some refreshment, he left the chamber, leaving Aznar and Yolande without any other company, and closing the door behind him, he bolted it. Finding himself alone with the damsel, Aznar laughed at the joke. 'Lady,' he said, 'if all prisoners have such a jailer as I have, they cannot fear death nor should they wish to leave prison. And if it please you and your brother, I should like you to be my wife.' The damsel answered that she would not deny him anything he wished.

So then Aznar got to his feet, went to the door, and shouted for Guillaume; and when he came he said 'Are you weary of my sister's company already, Aznar?' 'I am not weary of it, Guillaume,' said Aznar, 'on the contrary, I ask you, if she is willing, to give her to me as my wife.' Pleased beyond words, Guillaume replied 'Not as a wife, Aznar, I do not deserve it, but I give her to you as a slave: take her away and do with her what you will.' But Aznar said again that he wished to marry her, and both Guillaume and Yolande were willing.

After the siesta was over, the King was informed of this agreement, and he was very pleased. He sent for Yolande, and the Queen decked her with jewels and other finery, and they were betrothed that very day, and not very many more passed before the marriage took place with great pomp and solemnity.

This Yolande was highly born and well endowed, and moreover the King, wishing to make a particular display of his royal munificence, gave Aznar many jewels and five thousand gold écus as well. Yolande's kinsmen bought her inherited property from her, so that Aznar could take away his wife's dowry with him, and then Aznar, with great joy, honour and riches, began to make preparations for returning to his native kingdom with his wife.

The Boar, who was ill-pleased with the world, had shown no sign of himself since the day when the knights had made their peace, and in fact he took the habit of a friar minor and stayed hidden away in his convent. However, on Aznar's wedding day he emerged with a companion, dressed in a very poor habit, and came to the hall where the marriage-feast was being held, and went to where Curial was sitting, asking him for alms. At first Curial did not recognise him, for he had no idea that the Boar would take such a step. 'Give me alms, Curial,' said the Boar, 'for the love of Jesus Christ'; and he wept. Curial looked at him closely and then recognised him. 'Oh, Boar,' he said, 'who has counselled you to do this?' 'God' answered the Boar. 'May He grant you salvation' said Curial. 'What?' said the Boar, 'Do you think that God, for whose service I have abandoned the vanities of the world, will not grant me salvation?' 'I do not doubt that,' said Curial, 'but I fear that despair rather than love has moved you. No more of this now, for this is not the place to talk of such things.'

The Boar left him, and went along the tables begging alms, and would eat nothing save scraps of bread. He was surrounded by people as he went along, some of them weeping, others surprised and almost struck dumb with amazement, while others stood aside meditating on the strange event.

The King too, and the other lords were very surprised and at a loss for words. But after a while the King began to talk about the Boar, and said 'Indeed, the Boar has always gone to extremes, and no one should be surprised at this because it is customary and very natural that when a gentleman of this nation finds himself in such serious misfortune that he loses his honour or becomes poor, he can always find a staff with which to go begging alms on a pilgrimage to St James. It is the contrary with the Spaniards, who as soon as they become poor turn thieves and highway robbers in their poverty.'

The Boar, however, did not remain in Paris but went away, and by stages he reached Jerusalem and from there he went to Mount Sinai, to the monastery of St Catherine, where he lived and died in sanctity, with the reputation of being a very holy friar.

★

The two foreign knights were fêted and feasted with great magnificence, and it was generally agreed that they were the two best knights in the world and that there was little to choose between them, for if Curial was a skilful and very valiant knight, Aznar was certainly no less skilful nor less valiant, and the King was so fond of him that he never tired of his company. But now Aznar took leave of the King and the dukes and the great lords, and received many presents of silver and jewels; and so with his wife and great happiness, he went away.

Curial accompanied him for twenty leagues of the journey, and when they came to the parting, he said 'Sir Aznar, I can do nothing now to repay the great favour you have done me or the honour that I have received through you. May God who repays all, reward you. I have divided my spoils, half and half, and here is the half which I have for you. Take it when you will; I beseech you not to reply in any way save to accept it, for if you are my friend as I am yours, and as you have been until now, you will do my pleasure and will, which is this.' Aznar struggled long not to take it, but finally he had to satisfy Curial's wish. Then Curial asked him to commend him to the grace and favour of his lord, the King of Aragon, and they commended each other to God. Then Aznar continued on his way to Barcelona, where he found his lord and many notable people.

I shall not describe here the reception that the King gave to Aznar and his wife, for I said sufficient when describing the return of the Aragonese knights from Montferrat; but it must be remembered that this King was the best knight in the world, and loved and honoured good knights. Whoever wishes to know about the King should read the seventh canto of Dante's *Purgatory*, and he will find him there. Dante was inclined to favour King Charles, the enemy of the King of Aragon, and in the comedy of the *Purgatory* this great and venerable poet and author seeks with all his ability and knowledge to sing the praises of King Charles (who was without doubt a notable king and a good knight, though not equal to the other); nevertheless he could not pass over in silence the courage and excellence in chivalry of that illustrious and most excellent, high and valorous King of Aragon. And he corroborates and confirms his intrepid feats of arms, worthy to be recorded with veneration, which are written in many long and truthful books by various great and learned doctors, saying of him, as the highest praise, and with sorrow in his heart, that *d'ogni valor portò cinta la corda* – 'his heart was girt about with every excellence'. Reader, mark those words 'with every excellence': he did not write them carelessly nor could he have said them unthinkingly. For Dante well knew that when the said King Charles was besieging Messina by land and sea with a great army, he fled in fear from this King, who was coming to attack him with smaller forces than his own. Again, when Charles had challenged him and they were to fight man to man in Bordeaux, the said Charles, against his word and the honour of chivalry which prohibits what he did, gathered together a large number of armed followers, which was easy for him to do because he was in France, in order to prevent the King of Aragon from coming to do battle by frightening him with a show of force. The King, however, not without danger, sought a way of going there and indeed he arrived and on the day assigned for battle presented himself to the Captain of Bordeaux, ready to fight. King Charles, however, did not appear to uphold his honour, and this was not hidden from Dante, for it was well known even to the blind.

No more of this, for it was famous throughout the world at that time, and will endure as long as the world endures. So I shall return to the matter from which I have strayed a little, for it is not relevant to speak of it more in this book.

★

Curial returned to Paris, where he had left the two old knights, whom he continued to entertain as he had begun. Ansaldo and Ambrosio were well pleased by this, and saw that Curial was so favoured and honoured that the Marquis of Montferrat himself would have been content with the half of it. When the King of France learned, as he did but certainly not from Curial, that he had shared his winnings with Aznar, he considered him an even better knight and did him yet greater honours than he had previously done, and gave him valuable presents.

Nothing was talked of save Curial and every day added to his honour, as the old knights observed; and although they made a show of pleasure at it they really wished him dead, dishonoured and degraded. What a slave is wretched Envy, for the more honour you do her, the more she will loathe you and wish you harm!

At this time the King of France returned to the question of the marriage of Lachesis and the Duke of Orleans, which had often been suggested. Lachesis was quite unwilling, and the King was informed that unless Curial left Paris for a while the match would never be made, as Lachesis had eyes and ears for no one but him. Thinking to act for the best, and hoping to find a way to achieve what he had set his hand to, the King sent for the two old men and told them that he was working to bring this marriage about but that the affair was held up because of Curial, for he had heard that the damsel loved him. He asked them to find a way of suggesting to Curial, and of bringing it about, that he should leave Paris on some excursion, or at least to prevent his continual coming and going to Lachesis's residence, so that she might become a little cooler towards him; and by thus making her believe that he had come to hate her, a better response could be won from her: for the Duke of Orleans was madly in love with her, and Curial gained nothing from it.

When the old men heard what the King had said, each invited the other to speak first, and then one of them began thus: 'Most high and most excellent sir, were I addressing anyone else I should perhaps not propose to make the following reply, but before so great, high and wise a king I will not hold back from saying in all truth what I feel about Curial. Sir you must know that he is the son of a poor gentleman, one who almost lived on charity, and that as a very young boy he came to the house of the Marquis of Montferrat, my lord, who was very taken with him, and dressed him and accepted him into his household, putting him among the pages of his bedchamber. He grew in age and in cunning and became very sly, and Guelfa, the sister of the Marquis, who is the lady of Milan, with the encouragement of a traitor called Melchior de Pando, fell in love with him. He robbed her not only of her treasure and jewels but also of her honour and good name, so that the lady has failed and continues to fail to remarry, for apart from this she is very rich and worthy and of incomparable beauty; and with the wealth of this lady he goes about the world. Similarly, when he went to do battle in Germany, being brawny and fearless, which is all the good that can be said of him, he fell in love with this Lachesis. If she knew him as well as we do, she would care nothing for him. He robs the lady, and so keeps up the state in which you see him, for of his own he has not enough to keep a nag. Now see, sir, what kind of a person is he to whom you do so much honour that his brain is being turned! Indeed, it has been turned, and he has so high an opinion of himself that he holds no man in esteem, but expects that everyone must do him homage. If he were wise, knowing that the Duke of Orleans is displeased by his frequent visits to Lachesis, he would keep away from her; and she shows herself a woman indeed in always choosing the worst, because she should be able to see the difference between the two of them. However, since your lordship wishes and commands that this fellow should go hence, we will see to it that he leaves soon, for we can arrange for him to be summoned away. Then Lachesis will give up hope and her affection will cool.' The other old man praised this reply, adding that it would not be necessary for Curial to know anything about it.

The King was pleased with this advice, but he realised that these old men wished Curial ill, and had he known it before he would not have taken them into his confidence. So he spoke to them thus: 'I was aware whose son Curial is, and about his father and his early career. It is true that the lady gave him much advancement, but I swear to you as a king that she has in him the best and most worthy servant in the world. If she has given and continues to give him money, there is no better way of spending it, and he well merits it. Tell me, who do you know or have ever seen, as noble and valorous as Curial? I tell you that of all the knights known to me there is not one who is his equal, for he is a knight in word and deed, on the exercise-ground, in the chamber, in the lists, everywhere. Moreover, he is intelligent and virtuous, wise and of good counsel; this does not surprise me, for I have observed he is held in high esteem by philosophers, poets and orators, and I can see that his affairs will go from strength to strength. He is so diligent that he never wastes time, and whenever there are exercises of arms he is one of the first to perform, and carries off the honours. If you wish for singing, dancing and courtly pleasures, I tell you no one is his equal in the chamber; and when he is not here, he studies ceaselessly, and treats books with such great reverence that everyone who knows him is amazed. I do not need to tell you that he is handsome and graceful of person, for if you are not blinded by malice or envy you can see it as well as I. I have heard him praised by many, and certainly not wrongly, for if my eyes have not deceived me, I have never heard him praised for anything that he did not do better than he was said to do it. What more can be said of him than that God and Nature have formed him and endowed him outstandingly? What you say of Guelfa, that she has not been able to remarry because of him, surprises me. I assure you that with his valour and the many virtues that God has richly bestowed upon him, he could make a marriage so good that you would be surprised, for there is no one, however great, who would not willingly be allied with him, as a man of great deserts. Lachesis has reason to make much of him, for he brought her much honour in Germany, and if he wishes to have her for his wife he would not have to ask twice: it would be granted at once, and I know that it would please her father the Duke. So give no importance to such matters, for it is the custom that chivalry and knowledge advance men of poor estate and make them great lords. All kings have their beginnings in chivalry and knowledge, for without these they would not be greater than the rest. I ask you again to put into effect what you have offered to do, and to forget the rest, for Curial would not have achieved the victories and honours that have won him advancement if it were not the will of heaven.' Thus the king ended his speech.

The other old man who had not yet spoken, replied. 'Sir,' he said, 'it is neither a wish to take away from him the smoke of vainglory that is his nor a desire to do him harm that has made my companion say what he has said of Curial, but the dishonour that he brings upon the Marquis and upon Guelfa, whose honour we are desirous of preserving. If it is possible, we wish that our lady, who is the most beautiful and worthy in the world, far from losing her good name on account of this fellow, should make a good marriage, and that is what we are here for. Think, your highness, what you would feel if in your house there were a knight who molested a sister or daughter of yours, bringing mischief and blame upon you! We would not care about it so much were we not afraid that the first day this matter came to the ears of the Marquis the lady would be lost, even though she has committed no other fault than to aid this knight's advancement; and losing the lady's favour, the knight too would be lost. For this reason we continually wonder how we can prevent this unfortunate consequence, which must come about if God, or good people, do not intervene in some way. Moreover, we are servants of this lady and her honour has been commended to us by the Marquis, and if this folly is not converted into wisdom, we must give him a bad account of it. Some time ago the Marquis had an inkling of it, and seeing the danger, we are not unfearful and cannot help expecting a day when it will become known and we must die with her or be imprisoned for ever.'

The King listened attentively to all that was said, and then he replied 'Good men, you take a great burden upon yourselves. Curial has no fear of the Marquis, who would not dare at present to undertake what you suggest. Curial has such friends that the Marquis would be ill-advised to try any such thing, and he would undoubtedly make him realise this by his actions. From what you have said, and from what I have heard from others, his sister has not yet committed any crime that deserves death or imprisonment, and if there were anything of the kind you may be sure that Guelfa would not lack someone to defend her and avenge her, with force if need be. If there were such a knight in my household and a sister or daughter of mine fell in love with him, I should give her to him as a wife, for by virtue of his chivalry and nobility of heart there was never a more worthy than he. If you seek a husband for Guelfa, go no further afield, for you have one in Curial, if they are both willing, and you could not find a better in all the world. Help them, therefore, and do not accuse them, for I know many things that you have no idea of. Now leaving other things aside, do what you have offered to do. If by chance you can find a more honest way than that, use it, I pray you, for I would not wish to do Curial harm for anything in the world.' Then he dismissed them and they went their way.

When Ambrosio and Ansaldo returned to their lodgings they found Curial waiting to take them to dinner. With a kind and cheerful face he said to them 'Now we can begin to talk of the matter for which you have come. Whenever you please you will find me ready to discuss and to carry out not only that but anything else that may serve the Marquis.' The old men answered that he already knew the reason for their coming, that they had come to him rather than to anyone else and it rested with him and he might set about it whenever he pleased.

So that same day Curial went with them to the Duke of Burgundy and spoke to him at some length, giving him to understand that the Marquis of Montferrat had sent the two old knights to him for this purpose and accordingly he begged and entreated him to ensure that the Marquis would not be discommoded by Anthony, monseigneur, his uncle.

'Dear friend,' replied the Duke, 'my uncle is not here. He is ill, and so ill that as I have heard today I do not think he will ever rise again from his bed. If he does recover, I will have him come here, and you may believe that for your sake I will ensure that the Marquis's affair will prosper. If he dies, which God forbid, I am heir to what he possesses, including the claim to the Marquisate, if there is any; and I shall always do as you ask, and not go a step further.' Curial received this reply with great pleasure and thanked him very warmly, offering his services for the future even further than that to which he was already committed.

So they returned to their dwelling, and it was decided that the following day Curial should see them off and they would leave on their journey, Curial taking charge of the matter agreed upon with the Duke.

Curial believed that these men were the same within as without, and had no idea of what they were contriving day and night. So early next morning he had tailors come with cloth, and had fine clothes made for them and for their servants, suitable for each one. When they were dressed and ready to go, he gave them letters to take to the Marquis in which he commended the old men for their wisdom and diligence, and asked them to confirm what he had said. He set out with them, graciously giving each a fine hackney and money for their expenses, which the old men took with great contentment, bowing and scraping to him, and so they left him. Curial returned to Paris, and they made their way to Montferrat, where they were welcomed with rejoicing and celebration.

When the Marquis had received and read Curial's letter he wished to hear confirmation, from which he learned the reply of the Duke of Burgundy, which made him very happy. The old men described publicly to the Marquis and Guelfa the position which Curial enjoyed, the honour that was done him and what he had kindly done for them, the battle he had fought with the Boar and the triumph which he had achieved: and the Marquis said that he did not think there could be a better or more valiant knight in the whole world.

The old men spoke of Curial in such a way that everyone took it for granted that they were very fond of him, and thinking that this was so, Guelfa liked to hear them. And in the presence of everyone

169

she asked them things that she wished to know, ordering them to come with her to her room to speak with her.

★

Until that day, Fortune had showed Curial a cheerful and smiling face, although she had been many times pressed and indeed importuned by false, wicked Envy, who always accompanies her. Now she decided to harm Curial with all her power so as to test him and his virtue more than she had been able to do before. Whereas she had formerly granted, freely and generously, all the good things and the prosperity he could desire, it was now her will to harm him, and indeed she was to harm him with all her might and knowledge, as much as she could. Accordingly she called the Misfortunes to her and spoke to them thus: 'I cannot deny, nor will I, that you are separate from me, for on the day I strove with Poverty I lost all the power that I had over you, with the result that I can no longer command or force you, according to the sentence that was then passed on me. But I am not denied entreaty, and so I beg you, remembering past times, to grant me a favour; and if you follow your custom and usage you will grant it, for you have never said no to anything I have asked you. The reason for my request is that I have striven with all my power to advance and raise to high estate a knight named Curial, who serves the Lady of Milan. I have caused him to find favour in the eyes of all who see him, with only two exceptions, whom I set apart so that you might perform your good office, and these are two old knights of the household of the Lady of Milan. My sister and good friend Envy, whom you see here, has kept close to them and never left them, and she has continually begged me to take from him all or at least some of the favour I have bestowed on him. Seeing that I cannot do this without your help and favour, I entreat you affectionately that, if you are favourably inclined to carry out what I have asked, you will assail him in all the ways in which I have lavished on him, so that nothing remains; and I beg that you will do this not at one time, for it would be a slight thing and little suffering for him to be destroyed at a single blow, but gradually, a little each day, as I have raised him up. Then I shall see whether he can feel gratitude, for he takes for granted that all the prosperity and the good things that he has had and possesses have come to him through his own merit, not giving thanks to the giver, nor does he think that he could ever be without them. If he bears with equal heart both myself and you, I shall know his virtue, for even if he has much to do in enduring good things and knowing how to behave in prosperity, nevertheless it is misfortunes which demonstrate the virtue of men.

Thus following me and the path I have taken to raise him up, by that same route do you bring him down – except that I do not wish him to be overcome in battle, but I do not want victory either to be of any profit to him or to bring him any advancement.'

When the Misfortunes had heard the words and entreaties of Fortune, their former mistress and preceptor, they set about their work. Before they replied, however, they cried out aloud invoking Juno, the wife and sister of Jove, and besought her to appear to them.

Juno broke open and shattered the clouds, and sent lightning and thunder and terrible tempests, the sky darkened and stones fell. Aeolus unhinged and burst asunder all the caves of Lipari, and stormy winds rushed forth through every crevice, casting down trees and high towers throughout the world. Neptune stirred the seas, the waters roared and fish fled in all directions, while ships, galleys and other boats perished. Pluto gave voice, flinging flames and rocks through the mouths of Vulcan and Mongibello, setting fire to gardens and vineyards in Sicily.

When all this had continued for some time, the fury abated a little and the gods sat down together. Then the Misfortunes, their officers, kneeling before them, explained fully the request of Fortune, and when their prayers had been heard, Juno, without asking leave, spoke first. 'Ah, how often, brothers and dear friends, have I experienced the ingratitude of this knight! And the fair Cyprian and her son Cupid are witnesses also, who have been good to him and gave him as his lot the most beautiful and rich lady in the world for his beloved. Once and many times has she been scorned and abhorred by him, and he has incurred the penalty for ingratitude by seeking the love of another woman with the wealth of the first. It is reasonable, therefore, that, not obtaining the one and losing the other, he should wander through the world in poverty, exiled and without honour. If it pleases you, this is the sentence I pronounce.'

Since all were agreed in this verdict, they ordered the Misfortunes to follow Curial and not to leave him until Fortune, whose prayers brought this about, should be satisfied and order them to desist. Then each returned to his kingdom, causing again the same tempests as before.

The Misfortunes returned to Fortune with the reply that they were content to obey all that she asked of them concerning Curial, and Fortune answered that she had already revealed her intention to them, and begged them to waste no time but to carry her requests into effect forthwith. She ordered Envy to go to the old knights and to remain close to them, and the Misfortunes to go to Curial and not to leave him. So Envy on the one hand and the Misfortunes on the other went their ways according to their instructions.

★

Obedient to the command of Guelfa, who was all unaware of the ambush they had prepared for her, Ansaldo and Ambrosio went to her chamber. She spoke first of other things, in order to arrive at the haven of Curial from as great a distance as possible, and at last, lowering her sails, she said to them 'I have heard with pleasure, God knows, of the honour shown to you in Paris, and I am as grateful to Curial for it as if it had been shown to me in person.' They replied, in Curial's favour, that the valorous knight made such efforts to honour and oblige all those who came from Montferrat that it was wonderful to see. And talking of one good thing after another, passing from one honour to another, they said so many notable things about Curial that Guelfa was all happiness. When they had spoken long and without ceasing – and indeed without being able to cease, for they had seen and observed so many things that even if they had spoken for ever they would still have omitted something – Guelfa continued to interrogate them, while they answered, now one, now the other, and related such marvels that Guelfa needed no other Paradise. However, as she pursued her interrogation, she asked 'Tell me, have you seen Lachesis?' 'Indeed, madam,' they said, 'we have indeed seen her: we had no choice but to see her, madam, for Curial never leaves her house, alive or dead, and neglects all his other business for her.' 'Is she beautiful?' asked Guelfa. 'She is certainly very beautiful' they said. 'I am surprised that she has not returned to Germany' said Guelfa. 'She cannot, madam,' they answered, 'she is so much in love with Curial.' 'I am sure Curial cares for her, too' said Guelfa. 'Quite right, madam, he neither sees nor hears anything but her; and on my word, it is not surprising, for she makes so much of him that many are envious of him. I believe that if she goes away to Germany he will not leave her for anything in the world and will go with her. Would you hear proof of how she loves him? We can assure you of it, for on his account she will lose a marriage with the Duke of Orleans.' 'How do you know this?' asked Guelfa. 'Because the King asked us to find some way of removing Curial from her sight so that he would not learn of it, and to arrange for him to come to you, since you are so fond of him and make him presents with such generosity; and thus Lachesis, not seeing him and knowing that he was with you, would grow cold and, despairing of him, would agree to the marriage.'

'Indeed!' she said. 'So that is how I am spoken of in Paris?' 'Yes, to be sure,' they said 'and with such freedom that it would be better for you to be dead than alive. And although we have tried to cover it up and remedy it for the sake of your honour and because we know nothing of it and do not believe it, such improper things have been said to us about it that anyone who wishes to serve you well must feel ashamed to hear them. We are not surprised, however, that these things are said, because Curial, in the way of young men who wish to win favour, has said, so they say, things that would be better left unsaid by such a noble knight as he. He could cost you all the honour you have, and it would be better if he had never gone to France. On the other hand, he is, in faith, a good and renowned knight, since in what pertains to a good knight no one besides him is ever spoken of; but as far as it concerns you, it would have been better never to have seen him.' 'And has he, by chance, said as much?' she asked. 'We know only what we have heard about it, but not from him' they answered. 'But so that you may know how matters stand, when, by order of the Marquis, we spoke about a marriage between yourself and the Duke of Orleans, we were told that you already had a husband, and could not have two; and when we expressed surprise at these words, we were told that you were betrothed to Curial and perhaps had already consummated the marriage, and that it was for this reason that you were giving him all that he was spending; and so we should give over such jesting.'

Guelfa was deeply disturbed, and made no answer. Dismissing the old men, she sent for Melchior de Pando and told him that Curial was now rich and in high favour, and what she had intended to do was now accomplished. Accordingly she no longer wished him to be sent any more money than he had already received, and the key was to be turned in the chest. Henceforward she would decide how to spend her money in the service of God, for she had already spent enough in that of the world.

Ansaldo and Ambrosio went away to their homes thinking that they had achieved something of what they desired. A few days later there arrived the damsel whom Guelfa had sent to Curial, but Guelfa did not fête her or question her as she had done the previous time, and if the damsel tried to mention Curial, her lady turned the talk to other matters and would not listen. Thus the damsel knew that the lady was angry with Curial, and dare not speak, and within her heart she cursed Lachesis, thinking that Guelfa had heard of her love and for that reason was angry with Curial.

But after a few days, Guelfa, as though it were a matter that she cared little about, said 'Tell me, does Lachesis make much of Curial?' The damsel, thinking that Guelfa knew everything, told her what she had seen and heard. Then Guelfa believed what the old men had told her, and again ordered Melchior de Pando, more strictly than before, that he was not to consider giving anything to Curial, for if he were not well provided with what she had already given him, he would not be so with all the Sultan's treasure. Melchior replied that he would do her command.

Some time later Curial sent to Melchior de Pando for money, as he was wont to do. Melchior replied that he dare not give it unless Guelfa ordered him. When Curial heard this reply he was very surprised, and secretly and in disguise journeyed to Montferrat, and went home at night. There he spoke with Melchior de Pando of many things, and showed him the letter he had sent him. Melchior replied that it was true that he had sent it, and that he dare not give him anything unless Guelfa commanded by word of mouth.

'Go to the lady,' Curial replied, 'tell her that I am here and wish to pay my homage to her, and may it please her to tell me when I may come to her.'

'He is not so courtly, nor does his name befit him as well as he thinks' Guelfa replied. 'Tell him that I care little for homage or words, that I do not care about his affairs. Let him go, in God's name, wherever he please, for I am in retreat and have no mind for vanities. To you, Melchior, I say that if you wish to remain in my service you will not speak of him to me again, for I am weary of foolishness. Curial would be too costly if for his sake I were to lose the world to come, and if I were to continue to give to him, to spend in baubles, what God's poor should have. I have given him enough, if he has been wise enough to keep it; and if not let him find someone who will henceforward do for him what I have done until now. If he knew the penance which has been imposed on me for these follies, he would speak to me of them no more. Go, for I do not wish to talk to him again. I regret what I have said to him in the past, if that could make amends.'

Melchior returned with this reply and told Curial all that he had heard. Curial was astonished, and could not think what the matter could be. So great was his anxiety that he said no more that night but went to bed, thinking over many things.

The next day Curial said to Melchior 'Sir and father, I beg you in God's name, go to my lady and find out further what the matter is.' Melchior said that he dare not ask. Curial begged him to go nevertheless, and even if he said nothing, to listen in case she said anything. Melchior answered that he would. So going to the lady, he stood in her presence; but stand as he might, she never opened her mouth to say a word of Curial, which surprised Melchior. When the time came for him to leave he returned home. Curial was waiting in the hope that Melchior would bring him good news, but when he

174

saw that he had nothing to say, he began to ask Melchior what had passed between him and the lady. Melchior replied that there had been nothing, and that she had not spoken to him.

'Ah, holy Mary!' said Curial. 'Have you no advice to give me?' 'Indeed, I can only suggest one thing,' answered Melchior, 'and that is that you go to the Abbess, who I know is very friendly towards you and wishes you well, and through her you may learn what is the matter. This is the best advice I can give you.'

Curial took his advice, and went in disguise to the convent and had word sent to the Abbess that there was a gentleman at the door who wished to speak to her. The Abbess went to the door, and seeing him in disguise did not recognise him, and was afraid to approach him. But he reassured her, telling her to come a little closer, and to tell the other ladies to move further away, and then he would tell her who he was. The Abbess did so, and went up to him, and Curial in a low voice said 'I am Curial.'

At once the Abbess took him by the hand and led him into the convent, embracing him and making much of him. They sat down together, and she asked how he came to be there. 'My ill-luck is not yet finished' said Curial. 'God forbid that it pursue me further', and showing her Melchior's letter, he told her that he had come to discover the reason for this change, and had learned that Guelfa was so angry with him that she could not be more so, and he could not think why. He begged her to go to the lady and to find out, if she could, how this had come about, for he did not believe that he had done or said anything for which he deserved this treatment. The Abbess answered that she would go and do her best to find out and to discover some remedy. Curial was a little relieved, thinking that the Abbess would find a solution, and he took his leave of her and returned home.

As soon as the Abbess had dined she went to visit Guelfa, who was very pleased to see her and taking her aside, asked her the reason for her coming. When the Abbess had explained, Guelfa remained in thought for a time and at first made no answer. But then she asked for a Cross and the Gospels, and made the Abbess swear that she would not tell Curial or anyone else what she was going to say. Next she sent for her damsel and bade her tell, word for word, all that she knew of Curial and Lachesis and of the reputation that she had in the court of the King of France. The Abbess was very distressed and said 'Perhaps, lady, Curial is not much to blame for this.' Guelfa replied 'My friend, I would rather be dead than hear what I have heard', and she went on to tell her all that she had been told by Ansaldo and Ambrosio, and said that because of this she had decided to give him nothing more, adding that if the Abbess valued her life

175

she would not go back to the convent so that Curial would not weary her every day in his desire for news, nor would she send any message to him.

So every day Curial sent to the convent to know if the Abbess had returned, and when they said she had not, hid himself away, waiting for her to come.

★

Fortune, who had turned her cruel and pitiless back on Curial, went off to the Duke of Orleans, and appeared to him in a dream, all smiling and joyful, and said to him 'My dear friend, in the past I favoured Curial with all my power but now, wearied of bestowing all my good things on one person, I come to you, as I know that Curial was proving a great obstacle to you in Lachesis's love. To succour and uphold your afflicted spirits, I give you my assurance that if you now return to thoughts of marriage I shall be so favourable that you will obtain your desire, and unless you are robbed of it by sloth there is no other way in which you can fail. As soon as it is morning, therefore, go to the King and beg him to send for Lachesis and her mother and to speak to them of it again. It will be settled at once, since Lachesis is displeased with Curial because he has gone away to Guèlfa without saying anything to her. Know too that Curial has fallen so low that he will never return here, or if he does he will stay but a short time and will not find favour. For I have disfavoured him and he is assailed by Misfortunes, who will not leave him for many years and will bring him to such a point that he will be spoken of by no man, those who know him will not know where he is, and he will be erased from the memory of all men.' So saying, she disappeared and, turning her wheel, went away elsewhere.

The next day the Duke remembered the dream, and thought that he should act in accordance with it. He went to the King and, without telling him what he had dreamed, besought him to send for the Duchess of Bavaria and to treat again of the marriage, as he had already done many times; for he knew for certain that it was Curial alone who prevented it, and no one else, and he was sure that Curial would not return to France and did not care, nor ever would care, for Lachesis. So he begged that he would graciously undertake this matter.

When the King heard these words he at once thought that the two old men with whom he had spoken had contrived that Curial should leave Paris, and he sent at once for the Duchess and her daughter. He so spoke and laboured in one way and another that, with Fortune

176

taking a hand, Lachesis grew angry with Curial because he had gone off to Montferrat without saying anything to her, and consented to the marriage; and before they left the chamber they were secretly betrothed. As soon as they were betrothed Lachesis transferred all her affections to the Duke with such fervour that she could not bear to be parted from him for an hour, or even for a moment. No one knew why this should be, being ignorant of the marriage, and Curial's friends regretted it on his account although they also thought that if he returned the Duke would lose favour again; and so they waited for him to come.

★

Curial remained some days in Montferrat, and when he saw that the Abbess did not return nor send him any reply he made a decision, and in that decision added one error to another. Thus it happens, that when men fall out of favour with Fortune and are persecuted by Misfortunes, thinking to remedy or to rectify their affairs they rather increase their error and work to their own harm.

Accordingly, Curial said to Melchior 'Sir and father, I am doing nothing here but waste my time. I have determined to return to Paris to find some way to keep the position I have there. I assure you on my word that if I had wanted to have Lachesis for my wife it would have been done long ago, and perhaps I should not be so crestfallen here, and if I were treated as they treat me and have treated me here, I should know where to go. Now I shall perhaps have perforce to do what I have been unwilling to do. I will go and set my affairs in order, for if I have no money to spend now, I have jewels and many other treasures with which I can help myself; and before the disgrace which I have encountered here becomes known, I shall contrive some remedy for my life, which, if I stay here longer, I shall lose through grief. Meanwhile, I beg you, if you can, to seek to improve matters here; for if you write to tell me to return, I shall be with you at once.'

Melchior was a wise man, and he answered 'Alas! I fear that you are taking the wrong path. That is not the way to treat women of feeling, especially great ladies who because they are unable and unwilling to punish those whom they love in any other way, deprive them of the opportunity of speech. They hide themselves away from them and say they do not wish to see them, but often it happens that they suffer more on account of the lovers with whom they are angry than do the lovers themselves, even those who believe themselves to be unloved, and since they are unable to bear it for long, the ladies find a way to make the peace. You know this

177

yourself, because it has already happened to you in this same place. Where will you go, then, what can you do that will be of any avail? Where will you find a lady as rich and as beautiful as this one, and how will you induce her to give you as much as this one has done? Open the eyes of your understanding, and if you have done wrong, mend and do not err again, for that error would be worse than the first. If she hears that you have done what you intend, she will perhaps think, as she reasonably may, that caring little for her anger, you are returning to Lachesis to spite her, or because you despise her. Then from being angry she will become cruel, and hating you, will perhaps bring about your ruin; for gifts such as Guelfa has given you do not come to every man at Christmas'.

Curial was silent for a while, and made no reply but went away to sleep. When he was in bed and could not sleep he found Melchior's advice good. As he thought of many things, his mind leaping from one fancy to another, and wearied by long wakefulness he fell asleep, and in his sleep a Misfortune appeared to him in this manner:

A lady of most noble and venerable appearance, accompanied by many persons of importance, came to him and said 'Do not be surprised if I sit down, Curial, for I have been travelling and am so tired by the length of the journey that for weariness I can no longer stand. Oh Curial! What have I done, that because of you I should lose my daughter? Answer and tell me, what have I gained in recovering Clotho through your efforts when I had almost lost her, if through you I am then to lose Lachesis, who is my life? My other daughter I had already forgotten, but this one will shorten my sad life. Tell me, Curial, is Lachesis not a fitting wife for you? There is not a duke or lord in the world who would not wish to have her, and I cannot think why you should despise her. If you do so on account of Guelfa you are very wrong, for Guelfa now hates you, as that false man who advised you not to go to Paris well knows: no advice in the world can avail you against such hatred. Moreover, if you compel me to say it, I can prove to you that she has tired of you and has taken another in your place, who holds her closer than you did and has perhaps received firm and secure pledges of her love, to keep her faithful to him, together with corporal possession: she gave you only wealth, to the other she gives wealth and her body. So I advise and beg you to give up hope of her as something that is vain, and to leave here at once. I have come while I am still able to give you my daughter: do not lose what is within your grasp for what you cannot obtain. Her suitors are many, those who seek to arrange a marriage are powerful, and I assure you that if you do not go at once either she will die for your sake or you will see her unwillingly in another's power. Your only comfort and your foolish excuse will be that of stupid people who say "I never thought it would happen".' And so saying, she disappeared and went away with the dream.

Curial awoke, and remembering the dream he took it for granted that he had lost Guelfa, and because he did not wish to lose Lachesis also he determined to leave Montferrat whatever befell, to go to Paris. As soon as day arrived, which to his mind took a long time coming, he sent for Melchior and told him that nothing could shake his determination to go to Paris, to give orders to his servants and provide them with the means of livelihood. He begged him to commend him to his lady and to excuse his absence as best he could, for he had not wronged her in any way, and if she harboured any suspicions about Lachesis she was very mistaken, because the truth was that he had visited Lachesis as many others had done and there was nothing between them more than could be seen by other people. Melchior replied that if that was what he wished he should go, but he should not expect him to agree. As for the lady, he would, as he was wont, do all that was in his power. So Curial went away.

Just at that time the Duke of Burgundy left for his own lands, and the Count of Foix likewise, so that of all Curial's friends at the court of the King of France none remained. When Curial returned to Paris he found the world changed. Finding none of the friends he used to frequent he began to feel sorry for himself, and in order not to be on his own he was forced to seek the company of those who used to seek his. Lachesis sent word to ask him not to visit her, since she was betrothed to the Duke of Orleans who would be very angry, and she bade him farewell. The King too would have preferred Curial not to have returned to Paris for fear that Lachesis had not forgotten him and might not behave with the discretion that befitted her marriage, and he did not make Curial so welcome nor show him such good-will as he had done formerly. As a result only men who were out of favour or of no account kept company with Curial, who became very dejected.

Curial saw that all the doors that used to be open to him were now closed, and realising his lack of favour he began to give himself up for lost and came close to despair. He could not eat or sleep and was so wretched that nothing in the world gave him pleasure; and he would talk to himself like a madman, making great gestures and waving his hands about, walking up and down in his chamber, answering many times when no one called to him and not answering when he was spoken to, like a man out of his mind and lacking all judgement. He had to be forced to eat, for he never had any appetite for food; he was pale and clumsy, and nothing he did or said had any grace.

179

But Fortune was not yet content and contrived another misfortune for him. As Curial realised that he was wasting his time there and was near to losing body and soul too, it seemed to him that he ought to go back to Montferrat before Guelfa learned that he had lost favour in Paris. So converting into money some jewels and other things that he did not need or could take with him, he set off and returned to Montferrat as secretly as he could; and leaving his servants in an out of the way place, he went to his home.

When Melchior saw him he was not as glad as usual, thinking that Guelfa would be displeased, but nevertheless he welcomed him and asked what he had done in Paris. Curial replied that he had done nothing save set his things in order so that he could leave. 'Is Lachesis married yet?' said Melchior. 'I do not know' answered Curial. 'I did not concern myself with her affairs. I should be glad if it were so, then at least she would no longer be a cause of suspicion.' 'Indeed it is so,' said Melchior, 'and I will tell you how I know. The very day you left Guelfa sent for me and ordered me not to let you live in my house any more. I answered that you had left to go to Paris to settle your affairs and would return here. Guelfa at once sent a squire after you, and he came back with the news of Lachesis's marriage and of your lack of favour, which made Guelfa laugh. The Abbess and I have done as much as we could to persuade the lady to take you back in her service, but we have achieved nothing. And when we objected that if Ansaldo and Ambrosio begged her she would do it, she fell to her knees, raised her eyes to heaven and swore to Our Lord and the Blessed Virgin and the whole celestial host that neither of her own free will nor at the prayer of any man in the world would she ever forgive you unless the whole court of Le Puy met, with the King and Queen of France, and they were all to beg her together (which is impossible), and in addition all true lovers there assembled were to cry mercy for you: and she would never go there. So now you see what your position is.'

Curial was silent, and yearned for death far more than for life. After a long silence, sorrow made him speak and he said to the worthy Melchior 'There is one thing that I would have, and then let death come when it pleases, that my lady would have the great goodness to hear me, once only, and then do with me what she will.' Melchior said that he would do all he could to persuade her to listen to him.

That night Curial could not sleep nor find any repose. The worthy man tried to console him, but in vain. The next day Melchior went to Guelfa and when he saw that she had heard mass he went up to her and knelt before her. 'Oh most noble and most worthy of all ladies!' he said, 'I beseech you to pardon these grey hairs if I dare

180

speak in the presence of such great and singular excellence, especially on a matter which only special leave from you should draw from my mouth. My old age induces me to do this in the thought that even if I must die for it I cannot lose many days of life, and also the long service which I have given you in the course of so much time and which I shall continue to give you as long as you wish it and my weary soul keeps company with this ancient and troublesome flesh. My request is that Curial, who arrived last night and is in my house, be heard by you one single time. Let me receive this one favour, oh most noble lady, I beg you, and grant this boon, which I think will be the last I ever ask of you, not to him but to me.'

The Abbess, also kneeling, added her entreaties and begged her to grant the boon. Seeing their insistence, indeed their importunacy, Guelfa granted it, renewing and confirming however the vow she had made and swearing a solemn oath that she would not change any point of it, and saying that as soon as she had heard him he was to go away and not come again within thirty leagues of any place she might be.

This reply was conveyed to Curial, and the following night Melchior led him to Guelfa's chamber. Guelfa went into a closet and shut the door, and told the Abbess that she should say to Melchior that the man who had come with him was to speak and say all he wanted to say because she was in a place where she could hear him very well. The worthy man asked the Abbess if it would be possible for him to see her and to speak to her face to face, and the answer he received was no. So Curial knelt down and began to make his excuses and to make entreaties and to beg for mercy and to beseech her that if he had sinned she would pardon him. He continued to speak for a long time, and if he were indeed very eloquent and a great orator he had certainly lost and forgotten all his art and knowledge, for the more he strove to excuse himself the more strongly it seemed he accused himself, making a crime and mortal sin out of nothing. See what it is when a man loses grace!

But Guelfa heard him out to the end, and when she knew that he had finished she left the place where she had been sitting and ordered the Abbess to tell them to go away. The Abbess begged her to make some reply to the words she had heard, but she answered that she had only promised to listen and she had done so, and that they must do without a reply because she would never speak to him again. So the Abbess told them that since the lady had heard them they must go away, for they could have nothing more.

I am sad and full of grief at the unfortunate and unhappy parting of Curial and Guelfa, and I assure you that if Curial, weeping as he knelt beside the hinges of the door of Guelfa's chamber, could have

181

burst asunder, I think that death would have been a sweet remedy to his sorrow, for death could have put an end to all his earthly sufferings. It is however true that Atropos, who threatens all living men with the sharp knife with which she cuts each man's thread of life, is so cruelly disposed that most often she kills those who wish to remain longer in this world and scorns those who invoke and seek her, and turns away her vexing face, wrinkling her nose a trifle and pursing her lips, and like a deaf adder pretends not to hear; feigning blindness, she ignores all wishes, killing some and leaving others for the time being. Her great sport is to bathe in the tears which by various means she contrives to draw from the eyes of the mournful. Indeed, when Curial departed from Guelfa's chamber on that sad day he thought he would die and as things were he had little wish to live. When I too think of it, moved by the tears of the wretched Curial, I am near to keeping him company.

When Guelfa had gone away from her door and Curial, unheard, vainly renewed his excuses, Melchior raised him from the floor, trying to comfort him, and with many words exhorted him to refrain from such weeping, telling him that the cause he was bearing away with him was certainly better than that which he was leaving with Guelfa, as he would show with powerful reasons before any just judge. Curial, however, not grasping the true meaning of these words and distressed beyond description, was for a long while dumb and speechless. But then he cried out to St Peter, asking him whether he had lost the keys of Paradise and begging him that if he had them he would carry out his office and not let a piece of wood prevent his entering. 'Hush!' said Melchior. 'This is not the Paradise whose keys are held by St Peter: that one is far away from this, and its laws are very different. But in any case, even if this is Paradise to you you may be sure that you cannot enter either one without going through Purgatory first. So let us go home,' said Melchior, 'and perhaps you will come to see that matters are not as bad as you think.' And almost by force he moved Curial away from that place, and they went their way.

Alas! How can I write of this parting without tears? Strength fails my fingers, my pen falls on to the white paper and blots it in several places. I forget myself in contemplation of the unhappy Curial as he goes away with tottering steps and contorted face. Oh Curial! Where is the grace and sprightliness of your carriage? Those are not your movements, return them whence they came, and recover your own. Why are you changing into another person? Are you not content with what God the artificer and Nature His servant have given you in such plenty? You are like a woman ill-content with her beauty, great as it is, who adds to it with all her art and knowledge, with dextrous skill, and then poses this way and that and, not content with mirrors which show her the truth, now questions others, asking them to tell their opinion, and now looks at herself behind, and is in danger of breaking her neck and turning her eyes out of their sockets as she twists round to see the tail of her dress, which still would not please her even if it had as many eyes as the peacock; nor would she think she could see well, and Argus would be hard put to it to please her, even if he lent her all his eyes! Be yourself again, Curial, I beg you, and regain your senses while there is still time. If you can judge dispassionately you will see that you have no cause for weeping.

When he reached home Curial fell into bed as a load of wood falls when the ropes have been loosed and the wood pushed with great force; and he groaned bitterly, cursing his unlucky fate. Seeing this, Melchior came and spoke to him thus:

'I know well, Curial, that your virtue has lost its strength and that you are in great need of counsel. If I were not restrained by the re-collection that I too have been young and have often wandered along the paths where you are now astray I should make efforts to re-proach you for your unwise actions. Do you think to make good your loss with tears? That way will not serve for anything, and if you wish to prosper you must leave it forthwith. The road you must take is quite another, for the one you are following leads man only to perdition. Regain your senses and return to yourself while you have time: dry your tears, listen to what I say. Prepare to receive advice, and take it from me, who desire nothing more than your good and your honour, and answer me.

Melchior	What injury does Guelfa do you if she denies you her help and not your own?
Curial	She does me no injury.
Melchior	Then why are you weeping?
Curial	I do not weep for an injury but because she condemns me wrongly, and if by chance I have done her wrong I do not deserve such heavy punishment.
Melchior	You have certainly done wrong, it cannot be denied, and punishments are not given at the pleasure of those who are punished. You had best be silent, for weeping pro-vides no remedy.
Curial	On the contrary, weeping lightens sorrow.
Melchior	That is something to the good, and I am pleased that you seek a way to lighten your sorrow.
Curial	It often happens, Melchior, that men die because their liver bursts with their weeping.

183

Melchior	Yes, but you are weeping as a remedy, not to burst.
Curial	Ah, Melchior, father! I beg you to seek, if you can, some other way to console me, and with the eyes of your thought consider the colour of my heart. You see Death threatening me, thinking that I fear her: she does not know that I am ready to follow her, or she would move more sluggishly to come to me. Oh, you three sisters who fatally dispose the lives of men! Let one break her distaff and spin no more, let the second fall idle and neither reel nor weave, let the third cut the cloth, severing the threads of my life, and all three put an end to my woes! See what great necessity makes me invoke you, see me on my knees before you! Do not turn your faces from me, hear me at least, and if you have any pity use it towards me, removing me from this world which is so harsh and cruel to me!

The second book is ended.

BOOK THREE

Since in this third book mention is made of the Muses, it must be explained that the poets imagined nine Muses, in the form of nine ladies or maidens, who dwelt on Mount Parnassus and to whom Mount Helicon was sacred; and they named them Calliope, Clio, Euterpe, Thalia, Melpomene, Polyhymnia, Erato, Terpsichore and Urania. In addition to these, Ovid in his fifth book tells of another nine sisters born in Greece, whose mother was Euippe and their father Pierus whence they are called Pierides; they learned to play and to sing wondrously, and on account of the delectable science known as music (of which they were perhaps not such great masters as they supposed) they became very proud and vainglorious, so that they despised all other experts in the art and not only wished to be compared with the Muses but to surpass them. When this came to the notice of the gods, they entered into contest, or battle, in this way: the Muses deputed one of their number, and the Pierides like-wise, to contend, and she who acquitted herself best would win victory for her side. When both sides had been heard, it was judged that Calliope had played and sung better than the one the Pierides had chosen, and straightway the Pierides were turned into pies, also called magpies. These are chattering birds who can learn to speak in all languages whatever they are taught, but neither know nor understand what they are saying.

Fulgentius, discussing the outer husk of this fable, says that the nine Muses are nine consonances of the human voice, and the nine Pierides are nine dissonances. Papias says that the Muses are called the daughters of Jupiter and Juno because every voice is composed of wind and water and 'Muse' comes from the Greek word *mousa*, meaning water, and no voice can sound without wind and water and their movement; and from these two things come all the powers of song and modulation. The voice is produced, then, by four teeth so placed that they are struck by the tongue, and if any of them is missing there will be a defect in the voice; two lips, like two cymbals, towards which the tongue bends, and as it curves it creates

185

a vocal breath in the hollow of the palate, which passes through the channel of the throat as though through a flute; the lungs, or pulmons, acting like bellows, force out wind and after it has been expelled, they draw it in again. And these nine instruments are the nine Muses, to which is added Apollo because all melody is formed of ten voices, and the instruments would be worth little if there were no instrumentalist. This is the explanation of singing.

Apollo himself is depicted with a decachord, which means an instrument with ten tuned strings, or ten harmonising voices, otherwise a cithara. A psaltery also is called a decachord, which means ten concordant strings, as has been said: and the Psalmist says 'Upon an instrument of ten strings, upon the psaltery, with a canticle upon the harp'. This is the meaning of the Muses with regard to playing and singing. The allegory of the Muses is explained in another way: the first Muse is called Clio, which means goddess of glory, or the glorious intention of seeking or contemplating knowledge: *cleos* in Greek is *fama* in Latin, which is consequent upon knowledge. The second is Euterpe, which means delectation, since we must first seek knowledge and then delight in what we have sought after. The third is Melpomene, which makes us persevere in that excellent intention; the fourth, Thalia, means ability and the fifth, Polyhymnia, means remembering well; the sixth is Erato, which means invention, that is, a man must discover something new on his own account; the seventh, Terpsichore, means instruction or judgement, since after invention we must discern and judge; the eighth, Urania, which is heavenly intelligence, the ninth and last, Calliope, which is eloquence, and if well-ordered and brought to a conclusion, the others acquire enlightenment, increase and fame from her, and she from the rest. And that is what the Muses signify concerning knowledge.

And no one should marvel if it so happened that the daughters of Pierides were, according to the poets, converted by the gods into magpies, because men who are lacking in knowledge and who think that they know a great deal like to argue or dispute with men of knowledge and venerable erudition, thinking to be their peers and equals, to whom they should listen and from whom they should learn. Then they are judged as foolish and of little learning and compared to chattering and garrulous magpies who do not know what they are saying, and their persistence brings them shame. Let us who know little be silent, then, in the presence of those who know much. It often happens, however, that men of great learning are proud and despise other men who are not so capable, and they are puffed up as though their knowledge took up room within them and their breast could not contain it; this is especially true of those

186

of noble lineage, of whom Sallust says 'Pride is the common ill of nobility'. St Gregory says 'We are all equal, and our first parents were made of dust', and the prophet Malachi in his second chapter says 'Have we not all one father? for hath not one God created us? Why do we deal treacherously every man against his brother?' So let them drive out pride, which is the cause of all evil, and let the smoke of vainglory depart from them; for if knowledge is a virtue and dwells within them, the vice of vainglory, being its opposite, must take flight, since two opposites cannot dwell together. Tully says against them, or perhaps wishing to excuse them 'Great deeds or great sayings repeated often with praise may blind not only the proud but also humble men excellent in their works or their learning'. Again, Valerius in his chapter on the desire for glory says 'No humility is so great that its sweetness is not touched by glory'; and Prosper in his book says 'When man has overcome all vices there is still a great danger that his conscience may glory more strongly in himself than in God'. So let great and noble men of letters grow humble and abashed and believe him who tells them 'He hath brought down the mighty from their seats'.

As for Curial, with whom we are now concerned, he should have remembered that King Hezekiah lost fifteen years of his human life for the sins that he committed; but when he recognised his faults, God restored and returned them to him. He also knew that when a Roman emperor had a triumph and rode through Rome in a chariot, he took with him the meanest slave to strike him from time to time on his neck, saying 'Know thyself and be not proud'. So when Curial became proud through his knightly valour and somewhat vainglorious through the dignity of his learning he was thrown headlong from the triumphal chariot of his honour and became a slave for seven years, so that he should recognise the difference between giver and receiver. However, acknowledging this, he was restored to liberty after seven years, and God returned him to his former state, like Nebuchadnezzar, who through the sin of pride and vainglory was for seven years turned into a kind of wild beast. Those who heed the fall of Curial, which you will learn about in the book which follows, will see that he suffered more than Job. For although Job lost all his goods, there yet remained to him a dunghill on which he lay, which was his own, and he was at liberty, for he was never sold for a price; while Curial, when he lost his goods lost also his body, or its freedom, because he was sold for a price and made a slave. But afterwards, having confessed and repented, he became heir and lord of greater wealth than he had had before.

If it is perhaps lawful for me to do as other writers do and have done and to invoke the Muses, I think that I shall not do so for it would be useless: they would not appear and manifest themselves to me however much I called them to my aid and support, for they care only for men of great learning, and keep them company without being asked, whereas I and those like me, being ignorant, are by them held in strange abhorrence. In this, as in everything I utter, I am like the wretched chattering daughters of Pierus, the principal enemies of those nine excellent sisters who live on Mount Parnassus. Moreover they consider themselves demeaned if they are introduced into base and low works because they attend only upon very lofty and sublime styles, written by great and grave poets and orators. If I had served them in my tender youth they would have aided and assisted me as they do their other servants; but I cared not for them and did not appreciate them, and accordingly they do not appreciate or care for me. Now indeed I should like to praise them, but knowing that they would laugh and mock at me I choose silence. Thus since I cannot help myself with the gifts of their grace, I will proceed as best I can to this third and last book, which is a trifle more complex than the first two, since in this one there will be some poetic fictions and vicissitudes written not as the matter requires, but grossly and crudely, which is all that I can do.

It is true that this noble and vainglorious knight with whom the present book is concerned was not a great captain or a great warrior or conqueror, as, for instance, Alexander, Caesar, Hannibal, Pyrrhus, Scipio or many others who by their industry combined with chivalry conquered, in some cases, almost the whole world, in others, large areas or parts of it; but I have not found in anything I have read, however hard I have sought, that any of those I have named took part in so many and such closely fought hand-to-hand combats, judicial duels and tournaments, with so many and such valiant knights as Curial encountered.

I have often heard and also read about the labours of him who in his day was the strongest of knights, the son of Jupiter and Alcmene, who slew giants, lions, serpents and destroyed monsters which he pursued to the ends of the earth; and also about Jason who, according to poetic fictions, like him tamed bulls, slew serpents, sowed teeth from which soldiers were born, and killed many men in battle.

It will perhaps be said that Hector killed many kings and great knights in battle and was never defeated by any knight who fought with him, but nevertheless being neither vanquished nor subdued in battle he died by misadventure, through Fortune's fell design. I answer and say that it is true that Hector, in battles in which many took part, was the best knight in the world as long as he lived, and it is true that he willingly agreed to do battle in single combat with Achilles and that it was not his fault that it did not come about. But

I have never heard or read or learnt that he or any of the others I have mentioned entered the lists or an enclosed field (the ceremonies of which are terrible and awesome) with any knight equal to himself, with similar arms, offensive and defensive, and that having entered he would leave only as victor or dead. I think that these I have named, and many others of those times who could be named, would have accepted to enter the lists if they could not die without doing so. But this is speculation, whereas Curial, as we have seen in the past two books, did it many times. We will not blame him who has not done it but would if the case arose; but neither will we pass over or conceal one who has done it not once but many times, for that would not be fair. Similarly, if Fortune, who was willing for Curial and the knights he fought hand-to-hand to enter the lists, had given him military commands as she gave them to the others we have mentioned, he by his victories would have become a great conqueror and a knight of outstanding fame and renown: because conquests increase fame, and the lists increase skill and strength.

In conclusion, then, since the most stringent and most extreme test of military deeds is in the lists, in which Curial, not of his own seeking but rather being sought there, performed more than any other, let us not say that his acts of valour were not worthy to be recorded with admiration. If by chance they had been written by Livy or Virgil or Statius or some other great poet or orator, they would have been read, remembered and held in high esteem by men of venerable learning. For the writers would have, as it is said, made gold the silver deeds, and if peradventure they had been golden deeds they would have increased the carats of that gold with the help of the nine companions of Apollo who have been mentioned, with the loftiness of a sublime and marvellous style. So let us continue the account which has been begun of the life of our knight.

★

Curial had ceased to complain of Fortune, but not to think of her anxiously, and in continuing distress he considered what he should do. On the one hand he saw that to remain in Montferrat was not only fruitless but might be harmful to his honour as well as to his pleasure, because to be idle while lacking the means to maintain himself in the state to which he had attained, and so to return to poverty, would be both dishonourable and distressing to him. Sometimes he thought he should perhaps return to Germany, but since the Emperor who had given him encouragement and honour was now dead he did not know whom he should approach or where to go. He also considered going to the King of Aragon, who would have been delighted at his coming and would have provided good companionship. This was the best and most useful course open to him, but the Misfortunes, who were persecuting him, did not allow him to make this decision.

So, sad and ill at ease, he did not know what to do or where he could conveniently turn. He knew that the Marquis of Montferrat would be pleased to see him receive honour, but was not willing for him to remain in his domain, nor indeed was the house great enough to contain him. So his thoughts were very perplexed.

Perceiving this, and fearing that the knight might altogether despair, Melchior de Pando could not refrain from approaching him. 'My dear friend,' he said, 'I beg you not to be disturbed by the unfortunate accident which has befallen you but to count it among your benefits or blessings, if that is a fitting name for them, and consider it one. If you think over the good things that have happened to you, you will see that you have no reason to complain but rather to be grateful to God, who is, or at least who commands, prosperous fortune, because He has bestowed them upon you irrespective of your deserts, and has allowed you to enjoy them for so long. Tell me, Curial, do you remember the day you first came here? I entreat you to bear it always in mind. You know well that you were poor, very humble and friendless, a lad of few years who would have been well pleased to tend animals and to trot behind some gentleman; but you were received and advanced in this house, taking a place which others of higher birth and longer service deserved more than you. Yet you were placed before all others of your own age and even older than you. You felt no regret for this but were glad and took it as well done, whereas others bemoaned your joy, and with reason. And when you were a little older, Guelfa set eyes upon you and, wishing to help someone on their way, she chose you: and as she determined so I executed, for she ordered me to give you some of her riches. You did not know whence or why this came about. The lady owed you nothing, neither your father nor yourself had any claim on her, nor had you served her or given her any cause why she should act in such a way. So if she was not moved by duty, we can truly say that the lady conferred a passing grace which brought happiness to her heart and profit to you, and set you on the way to prosperity. At her own cost she has brought you to your present state, and she has paid a great price for the honour and favour you enjoy. What profit has she from the honour you have won? None at all, in sooth, indeed she has harmed herself, for if it were not for you she would have kept her treasure and her house would be the richest in Italy, which now it is not. She has given you her wealth prodigally, beyond all reasonable gift, and you, like a prodigal,

190

without counting the cost and without restraint, have spent unwisely and wasted it. You know well how you lost your senses over Lachesis in Germany, and forgetting what you should not forget, you grew heated with love for a stranger. I, who dragged you away from there with difficulty, know this well. Ah, Curial, how hard a thing to bear is prosperity! Remember your dream of the ungrateful man whom you wanted to kill, and reflect that he was yourself! You knew that if Guelfa had not helped you, you would never have gone there, or at least not in such splendid state, and your name would have been heard no more than that of any other poor man. Think of Lachesis as an infernal fury, come to destroy you, and expecting to do so; and who would have done so had it not been for this old man who stands before you, who prevented her. You were angry with me because I advised you to leave, fearing what now, with some delay, has come upon you – for you were due to drink this cup many days since. Yet this lady, who well knew all that was going on, shut her eyes and, as one who takes medicine, was willing to swallow this bitter pill. She strove against her wisdom, which counselled the contrary course, and by overcoming it added loss to loss and expense to expense, sending you to France to win honour and profit with your labours, and fame and renown with her wealth, giving you her treasure in accordance not with your needs but with your prodigal will. Indeed, the Marquis with all his state has not consumed half the wealth that you have. You have achieved your own ruin as though you were using your own revenue and it could never fail you. Moreover, unaware that woman's jealousy and suspicion will not for anything in the world admit another to share the affections of the loved one, and forgetful of this mine of gold, you returned to Lachesis as a dog returns to his vomit. You have committed these two foolish faults against yourself, for I have told you that no harm comes to Guelfa by them, indeed she gains much by your ingratitude. We will not speak of the tears that she has shed for you without your deserving them in any way; for a price cannot be set to those. Let it suffice, as indeed it must, that you left her as a sinner leaves a confessor, the one leaving behind sins and abominations while the other grants indulgence; for you depart rich in honours and fame, and she is left poor in both wealth and honour; you have bought it from her, with her money, which cost you little. And with all that she possesses, she has little need of the infamy she has acquired through giving you honour and her wealth. Lastly, remember what I told you: that she does you no injury if she denies you her help – not something that is yours. Remember too the condition she laid upon you when first she began to give you advancement, that the first day you gave yourself out as her servant you would lose her for ever. You know well whether the story is spread through the world, that she gives you all you spend: she has not said so, nor I, so it is a reasonable assumption that it must have come from you. Go, then, in God's name, for now you will find many of both sexes who will be happy to see you, which would not have been so the first day I spoke to you. And in conclusion, as I said in the last book, you go with more in your favour than Guelfa is left with.'

Curial listened patiently to all that Melchior said, and then, sighing a little, replied 'I cannot nor will I deny the things you have said, indeed I say and confess that they are true and contain truth. But it is not true that I have disobeyed the condition she imposed, because not a word of it ever escaped me. It may well be that others have thought it and have declared their thought to others and that it has become spread abroad and so, I think, has come to her ears. Since I can find no other remedy, it is better that I should go away than stay here. I have many robes and jewels, which I shall leave to you, and I beg you to lend me some money so that I may go.'

Melchior replied that he would willingly, and estimating the jewels as worth a considerable sum, he lent him twenty thousand ducats on that surety, and of his kindness gave him another five thousand. So taking the money, he departed secretly, and went to the place where he had left his servants, who were very glad to see him return.

He dressed himself in mourning clothes, and by stages they came to Genoa where after a few days he boarded a merchant vessel bound for Alexandria, with all his servants, and sailing from Genoa set off upon the journey he intended to make.

A Genoese corsair named Ambrosino Spinola came to hear that Curial was very rich, and desirous of acquiring such possessions and thinking he could do so with little difficulty, he got ready a ship which was lying at Portovenere, and made for a place where he was likely to meet the galley in which Curial was sailing. So as Curial, full of cares and sorrow, lay in his cabin, the master and others saw in the distance the pirate ship coming towards them. Seeing it approach with an evil intention, they began to arm and to make a great clamour throughout the galley, and when Curial heard this, although he was suffering greatly from seasickness, he raised his head and asked what the noise was about. He was told that a pirate ship was drawing near and that he should get up and prepare to help defend the ship or perhaps he and all his men would perish. When he heard this, Curial at once leapt up and with his men, most of whom were also seasick, he went out on deck armed, and saw the pirate galley close at hand. As the ships drew together, they each sent out a shower of arrows, by way of greeting, and then they began to exchange cross-bow fire, and those of the pirate ship wounded several of Curial's men, while Curial and the gentlemen with him stood idle on the poop, unable to help in any way. So Curial shouted to the master and the master of the oarsmen to bring the galleys alongside, thinking that in that way they would have the better of the corsair; but it made matters worse, for the pirate was a valiant man, and very skilled in seamanship, and with the help of his men he leapt on to Curial's galley, followed by many men and in a moment, before Curial had time to do anything, they had taken possession of almost half the ship, and his companions were on the point of surrendering.

But Curial, leaping from the poop and followed by his men, some with axes but most with swords in their hands, made their way forward, and whoever they could reach fell dead or wounded, or else turned back. At this, the men on Curial's ship rallied, and struck out without mercy at those of the pirate ship, winning back the ground they had lost, and so effectively did they fight that the pirates who had boarded the galley longed to be back in their own vessel. They showed this because many of them flung themselves into the sea to escape sword and axe blows, and there they perished, struck by many arrows. Meanwhile, the pirate ship, to save their leader who was still fighting in the other galley, came so close that Curial's men were able to board her and those who had remained there, seeing that many of their comrades – and the best of them – had perished, could not long defend themselves, and surrendered as best they could, and all were taken captive. The pirate leader, who had two slight wounds on his face, was also captured.

So Curial reached the island of Ponza with the two galleys. There he rested a few days, and then sent the corsair ashore and made a pact with his men that the pirate galley should be his. He transferred his men into it, adding to his company some men from the galley who, with permission of its captain, wished to leave it, and taking his leave sailed for Sicily. There he spent money to arm and provision his ship, and prepared to set off on his journey to the Holy Sepulchre.

★

At that time there ruled in Sicily a noble and most valorous king named Conrad, a young man who was son of the Emperor

Frederick, King of Sicily and a nephew of Manfred, who also had been king of that realm. When he heard the news of Curial's arrival and of his victory over the pirate, he showed great joy and desired to have him in his service. It would have been well for Curial if Fortune had permitted this; but the King, for all his generosity and nobility, had no power to do good to Curial because the Misfortunes, who followed Curial closely, gave him no chance. So when the King asked him to remain and serve him, offering him good company, Curial replied that he was unwilling to stay as he was going to the Holy Sepulchre and would not turn aside from his aim. So the King let him alone.

A Neapolitan knight named Enrico Capete, who governed Messina for King Conrad as he had for Manfred, coveted Curial's galley and petitioned the King to grant him the vessel. The King answered that he could not give it to him because it was not his. Enrico answered 'Sir, the galley is yours, and that is why I ask you for it; otherwise I should not do so'. And then he told him that the galley had belonged to Ambrosio Spinola, a good and loyal servant of the crown, and that Ambrosio on his way from Sicily had been in a great battle and had been captured and robbed by this pirate, who had taken the galley; and that he should certainly take it from him; and he supplicated that this should be done.

When the King heard what the Captain of Messina had to say he sent for the master of the galley and the master of the oarsmen and asked them where the knight came from and how he had come into possession of the vessel. They answered that he was from Montferrat and was on his way to the Holy Sepulchre, and then went on to tell him all that had happened with the pirate. The King listened and then told them they could go; and he called for the Captain of Messina and told him that on no account would he allow or suffer the galley to be taken from the knight; and so let him ask for something else, for the ship would not be his.

As soon as conditions permitted Curial left harbour. But when he was in the straits of Messina he encountered nine of King Charles's galleys, and these surrounded him so that Curial had to raise oars. The commander of the galleys sent for him and he went aboard his ship and was taken to Naples, to King Charles. But he took a liking to Curial and no harm was done to his ship. The commander went to the King and told him that he had seized one of Conrad's ships and had captured a knight who must be one of Conrad's knights, and he asked Charles what he should do. The King was very wise and valorous, magnanimous and of outstanding generosity, and he sent for Curial and asked him whence he came and where he was going. He answered that he came from Montferrat and was on his

194

way to the Holy Sepulchre. 'How came you from Messina, then?' asked the King. Then Curial told him all that had happened with Ambrosio Spinola and how he had come by chance to land in Sicily. 'Tell me, Curial,' said the King, 'did Conrad ask you to remain with him?' Curial answered that he had, and that he had replied that nothing in the world would make him renounce his journey.

The King at once gave orders that Curial should be well lodged but that care should be taken that he did not go away, because he wished to question him more fully. He was accordingly given a splendid apartment, but no one showed him honour because his condition did not warrant it.

The King was heard by many to say of Curial 'I am indeed much taken with this knight, who has done me a great service in defeating that rascal Ambrosino Spinola, and were I not afraid that he is in the service of Conrad, I would ask him to stay here.' 'Sir, that knight is no Sicilian,' someone said, 'nor has he ever been to sea, except that being on his way to the Holy Sepulchre, as he says, he encountered the pirate. Then he went to Sicily, and he would not stay with Conrad although pressed to do so.' Others, who were Italians, said that he must be a traitor, and that the galley should be taken from him and he be put to torture, and then the truth would be known. Others, who were French, said that nothing of that kind should be done, but he should be allowed to go his way freely.

Having heard many opinions on the matter, the wise King said 'The knight has not yet done me any disservice, nor anything for which I should ill-treat him. If Conrad did not destroy him when there was some reason, how can I, when he has given no offence either to me or to any of my vassals? Give him back the galley, and let not a nail be missing from it, and he may go hence. By my faith, I swear that if he were willing I would gladly keep him in my service, although I fear that I should always have some suspicion of him. Give him too a safe-conduct, so that if he falls in with any of my vessels they will do him no harm.'

★

As soon as Curial had recovered his galley and received the safe-conduct he departed, and sailed on until he reached Alexandria, where he landed. He then went overland to Jerusalem, and visited the holy place where our lord Jesus Christ was laid in the tomb, and Mount Calvary and all the holy places where Jesus had been. He travelled about in that country accompanied by informed and prudent guides, who took him to all the places he wished to visit.

In the course of his travels he came to the monastery of St

Catherine on Mount Sinai, and there he spent nine days in devotions. All the friars of the monastery made much of him, especially one holy friar who never left his side and with whom Curial liked to talk because he spoke French and was considered a very saintly person. This friar knew Curial well, but Curial did not recognise him. Because they were often in each other's company and the friar asked him many questions, Curial told the friar, as though it were in confession, all about Guelfa and the cause of his despair, complaining much of Fortune who had brought him to this pass.

When the friar, listening patiently, had heard the whole story, he answered. 'You have good reason to speak ill of Fortune,' he said, 'and I should not blame you for doing so, indeed I am surprised that you do not complain more strongly. She has laid many snares for you of different kinds and in different places, and it is a wonder that so long has passed before you were caught. But let us forget her, for she is deaf, blind and treacherous, and does not know what she is about, from whom she takes or to whom she gives: let us not curse her because we must also praise her. Tell me, Curial, are you not indebted to her for sustaining you for so long, and for making you – if we speak in accordance with worldly vanity – the best and most valiant knight in the world, and for favouring you above all other knights? You have been honoured by an emperor, by kings and lords far more than any other, and she has showered you with riches, and indeed all her gifts, freely and abundantly. And then, so that you should not drown in this gulf of vanity, so that you should not lose your soul, so that you should know your Saviour, she has brought you to this state. Yet you speak ill of her, from whom you have received honour in this world and who now offers you that to come! You have prevailed on earth and now, if you will, you shall prevail in heaven. You speak ill of Fortune? Oh, Curial! God loves you! If the vanities of the world are worth anything, you have had them, and if after earthly glory comes that of Heaven, which you would not know if Fortune had not shown you her dark and cruel back, why should you speak ill of her? You can complain of her on one count only, that she has left it so late, and your peril has been great. If you had died before now, you would have gone straight to hell, which you have won with great bodily toil and danger. They await you there with joy and have a place prepared for you befitting your errors. Leave the vanities of the past, then, which are as nothing! See how close to you is the kingdom of God! Repent what you have done, brother, confess and weep for your sins; ponder and contemplate the new heaven and the glory of liberty, and like a new-born child take the road to Paradise. Do not let earthly pleasures

196

beguile you; taste celestial bread and behold the glory of the angels; delight in the service of God, and if you speak ill of Fortune, let it be only because she caused you to slumber so long among the vanities of the world, not because she has roused you and offered you celestial and eternal riches and honours. Consider, brother, the martyrs of Jesus Christ and the sufferings through which they soared to heaven. They laugh at our vanity and rejoice when one of us acknowledges it. Chastise your body, which wars against you; do not desire transitory things of little duration. Come, brother, and hear the divine voice. God who created you sees you, and commands you to be His; choose the kingdom that has no toil or danger. There you need have no fear that enemies may kill you, and there wretched envy has no place. No one will covet your goods, you need have no thought for maintaining your state. Leave your chains, brother, pay the jailer, who will be silenced with a drop of water and can ask no more of you. Leave the meats which cost much money, and choose those which are given without charge and satisfy the soul: flee from hunger and thirst, flee from toil and vain thoughts. How great is the folly of men who with their labours conquer hell and eternal suffering! You weep over Guelfa? Do not weep for her, but for your sins and the offences you have committed against God. Offer your vile and stinking flesh to labour for our Saviour; consider what He did for you, open your arms and embrace the celestial glory that is offered you, go to meet it, and take it while there is still time: you are robbing no one of it, it is for all, and it is yours. Do not lose it. Alas! how long I myself lay in that ditch! You must know, Curial, that it was you who raised me from death to life, who made me forget the vanities for which you weep and are sad. Amyclas did not weep when great lords and rich men fled fearfully to seek shelter in caves and solitary places in the forests, where they hid with their possessions when there was no hope of safety in great and well-walled cities: he showed himself and sang in the streets, with no fear of the anger and fury of kings. So leave of your own free will what you must perforce leave; if you do not, it will be taken from you with your life, or before it, and when you leave this world you will not come into possession of the other unless you are willing and ready to do as I have said. Make use of the vanities of the world as a boat which serves you to cross a river: you pass over, and when you have paid the ferryman each one takes his path and does not return to the boat unless he needs to cross again and leave it again. Use this world as you need it, and erase from your mind all that is not necessary. Do not desire great things which, even if you attain them, you must lose, so that they sadden the heart. Be humble, then, and God in heaven will raise you. You who have fought for vain things,

197

fight now against the devil in defence of your soul. He is a strong and a fierce knight and wars against you continually, and if we do not guard against him with the arms of Christ the victor, when we die he will bear away the spoils.'

When Curial had listened with great attention to these words, he raised his eyes and gazed at the friar and said 'You say, father, that I dragged you out of the ditch: I beg you to tell me who you are.' 'I am the Boar,' said the friar, 'whom you fought in Paris.' 'Mother of God!' said Curial. 'How can you have so lowered and humbled yourself as to spend your life in this way?' 'Christ our Lord, who being of royal descent owned a kingdom, and being God was lord of all the world, has shown me the way, for He chose to be poor for our sakes; and then St Francis showed me it, who followed Jesus in poverty and humility and deserved to bear the marks of the Saviour's wounds. There is not a friar in this monastery, Curial, who would exchange his way of life for that of the King of France, and everyone who lives here esteems as worthless more than all the kings in the world together could possess. Here we see in our contemplation the kingdom of God, the glory of the angels, the divine and eternal court. What can be seen in the world but trivialities and folly and things of little duration, which cannot be obtained without great labour and cannot be held without more, vile, despicable and transitory though they be? He who barters dross for gold is no bad trader, and to exchange earth for heaven does not seem to me a bad bargain. Leave these foolish cares, Curial, and cast them out of your heart: make room for the words of God, which only enter where there is readiness to receive them. Do you remember how you went about heaped with pearls and gold and precious stones? Where is that vanity now? I tell you that if their glory was visible, all those around you saw it better than you, and you had only the labour of carrying them on your person and the anxious care of guarding them. Do you not know that they had belonged to others before, and they are now or will be hereafter another's? For whom did you guard them? You do not know, I think. Consider well what I am saying to you, for I assure you that if you are prepared to think of God and His works, you will abhor what you now desire, you will despise the wretched things you think are good, and you will consider yourself very foolish for having delayed so long. But our merciful Saviour has arms so long that wherever and whenever the sinner repents, He will embrace him and draw close to him, and make him a citizen of the eternal glory of the kingdom of Paradise. Tell me, pray, what is left to you of the multitude of delicious foods you have eaten, of the dances, jousts and tourneys you have taken part in? Where are the festivities in which you joined? Show me

198

them, brother. Where is yesterday? Show me. Where is the glory of precious ornaments? Do you not know that these things must have an end? One thing alone can be of profit to you if you repent and achieve a state of grace: if you have done any little good for Jesus Christ's sake, some small act of charity, that is, of pity or mercy to the poor, though I think it will be a small thing; yet if you are lost, which God forbid, it will ensure you less punishment, and if you are saved it will win you greater glory, provided that it is done in due time and from wealth justly won.

'Oh wretch, are you not sorry for the battles you have fought for the vainglory of the world? You have killed men, you have sent souls to hell. Where is the smoke of that vainglory? Where are those transient things? No one speaks of them any more, no one mentions your name. You cannot show me anything that remains to you of all that, but I will show you, I will remind you what it is: a savage sin, stinking and abominable to God, a persistence in damnation; for in your heart you are glad and you hold it a glory that you have committed these sins, and you do not repent. You are proud, you glory in them: and thinking that for their sake you deserve honour and favour you are making straight for hell, and every day you travel a thousand leagues in order to arrive there sooner. You need not worry, for although others may arrive to take a place before you, there will always be a place for you, no one will take it but you will have ample room. You may be sure that he whom you have served will not fail you, indeed he has already given you reward for each and every thing you have done for him. Tell me, do you believe that the devil, who counsels you to do ill, will harm the soul in hell, that he will punish it, if that soul has served him here in this world? How can it be, that because you have served him he will punish you? Open your eyes, dear brother, and sharpen your wits, for he is not punishing you for the service you have done him, indeed he has already given you reward, glory and worldly honour in this way. For you have gloried in committing the sins I have spoken of, and for this you have won, through the devil's means, worldly fame and honour, if it deserves such a name. You have had the devil's reward in this world, and if in the next he gives you punishment, this is not because you have served him, but as the executor of justice, for offences committed against God and the harm done to your neighbour, and this is how it seems to me that you should see it. Everything passes, I tell you, and is nothing but smoke. Where are those great kings who ruled the world, tell me? Where is Electra, from whom came all the kings of Troy? Where is Priam? Where are Hector, Paris, Troilus, Deiphobus, Helenus and his other thirty sons? Where is the glory of his daughters-in-law? Where is the duchy and empire of Agamemnon? Where are the kings of Greece? What remains to them of their victory over the Trojans, and the cunning and false trick and treason of the horse, and the destruction of that great city? Shall I tell you? All are in hell and in the power of the devil, and their reward was that the most and the best of them died in that siege; and those that remained found their wives with child by other men, and afterwards some died at the hands of their wives, or by their design, others at the hands of their daughters or step-daughters, so that they all, one after another, came to a bad end, and suffer in hell. What esteem does the world hold them in today? Are they tolled for in churches? Do people universally celebrate their feasts? Do their sons reign after their death? Come, Curial, be a courtier in heaven, follow the footsteps of the poor fisherman, for Jesus Christ has entrusted to him, and not to Sardanapalus or Artaxerxes, the keys of Paradise. Consider the holy apostles, the holy martyrs and confessors, whose feasts are celebrated in heaven and on earth: theirs is the achievement that endures. Shed your shoes and follow the son of Ser Pietro Bernardone, who making himself less than others is made great in heaven and great on earth (and all deeds are nothing save the service of God and having pity for His poor); embrace the virtue of charity, which is very pleasing to God. And if you cannot achieve other virtues, at least aspire to the cardinal ones, prudence, justice, temperance and fortitude. According to Macrobius, from these spring like rays of light, reason, understanding, circumspection, providence, obedience, caution, friendship, innocence, concord, pity, piety, affection, humanity, modesty, shame, abstinence, chastity, honesty, moderation, patience, sobriety, propriety and steadfastness.'

While they were talking thus a little bell was rung in the monastery, and when he heard it the Boar said 'Curial, I can stay no longer. Go with God. I pray that you will remember my clumsy words. It is true that I wished to speak to you a little of the other virtues which are very necessary for the salvation of the soul, and to say other things to you, but obedience compels me to follow the sound of that bell.' And turning away he went, saying 'We shall meet in Paradise'.

So the Boar departed, leaving Curial in confusion. If he had listened to many such lessons I think that, despising the world, he would have followed in the steps of the Boar. But his men were waiting for him, tired of being in that place for the nine days were now over, and they entreated him to leave. The devil was spurring on these gentlemen, as they were Curial, to make him go away from that place. So he made his way to Alexandria, where he had left his galley, full of thought for what he had heard and of remorse for his ill deeds, with an anxious soul. When they were aboard, he had hardly spoken a word before all the young men laughed at him saying: 'Oh what a beadsman! Oh what a holy person is our master!', and they all teased him, so that within a few days, forgetting all about the warnings of the Boar, he returned to his usual self.

And he decided that he would like to see Mount Parnassus, where there used to be poets and philosophers, and to know where were the temples of Apollo and Bacchus who according to the ancients were the gods of wisdom and knowledge.

★

But Fortune, not yet satisfied with the dance she was leading Curial at the request of Envy, desired that he should perish after leaving Alexandria. Seeing the weather fine and pleasant and Curial going his way with favourable winds, she leapt forward and shouted with loud cries to Neptune, god of the sea, and with an angry voice spoke to him, saying: 'What idleness and negligence is this? Will you not see that Curial is one of the best and most valiant knights in the world, and do you not realise that he will make himself lord of everything, of the wrath of the heavens, of the winds, the land, of hell and even of the sea, of the names of Jupiter, Juno, Pluto and of yourself? Think too that this man will never let the Moorish people fill the flaming house of Pluto, but with the holy name of Him whose sanctuaries he has visited, within and without the walls of Jerusalem, will turn them to believe in that Lamb who bore the sins of the world. And you, who with your brothers are worshipped in those lands, will lose dominion over the sea, and they will lose the kingdoms they rule. Think that Venus has already lost the name of goddess, and all Christians affirm that she is not placed in the third heaven and that her son Cupid is nothing, that he has no bow, no arrows to strike with and, in short, that the gods of the pagans are nothing at all. Strike him before he occupies your kingdom, torment him! Let the sea yawn and throw out foam from all its mouths and send the submerged sand high in the air to see the sky, and let the waves show themselves to be mountains and valleys: for his sake let all who sail be tempest-tossed. Do you not see that you are already considered of no account because until now the seas have shown a smooth and mild back and he has sailed along calm and peaceful as though he were gliding. Oh, lazy one! Will you still not move? Are you afraid he may strike you with his invincible sword? Alas! To whom do I speak? I was not afraid to take away all that I had lent him, and yet you are afraid and tremble as soon as you hear his name, and dare not stir! Remember, I beg, that you are a spirit and his sword cannot harm you. Awake, then, let the sea be stirred up, and all the storms come that you are wont to display in the oceans and in the straits of Gibraltar, let them all come; and the roaring of the fierce, bold lion that lives between the islands of Majorca and Sardinia, let that be heard here, not forgetting the tempests of the straits of Messina and the gulfs of Adalia and Crete, let them all unite to strike this galley! Show that you are mighty enough to rule your kingdom, terrify the heart of him who never is afraid, who never grows pale nor alters his mien in whatever danger he finds himself. Have no fear! See, a woman has taken the land from him, although it is not hers, and will you not take from him the seas which have been yours until now? See how Jupiter from the heights of his kingdom is watching you, judging you unworthy to rule: young boys mock at you and with their little skiffs ride over your seas and take possession of the realm which formerly was forbidden ground. If these things cannot move you, then fear the harm which will befall you through your idleness: for you will be held in derision and contempt among the infernal spirits as unworthy to rule, and you will defile the resplendent house of Jupiter, Saturn will deny that he is your father and Pluto will deliver you to the darkest and cruellest prison of hell, perfumed with sulphur and stinking gum, and your name which has been written in letters of gold will now in that realm full of smoke be read in dark and gloomy letters. You will burn in the living flames which turn almost white in the quivering of their sharp tongues which, already spluttering, warn you of punishments and continually menace you; and the fame you leave behind will be of that idleness through which you have merited this great affliction. Hecuba will not bark around you with her rabid dog's mouth, nor will Megaera entreat Hercules to strike you with his club, for it would be too great an honour for you that souls born of such noble blood should serve you with torments; but others, damned for filthy, vile, stinking crimes, will goad you continually. If you say that my words are lighter than the wind and that I have no power to do harm, I grant that this is so; but know that I have knowledge and skill, and that I am instable and diligent and know not what repose is, turning my wheel with continuous movement and sending my good things and prosperity where I will. I hold my office dear, and I know how to entreat and to sue. So not only diligently but also unrelentingly I shall persecute you in every way I can harm you, and you will know that I do not deserve to lose my dominion through laziness, as you do.'

As Fortune was silent, awaiting Neptune's reply, the sea shook and murmured, and in its depths began to shift and move. The waters were troubled, and threw up seaweed mixed with sand, and

Neptune thrust out his terrible and fearsome head, opening his mouth so that it seemed that all the ships in the world would not make a bite for him, but he could gulp them all down at once. He spoke with a great, frightening voice and said 'What is all this, false traitress? Do you think I am your wheel, that you should spin and turn me as you will? That will certainly not be so, indeed to spite you I grant guidance and safe-conduct to the knight, and you shall not ill-treat him in my kingdom. Use your malice where you may, for here and now there shall be no opportunity given to your changing will. Truly you are a woman in all your deeds: now you will, now you will not, now you weep, now smile, now you give, now take away, and in brief you are not constant for a single hour. Go, false and fickle woman! If you have been willing to give him your support for a time, admitting with your treacherous tongue that he is noble and valiant, so too will I, who am also noble, help another noble. Even if I wished to harm him I should not do it at the request of so fickle and false a woman as you, for I have always regarded you with suspicion; nor do I wish to be thought womanish, letting myself be ruled by you.'

When he had said this, the waters began to roar, and the whale on which Neptune rode bellowed and struck the water with its tail, preparing to dive and plunge down to the bottom. But that wicked and fickle Fortune cried in a loud voice 'O Juno, my friend, where are you? Come to me, appear! Here I am, waiting for you! Do not lose the respect that you have always shown me and the obedience I have always found in you; do not think, my friend, that I am summoning you for matters of my own, for this business concerns you yourself.'

When these words had been uttered, Juno began to set in motion a great tempest and to send arrows of lightning in all directions. The winds stirred up storms and struck the sea with goads, driving it onwards. Then, sitting on a black throne, surrounded by many servants, she began to speak.

'My very dear friend,' she said, 'I heard your supplication to Neptune and I am not surprised at his curt and rude reply, because he was always like that and will not let himself be ruled by anyone in the world. In any case he would not listen to your entreaties because he knows what sort of woman you are; for you will not listen to anyone's prayers and have no spirit of compassion, and you grow angry in a flash, and want everything done when and as you will – and Neptune likes to rule his kingdom in the very same fashion. I am surprised that in this case you were moved to beg Neptune to be cruel to that knight, because he himself is as cruel as it is possible to be, and cannot let a moment go by without being cruel and doing harm. Do you suppose that although at this moment the sea here is peaceful and shows no sign of storms, in other places it is not awesome and terrifying in its movements and that many are not perishing with all their goods? Such is the greed of Neptune, I assure you, that if men continue to make voyages he will snatch away all the goods and all the riches in the world – if they deserve to be called such – and his insatiable voracity will swallow them up. I do not believe that the wealth and possessions of all men now living added together equals what Neptune has taken away from them. He owns wealth without comparison greater than Jupiter, my brother and husband, and than all the gods of the past. It is true that you dispose of prosperity and award it in due course as you please, but you are poor, you have nothing and you can prevent nothing. With Neptune it is the contrary: he cannot give, and he takes away continually, and all the time he is roaring in one place or another, threatening those who sail; and although they know him well, they never learn. So Neptune, knowing that if they sail a great deal sooner or later they will fall into his hands, sometimes shows them a kind face and lets them return home in peace. He thinks that if he always used them ill some would cease to go to sea and he through little wisdom would lose what he hopes to have if he bears with them for a short time. You may be sure that even if he has allowed this knight to travel for a little while he is keeping him for a greater loss, which will rob him of that scrap of wood in which he sails, and in the end he will have nothing to laugh at. I ask you therefore, to be silent and cease to molest him, and to trust enough in the covetousness and avarice of Neptune; for when he thinks the time is right, the knight will not escape. If you knew him as well as I do, you would not encourage him to do mischief, because he himself is over-ready for it. Finally, pardon me for what I am about to say: when you seek to ask someone to do something for you, do not do so with threats and insults, because that would only remove any wish to please you. I heard the arrogant and haughty menaces and the slander and abuse you uttered, and for that reason I have no intention of asking Neptune to do what you now request. Later it may be that he will do so even if you do not wish it, for I will make a note and I shall not forget.'

When Fortune was about to reply, Juno, annoyed by the insults offered to her brother, would not hear her and, turning her back, went away.

In spite of all Juno had said, when Fortune saw that she had no longer any respect for her and had gone away without listening to her, she was beside herself with rage and began to call out, or rather to shout, and to fling after her words that were confused, deranged and incoherent.

'It is useless to flee, false woman' she cried. 'I am here and shall beset you together with all the enemies who assail you in this world, and in the other I shall ensure that they do not pardon you. O Europa, daughter of King Agenor, whose beauty, desired by Jupiter, merited that you should be a third part of the world! And you, Ocyrhoe, daughter of Chiron, who were converted by Jupiter into a mare because you prophesied things to come and placed yourself before the gods! And you, Tyresias, whose bodily eyes Juno took away, and you Danae, daughter of Acrisius King of the Argives, who were shut up by your father in a windowless tower for fear of Jupiter; and the god turned himself into a shower of refined gold and entered, and begot in you Perseus, the good knight! And you, Carmentes, whose first name was Io! When Jupiter deflowered you, you were changed into a heifer and given in charge of Argus, and his hundred eyes were placed in a peacock's tail when he was deceived by Mercury. When you fled to the sands of Libya you wrote your name with your hoof at every step, and then, when Jupiter had turned you back into a human, you were worthy to be Queen of Egypt! You, Queen of Macedonia, who, it is said, through the means of the great astrologer and philosopher Nectanebo, had a son, Alexander, by the god Ammon, and that god was Jupiter turned into a ram! And you, Leda, daughter of Thestius, who lost your virginity beneath the wings of the god Jupiter when he changed into a swan to take you! You, daughter of Asopus the river god, ravished by Jupiter when he appeared as a flame! You, Alcmena, daughter of Amphitryon who, deceived by Jupiter, gave birth to Hercules the strong, and that night was doubled into two nights! You, daughter of Nycteus, who were deflowered by Jupiter in the form of Saturn, god of the sea, and brought forth twin boys! You, daughter of King Alcidamas, who, being pregnant by Jupiter, so that your father should not know, gave birth to a dove; and all the people of Aegina who were destroyed by Juno because her husband lay with Aegina, born of that people, which Jupiter later restored and made another far greater people from the seed of ants! You, Ganymede, son of Ilus King of the Trojans, who were carried away up to heaven by Jupiter in the form of an eagle, and made his cupbearer! And you Ceres, goddess of the land, who were ravished by Jupiter and gave birth to Proserpina, who was carried away from Sicily by Pluto and made goddess of the infernal regions! And you birds, who mourn and were born of the ashes of the body

205

of Memnon, son of Aurora, who during the Phrygian combat was cremated by fire sent by Jupiter, and who seem to lament for the said Memnon! You, Mnemosyne, who were taken by Jupiter in the guise of a shepherd, and you, Deo's daughter, whom he deflowered in the shape of a snake! You, Menephron, whom Jupiter turned one night into a wild beast because you indulged in lechery with your own mother! You people of Thebes, whom Juno destroyed because Jupiter lay with Semele, the Theban maid, who gave birth to Bacchus, the god of wine, and whom Juno caused to perish in ashes! You people of Corinth, whom Jupiter turned into mushrooms because you had become excessively lustful and only two virtuous youths, Crocus and Smilax, escaped, and they were changed into flowers! Come, all of you, come male and female together, with all the others loved by Jupiter! Occupy and sully Juno's bed so that the god of fire will have no desire to enter it and that false, ungrateful and wicked Juno will not rejoice in the divine embrace but be despised and detested by her husband! Let her keep only the name of sister, which for her arrogance and ingratitude she does not deserve. Come to me, then, for I shall be with you and shall help you to wreak vengeance on that wayward and iniquitous Juno. Have no fear of her, she is nothing, and has lost all the glory of her divinity. Come to me, then, for my weapons are prepared and ready to assail that odious and tiresome woman; and I am sure that with my help you will have revenge, cruel and harsh, such as was never seen or heard of before.'

★

'And you Dione,' she continued, 'Queen of Cyprus, who through my doing gave birth to your daughter Venus by the god Jupiter, who was endowed with singular beauty. By the same god she bore her son Cupid, and she was made a star and placed in the third heaven. She is called Lucifer when she appears at dawn and when evening comes she appears in the west and is called Hesperus, because she sets in the realm of Hesperia. Remember the happy destiny that was yours through me, for I gave you as lover the greatest of all the mortal gods, and your daughter, a goddess, had a son who is the god of lovers and wounds with arrows from whose invisible aim none can guard himself. When he strikes with the arrow of gold he causes love and ardour, and when he strikes with the leaden arrow he causes aversion and coldness. There is no nation in the world that is not subject to his rule or that can avoid his hidden blow. Since it is to your great glory that I have not forgotten the names of that excellent goddess your daughter, who in many places is called Dione because of you, I shall repeat before you the splendours of her godhead, which I think should give you no little pleasure, so that you can see how she is considered in the world and placed in heaven, and how great is the honour and renown in which she is held universally throughout the world.

'The poets imagine, my dear friend, that Caelus had no father, and that he had a son named Saturn, who was king of Crete, and his genitals were cut from him because he devoured all the children born of Ops Rhea, or Cybele, his wife. His genitals were thrown into the sea near Cyprus, your realm, and from the foam was born Venus, your daughter, who by the same Jupiter was deified in the third heaven and converted into a planet. This planet of its nature signifies sweetness, is amiable, it brings love, happiness, gain; it tempers the malice of warlike Mars; it spends twenty-nine days in each of the Signs, according to Ptolemy; it is hot and moist; Taurus and Libra are subject to it, it reigns in Pisces and its house is Virgo. Sometimes it precedes the sun and sometimes follows it, but it is always so close that it is never far away, and it supports the sun in its nature. It is burning and hot: all lust and sensuality have their origin in it. Its journey takes three hundred and forty-eight days, and it touches two parts of the zodiac. It makes men amorous, watchful and solicitous; and as I have said, from its birth it takes the name of Venus. It is called Diana by the people when it appears in the east in the morning, because it announces the arrival of day, and the common people call it the star of dawn. It is called Cyprian because Venus was born in Cyprus, and after her passing she was changed into a star, and that is why it is so named. It is called Hesperus when it appears at evening, close to the sun. In Greek it is also called Phosphor, which in our tongue means "light", and is so called on account of the bright light of its rays. She is called Aphrodite from Greek *aphros*, which means "foam", because she was born from the foam of the genitals of Saturn thrown into the sea of Cyprus; and she is called Dione for your sake, as Dante says in the third book, *Paradise*, where he writes "But they honoured Dione and Cupid, the former as her mother and the latter as her son, and they told how he sat in the lap of Dido". She is called Cytherea from Cythera, a mountain where it is said she was born. She was the wife of Vulcan, the god of lightning. This your daughter turned the women of Cyprus into cows, and a stone image into a noble and most beautiful woman.

'So, my sweet friend, I beseech you to hear me. You know that tiresome and despicable Juno with invincible arrogance has turned her cruel savage back on me, has disregarded my entreaties and refused to molest Neptune, the god of the filthy, stinking kingdom of the sea, god of eternal weeping. He disdainfully turned his loathsome dark face towards me, and while I spoke horrible sulphurous fumes poured from his mouth, his nose and his eyes, which were like spills when they begin to flare; and down his beard ran bloody slaver, like crimson foam in the light of the fire, which bubbled and seethed with a noise like a little hot oil in a pan when something cold is put into it. Think of the wicked persecution to which you were subjected by Juno, a mortal and cruel enemy to you and your daughter when you lived in the world: if she had been able to annihilate you and to erase your memory among mankind, she would have done so. See these others, beloved of Jupiter, who like you were ill-treated by her. With hair erect and gnashing teeth, they clench their fists and look from afar with eyes like burning coals! Their fiery glances flash, and sparks of ardent fire, blazing and keen, shoot from their eyes: they threaten Juno, their foe! Now we shall see what false, proud Juno will do, for she has no friend or kinsman who wishes her well, indeed we can say now that the doctors have given her up! Come then, sweet friend, leap forward and take the foremost place: you merit it for many reasons that I have no time to explain. Take her by surprise, drive her from heaven to dwell in the filthy stinking mud of marshes or bogs as a tadpole or polliwog, let her live in loathsome swamps or marshes with little water and come to life only in the summer, and be as nothing in the winter. For she who desires to be glorified above all living things justly deserves to be deformed, despised, degraded below all creatures that live! If I could compare her to something else more loathsome and less useful or of less worth, and turn her into that, I would not for the world desist.

'Come, then, all together! You see that all the others are waiting for you and longing for your royal company, they are eager and ready with their weapons. See their shining swords and resplendent arms! Do you see Tyresias and Manto his daughter? Do you see Aronta, Erythrea, Pythia, Herophile and all the other soothsayers, with owl's heads and eyes, gnash their beaks and open their mouths, wishing that ill may befall Juno? And here already are the Eumenides or Erinnyes, Tisiphone, Megaera and Alecto, the infernal Furies. Look how the cruel Harpies, Aëllo, Ocypeta and Celeno, fly to assail her. What, then, are you waiting for? Come, advance! The proud arrogance of Juno must now surely perish. Ah, how many damned souls with serpents for hair come to attack cruel, proud Juno! The roads are full of them. But wait, and come no nearer for a moment! Make way for Dione, mother of the great goddess, who comes to aid us, accompanied not by poor people of no account but by gods, Venus and Cupid. Let proud Juno show now what deeds

208

she is capable of, let us see if they can resist. Surely they are worth no more than the works of Arachne, which were turned into nothing. Now, dear friend, I beg you to stir yourself, to raise your resplendent and fortunate banner in the midst of the field, and the gods will follow it. For I am certain that Jupiter will at once come to your assistance, as you know full well he has often abandoned the marriage bed of that sullen, ugly Juno and kept you company in yours, where you have rejoiced in the embraces of the greatest of mortal gods, depriving Juno as unworthy of them. Do not be idle, my dear friend; come, just for a little while. Do not spurn the honour the other gods show you – go to meet them, and greet them with reverence. Do you expect to receive such honour every day? That is impossible; and if they see that you do not take it when it is offered, perhaps they will be angry against you, and with reason, and you will have lost it for all time. Now you will see what you wish to happen to that wicked woman. Do you still hesitate? Why do you not stir? He who is unwilling to behave masterfully does not deserve the name of master. So, dear friend, master the proud Juno, who has as much as she can do to master the humble who stay kneeling, with folded hands. No, no, it is no glory to the gods to master the weak who do not defend themselves but those who are or who think they are strong, and who strive to combat those who are greater than them, or who are their equals, or at the least are strong and valiant. Let the pride of pestilential Juno be cast down, and when they see your victorious and unsurpassable excellence, all the gods, despising her, will make way at your coming and you will gain the place among the gods that is reserved for you to all eternity!'

When Dione had heard all the prayers that Fortune could make to her, she answered in a very sweet, soft voice. 'Lady and dear friend,' she said, 'I will not deny or forget the gifts which you, kinder to me than I am to myself, have offered me, nor will the glory which you have bestowed on me ever be lost in oblivion. I know and acknowledge that you, the goddess and mistress of all prosperities, lend them to everyone, to some more, to others less, to some for a little while, to others for a long while, according to the disposition of your untiring will. Every day you must give and take and exchange earthly goods from one dynasty to another, from some men to others. And because your realm is widespread and you must continually dispose of worldly riches and have much to do in many parts of your domain, my reply must not be a long one. Nevertheless, I beg you to hear me with a pacific ear. Tell me, lady, who moves you to make these requests? What is the cause of your anger against this knight? Have you not troubled him enough, have you not struck him and harassed him and cast him down from the position to which you

209

had raised him? Is it not enough to have taken from him all his worldly goods – why do you wish to take his body also? You are not wont to be a murderess, you are more of a thief, so why do you wish to do what is not proper to you?' 'I am surprised at you,' said Fortune, 'why do you ask me this? You are not ignorant, as it appears from what you have just said, and my anger cannot stand delay. Yet I will tell you, briefly: you know that I am not constant or stable but I needs must give and take away, change and exchange, as you know well. So why do you ask? Come sweet friend, help me to destroy that wicked, false woman, and then perhaps I will account to you for what I do, although I am not obliged to.'

'I do not speak of Juno,' said Dione, 'she is a spirit and so outside your power: I speak of the knight. What has he done to you that you should persecute him?'

'Alas!' said Fortune, 'is this the result of all my prayers? It would have been better to be silent and do my own work as far as I could! Go, men of the world, beg your friends to help you in your needs, and when you are most hard pressed they will fold their arms and ask, with concern not for your anguish but for their repose, why you need to borrow! To ripen is good, if time permits, but to rot is damnable: he who has no will to help lays hold of a twig so slender that it could not support a fly, and makes show that he is bearing the affairs of the whole world. I beg you, Dione, to help me when I need help; if I wished to argue with you now I should lose my right, which is in contention, and if you will not, do not keep me here gossiping, do not make me waste time, because delay would consume my goods and then I should not be able to supply my needs. I should lose my friends, who are now in the field ready for combat, and knowing this, my enemies would regain heart and would think little of me. Remember, Dione, there are some things which bear ripening and others which must be taken by surprise, and one of the latter is this of which I speak. If you do not intend to help me, make haste to answer, so that you and the others do not lose by delay.'

'O goddess of the mortal gods, who have won primacy and pre-eminence among the rest! Do not be angry with me, but judge if I am capable of doing what you ask of me. You know well that my daughter Venus is the goddess of concord and that she induces people to love each other and to wish each other well; and Cupid her son forces, constrains, excites and rouses them to love. I am of the same condition, for I have never loved discord nor had any desire for vengeance. Also my daughter takes after her father, Jupiter, who, as you know, is a very pleasant planet, an enemy to wickedness and a friend to peace, the king and lord of justice, the fountain of truth and righteousness, amiable and virtuous; he tempers the fierceness of

210

Mars and Saturn, and of him Dante says in his third book "Then appeared to me the tempering of Jove between his father and his son, and thus the variation they make in their position was clear to me". And so if of my own nature I have no desire for discord, sedition, vengeance, how do you think that I can become cruel, and against my nature do what my nature forbids? It would be impossible for me to do as you ask. However, if you will let me, I will try to rid you of this preoccupation (and it is a true friend who guards you from dispute and from wrongdoing) and this I will do with all my knowledge and power, provided that you will give me the opportunity. This is true and not common friendship, as the philosopher says in the fourth book of his *Ethics*. If this does not please you, then call on Mars to help you, who is a warrior, and let me go, who am love, peace and concord. I can be of no avail to you in deeds such as you summon me to do, for he who wishes war should not bear an olive branch.'

Hardly had Dione finished speaking when Fortune began to tear her hair and rend her robes across her breast. 'Woe is me!' she cried. 'I did not come here for advice, I wanted help, not advice! Tell me, Dione, did I give you advice when you asked me for help? Be a friend to whom you will, Dione, I do not need such friends. I should have to be very short of wisdom to ask advice from such as you: you could not give it to yourself when you had need of it, and now you seek to advise me, without being asked! Ah, Dione! If I were to summon you to commit adultery again, as you did with Jupiter, I am sure that you would be ready and not need much asking. Thanks to God, you and your daughter have been revealed for what you are, for I made your daughter the wife of Vulcan the god of lightning, and an adulteress with Mars, and when the sun saw them through a narrow window she was shamed (if it can be said that a whore can feel shame) and was shown to all the gods, who mocked at her. So your daughter is not the goddess of love but of lust and strumpetry, and because she was far more lecherous than all the women in the world together, she was more degraded and defiled too: not a star in the sky but a dirty, vile, stinking sow, and she does not dwell in the heavens nor is she a star, because the star was there before she was born; but she lives in bogs and loathsome stinking places, which she puts her snout in before her foot. I have tried you, and I have found you one of those friends with whose aid one can threaten but not strike: such you may remain, and I will be victorious over my enemies without you. God lends me Envy, my friend and kinswoman, who is here and will not be parted from me. May I never see you and your like in my house, for in faith it would be a great honour for you and a great shame for me if we were to be found

211

together. Let the knight sail as much as he likes and the weather will let him.' And she went away and disappeared.

★

So Curial boarded his galley and sailed away, for his desire was to see the ancient and celebrated city that gave laws to Rome. He saw there the famous school where the science of the knowledge of God was taught, and being a man of learning who was continually studying, he was delighted with all that he was shown and told there. Then he went on to see the city which was first given walls by Cadmus and of which so much was written by Statius in his *Thebaid*. He visited the tomb of Eteocles and Polynices, the cruel brother-sons of Oedipus and Jocasta. Then he visited the mountains called Nysa and Cithaeron, the laurels sacred to Apollo, god of wisdom, and the vines sacred to Bacchus, god of knowledge, and many antiquities he knew of from report.

Although this bold and great and valiant knight had in truth never felt fear – or at least no one in the world could tell whether he had ever before been afraid – as he approached the temple of Apollo he turned pale, and there was not a hair on his head that did not stand on end. However, he continued on his way. His companions, fearful and afraid, all fell silent; their strength and valour failed, and they were unable to take a step forward. So frightened were they that when they looked at each other they became more so, seeing their companions mute and speechless, their faces the colour of death, without strength or vigour and with nothing to give them cheer or to rouse their spirits. They were compelled to sit, even to lie down, for they could not stand upright. They remained thus a long time, and Curial, who had gone on ahead, grew tired of waiting for them. Unable to go further, he sat down on a marble step, leant his head on a stone and, weary from his efforts, fell asleep. As he slept it seemed to him that he heard loud shouting and, so it seemed, he awoke (although he was so fast asleep that it would not have been easy to rouse him). In his sleep he saw Hector, son of Priam, whom all his life he had wished to meet; and he was so afraid of him that if his mother Honorada had been present he would have fled in shameful terror back into her womb to hide, if it had been possible, or at least beneath her skirts.

Oh Curial! Would that you yourself could write this account of what you saw in your dream, so that the pen that now turns red for shame in my hand need not write what is to follow! For what it recounts has no witness and some will not believe it, and if I could leave it in the inkwell I would not mark the paper nor stain it with

212

ink. See how my hand refuses to write, and will not do so! However, Dante counsels me with his lines, saying 'To that truth which looks like falsehood a man must keep his lips closed as long as he can, because it can bring shame without fault: but here I cannot be silent'. And you force me to tell it, citing by way of example the book of Macrobius on Scipio's dream, and Joseph's explanation of Pharaoh's dream expounded by Jean of Limoges in twenty epistles. You say too that it is impossible for a man to dream of something he has never seen or heard tell, and everyone knows that, and there is no compulsion for everyone to believe it; it is not an article of faith but merely a dream, dreamt in the way that everyone dreams. So I will speak boldly and not omit so lofty and noteworthy a deed as that which is described here. That you should say that you dreamed, and that I should write what you made known to many people, as I have heard, seems no great fault.

Curial opened his eyes when he heard the shouting and saw before him nine beautiful and venerable maidens comforting a most worthy, reverend man, who had been called to judgement and was reluctant to appear for fear of the verdict he knew would be pronounced against him in the case for which he was summoned. One of the maidens came to Curial and said 'Wake, you sleeper! It is you who have been appointed as the judge. You must hear the parties and pronounce sentence on the case which will be explained to you. We are sisters, the daughters of Jupiter, and we dwell here upon Parnassus. We are at present attending upon Homer, this worthy Greek poet of whose fame you must be aware; for while he lived he loved us and for that reason we helped him to write the noble book called *Iliad*, and many others worthy to be remembered. But do not think that because we are now in his company we hate and abhor his accusers and adversaries Dictys, the great historian, and Dares, the great poet, who will soon be here. We commend to you, nonetheless, the honour of this poet, who well merits it as the greatest of Greek poets, by whose mouth has been said all that is possible to say in the Greek tongue. We know indeed that this request is superfluous to you, who give honour to all people, especially to those who deserve it. But because we are beholden to him, I wish that you should know our mind. We do not ask that you should not give a straw for the just deserts of the others, only that you treat him with honour. The truth is that he, the greatest master among Greek poets, writing with our help the book which I have named, says many things in favour of Achilles, a Greek like himself. For this he has been found fault with by the other two, who are men of great learning but not equal to or comparable with him; and they say that in many cases he has stated things that are not true. They say that

213

Achilles, of whom this man has told so many great and excellent things, did not attack Hector honourably and as a knight should; and that with the loftiness and sublimity of his wonderful style he softened the hearts of learned men and thus of those who listened to them, and so has made them believe many things that Achilles did not do; and that they did not happen as he describes them, so that the excellences of the incomparable Hector came to diminish in fame and renown. Soon they will all be here, you will hear their reasoning and by giving your decision you will resolve the dispute that exists today among living men on this matter.' Having said this, she fell silent.

Curial replied in some confusion 'Oh most noble and excellent lady, I humbly beseech that I may find such favour in your eyes that you will tell me your name and those of your illustrious sisters, so that I may know to whom I speak.'

With a benign face the goddess at once answered 'We are, as I have said, nine sisters, and daughters of Jupiter, father of the great Alcides. My name is Clio, and the others in order as they come are Euterpe, Melpomene, Thalia, Polyhymnia, Erato, Terpsichore, Urania and Calliope. We are daughters of the father of mighty Alcides and of Rhadamanthus, and we are called the Muses. We changed into magpies the daughters of Pierus. We are companions of the god Apollo, who tempers with love the seven-stringed viol and with love sings sweetly and softly, tempering the harmony of the seven planets. If you would learn more, speak, for my sister Calliope, goddess of eloquence, will answer you.' And Calliope approached Curial.

Then Curial, with great reverence and not without some timidity, spoke: 'Oh most celebrated lady! What destiny has willed that I should receive such honour, that the nine sisters, daughters of the greatest of mortal gods, should come to me and visit this sepulchre of ignorance? I know indeed that you attend Homer, Virgil, Horace, Ovid, Lucan and many others whom, to be brief, I shall not name; but what reason have you to come to me, who am no man of learning nor deserve, nor ever deserved, to be visited by maidens of such excellence. Do you leave Aristotle and Plato and come to me?'

'Do not be surprised at that,' answered Calliope, 'for we are always close to those who wish for us and while we are present here with you we do not leave the others but are always with them. By the power of God we are such that we are in every place we wish to be. Sometimes it happens that all or some of us attend men who may not realise our presence, and help them to do or say what they are doing or saying, some more and others less, according to the disposition that we find in them. Now, however, as my sister told you,

214

we have come with Apollo to comfort this poet, who with our help said all that can be said in the Greek tongue, and we wish to hear the accusation made against him by two venerable men. You have been chosen as judge to examine the question. Because he loved us while he lived and never left us, we do not want to desert him in his need, so that we cannot be accused of ingratitude.'

'Most revered lady,' said Curial, 'all that you have said is true. But how can I judge what I do not understand, for I am not competent to do so? How shall I judge such great knights as these, and how shall I know if Homer spoke truly or not, if I never witnessed the deeds of which he tells?' 'Fear nothing' said Calliope. 'All will be disclosed to you as though it were the work of your own hands or at least done in your presence, so that you will be fully informed and instructed.'

While they were thus engaged a sweet harmony of soft music fell upon Curial's ears, for Apollo was singing so sweetly to the sound of his viol that I cannot believe that the Sirens who delayed Ulysses would not themselves have been held by such sweetness. Phoebus began to fire his arrows over all the world, lighting up the face of the earth and gilding the place where Curial sat. Curial was roused and opened his eyes very wide and strained his ears towards it: he saw the laurels bend low and the sun with its four-wheeled chariot drawn by the four horses Titan, Etheus, Lampaus and Philogeus approached swiftly. Curial was sure that this was the brightest day he had ever seen, and his eyes were able to withstand its splendour, tempered by mist, for a long while.

★

When the noble court had been arranged and seated in a place consonant with its dignity, Curial was first escorted by the nine maidens to a seat befitting his function and dignity as a judge, and the said nine excellent sisters stood around him and encouraged him, telling him to have no fear. Then Homer came before him and called on Achilles, who immediately appeared. Homer said to him 'Oh, you who were king and lord of the greatest kingdom in Greece, the flower and light of chivalry! You know well that I wrote and made a book which contained the great deeds which you performed, where I strove with words to make known, if it were possible, the glory of your victories, which I believe were greater than my pen was able to express. I beg you, in recompense for my labours, to speak in my favour and, knowing the truth, to be my witness in this court as I have been yours in the world. Here you see the accusers, two strong and worthy men who have worked to prove, against what I have said, that the praise which I gave you was not entirely truthful, and

215

that Hector was a better knight than you. If he died by your hand, they say, you struck him treacherously. They have written much concerning this, and I have seen what they wrote; and although it is not read as often and with such respect as what I have written, nevertheless many people come to know of it. Indeed, if it were not for Virgil, greatest of all other poets, who for your sake, I believe, and because he loved truth, followed and defended you among the Latins, I think you would have lost much of your reputation. Therefore I pray you that as when you were in the world you defended all the Greeks, and were the cause of their victory over so many notable peoples, so now you will defend a single Greek, your servant, against these two men who, although they have spoken behind your back, will grow silent before your face, and their despicable writings will lack effect and value.' Having said these words, Homer was silent.

Achilles at once grew angry and his lips began to tremble, and unable to keep his hands still he moved forward to speak. But Apollo said 'Silence, Achilles! I already know the truth, so keep away. You, Homer, go with him, for there is no need for many words: here is your book and your cause. Say no more than you have said.'

This Achilles was suitably tall in stature, well proportioned and of noble mien, white-skinned with red hair, well-spoken and quick-witted, swift to do all things, strong, a great striker with the lance, bold and enterprising, who feared nothing that ever appeared before him; a great philosopher and astrologer, singer and player of instruments, well-dressed and adorned, a man merry and ready for love, knowledgeable about herbs and all kinds of medicines, a good friend and a fervent enemy; skilled, expert and very energetic in all kinds of military exercise, a great hunter of lions, generous in giving and prodigal in spending, so that as long as he lived none among the Greeks was equal to him. But he was also lecherous, covetous and desirous of glory in all that he did, and he was ready to boast and to threaten; and it is said in the *Fiorita* that he was a liar and false: but I do not say this because I have not read it anywhere else.

So Achilles and Homer moved away, among the laurels; and Achilles began to sing very sweetly, and both he, as a ruler, and Homer, as a poet, made crowns for themselves from the branches of the trees sacred to the god.

When these had departed, as we have described, the other two were called: Dictys and Dares, great and serious historians and poets. They appeared in that solemn consistory accompanied by Hector, the lofty, exalted and excellent eldest son of Priam, concerning whom they had written with great reverence; and they put into Curial's hands two books, written in Greek and Latin, which contained the victories and feats of arms achieved by Hector in the brief time during which he had lived, describing how he had compelled all the kings of Asia to become tributaries to Priam. Furthermore they described in good order the buildings and constructions of great Troy and everything that had happened up to the time of its destruction, and thereafter what has become of all the Greek princes, as has been related by Guido delle Colonne, the faithful chronicler of all these events.

Preceding this supremely great and courageous leader came the forty-seven kings whose natural days had been ended by him either during the siege or outside the noble and supreme city, and similarly captains and princes and legions of men of lesser estate, amounting to a great number who, like the kings slain in battle, had been sent to the kingdom of Pluto by Hector's sword.

When Curial saw Hector he thought he would fall from the place where he sat, and such terror filled his heart that all his limbs began to tremble. The wise and courteous Hector, however, aware of Curial's emotion, moved a little further away from him and spoke to him thus: 'I am not surprised, Curial, that you should feel fear finding yourself in authority among such people, for there is no man in the world today who could feel safe in such a situation. Be assured, therefore, that no one of us here present can harm you. I have been told that you wished to see me: here I am. I am he of whom so much is told, and perhaps it is true that my deeds did not deserve that they should be so much spoken of. If it were possible for me to do anything for your honour, I should not fail to do it, but I cannot, and I can serve neither you nor anyone else. This is the punishment that I endure.' And he was silent.

Curial was quite unable to reply, and he would have fallen to his knees if he had been allowed to: but he was the judge and it behove him to sit and not to move from his seat.

Then Apollo said 'Hector, there is a great argument among living men as to whether yourself or Achilles was the better knight, and also concerning which of these two writings is the more truthful. It is therefore my wish that you be judged by Curial, who today holds, among those who know him, the crown and primacy of chivalry – and not wrongfully, for I assure you that he is praised for no deed that he has not performed better than the tongues of those who have seen it are capable of expressing. If he were not present I would tell you many things, about which I must remain silent if I am not to fall into the vice of adulation.'

At this Hector looked more closely at Curial than he had done before; and to him he seemed a little man, almost a dwarf compared

217

with the men of his own time, and it did not seem possible that he could be such as Apollo had described. But Apollo knew what Hector was thinking and said 'Do not be surprised at what I have said, for all the men of today are small in stature, and this man is, among the living, tall and even very tall.' Hector said nothing.

Then Apollo said to him 'Leave us, go to the far end of the temple. I wish to instruct this knight so that he may give a just verdict.' 'I have never wished for vain praise,' Hector replied, 'and now less than ever do I wish it. Let those who deserve it receive it, for I renounce it utterly.' And turning his back he withdrew from the place, with all his venerable company. Then Apollo, retaining Dictys and Dares, sent for Homer, and when he had arrived, addressed him thus:

'I did not make you my partner and sharer in my godhead, Homer, nor did I give you these noble maidens to accompany and serve you, who have been with you and honoured you as long as you lived, in order that you, with their aid and profiting from my divinity, should write with more regard for your own glory than for the truth of the matter. You sought to display what you felt of my power, and using the science of Bacchus in poetry, you strove in your writing to contrive poetic fictions and rhetorical colour, feigning many things that had no substance, giving to some what was not theirs and concealing what was publicly known to others. Raising to great heights your wonderful and noble style, you with your pen have caused all the poets who came after you to marvel and to think that things happened as you described them. Such a one was the great Virgil, indeed the greatest of all Latin poets: like you he sought out and wrote in poetry things coloured by falsity, saying, among other things, that Dido Queen of Carthage killed herself for Aeneas' sake: which did not happen and is not true, for Aeneas never saw Dido nor Dido Aeneas, since nearly three hundred years separated one from the other. That modest, chaste and honest widow never broke faith with the ashes of Sicheus her husband, and indeed when Iarbas, the king of musicians, wanted to take her by force to be his wife, and for that reason fought against her and laid waste almost all her country, when the noble queen saw that she could maintain her liberty in no other way, she voluntarily killed herself rather than let her body be touched, against her will, by the hands of a foreigner. It does not seem to me that she broke faith with her husband, who had been dead a long time, but rather that she died in order to keep it: and so wrote St Jerome, who does not make mistakes, in one of his letters to Jovinianus. To write poetry is good; but to write contrary to the truth is not, I think, to praise. I have read all that you wrote, and likewise all that has been written by these two here, who have

218

treated the same matters as you. I have shown the books to this knight, who is a great poet and a solemn orator, and he must decide between you. But I must ask you if you have anything to say.' The great Homer answered that he had not, for he had said enough and neither could nor would say more; and the other two also declined to speak. Apollo therefore ordered them to move aside and not to return until they were summoned to hear the verdict.

When they had gone, Apollo took some branches from the trees consecrated to him and made a garland for Curial's head, saying 'Best and most valiant of knights, and greatest of all poets and orators here present'. And he bestowed on Curial all the wisdom of his godhead, so that Curial was fully informed of the virtues and might of the knights and of the composition and disposition of the volumes. So when he had decided upon his verdict and the parties had been summoned and assembled, he pronounced his judgement:

'I find Hector to be the best knight among the Trojans and Achilles the best among the Greeks; and that Hector performed more, greater and weightier deeds, possessed more virtues and was less given to vice. Achilles struck Hector justly, for in battle everyone must seek his own advantage. Homer wrote a book which I direct must be held in great esteem among men of learning: Dictys and Dares wrote the truth. This is my verdict.' Everyone bowed their heads, praised the judgement, and disappeared from the spot.

★

All this had taken a long time, during which Curial's companions, who had fallen in terror to the ground, first rose up again, and then, hearing the sweetness of the music, lost all consciousness and knowledge of where they were, for the angelic voices and the sweetness of the stringed instruments fell so softly on the ears of those who heard them that they did not know whether it was day or night. As the brightness of the place became dimmed, a kind of shadowy darkness covered their eyes so that they could see nothing, while they felt fresh and rested as though they had never striven.

Then, as they began to recover the power of sight, they went towards Curial, who was sleeping profoundly, and they saw that he was crowned with laurel, and that the place where he lay was full of a delicate and pleasant perfume. It indeed seemed a place where gods might have dwelt, and they were conscious of nothing save the celestial aroma and the sweetness of Paradise. The heavenly dew which bathed the grass around gave out so delightful a scent of such fragrance that the memory of man is powerless to recall it, and the pen to describe it. Consider, reader, that human knowledge fails when it seeks to convey and to remember divine acts for which the wisdom and memory of man are inadequate.

So the gentlemen of Curial's company awoke him, and he, raising his hands to his head, found there a garland of laurel with an inscription which read: 'The best and most valiant of knights, and the greatest of all poets and orators in the world today'. The gentlemen questioned Curial time and time again, but he gave no answer but stood as though enchanted, looking about him, not knowing what had happened to him, and not daring to speak. He kept raising his hands to his head, and he did not know whether his gentlemen had played a trick on him by putting the wreath on his head, as though he were mad. Then he remembered his dream, and he was amazed and did not know what had befallen him.

One of his gentlemen said to him 'Where are you, Curial? Do you recognise this place? Have you lost your memory? Take thought, and counsel with us so that we do not get lost ourselves!' 'Come away!' said another. 'Let us leave this place, for we have tarried enough. Back to the galley, and on with the journey!' Curial again put his hand to his head, and taking off the wreath read the inscription on it. He looked at his men and said 'Why have you shamed me so? Am I drunk? Why do you mock me?' Then they all declared with oaths that none of them had been near him but that they had found him like that, and that no mortal hand was capable of making that garland or writing that inscription.

So Curial, like a man who rises from a long and severe illness, very weakly rose to his feet, and he could hardly walk or even stand erect. But with the help of his companions he was slowly taken to the city and thence by daily stages they came to the galley. When he was aboard he ordered that he should be taken to Genoa, and the captain of the vessel gave orders to make for that port. And for many days they sailed on safely and prosperously.

So calm was the sea that Curial and his company never thought that the weather would ever change, and for many days it continued fine. But Fortune and Envy were not sleeping, and by various means they roused the anger of Neptune, god of the sea. With great fury he sent out his heralds, proclaiming war and tempest against them, and the heralds, turning their backs on the travellers, returned to their king. Then Neptune, mounting his chariot drawn by four dolphins, rushes through the depths of the sea, stirring them up. Aeolus breaks and breaches the caves of Lipari, of Ponza and of Sicily. Tempestuous winds rush forth, lashing the face of the calm, smooth sea, shaking and tossing it about, and the sea moans and howls beneath the blows; tormented, assaulted, harassed, the wretch laments that it has so cruel a tyrant for its lord and master.

When the mariners see Neptune's heralds, they make ready and prepare to defend themselves, binding the galley about with strong ropes and cords, and they lash down the galley-slaves so that rapacious Neptune will not carry them away. Seeing in the distance a dark black cloud approaching them, menacing and muttering, the sailors and the master of the oarsmen, using the shafts of their spears as well as entreaties, urge the galley-slaves to row hard so that they may reach a safe harbour. But the rain falls heavily, the clouds roar, and the darkness increases. Night shows her black and shadowy face, the waves heave and form mountains and valleys, striking against the galley which is as yet unaware of how bad things can be; they beset it all around, thrusting now this way, now that, now upwards, now downwards, now on the highest summit of the waves and now in the lowest depths of the sea. The sailors are distraught and do not know what they are doing, and lose all hope of safety; nothing they can do is of any avail, for the tempest of waves and contrary winds, striving with one another like mortal enemies, is so fierce that the oars snap, the bonds burst, and the galley, running between two walls of water, sometimes disappears and cannot be seen, so that the sufferings undergone by the wretched sailors in a short space of time are truly marvellous. They have no time to pray to God or to call on any saint to change the weather for them or to have mercy on their poor souls, but in a moment will be food for the fishes. Now one man goes, now two, they lose all control of their vessel, the galley cracks, the nails fall out and it breaks asunder, shudders, and doubles up like an eel. And the night, although it was August, seemed very long.

I cannot describe to you the thoughts of each man, because I could no longer see them. When God willed the day came, and they were in hopes that things might become better because the force of the wind began to lessen a little and to lose some of its might. But the waves grew higher and the sea roared fearsomely and tossed the wretched galley hither and thither so that it took on a great deal of water and was on the point of being lost. So passed all that day and the following night, until the third day, when it ran aground off Tripoli, in Barbary.

The whole coast was on the alert because some galleys and frigates of the King of Aragon had recently done damage along the shore, carrying off many souls and two armed galleys full of Moors into captivity, and had burnt many other smaller vessels. So the Moors who saw Curial's galley come ashore broadside on ran to the place, and seeing that they were Christians put to the sword all those whom they found alive, and cut them all into pieces. Only Curial escaped, and a Catalan gentleman named Galceran de Mediona, a valiant and strong man; and they escaped only because the Moors thought that they were already dead, for they lay in their cabins like corpses. However, by the time the Moors found that they were alive, their fury had abated, and so they dragged them from the galley in a shameful manner, with their hands tied, and they were sold at a low price because it was not thought that they could possibly recover. They were bought by a Moor who was not of that district, who took them more than forty leagues inland. Then the Moor sold them to a gentleman of Tunis, young and very rich but miserly, who soon after took them, laden with chains and leg-irons, to Tunis, on foot and quite naked, with little to eat and less to drink.

This gentleman owned a noble and beautiful house among gardens half a league outside Tunis, a brand-new house as white as a dove, with a large and fair orchard around it well-planted with many trees and with much other land besides. This man loved his house, and he had purchased the two prisoners to cultivate the garden and land. When he had taken them thither, he had them each given a hoe, and they were shown what they had to do. When he commanded that they should tell him their names and what country they came from, Curial answered that he was from Normandy and that his name was John, and the other said he was Catalan and his name was Berenguer. The gentleman asked them what they were able to do, and they said that they could look after animals. 'Look after yourselves, then,' said the Moor, 'for there are no other beasts to tend here.' And he ordered them angrily to dig and to look after the garden.

So John and Berenguer began to take pleasure in digging and cultivating the garden and other pieces of land and in short they became good husbandmen; and because they were very strong and worked very well, their master, whose name was Faraj, was very pleased with them. His pleasure, however, was of no help to the slaves, indeed he loaded more irons upon them and gave them more work to do, and they were never allowed to go to the city. Thus the poor men were never seen by other captives or by merchants who perhaps might have recognised them, and no one gave them any help. And so these wretches, sad and unfortunate, lived a life full of toil.

Curial sang marvellously well, and so also did his companion, and sometimes when they were weary they would sing to cheer themselves, with a cheerfulness from which God preserve me and everything good; for the poor slaves had little bread and less meat

222

and they were not given wine, and every day they were fed rather than satisfied, and there was no shortage of work. Because of this they were soon so changed in appearance that if the men who had been their companions in the galley had seen them, they would never have recognised them. So there was no witness to their captivity, since all in the galley but themselves had perished. Thus it was generally accepted that Curial's galley had been lost and that all in her had died without anyone having escaped, as though all had perished by the sword. The news was taken by Genoese merchants to Genoa, and thence to Montferrat, that Curial was dead and his galley run aground in Barbary, and that all in her had been slain and no one had escaped. This was taken as certain in all parts where they were known.

★

The news came to the ears of Guelfa. She sent for the weary old man Melchior de Pando and asked him if he had heard anything of Curial. Before replying, the good old man wiped away his tears and said as best he could through his weeping 'Indeed, lady, you have done your work, and your hatred has now no object; if Curial vexed you in any way, the Moors of Barbary have avenged you well. He and all those who were in his galley have been miserably and wretchedly slain, with no chance to defend themselves. Their fate has been even worse, in that their bones lie unburied and their flesh, eaten by dogs and wild beasts, has left them bare and uncovered. They had no time for confession. Indeed, madam, your curses have pursued him. Now those false old men can rest in peace; Envy will pursue them no longer, and at least his spirit will be spared their persecution. Ah, false, evil old men! Rest henceforth, for Curial, whom you have harmed without his harming you, is dead. You need have no fear of his return now. Now you may see how you profit from his death, how many years will be subtracted from your senility, how much your worldly goods will increase by his death! And you, madam, must seek another servant, for that loyal, noble, virtuous one has died in the exile to which you so wrongfully condemned him.'

Guelfa listened to all that Melchior had to say, and then, without showing any change of expression, without replying, she dismissed him, and he went away. As soon as the doors of her chamber had closed, however, she shut herself away with only the Abbess for company. And when they were alone, she called out with a loud voice, saying 'Curial, my own, where are you, where have you gone? Wait for me, I shall follow you! You have died because of me,

223

I have severed your soul from your body, I have given your flesh to dogs and lions and your bones lie unburied. Oh pride of all knights! Where are you going, show me the way! Tell me how shall I follow you? Where are you, my soul, my life? Where do you dwell, what palaces are worthy to house you? Oh, Guelfa, harsh and cruel, how could you so rob yourself of the light of your eyes, why did I not tear them out so that I should see no other man? Oh, Oedipus, I beg you to lend me your fingers, bold and experienced! Alas, how shall I live without Curial? Oh false, cruel one! I have slain him whom other knights could not slay, I have overcome the conqueror of all, sending the most virtuous and best knight in the world into exile!' And as she spoke thus, she paced up and down her chamber, remembering all Curial's virtues.

But her eyes would not dry up. She tore the veils from her head, and did not spare her hair but drove her white and cutting nails through it, dragging out with her snowy fingers the hairs which seemed threads of beaten gold. She went to and fro, saying so much and weeping so long that at last, overcome with grief and tears, she lay exhausted on her bed. The Abbess, full of sorrow and wretchedness, knelt down beside her and tried with all the best arguments she knew to console her. But she strove in vain, for the lady's spirit was so afflicted that she was inconsolable, and if for a little while she was silent she would begin to weep again, so that her tears had no end. She praised Curial for all the virtues for which that noble and virtuous knight could be praised, and they were endless, affirming that if chivalry were personified then the day that Curial died it must have been buried alive with him; for it was he who gave chivalry the great esteem in which it was held. And so she wept for many a long day.

Nevertheless, since the passage of time drives tears away, she ordered Melchior to send wise and prudent men to the place where Curial's galley had been wrecked to find out if anyone had escaped, and if not, to try to bring back his bones, if they could be distinguished from the rest, so that they might receive the burial that his valour merited. As secretly as he could, Melchior at once sent wise men to Tripoli to do discreetly what was ordered.

When they reached Tripoli they learnt that when the galley was wrecked all who were in her were killed save for two men who were sold to a merchant who was not known in those parts; but it was thought that they would not be able to escape because they were almost dead when taken from the vessel, and they were not expected to live. What was worse, they could discover neither the name of the merchant who had bought them nor where he came from. Then they went to the place where the murders had taken place and saw many bones. But they inquired about the build and stature of the two captives who had been sold, and the clothes they had been wearing when found, and they were told that they were well-built, especially one of them who was very tall, with a very handsome face and white skin, wearing a silken doublet; and this was shown to them, and on the thumb of his right hand had been found a gold ring with a lion on it, with which he sealed letters. With great difficulty they managed to obtain the doublet and the ring, buying them at a price far higher than their value. Then they left Tripoli and visited many towns and villages in search of the captives, but they found nothing. Returning to Tunis, they made inquiries in the city, of residents and Christian slaves, whether they knew where the two captives who had escaped from the wreck of Curial's galley in Tripoli might be, but they could not find a trace of them. They visited many villas and estates in the countryside, but they never came to the house where they were, nor, even if they had done so, would they have recognised them, so changed and altered were they; nor would Curial have revealed who he was, for he had no desire to leave his captivity, but rather wished to die there.

Having searched widely without finding any trace of Curial, they returned to Genoa in a Genoese ship and thence by daily stages to Montferrat. There they presented themselves to Melchior de Pando and explained to him all that they had done, and gave him the doublet and the ring they had purchased. Melchior was sure that the ring had been Curial's because of the lion carved on it, for Curial always wore a lion for Guelfa's sake. Melchior took the doublet and ring to Guelfa and told her what he had learned and showed her the doublet and ring. She too was sure that the ring was Curial's, and the doublet too, and she asked Melchior if Curial had left any doublets behind in his house. Melchior said that he had, and they sent for another doublet and compared them for size, and they found that both had been made to fit the same body. Knowing that the owner of the doublet and ring had been taken from the galley alive and had been sold, they thought it was possible that he was still living but that he had not been sought for thoroughly, otherwise he might well have been found. Accordingly Guelfa ordered Melchior to send envoys again, to seek the slaves with the utmost diligence, and that they should be redeemed at whatever the cost: but that Curial should not return to Montferrat. So Melchior sent his men back to Tunis.

There they set about inquiring as thoroughly as they could, to try to discover something about the two slaves. But they could find no trace of them, because they were not in the city nor ever entered it, and those who were seeking them never chanced upon the house where they were. So time passed without the slaves receiving consolation or the seekers rejoicing in the discovery they hoped for; and they returned to Montferrat saying that it was not possible that they were alive since they had sought with all the diligence in the world, not only in Tunis but in many other towns and villages, and they had not found the least trace of them: and it was certain that they were dead.

★

Meanwhile the two slaves were working hard and serving their master well, and this Faraj would not have yielded them up for anything in the world. He was very pleased with them and trusted them, so that he did not trouble whether they did much or little work, taking for granted that they were never idle. He went off to Tunis and often spent the whole week there without returning to his orchards, where he kept his wife and daughter, who was a girl of some fifteen years. She was so beautiful that according to the opinion spread abroad by those who had seen her, she had no equal in the whole kingdom of Tunis. This was no untruth, for if Curial's eyes were not deceived nothing was claimed for her beauty that was not exceeded by the reality. Her name was Camar; and her father was so jealous, not only on her account but also on that of his wife, who was a most beautiful lady, that he never allowed them to go to the city but kept them in his house not only in seclusion, but hidden away. He would go off to Tunis, where he had another home and other wives, and indeed other women whom he frequented, because he was very lustful and much inclined to that sin, and sullied and stained with it; and such was his way of life.

His wife, whose name was Fatima, fell in love with the Catalan slave who gave his name as Berenguer, and she began to give him better food than he was wont to receive, and when Faraj was not there the slaves were held in greater esteem and were better treated. But their labour did not cease but increased every day, and the weight of their irons also. The Catalan, however, had better nights and more enjoyment than Curial – who was calling himself John.

Six years passed thus on the estate, and their captivity had become natural to them and they gave no thought to the possibility of freedom nor thought that they would ever leave that place or their servitude.

Camar was aware of the love of her mother and the slave called Berenguer; and seeing her own solitude and the jealousy of her father, who gave no thought to providing her with a husband, she realised that she was defenceless, and had no hope of companionship

of men or of anyone except the two slaves. So she used to leave the
house and go out into the orchards and spend the whole day with the
slaves who sang so well. So too did her mother, who accompanied
her. Camar would sing very well and John taught her new songs and
would sing in harmony with her.

So often did the tender maiden do this that she grew aware of the
beauty of Curial's body and the brilliance of his eyes, and she looked
at his mouth, and all the features of his face, and it seemed to her that
there neither was nor could be a nobler man in the world; for Faraj,
who was adjudged one of the most handsome men in the kingdom,
did not come anywhere near the beauty of John. The girl thought in
her heart that if he were not a slave, and if he were dressed well and
had pleasant things to do instead of unpleasant ones and hard work,
he would be quite another person from what he now appeared. And
for this reason she began to give him better and more delicate food
than he was used to, and in greater quantity, so that life for the slaves
was incomparably better. If Fatima kept close to Berenguer, Camar
did not forget John, but kept him company and never left him.
Fatima never thought that Camar would fall in love with John, but
believed that she spent her time with the slaves to please her, because
she knew about herself and Berenguer; and her mother was very
glad of this and encouraged her, in order to cover up her own ill
deeds.

When Camar left the slaves she would read Virgil's *Aeneid* (which
she possessed in her mother tongue, with good glosses and moral-
isings, her father having received it from the king) and many other
books, which she read as a pastime. She was marvellously intelligent
for her tender years, and John, who knew Virgil well, and the other
books, explained many things to her that she did not know or
understand. And I can tell you that she repaid her master as best she
could, for John spoke the language of the country well, and Camar
showed him how to read and write it. And in this way, when Faraj
was not present, she and John were never apart.

When Faraj came, however, they dissembled so that it appeared
that they never spoke to the slaves, and Faraj would go to see them
and they would complain of the bad food they were given and the
little attention that was paid to them, and Faraj at once ordered that
they were to be given food, and reproved them for not taking care of
the two slaves. 'It seems that you care more for them than for us',
answered the mother. 'I do not think that Moorish captives are
treated so well by Christians, and you know well the bad time my
cousin had in Barcelona. In faith, these men will pay for that!'

Faraj laughed and said 'What harm do these deserve? Indeed, I do
not believe there are better slaves in the world. They do what they

have to do well, and each one of them does the work of two. So please feed them well, and let them enjoy themselves a little.' The next day Faraj returned to Tunis, and the women were glad because they liked to see his back more than his face. They went at once to visit the slaves and found them well, if slaves can be said to be well.

John, however, did not care for Camar in the way she would have wished, and the wretched Camar, who was afire with love for Curial, which burned in her like a glass-maker's furnace, wasted away more every day. What she lost, the slaves gained, for she could neither eat nor sleep, and they ate well and slept better, and rejoiced that Faraj was in Tunis: for when he came back they lost all that they enjoyed when he was away.

★

The fame of Camar's beauty reached the ears of the King, and he sent for Faraj and questioned him about his daughter's beauty. Faraj replied that no one could judge his children rightly, and that she seemed beautiful to him but perhaps she did not appear so fair to others. The King commanded him to show her to him, for he wished to see her. Faraj went home very pleased and happy because the King had asked to see his daughter, and he took his wife aside and ordered her to make Camar ready for him to take to the King.

The next day Fatima called her daughter to her. 'Camar,' she said, 'I think that today you must be the most fortunate girl in the whole kingdom. The King is in love with you and has told your father to take you to him, and you will be his wife. Come then, and make ready, so that you can soon depart; and, dear daughter, I beg you that when you are queen you will remember your father and me.'

When Camar heard what her mother said, her heart at once filled with deep sorrow, and she answered 'Madam, I do not wish to be the King's wife, nor anyone else's. Indeed, if I had to take a husband, nothing on earth would make me marry the King, certainly not now that he has already a thousand wives; but even if I were sure that I should be his only wife, I would not be his. He may put me to death, but such a marriage will never be with my consent, for I have made a vow of virginity which I shall keep with all my might. He who would take my virginity must take also, at the same time or before, my life. Let us speak no more of this, madam, for this answer you will have from me as long as I live, which will be but a short time. It would be more honourable for my father to kill me than to seek such a marriage for me.'

Her mother was very distressed to hear her speak in this way, and said 'My sweet daughter, can you despise your King, who is a very

228

noble lord, and young? I know that you will be very well treated by him. You must prepare to do as he wishes, for I promise that you will not regret it. Is it not a great thing, that the King asks us for something which we should be asking of him?' Camar said again 'In faith, madam, my intention is not to give him or anyone else their pleasure in this matter, so let there be no more words. You will soon see my intention in deeds, perhaps this very day, if you continue, and you will see what you are asking of me.'

Faraj thought that his wife was busy making Camar's beauty yet greater, and that she was taking a long time. He went to the chamber in which they were and said 'Are you still there? Come, hurry, for I have already kept the King waiting too long, and he will be angry at the delay.' 'Your daughter is unwilling to go, Faraj', answered Fatima. 'Here she is, you order her to prepare, or take her as she is.' 'Tidy yourself and make ready, daughter', said Faraj. 'You know that the King wishes to see you. I assure you that you will be treated honourably and well, and we shall receive honour and advancement because of you. So come with me, and consider that there is no king in the world who would not give his daughter to such a king and lord as ours. He will leave all his other wives for you, and your sons will be kings. So hurry, daughter; you know I have no treasure but you. And if I do not take you to the King, I must die on your account, or at least be ruined for ever.'

Camar was so aflame with love for the slave that she would have given the life not only of one father but of a hundred in return for a single kind word from John, and she answered 'I will not deny, sir, that I should obey your command, and I shall do so in whatever way is possible as long as I live, which will be only a short while. But you must know that I have offered up my virginity to God, and I will not take it back from him for anything in the world. I beg you therefore to provide for my death rather than provide me with a husband; for I already have a husband, as I have told you, and, please God, will have no other. I shall be very grateful to you for it. If not, be assured that if you pursue this any further, my own two hands shall remove me from your power and from the King's. If you want me to paint myself, I shall wear the paint that pleases God.' As she said this, she raised her hands to her face and scored it so that in a moment it was covered in blood; and she began to weep piteously. Her mother and father were greatly distressed, and her father especially was very apprehensive at the thought that he would not be able to bring an answer to the King, or that if he did it would be an answer that displeased him, and then the King would be angry and give orders for him to be killed, or at least would bring him to ruin. For the King was a very lustful man, and as soon as he heard of any maiden that

229

she was beautiful, he immediately wanted to possess her and her father had to give her to him at once or face his anger, displeasure and hatred, and he would not be pardoned without being put to death.

So Faraj said to Camar 'Tell me, my daughter, do you believe that God is greater than the King? To what god can you offer your body who would give you greater honour and wealth? Do you not know that what this lord wishes to be done in his kingdom must be done? How shall I say no to one who can make and unmake me according to his will? I beg you, my daughter, put aside these whims that can profit you nothing. Serve the King, since such is his wish, for to serve the King is to serve God, and the King is God on earth. If you could escape by doing as you are doing, it would be understandable, but it will not prevent the King's command being done, even if it has to be done by force. If a father's order has any power over a daughter, I order you to dry your face and make yourself as beautiful as you can. Nothing will prevent me from obeying the King's command, and I would rather endure your unjust tears than incur the wrath of the King, which knows no end.'

When she heard her father speak thus, Camar thought and believed that he meant to use force and to take her to the King against her will. She looked around, and seeing a knife lying on a bench, she ran and picked it up, saying 'You will defend me from the King!' and she drove it into her bosom. As she struck the blow, doubtless because she feared that she might be prevented, the knife did not enter straight but turned under her left breast, and did not penetrate into the soft part of her body. Even so, the wound was a large one, deep and frightening, and when poor Camar saw the blood her heart failed and she fell to the ground half-dead.

When her mother saw this unexpected act, she ran to her daughter shrieking like a woman out of her mind. 'Traitor, you have killed my daughter! Oh betrayer and denouncer of your own flesh, why have you slain your daughter, and me, and yourself too?' The wretched father, in great distress, did not know what to say. He mounted his horse and rode to the city and sent the King's surgeon to his house, begging him to heal his daughter. The surgeon set out at once, and riding hard came to the house, where he saw the large and dangerous wound. He said, however, that with the help of the Lord she would mend, although she was still in danger; and he stayed with her for four days.

When four days had passed the surgeon returned to Tunis and went to pay his respects to the King, who asked him where he had been. He replied that he had been to tend a daughter of Faraj Abdilbar, who had a large wound in her left breast which she had inflicted on herself with a knife, and that it was a very dangerous one. The King then asked him how it was that she had wounded herself with her own hands. 'I do not believe it', he said. 'I had commanded her father to bring her to me here, and the traitor must have tried to kill her so as not to give her to me. This must be the case, for I have known for a long time that the man was not open with me. But he will pay for it.' And at once he sent for Faraj, and without saying anything to him or allowing him to speak, he had his head cut off.

With the same fury he mounted his horse and rode off to Faraj's house, where he found Camar very weak in her bed. He said to her 'Camar, my dear, why did your foolish father wound you so grievously?' 'My father did not wound me', the girl answered. 'Then who did it?' asked the King. 'I did myself, with my own hands, hoping to put an end to my days: but although they will continue a little longer than I wished, I am certain they will not be many, and I shall find some other way to end my sorrowful life.' 'Camar,' said the King, 'I am very sorry for your injury, and if I could find a remedy for your suffering, I would do all in my power.'

He sent at once for Yunus, a notable knight, brother to Camar's mother, and said to him 'I am in love with Camar, Yunus, more than I can say. Believing that her father had wounded her – and indeed I still think so – I ordered his head to be cut off. Do not leave her, I beg, and make sure Camar does not learn of her father's death or else it may double the grief that she is suffering, and she may die as a result. I beseech you to work little by little upon her so that she comes to feel that she would like to be mine. I promise you that she will be chief among all my wives, and, if she so wishes, I will leave many of the others, perhaps even all of them, then you can rule my kingdom and I shall do only whatever you will.' Turning to the girl he said 'Camar, God be with you, and if I can do anything that would give you pleasure, I beg you to tell me and it will at once be done.' Camar made no reply.

The King returned to Tunis and summoned one of Faraj Abdilbar's brothers and said to him 'Abdullah, I asked your brother Faraj to give me a daughter of his called Camar to be my wife, and then I was informed that to spite me, so that I should not have her, he had killed her. Now I know that this was not true, and I am sorry for what I did and beg you to forgive me. I shall do all I can for you and your family and all your kinsmen.' 'My Lord,' answered Abdullah, 'Faraj did not wound his daughter and I have not been able to discover why it happened. Your lordship should not have imagined that any man in the world was cruel enough to kill his own children. Moreover, he was so faithful a servant to you that he would never

231

do or say anything that might cause your annoyance. That you should have asked for his daughter was a great honour to him and all his lineage. Your error was to believe too easily and then to have ordered the execution too soon. However, since nothing can be done about that, the remedy lies in oblivion.'

The King said again 'Abdullah, the truth is that I am in love with your niece Camar and I must have her whatever befalls. I ask you to contrive that she becomes mine, and I promise you on my word that I will be good to her and will make you prosper in estate and honour, so that you will be content with what I do for you.' Abdullah replied that at present the girl was not in a state to serve him in any way, but that as soon as she was restored to health he would contrive to satisfy the King's wish.

From that day forward the King rode out through the country-side every day to the house of Faraj, and thinking to cheer Camar he would sometimes pay her a visit. But she found this so irksome that she thought she would die of melancholy, and when that happened they could not make her speak or eat anything all that day.

★

One day as Camar lay pensively on her bed she saw John enter her room. Looking round she could see nobody else, and she decided to take her opportunity. Calling him closer, she spoke to him, stammeringly 'Oh John, have pity on me! This great harm is come upon me for your sake. Do not let me die, for I do not think I deserve to do so because of loving you.' In distress, John answered 'Tell me what harm has come to you through my fault, Camar, for I never wished to do or to cause harm to you or to anyone else. Tell me, for I am innocent, and I cannot think how harm can have come to you through me.'

Then the poor girl said 'Oh enemy of my health! Oh shortener of my life! Do you not yet know that I am in love with you and for this reason have abhorred my father, mother, friends and kinsmen, and even my honour? Do you not know the cause of the wound in my breast? Do you think that the iron blade I buried in my tender bosom is all my suffering, all my trouble, all my sorrow? The wound that your pitiless heart causes me is greater than the one I caused myself, and it increases every day. The one wrought upon me by you can only be cured by you, whereas the one I brought upon myself can receive remedies from every hand. My sorrow grows greater because there is no one with whom I can talk of you, or to whom I can confide so dear and so great a token as is this secret. But since God has granted me the grace of being able to reveal my suffering to you,

232

know that I had given you my love, in my heart, when my father required me to marry the King, who desired me for his wife. When my father wanted to take me to the King by force, after many words had passed between my father and myself, I knew that there was no other way to avoid it, and so I plunged the knife into my breast and made a great wound, although to my eyes, in comparison with what I would do for you, it was a slight thing. The wound you have caused in me is a far deeper one, which only you can heal, because it is in the heart, whereas the other was only in the body. And if I realise that I must die in order to preserve myself for you, at least have enough pity, let me find enough mercy in you, to slay me with a single blow by your own hand, so that I do not have to suffer many days of pain in dying, and you need not fear that my hands be my own executioners; and I should hold it a singular favour.'

When John heard these words it seemed to him that Camar was taking a wrong road and that he should not yield to her, for reasons it would take long to relate. But he thought that if he did not give her any hope, she might perhaps go to perdition. So he said 'I never thought, nor should ever have thought, Camar, that you would have had this in mind. Since it so pleases you, however, try to get well and then I shall respond to you in such a way as to make you reasonably content. Meanwhile, I beg you not to seek to talk with me so that the cause of your illness does not become known.'

When Camar heard John's reply she was very happy, thinking that once she was restored to health she would delight in his longed-for embraces. So she made great efforts and in a few days she was much better. The King's physicians were very pleased, and the King too was very happy and sent her jewels and many things to win her love. But she accepted nothing he sent her, she did not care to look at his jewels nor even to hear them spoken of. Her uncles, who were notable lords, encouraged and begged her to accept what the King sent, but she still paid no heed to them. Since they continued to insist, she had perforce to address them with the following words: 'Sirs and uncles, I have no suffering other than that caused by the King, and if he would leave me alone I should quickly be cured. If he persists he will strike not merely a single blow, as my father gave me when he first spoke of this matter, but a hundred and a thousand – if I do not die from fewer blows. I would strike them myself, and shall do so in order not to come into the King's hands. Now you know the cause of my suffering; and I have no other save what I have just told you.'

Her uncles and her mother were very troubled, and they told her that they were astonished at her audacity; that she did not deserve the great honour the King wished to bestow on her, and that there

233

was no other king in all the world who would not consider it as good fortune if the King of Tunis wanted to marry his daughter; and that the King, wishing and asking for the daughter of one of his vassals, however rich he was, should not be refused, nor should she show such contempt for the King; that she should be careful what she did for it might happen that she would repent too late, and perhaps this folly of hers could bring destruction on all her kindred.

★

When her mother had heard what Camar had to say, she told the others to withdraw so that she might speak to her daughter for a while, and perhaps she would be able to discover the cause of her aversion. When they had left, she went close to her daughter and said 'My sweet daughter, I am very surprised at you! The King wants you for his wife and you reject him? What woman, young or old, in the whole kingdom of Tunis would be so bold? I promise you on my word, I do not know a more handsome, more gracious figure of a man. All the noblemen of the kingdom beg him to accept their daughters, and it is he who is begging us! Shall we say him nay in a matter in which we should be entreating him on our knees? Do not behave in such a way, my daughter, or you may be sure that the King will inflict the greatest possible punishment for this.'

Camar	Nothing in the world will make me do what you ask of me. The King with all his power cannot give me suffering that I should not bear more willingly than he could inflict it. I beg you to find a way, if you can, to make him not care for me, and for that I shall be very grateful to him. If not, I myself will do something which will free me from this oppression.
Fatima	Then, daughter, you and all of us are as good as dead. As soon as the King heard that you were wounded in the chest, he had your father killed, severing his head from his shoulders, thinking that he had wounded you so that you should not go to the King. Think what he will do if he knows that the delay is due to you yourself.
Camar	Then Faraj is dead?
Fatima	Yes, indeed.
Camar	And I with him.
Fatima	Why, daughter?
Camar	Because after the death of such a father I do not wish, nor ought I, to remain alive.
Fatima	Daughter, keep this constancy of your noble heart for

	some other occasion, for in this it can profit you nothing, and you will not be able to have your way.
Camar	I shall certainly not insult my father's blood by subjecting myself to a man who has willingly let it flow.
Fatima	Ah, daughter, what will you do, what heart will help you bear the harsh and cruel torments that he will have inflicted on you?
Camar	Let all the sufferings that he can bring upon me come now, at once, for it is a greater suffering to wait for them than to endure them, and to continue in this life, it seems to me, is to commit a wicked crime.
Fatima	Ah, daughter, do you not fear the fury and cruelty of the King who whenever he wants something pays no heed to reason or counsel, making a law of his evil will, fearing no superior nor reproach from his subjects? He gives an order and what he wills must be done, and he kills those whom he holds in hatred, perhaps unreasonably, and no one dares contradict him.
Camar	If the King's cruelty has not power to drive me from this world, my own hands will do it.
Fatima	Do you not know that a woman's heart is weak, and that her hands tremble?
Camar	The contrary is true, for it is written, and not by one learned man alone, that knights should have the daring of a woman and the heart of a lion. So said Hercules to Philoctetes when he was a knight in Spain. And so my heart, harder than stone, orders my hands to execute now what before and with less reason they have already attempted. They will not let me be vilely sullied by the murderer of my father.
Fatima	Do not die, my daughter, for death is no vengeance. If you by your death were to murder the murderer it would be some glory to you, but not a great deal. But that you should die and the other live and enjoy all the pleasures the world offers, it is a foolish thing to contemplate and greater foolishness to carry out. When you were dead, the King would not lack wives, and you would be judged foolish, and you would die without virtue.
Camar	The fortitude of my heart is virtue. Cato, the pride of all the Romans, showed me in Utica the road to liberty and I shall follow that path and be a true disciple of such a master.
Fatima	Do you think that Cato, when he had wounded himself in Utica and had opened with his sword a path by which his

235

fearful, indeed, terrified spirit could flee from Caesar, did not regret having caused his own death, although at the last he could not say so? What harm did it do Caesar? And do you think that death is liberty? You may call it rather a dark and gloomy prison, an exile without hope of return. But if it is the case that your heart is bestowed elsewhere, tell me, daughter, and I will find a way to make you happy.

Camar   And where could I bestow my heart? You know well that it is seven years since any man came here other than the slaves.

Fatima   You know that there are many women who when they do not have the opportunity to consort with men befitting their honour do so with those who are to hand, as I do with our slave Berenguer; and would to God it could begin all over again!

Camar   It would be better if it were yet to happen. But you are not the only woman to have fallen into the acts of Venus, and you have had the good fortune to have done so with a virtuous man; for captivity does not take away virtue, although on the other hand virtue lessens captivity. We read of Plato, the great philosopher, that he was made prisoner by a tyrant and sold at a price; and he said to the man who had bought him 'I am greater than you', and he said this only because he had greater virtue. Also St Jerome, in an epistle to Paulinus (so I have learnt from our slave John) concerning the study of the holy scriptures in praise of the virtuous man, wrote of Plato: Given that Plato was a captive and sold into slavery, because he was a philosopher and wise he was more free than the man who bought him.

Moreover you have not sought unlawful beds for those acts of yours, as many others have done: for we read that Pasiphae, wife of Minos King of Crete, was enamoured of a bull and through the skill of Daedalus lay with him and had a son half man and half beast called the Minotaur; nor have you done as Phaedra, the wife of Theseus, who loved the chaste Hippolytus her stepson who, pressed by his stepmother to lie with her and not wishing to defile his father's bed, killed himself to keep faith with his father; nor like Semiramis Queen of Babylon, who took her son Ninus as husband and made a law that every woman could marry her son; nor like Jocasta Queen of Thebes, who lay with Oedipus her son and had two sons by him, Eteocles and Polynices, who slew one another in the sight of their unfortunate mother; nor yet like the bitter Myrrha, who loved her own father and, by the contriving of her nurse, when her father thought he was lying with another woman he lay with his own daughter; when he realised the deception he killed her, and the gods changed her into a tree which weeps perpetually, and its bitter tears bear the same name of myrrh; and then Juno, did she not lie with her brother Jupiter and hold him as her husband, to the scorn and contempt of all the world? And there are many others, as numerous as the hairs on my head, whom I shall not name so as not to lengthen my life. Thus your error is not as great as you make out, and if it were, it is your choice: no one forced you, but you have used your power of choice to give yourself pleasure. It would be the opposite with me, because the King killed my father on my account, and not by my fault. And now that my father is dead for this reason, how can I do what I would not do when he begged me? I have shed my father's blood and may well be called a parricide; should not my own be shed? Ah, what a happy fate it would be if the two bloods could mingle! Since that cannot be, our spirits will merge together. Oh sorrowful spirit of my father, wait for me, I shall soon join you! I shall not be long, you may be sure, and if you dwell in the deepest dungeon of infernal Styx, I choose to be with you, for I do not believe it is a worse place than this, nor that such suffering can be inflicted there as is endured here by those who live in a tyrant's power! Go, then, and do not speak to me of this again, and be assured that I shall accept no counsel that could lengthen my life.

Fatima   Ah, daughter, do not drive me from your sight! Have mercy on me, and at least live as long as I do! See how I bathe your face with my bitter tears!

Camar   Hide them, and do not let them flow, for the time will soon come when you will have need of them. But of one thing you may be sure: they shall not call you mother of an adulteress or of one who has been defiled.

Fatima   You will not be an adulteress or defiled, for he chooses you as a wife and will marry you in the form ordained by our Lord God.

Camar   That is no marriage which is made by force, for it is a contract freely made by free persons; if force enters into it, it loses the name and the effect of marriage.

Fatima   Consent to it, my daughter, and do it of your own free will and agreement, and it will be marriage.

237

Camar   Take a knife, rather, mother, and give me freedom with that! Have pity on your own flesh and send it from this world so that it does not fall into the power of my enemy. Let me not fall short of the example of Virginia, the Roman maiden whose father killed her with a knife to save her from dishonour at the hands of the consul Appius Claudius, preferring to be daughterless rather than father to one who was sullied, defiled and despised.

Fatima   Ah daughter, I am dying, and I shall die before you.

Camar   You will not die, but live, and will be known as the honoured mother of an honest daughter.

Fatima   Indeed, if you die, I wish to die.

Camar   Ah, mother, then kill me with your own hands so that I shall not fall into those of a tyrant! Have for me that pity which other mothers have had for their sons! Remember Medea, daughter of King Aeëtes, who killed her own sons to spite Jason. Remember too Procne, daughter of Pandion, who killed her son Itys and gave him to her husband Tereus to eat, for a single grudge, because he had forced Philomela, her sister, to lie with him and then cut out her tongue; whom then the gods turned into a hoopoe, and Philomela into a nightingale and Procne into a swallow. The sons of Jason and of Tereus, however, did not beg their mothers to kill them, but wept to stay alive. And if I beseech you with tears, will you be so cruel as not to grant my prayers?

Fatima   Daughter, I will kill myself rather than you; and if you take that path, your unhappy mother will follow you.

★

Then her mother returned to the others with this reply, and told them that after all she could discover nothing except that her daughter was ready to die rather than live, and that she would die without fail if they were to deliver her into the King's power. They were all very surprised to hear this, and took it as certain that the young girl's life would be a short one, for as soon as she had recovered the King would have her, and if she did not consent the King would wish to hear it from Camar herself and she would answer in a manner that would make him kill her. So they were very sad. From time to time the King sent to have news of her, and sent her many things to cheer her. The more he laboured to give her pleasure the more she was troubled, so their wills were far apart indeed.

238

Camar, however, thought of only one thing, and believed that she would never attain what she wished from her John, for as soon as she was a little better the King would take her away by force. So she determined to do, while she could, what in her heart she desired to do. This was to give John all her father's treasure so that if she escaped from the King's hands John would have the means to procure his liberty and to seek some means of taking her away; and if perhaps Fortune was so hostile to her that the King had his way by force, John would have the treasure and would not lose both her and the treasure in one day.

Several days passed during which Camar had the opportunity to see her John, and the sight of him was a great consolation to her. One day, seizing a moment when no one could see or hear them, she called John to her and when he had come, she spoke to him thus: 'In a corner of the orchard, opposite the tallest peach tree, my father – who has lost his life because of you – kept all his treasure buried in some pots. You will find three marks made by a hammer in the wall, and the pots are buried beneath these. No one in the world knows this besides myself. I beg you to provide for your freedom and to make your way to your own country. I am dying because of you and do not think that I shall leave this bed alive. If they take me from it by force, my life will be of short duration. Ah, murderer of the person who most loves you in this world, on whose account I have killed my father, robbed his house, shed my own blood and sent my soul to the other world! I beg you, if any spirit of pity lives and reigns within you, that after I am dead you will remember me. As soon as my soul is freed from this prison it will come to you, wherever you may be; and if you take my bones with you to your country, I wish for no other paradise – this I beg you to do.'

'Camar,' answered John, 'keep the money for yourself and be of good cheer. I do not want to leave my captivity but shall live and die your slave. God forbid that I should live so long as to gain my liberty or to leave your power. Nor do I wish to return to my country, for even if I were to return there with all the King's treasure, I should lead a worse life than I do here. You will find me here in these gardens, your slave as long as I live, and only death will remove me from your power.'

These words were indeed of great comfort to Camar, and if she had been sure that the King would not ask for her she would have risen from her bed that very moment, thinking that John had said them because of her. But she was far from the truth, for John's thoughts were elsewhere; and he was greatly troubled by the meaning that Camar had given them. She said 'Please set this bandage right, it has come loose. I am afraid that the ointment may slip and that some harm may come of that.' John went to her, and in a flash Camar had put her arms around his neck and fastened her mouth to that of John. As gently as he could John freed himself from her, and she said 'Oh blessed day, oh holy hour, in which I have attained this pleasure I have so long desired! Oh King, cursed be your life and the way you make me lose mine!' Her pale, yellow face flushed, and she turned red all over, and she said 'I beseech you, John, visit me sometimes; and since I have stolen a kiss from you by force, I ask you to give me another freely and of your own will.' Then John went close to her, almost reverently, and bent his head; and those weak, frail arms, which seemed no more than pulp, clasped him round the neck and she drew herself up by the arms which clung to John so that her whole back was lifted from the bed, and her thin, enfeebled body embraced him, and her inner lips kissed him so closely that neither could breathe out or draw breath, locked in that long, coveted kiss. They remained thus for a long time, and finally parted. John took his leave and left the room and returned to the gardens, and Camar remained in her bed, wiping her lips with her tongue to savour the sugar of the little saliva that remained there from John's lips.

Her mother came to her room and thought her daughter had a better colour than she had had before, and going to her, found her pulse throbbing. 'How are you daughter?' she asked. 'I have been a little frightened,' Camar answered, 'and now I think I shall have a fever, for I feel upset.' 'Do not be afraid, daughter', said her mother. 'It is probably nothing. You have perhaps got a little cold, or something you have eaten may be causing you pain; but it cannot be anything serious.' Camar was the happiest person in the world, and so that she could dwell upon it, she asked her mother to leave her and to send everyone away from her room so that she could sleep for a while. This was done, everyone went away, and she was left on her own.

Let everyone who has ever been in love think how pleasant are such thoughts and how sweet that solitude! In her imagination Camar saw John again, felt those sweet, delicious embraces and kisses, such that all pleasures she had ever before enjoyed seemed tedious and unpleasant in comparison. 'Ah love, love!' she said, 'how delightful are your hopes and how pleasant the flowers of your amorous fruit!'

When John returned to the orchard, as we have said, he spoke to Berenguer and told him all about the money, with which they could do what they had no means of doing if they did not make use of this; and they made their plan together. The following night Berenguer said to Fatima 'What do I gain from the favour you do to me in allowing me to lie with you if you always keep me laden with irons and neither I nor my companion ever have a day's pleasure? I beg you at least to release us from our chains and give us food, and we shall serve you all our lives. We have been your slaves for seven years today: we do not know, nor wish to know, another master, and you know our loyalty and good faith. After so long a time let us receive from you this grace, which is little to you and much to us.' Fatima said that she would willingly do so, and sent for a smith to remove their chains; thus their condition of life was improved, which had been worsened while Camar lay in bed. But they continued to sleep outside, for which they were very thankful, and they looked for what Camar had spoken of to John, and found it. They estimated that with that money Curial could return to a position greater than he had ever had, if it were possible for them to get it away to a Christian country. The slaves were very happy, but they continued to serve and to work better and harder than ever, and for this reason they were liked and favoured in many ways.

The family of Faraj was the richest in Libya and perhaps even in all Africa, for Faraj's ancestors had all been treasurers to many kings and had amassed great wealth for themselves, so that the money they possessed was almost inexhaustible. They were also all avaricious and miserly in the extreme and so mean that it grieved them to spend a single farthing. Their appetite for trading and earning money never failed, and their covetousness and avarice continually increased.

The King, who was so much in love with Camar that he could not forget her, sent for Yunus and said to him 'How is your niece, Yunus?' 'Sire', replied Yunus, 'there seems no way of improving her health and indeed I fear she may somehow slip from your hands and pass to the other world.' 'How can this be?' said the King. 'My doctor says that her wound is in a very good condition.' 'That is true,' said Yunus, 'but she does not eat or sleep, and she does nothing but cry. She is now so very weak that she is nothing but bones, and in faith, I cannot believe that she will ever be well again, and if she does recover it will be a long time before she returns to her normal condition.' 'Tell me, Yunus,' said the King, 'why does she weep so much?' 'Although I have tried to keep it from her, sire, I have not been able to prevent her learning of her father's death', he replied. 'The poor child loved him more than her own life, and does nothing but weep and, as I have told you, has lost the will to eat, and grieves so bitterly that no one can console her.' 'Who told her?' asked the King. 'I have not been able to discover, sire, for many people have visited her and visit her every day; and though I have tried, I have not been able to prevent it. However, if God wills, the passing of time will dry her tears and give place to other things, and

241

she will weary of weeping.' 'That is true', said the King. 'But I should like to know who told her.' 'Perhaps she herself will say, sire', said Yunus. Then the King said 'Yunus, I beg you to make sure that Camar is tended and served as well as can be done so that she be soon restored to health, for on my word, I am impatient to see her well again.' Yunus answered that he would do his best.

Meanwhile the slaves were going into Tunis every Friday and sought to make friends there. It so happened that they came to have confidence in a well-known Genoese called Andrea di Negro, and entrusted to him a thousand doubloons, asking him to look after the money for them and to find a way of ransoming them and freeing them from captivity. Berenguer also made the acquaintance of some Catalan merchants and among them one called Don Jaime Perpunter, a very good and honest man, a native of Solsona but living in Barcelona. He told him that he and another gentleman who was with him were slaves but had some money with which to pay a ransom; and he gave him another thousand doubloons, asking him to look after them because they intended soon to leave their slavery, and once they were free they could then make use of this money of theirs. The merchant answered that he was happy to do so. He asked Berenguer what his name was, and he answered that he was Galceran de Mediona, the son of Asbert de Mediona, although at present he had taken the name of Berenguer; and that the other slave was called John, and was a Norman.

When the merchant learned that he was Galceran de Mediona he made him a deep bow, and he took the money and put it in a safe place; and he gave the slaves a strong box. Then they spent most of their time going at night into Tunis laden with money, so that with the help of the merchant, who worked diligently with them, all the doubloons were brought to his house and filled the large box, and another which became necessary, and also many jewels of gold and precious stones, and large pearls, which they found with the money. Jaime Perpunter helped them loyally and guarded it faithfully with his own. The two slaves were very pleased when all the treasure was safely in the merchant's house, but they did not cease to work in the gardens, indeed they worked better and harder than ever, and received more consideration than in the past. They began to sing and enjoy themselves, thinking that they would not continue to be slaves much longer, and that they were rich and fortunate. Such was their happiness that Curial, who had taken the name of John, thinking about Guelfa and his exile from the marquisate of Montferrat, and of what Guelfa had said – that if the court of Le Puy and the faithful lovers there did not beg her to forgive him she never would – because he was a great troubadour, he made a song. This is how it went;

Just as the elephant
When fallen cannot rise
Unless others come
To help with calls and cries,
So must I seek aid.
So great is my error, so grievous my fault,
I'll never find favour by pleas of my own.
But all faithful lovers at court in Le Puy
Must deign to cry mercy and to plead for me.
If through these lovers
I cannot regain peace,
Nothing is left me:
Even my song will cease –
I shall be a recluse.
Alone, without solace, for such is my wish,
My life will be suffering, anguish and grief,
My pleasure be pain and my sorrow be joy:
I am not like the bear which when beaten grows fat.
I know Love is so great
That a fault he'll forgive,
Like Simon the Mage,
Presuming, excessive!
He claimed to be Jesus,
He tried to fly heavenwards in his great pride,
And God humbled his rashness and temerity.
My pride however is only in love,
Mercy must succour me, pity prevail.
I admit freely
That my words have been rash.
If like the Phoenix
I could rise from ash
I'd set myself aflame!
Such is my vileness, my false, lying words.
I'd rise again in weeping and tears
There where is beauty and virtue and youth –
Only mercy is lacking to make up perfection.
My song will speak for me
Where I dare not draw nigh,
Nor look directly,
So base and contrite am I:
None will plead for me.
Oh, More-than-Lady, after seven long years
Now I return to you, suffering and in pain,
As the stag turns to die midst the cries of the hunt.
Alas, you care nothing, you have forgotten love!

My lady has such virtue that the day I see her
I cannot fail.

Meanwhile Camar's wound had healed, but she was still so weak and thin that she seemed to be nothing but spirit, and they could not get her to eat. After a few days had passed, the King, thinking to make her better, ordered that she should be taken to the city. She was taken from her bed and at her request she was sat at a high window overlooking the orchard. There she sat for a long time watching John, who was digging there, while her mother begged her to eat something so that they could take her to the city in a litter. When the slaves were called to make ready the litter, poor Camar ordered that they should prepare it there in the orchard, close to the wall below her window, so that she could watch while they arranged everything. And because they did not do it to her mother's satisfaction, Fatima went down to set the litter right.

Finding herself alone, without her mother, and knowing that she would be taken to the King and would never see John again, she cried out with a loud voice, saying 'Oh granddaughter of Abas, King of Tyre and Sidon, niece of Acrisius, King of the Argives, and daughter of Belus, King of many kingdoms! You who swore on the ashes of Sichaeus to be faithful to your husband after his death and then, fleeing for fear of your brother Pygmalion, broke the promise made to the royal ashes for a new love which against all reason grew within you! I am ashamed to have been born in your Carthage because of your inconstancy, of which Virgil wrote. If it had not been for your second deed, by which you set right your great error by your death so that you were not twice a false liar, I would not call myself your compatriot nor wish to be known as a Carthaginian lover. I, Camar, your daughter, following the footprints of your second burning passion, shall come to serve you in the unknown realm, for it is not right that so noble a queen should wander alone among souls born of noble blood. I know that many hundreds of years have passed while you have awaited some vassal of yours who would dare to set out in the same path as you took in your intrepidity, to follow the light which shone in your heart. It is true that it was not too great a thing for you to die for love, since to think of dying and to die was the work of a moment, and execution was not preceded by deliberation. But it is no wonder that you chose to die for a man worthy of your love, your peer and your equal, especially because he left you and no longer wished for your company. You chose to die as one in despair, for whom all remedy had disappeared, unreasonably, in a frenzy so great that you died not knowing what you did. Thus it should not be accounted a virtue to you for you were merely unwilling to hear the shameful word 'rejected'; and that alone excuses your wicked severity. But I, punished and tormented by the insane flames that parted your sorrowing soul from your

244

tearful body, I pray and beseech you to receive my soul which comes to serve you, not through a sudden whim but after long and mature deliberation taken by me during many days. I know for sure that Artemisia wept as I do, but by her tears she conquered and Madreselva, her adversary, died of grief in prison. Alas, this deed of mine is not like that of Arachne, who was turned to nothing by the goddess Athene, but it will be a cruel and harsh death which, however, will put an end to my suffering. So, most dear lady and queen, do not think that I come to you through longing to see you because, if you will pardon me, I should happily live here with one of my slaves for ever. Since I cannot do so, I prefer to come to join you rather than to deny the faith that in my heart I have pledged to him. So John, get ready your arms and make them my death-bed. Receive me, Lord, for I come to you. I am a Christian and my name is Joanna. Commend my soul to your God, and let my body find a grave in your country.' And she threw herself from the high window to the low ground, her head struck the edge of the litter and the bones of her skull were shattered into several pieces, her brains spilt out in many places, and on the litter she died.

Her uncles, who were close at hand, ran to the stairway, but as they reached it she was already dead. Her wretched mother, who had no other treasure than her daughter, began a long lament over her body, rending her veil, tearing her hair and her clothes, and longing to die. Camar's uncles restrained her but they too were weeping piteously, and among them all was nothing but tears and weeping which grew ever greater. On the one hand they remembered the death of Faraj, on the other they saw the death of Camar, and they had no hope for their own lives because they thought that as soon as the King knew of it they would all die; and their sorrow was the greater on this account. Some lamented the misfortunes of the past, others those of the present, others those to come, so that their spirits were afflicted and they had no moment of relief or repose. They feared the King's fury and the consequent severity of harsh execution, and if they could have died then and there they would not have asked God to prolong their days.

★

The King learnt of Camar's death and of all that she had said, and so he knew with certainty that he had lost her on account of the slave, and he was so angry that he blazed with flaming fury. He sent for her mother and uncles, who came and gave him an account of the manner of Camar's death; and he ordered that the slave John be brought before him, together with the girl's body. As soon as the

245

King saw him he said 'Tell me, slave, did Camar fall into your arms?' 'No, sire', replied John. 'Once the litter had been prepared I went back to digging. When I heard shouting I looked round and I saw her fall through the empty air, twisting down from the window. I ran to help, but I was too late – she was dead before I reached her.'

With the King was an ambassador from the King of Aragon, a very noble and valiant knight named Ramon Folc of Cardona, whom the King honoured and made much of. He saw that the slave had the noblest appearance that, in his opinion, any man had ever had, and he looked at him closely and was as pleased as he could be with what he saw. The King was raging with fury, and ordered that the slave and Camar should at once be thrown to the lions. Sir Ramon Folc said to the King 'Sire, allow me to speak to him for a moment'; and taking him aside he said to him 'Tell me, friend, where are you from?'. 'I will tell you, sir,' answered John, 'on condition that you never tell my name to anyone in the world.' 'Friend,' said the Ambassador, 'have no fear. Tell me who you are.' 'Sir,' he replied, 'my name is Curial.' The Ambassador looked at him well and asked 'Are you the man who was in the tourney at Melun with the King of Aragon?' 'Yes', said Curial. 'You surely shall not die,' said the Ambassador, 'or I shall die with you this very day.' 'And who are you, sir', asked Curial. 'I am a knight of the King of Aragon,' he said, 'and your friend, even if I have never seen you before now.' The slave took heart.

'Come, come, it is time', said the King. 'You shall see the finest and fiercest lion that has ever been seen.' 'Sire,' answered the Ambassador, 'I beg you to grant me a favour.' The King said he would, but that he must not ask for the slave's life. The Ambassador replied that he would not do that, but begged him that since he was not taking from the lion his natural weapons he should not deny the man his artificial ones, and that he should order that he be given a sword and a shield. Very reluctantly the King agreed, and so the slave was given a good sword and a shield and then, his other clothes being taken away, he was put into the enclosure wearing only a shirt.

The unfortunate Camar, quite naked and hardly looking like a human being, had already been put in the enclosure, tied to a stake so that she would be upright. The Ambassador saw another sword and shield beside the King's couch, and in a trice he seized them, took off his doublet and went to the balcony where the King stood. When the King saw him he said 'What do you want to do?' 'You will soon see', said the Ambassador. 'The slave will not die without me.' As matters stood thus, and the King was ordering that the slave should be taken out of the enclosure, the lion had already come out, and although Sir Ramon Folc, seeing this, tried to jump down, the King held him back by main force.

When he saw the lion, the slave set his back against the stake to which Camar was tied so that the lion could not approach her. The lion did not come straight towards him but went off towards another part of the enclosure but still looking at him. Then Curial said in the Arabic tongue 'Camar, as it is said that you died for me, to give you what reward I can I promise that I will die before the lion comes near you' and, raising his arm, he brandished the sword. The lion, seeing his movement, came swiftly towards him. Curial waited with the shield before him and the sword raised, with his gaze so steady and his expression so confident that everyone was amazed. The lion looked at him, and at the brightness of the sword which was flashing in the sunlight, and began to be a little bewildered. Curial gave a great shout and rushed at the lion and reached it in two strides, striking it such a mighty blow with his sword across the eyes that the lion turned to flee. But Curial gave it another blow across its back, which nearly cut it in two.

When the King saw the lion was dead he thought he would die of rage, and ordered another to be brought. The Ambassador told the King that he was cruel, and begged him for mercy for the slave. The King was very ill disposed to grant this. But there was a Spanish knight there, Don Henry of Castile, who led a thousand Christian horsemen in the King's service, and he begged the King to grant this favour to Sir Ramon Folc. The King, hesitating not only what to do but also what to say, said 'Well then, I have ordered another lion to be brought. If the man wins, he will be quit and you may take him away.' Sir Ramon Folc was longing to jump into the enclosure, and Don Henry said to him 'If you jump, I shall too.' The King begged and commanded them both not to move, and restrained them with great difficulty, for as a matter of honour both of them would have faced any kind of danger.

The lion came out. John, who had already wiped his sword on the body of the other lion, looked the second one in the eyes as it came straight at him; but he did to the second what he had done to the first, or worse. The two knights ran into the enclosure. Sir Ramon Folc took off a very rich mantle and put it on the slave, but in a flash Curial took it off and placed it on Camar, covering her naked body with it, and kneeling on the ground before her in tears, he said 'Oh Lady Camar, God has given me no grace save in your life. If you see it, accept this small service from your slave, who is innocent of your death.'

★

The King had the slave brought to him and asked him whence he came, and he answered that he was from Normandy and that his name was John. The King asked him many questions about Camar's death, and he continued to answer that he knew nothing about it. Then the King said to him 'Go now; in honour of these knights who have entreated me for you, I make you free. Henceforward go where you will, but do not remain in my kingdom for more than two months.' Curial and the knights thanked him, and Curial asked for Camar's body, which the King granted. It was taken from the enclosure and carried with great honour to the Ambassador's house, where it was embalmed and anointed with myrrh, with all the attendant requirements, and laid in a rich coffin, and later it was taken to Christian territory and honourably buried.

The Ambassador said to Curial 'More than anything in the world I have wanted to meet you, and I swear to you that I have wished for your company more than that of any knight living. God be praised, who has allowed me to find you. My name is Ramon Folc of Cardona, and as long as I live I am ready to serve your honour and pleasure. I have money here with which you can equip yourself, not as you are accustomed to do nor as your valour merits, but you may at least accoutre yourself in a small way.' And he had some of his own clothes brought to dress him. But Curial said to him 'Sir, I would not for the world take anything, nor do I wish to relinquish at the moment the poverty in which I find myself.' Then the Ambassador asked him how he had been captured, and Curial told him the whole story, and how he had a fellow captive whom he did not wish to forget, and that he had enough money to pay his ransom. And the Ambassador took steps to free the other slave, who called himself Berenguer, so that both slaves had their freedom.

The Ambassador looked closely at Berenguer and thought that he knew him, and so he said 'Where are you from, friend?' Berenguer began to laugh, and answered 'Do you not know me? I have not forgotten you!' 'I have surely seen you before,' said the Ambassador, 'but I cannot remember who you are.' Then Berenguer said 'My name is Galceran de Mediona.' With a loud cry the Ambassador said 'My cousin! And you were a slave and neither I nor any of your kinsmen knew of it! Blessed be God that I have found you! In all Catalonia it is thought that you were dead. God be praised that it has fallen to me to find you! Come with me, or at least I will take the good news to Catalonia, and your mother, who thought to lose her mind and even her life because of you, will rejoice in what I shall tell her of you.' Galceran told him that on no account would he leave Curial then in that state, for he knew well that he for his part wanted to return home in the condition of a captive: however, if God gave him long enough life it might well be that he would go to see her.

Great was the Ambassador's joy in finding his kinsman, and he did him much honour (as you know, all the family of Pallars is descended from the lineage of the Mediona, who were the head and founders of all that house); and he asked him why Curial had been unwilling to accept money or clothes or anything he wished to give him. Galceran told him that he thought that he wanted to return to his own country as a captive, so that he would not be recognised. 'As for you,' said the Ambassador, 'I know that you cannot be allowed to appear like that, to my shame and that of all your kinsmen!'; and he at once ordered clothing and money to be brought, and asked him to accept them. Galceran answered that he had not become Curial's companion to move an inch away from what Curial chose to do, and so he would follow only where it pleased Curial to lead. The Ambassador tried again to persuade and beg Curial to accept something from him, adding that if he were in Curial's position he would take from Curial or from any other knight who wished to succour him in such circumstances. Curial answered that for the present he should allow them both to continue to look poor, and that it was necessary for him to return thus to his own country, and he could do nothing else.

The Ambassador had heard about Curial and the sister of the Marquis, and he suspected at once that he was doing this on that account, and he said no more, so as not to trouble him further. Then Curial said to him 'Sir, you have done me a great favour and much honour in setting me free, and you have given me my life, which, had it not been for you, would now be over. I pray that God will reward you, since I cannot, and God grant that I may do something in your honour to repay the debt I owe you. Excuse us now, for we must go to the house of a merchant who is our friend. If we are seen with you we should be recognised, which I would consider a worse fate than was mine when I was a slave.' And after exchanging many offers and promises one to another they left that place and went to the merchant's house.

Sir Ramon Folc was very pleased to have obtained freedom for Curial and Galceran, and thought in his heart that he would be honoured for it wherever it was known; but however much he desired that honour it did not become him to say anything at all about it. The captives were very happy to have acquired their liberty, but on the other hand Curial was very sad because of Camar.

They stayed in the Catalan merchant's house, and discussed with him how they might leave Tunis, asking his advice, and in what way they could take with them the doubloons they had. The merchant answered that when the Ambassador had concluded his business

249

they could go with him in his large and well-armed galley as far as Ibiza, where there was a large ship carrying salt, which belonged to some Genoese merchants. He said that the Ambassador was so worthy a knight that if they asked him he would set them aboard that vessel with a safe-conduct, and they could go from there to Genoa and so to Curial's country. And that is what happened, and their money went aboard the galley. But Andrea di Negro denied that they had given a thousand doubloons into his care, affirming with oaths that he knew nothing of such slaves and that he had never received any doubloons from them.

The galley did not leave for some time because the Ambassador could not leave yet, so the Ambassador ordered the master of the galley to take the two slaves, with their possessions, to Genoa while he was concluding his business. So they left and sailed to Genoa, which they reached in a few days. The master of the galley had a kinsman who was a merchant in Genoa and had a business there, although he was from Barcelona, a wise man, industrious, loyal and of many virtues, and he was in correspondence with many merchants in Barcelona. The master, who had observed the honour paid to the slaves by Ramon Folc, and apparently knowing that one of them was Galceran de Mediona, commended them warmly to the merchant, telling him that one of them was Galceran de Mediona. The merchant was pleased, and gladly offered them his services; so with great secrecy they brought their possessions from the galley to the merchant's house. The galley, well and nobly rewarded, sailed away, and they remained, and rested there for several days.

★

After not many days had passed they left Genoa and came to Montferrat and lodged in the hospital. Every day they went to receive their share of the scraps given to the poor at the gate of the Marquis's palace, and as they waited they often sang. The Marquis came to hear of it, and ordered that they should be brought to him. When they came, the Marquis heard them sing, and the singing so pleased him, especially the song about the elephant, that his pleasure was wonderful to see. At once he sent word to his sister, who was lying sick, that there were two men who had been captives who sang very well, if she would like to hear them. Guelfa answered that she would, and so the Marquis ordered that they should be taken to her. Guelfa thought that Curial had escaped from the galley but that he had died, together with his companion, for the men who had been sent in search of them had said, though wrongly, that this was so, and Guelfa had suffered greater grief over this than she had for the

250

death of her husband. When the two captives were brought to her, she ordered them to sing, and they began to sing the elephant song. When Guelfa heard it she was very surprised, and she told them to sing it again, as they did. And were it not for the certainty that Curial was dead she might well have thought that one of them was him; but the assurances she had been given did not allow her to believe it, nor even to think that that was the case. Yet all the time she remembered Curial and what she had said to him as she sent him into exile, that unless the court of Le Puy and the faithful lovers there besought her, she would never forgive him; and she began to weep. She ordered Melchior to take the captives home to his house and to give them food and good clothes and alms, so that God would have mercy on the soul of him who had died in captivity.

So Melchior de Pando took them to his house and gave them food. He tried to give them clothes but Curial would not accept any, saying that they must first go to Le Puy-Sainte-Marie, and that perhaps when they had been there they would come back and then might take what he wished to give them. Melchior returned to Guelfa and told her that the captives had not wanted clothes or anything at all, and that he had asked them if they knew anything of Curial and they had said no.

Guelfa ordered him to tell them to come again, and when they arrived she commanded them to sing that song again, which they did. When they had sung it Guelfa called Curial to her and asked him where he was from and what his name was; he answered that he was from Normandy and that his name was John, and all the while he was speaking French. His beard, which came almost to his waist, and his terribly altered appearance made it impossible for Guelfa to think he could be Curial. However, she ordered him to speak the song, rather than sing it, which he at once did. When she had heard it, she asked who had made up the song. He answered that he did not know but that he had learnt it from some merchants in Tunis. 'Woe is me!' she said, 'I knew the man who made it'. 'If you knew him well,' answered the captive, 'you would not have sent him into exile.' 'How do you know that I sent him into exile?' asked Guelfa. 'I should know,' he answered, 'who have been a slave for seven years because of your anger.' And this he said in the Lombard tongue.

Then she looked at him closely and recognised the features of his face. 'Traitor!' she said. 'Who brought you to my house?' 'You, lady,' he replied, 'you sent the command that I should come.' 'Go away, go to your host's house, and do not come here again!' she said. Curial bowed, and reverently taking his leave returned, rather happy, to the house of his host.

As soon as Curial had turned away Guelfa called to Melchior, and

251

wanting to appear angry, although she was not able to, she said to him 'And do you know who he is, that captive to whom I was speaking?' 'No, madam', answered Melchior. 'Well, ask him and he will tell you. Your guest is not what you think.' At this Melchior knelt down and said 'Ah, madam, mercy, for God's sake! Tell me who he is.' 'Go to your house, and there you will find that false friend of yours, Curial.' 'What, madam? Is it he?' 'Yes, truly it is', she said. 'Alas, I had him in my house and did not know him!' and he ran home and found Curial there and embraced him and kissed him and wept for joy with him; and he told him what he and Guelfa had done after he went away.

The Abbess could not restrain herself as soon as she heard the news, but secretly left the convent and came to see him, and it was natural that their joy was great, so great that they could not govern it in any way.

Guelfa, in great trouble, sent for the Abbess, and she was found in Melchior's house. She went to the lady, and with her face all red told her the things she had learnt from Curial, begging her to send for him, for without fail he would be able to acquit himself of the unjust charges made against him, and that in any case he was innocent. 'My dear friend,' said Guelfa, 'I am very happy to know that he is alive and I am sorry for the bad times he has had. And I am certain that if I were to listen to him he would be able to cover up his errors, rightly or wrongly. But, please God, I will see him and hear him no more. I am sorry for what has happened, although my conscience is clear because it happened by chance; but I will keep my vow and will not break faith with God, since I have made a promise. Tell him at once to leave this place so that nothing is known of his return. Let him go where he will, in God's name, and lose all hope of me, for I vow again to God and the Virgin Mary that as long as I live I shall not shift from the resolve that I made when I sent him away.'

Abbess	Where are you sending him? Where do you wish him to go? Name some place where you would want him to live.
Guelfa	Let him go where he will. The world is large and wide, and there is still room in it for him, as there has been until now.
Abbess	Yes, but if you order him where to go, he will go there.
Guelfa	I gave him orders when I thought he was mine; now I will not, because I have no right to.
Abbess	I tell you, madam, that he is yours, and will be as long as he lives. The unfortunate Camar, who refused a king and lost her life for his sake, is proof of this.

Guelfa	She ill deserved her death, because she killed herself for a cruel and ungrateful man. If she had known him as well as I do, she would have preserved her life better.
Abbess	She died, to be sure, for the most faithful man in the world, and although he was the cause of her death it was not his fault, for he could not do her wish and keep the faith he had pledged to you.
Guelfa	So according to you, I killed her?
Abbess	You did not kill her, but she would not have died had it not been for you!
Guelfa	Woe is me! It only remained for the soul of that silly Moorish girl to be laid to my charge! Would to God that she were alive and that Curial was happy with her!
Abbess	Curial can only be happy with you.
Guelfa	And, as I told you, he will not be happy with me.
Abbess	Since you are so eager for him to go away, have pity enough not to send him to beg for alms at people's doors. Give him enough money to go away in some reasonable state, until God wills that his ill-luck comes to an end, for I do not believe any man was ever born into the world as unlucky as this one.

Guelfa sighed and said 'I have had no more luck with him than he with me. No more of this. Go, and let Melchior give him what he needs for a company of twenty horsemen and sufficient to maintain himself. And he must give him the jewels and clothes that he left in pledge when he went away. Let him go in God's name and seek his fortune, not hoping for pardon from me except in the way I have said. Let him have silence in his mouth, and not write to me nor care anything about me; for I have hated him utterly, and the more you speak to me about him, the worse his case stands.'

The Abbess took her leave and went to tell Melchior Guelfa's wishes. The good old man at once restored to Curial all his possessions – and he would have given them without her command. Then between the three of them they discussed and arranged many things. Then when Curial had set himself in decent order and they had decided what he should do, he and his companion departed, well provided with money and bills of exchange. The good old man accompanied them for a day's journey, during which Curial told him all about the treasure that he had in Genoa, and they determined that in a few days it would all be transferred to Melchior's house.

★

Curial went to Marseilles and there he began to equip himself, and thence to Avignon, where he bought more furnishings and increased his company; and he continued through France until he had twenty horsemen. He went to Le Puy-Sainte-Marie and kept a novena in the church; and he stayed there for a time, taking what pleasure he could.

Meanwhile Melchior recovered Curial's treasure, and when he saw it he judged that Curial, although he lacked vassals and land, was one of the wealthiest lords in the world, and he was glad for him. Curial too was mindful of his wealth; and believing moreover that he had won back Guelfa's favour, he took to a soft and lascivious life as though he had been an archbishop or a great prelate, forgetting that he was a knight and a learned man. Banishing both military discipline and vigilant study, he spent all his time in banquets, entertainments and revels, in rich clothes and other vanities, and in the acts of Venus. Such was his study and his sport and all his delight, and in short he gave no thought to anything other than these irksome pleasures.

While he was engaged in this way, so that anyone who came to know him judged him a mere glutton and a man lacking all virtue, dedicated only to the dishonour and vexation of the vices of the flesh, there appeared to him one night in a dream the following vision. In a large and sumptuous palace decorated with vine-leaves and grapes, that god whom the pagans called Bacchus, son of Semele, the god of knowledge, manifested himself to Curial, amid a great company of people in the manner and order that follows.

In front of the god but to his left there stood a queen, with a young, girlish face and a crown, not very precious, on her head, surrounded by many children, some of them reading, others weeping. The queen had a whip in her right hand, and in her left a crust of bread. Before her stood four fair maidens, whose names were embroidered over their breasts, so that Curial knew the names of each, which were Orthographia, Etymologia, Diasyntactica and Prosodia.

Beside her, but nearer to Bacchus, was another queen, with a sharp face, who could not be still; and she held two snakes, one in either hand, which continually tried to bite one another and indeed would have done so if the queen had not held her hands apart so that they could not. Their tongues flickered so swiftly that each seemed to have seven tongues. In front of her stood three maidens, also with their names written across their breasts: Probabilis, Demonstrativa and Sophistica. Next to her was another queen, clad in many different colours but very richly apparelled, and she was singing so gaily that it was a great wonder. In her hand she held a paper on

254

which was written music and words, which she continually studied and emended with a pen. Before her stood three beautiful maidens who, according to the letters on their breasts were called Judicialis, Demonstrativa and Deliberativa.

Beside her and nearer to Bacchus stood another queen, who held a level in one hand and a pair of compasses in the other, and three maidens were in front of her, whose names, according to the letters on their breasts, were Altimetria, Planimetria and Subeumetria.

Beside her, and closer to Bacchus, was another queen, playing on an organ and singing with such great sweetness of melody that I do not believe any better sound or better song has ever been, is, or shall ever be. In front of her were three maidens singing with different tones but in harmony with her, and certainly if the angels were singing before the Saviour they could produce no greater sweetness; and the names of these maidens, according to their lettering, were Organico Flatu, Harmonica Voce and Rhythmica Pulsu.

The seventh and last queen, who stood closest to the god, held a sphere in her hand and a quadrant at her breast, and with one hand held high she was gazing at the sphere, and her sight was so keen that it penetrated and passed beyond the heavens. And before her she had two maidens, called Motus and Effectus. Behind the god there was such a throng of people from so many parts and such remote lands that were it not that they all spoke Latin they would never have understood one another. At the foot of the first queen sat Priscian of Caesarea, Uguccione of Pisa, Papias, the author of the *Catholicon*, Isidore of Seville, Alexander of Villedieu and many others; and in the same way the other goddesses had many servants and followers in great number, whom for the sake of brevity I shall not name.

But when Curial saw beside the last goddess Hercules, the son of Jupiter and Alcmena, who while he lived was the strongest and wisest man in the world, clad in a lion's skin, and with that terrifying face, he was filled with fear; never before had he felt fear, except of Hector son of Priam, and now of this man. However, he approached Bacchus, who gave him assurance, and kneeling before him Curial paid him great reverence, offering himself as his servant.

Bacchus received him joyfully and said the following words to him: 'Curial, you have received honours and advancement in the world through me, and through me you have become aware of what is reason and what justice. I favoured you greatly in your studies, and seeing your disposition it pleased me to dwell within you and to ensure that these seven goddesses accompanied you and instructed you, each one in her competence; and as long as you loved them they did not leave your company. But now the truth is that you have driven them from your house with shame, you have forgotten them,

255

have turned your back on them, giving up your life to lascivious things ill-befitting you and living in vice, so that you have become a stinking sepulchre full of corruption. You who shone in the world both for your chivalry and your learning have now won ill-repute in those places where you are but newly known, and if you do not return to your former ways this will become even more the case. I beg, require and warn you to return to your studies and to give honour to these goddesses who have honoured and favoured you, and to leave the life that leads men to penury, shame and dishonour. Do not exchange the divine and eternal gift of learning for earthly and temporal brutishness and filth. St Gregory has told you, if you have read him, "When you contemplate eternal things, temporal things become despicable". Let these goddesses, who with reason complain of you, return no more before me on this account, else you may be sure that Camar's treasure will not profit you as much as your ingratitude and thanklessness will harm you.' And so saying, he departed.

When Curial awoke he was full of wonder, and he thought well over what he had dreamed; and he judged that Bacchus had spoken truly. As soon as it was day he sent for books in all the disciplines and returned to study as he was wont, considering as wasted all the time he had spent without study.

★

The news that Curial had returned spread everywhere, for many who had seen him at Le Puy and in other places in the kingdom of France spread it in all regions. When the Marquis came to hear of it he showed great pleasure, and indeed he was very glad. Thinking that his sister did not know of the report, he went to tell her that Curial had been seen, and she laughed at him, saying 'Wretch, how can that be, for it is seven years since he was said to be dead. This is a greater miracle than the resurrection of Lazarus, for that was four days after he died, and this is seven years! I tell you, I have never heard such a miracle!' 'He did not die, it seems,' said the Marquis, 'but he was a captive in Moorish territory. God helped him and he has escaped, with honour, I believe. May God fail me in my hour of need if it was not a great pity that such a knight should be lost in such a way. I feel greatly to blame that I took no steps to look for him and redeem him, for he deserved it of me.' 'Now he will be able to tell good from bad', replied Guelfa.

So the Marquis wrote to him at once and sent one of his gentlemen to him, begging him to accept his help in everything he had need of, and making him many offers. When the squire was about to leave, the Marquis told his sister that he was sending him to Curial, if she wished him to take any message. Guelfa however answered 'Not I. It is enough for me to know that he is well, as you have said, and we shall know that with more certainty from the squire.'

The squire departed and rode until he found Curial, who was at Angers. He knelt to him, and gave him the letters from the Marquis, which gave Curial great pleasure so that he honoured the bearer of them and gave him clothing and money. He wrote back to the Marquis at once, thanking him for his offers, and saying that he was sure that the Marquis would help him even if he had not sent to say so, because he was his former retainer and his loyal servant; and that he should command him in whatever he wished, because he would seek to please him in all that he could, and would do more for him than for any man in the world. And so the squire, having learnt much about Curial's deeds, and very happy with the treatment he had received from him, returned rich and contented to Montferrat.

When he had delivered the letters he spoke of Curial with affection beyond words, and everyone rejoiced except the two old men. They were still unable to bear with patience that the squire should speak so well of Curial, and they muttered and said in private places that he lied. But the squire knew nothing of this and continued in the same way. Guelfa felt great joy in her heart, and although she asked the squire no questions, she liked to listen to him, and thought she would be driven to despair by the old men's grumblings. They, thinking that she hated him, said all the ill they could of him, and although Guelfa laughed she certainly was not pleased, and showed them no favour and each day kept them away from her a little more.

So things continued until Fortune grew weary of persecuting Curial and, while not repenting of the ill she had done him, determined to turn to favouring him again. Although Fortune observes no order in her actions nor justifies her cause, she cannot harm the diligent sage as she can the heedless fool; indeed, it often happens that those who persevere may defeat her and stand firm against Fortune, not perhaps doing so well as if she were their friend and helper, yet not as ill as if they submitted on their knees before her and resigned their affairs to nature. So she herself sought a way to raise Curial up again, as she had begun to do in the theft of the doubloons; and seeing that she could not succeed without the favour of Venus, although she was rather angry with her she decided to petition her that they should both together help the knight. So Fortune went off to the kingdom of Cyprus and climbed to the temple of Venus. As she approached its doors, she knelt, and spoke in the following manner: 'O heavenly pearl! O resplendent Diana!

257

O Lucifer, who precedes the sun and proclaims to the world the coming of day! O Hesperus, who descends into the kingdom of Hesperia, sometimes later and sometimes sooner, as necessity requires! Behold me here, repentant of all that I said in my rage against you and against your excellent son. Look well upon me, turn your merciful eye upon me, contemplate me with the benignity and mildness which you showed to him who violated the mouth, for whom the reply was "If we slay those who love us, what shall we do to those who bear us mortal hatred?" I, your devoted servant, crave your pardon a thousand times, and beg that you will not emulate the cruelty of the Fates, but be merciful to me. You are wont to pardon those who do not ask for pardon; how can you then deny it to me, who beg it on my knees? I acknowledge your divinity, and I am certain that there is no one in the world who can appeal against your sentence but, whether they will or no, what you ordain must be done throughout all the world. So great is your power that you can circle the world in a moment of time, you enter into every man's heart and induce him to accomplish what you command. I say induce, because your might is pleasing to all who feel it, and if it so happens that some speak ill of you, it is because your son has not wounded them with his golden arrow but hates them, and will not welcome them into your royal palace. I, who persecute and ill-treat the righteous, who give no thought to my deeds, neither see nor hear entreaties, nor have any spirit of mercy, but only will, which I use as I please, I have now wearied of persecuting a valiant knight and wish to turn my wheel, and as I have kept him low and downtrodden now desire to raise him to the very height of my sphere: and so I have begun to do. And I wish to pray you, and I do pray, that you yourself will beseech your son that with his golden dart he strike the Lady of Milan in the deepest part of her heart, and fire her with such ardour that she can nowhere find repose. May she long for this knight, and against her will seek out a way to win him, and may a day seem a year to her as she hopes and waits; may she beg those who have begged her on his account, and may they be reluctant to grant her prayer: let them make the time longer, and behave towards her as she has towards them. Let her learn that the vows and promises she has made which offend against your divine jurisdiction, without your permission, cannot be kept any longer than it pleases you.' And she fell silent, awaiting a reply.

There was little delay before a sweet and gentle voice issued from the temple saying 'My very dear friend, I have heard your prayer: what you ask shall be done.' Thereupon Fortune went her way.

★

At this time there was in London a valiant Breton knight called Guillaume du Chastel. He dare not enter the kingdom of France because he had done something to displease the King, and so for many years he had been living in England. Both in reputation and in fact he was the strongest and most valorous knight to be found in all the kingdom of France, and in England he had no peer or equal. His brother had been Bertrand du Chastel, the knight who had fought Curial when he was making his way to the tournament at Melun as a knight errant.

As a result of that combat, which we described in the second book, after he had left the convent Bertrand du Chastel had lost first his reason and then his life, and because of this Guillaume du Chastel, being his brother, had angry feelings against Curial; and when he learnt that Curial had returned, he sent a herald to him with a letter in which he demanded satisfaction by combat in the presence of the King of England (since Guillaume dare not go over into France). Although Curial wrote twice to excuse himself from such an encounter, explaining the whole truth of the matter between himself and Bertrand, nevertheless Guillaume, who was very bold and strong, very arrogant and extremely proud, replied to him in such a way, with such a choice of words, that, in accordance with the rules of chivalry, Curial would rather have died in captivity than continue to refuse to fight. So against his will he had to accept; and as soon as he knew the knight's wishes, he agreed both to his choice of arms and to the choice and nomination of the judge. The weapons chosen for the battle were the common ones of war, axes, swords and daggers, on foot; and the length of the weapons was also determined, and the King of England named as judge. Curial wrote that he was content with all this, although according to the rules of combat and the rights or custom of chivalry the choice of judge and the designation of arms really belonged to Curial himself.

The Breton, in high fettle, went with his company to see the King, who was young and eager to witness the deed; and the King replied at once to Curial to come on a certain day to England, and to be in London on the day appointed for the battle. Curial received the letter, and after contenting the herald replied that he was willing, and straightaway prepared to make the journey. He travelled to London with the equipment that Guillaume had named and with only a small company, but he was welcomed and received and feasted by the King and many lords of that kingdom.

And because we are short of time I will come to the point, for we have already described sufficiently the ceremonies proper to these combats. The field was levelled and the lists prepared, but not with such solemnity as in France, for I think that at that time they did not use such great ceremony in England when two knights fought each other.

Curial knew that Guillaume had been speaking of him contemptuously and with no little abuse, and was threatening to kill him in the coming encounter, using intemperate words quite out of keeping with the custom of chivalry, and that he was arrogant and longing to fight him and to kill him, and even himself with him, before the appointed day. Whenever they passed near each other Guillaume would say insulting words about Curial in order that he should hear them. One day when Curial was walking past Guillaume in the King's palace and Guillaume said something of this kind, as he had done many times, Curial went up to him and in the presence of many notable people said to him 'Guillaume, if you were to remember that very soon you and I are to give account to one another for what we have said and done, you would not speak as you do. So God help me, the words which you utter are not befitting a knight such as you believe yourself to be. If you are as willing to act as you are to speak, ask the King to shorten the delay, and let the day be tomorrow. Or else, you have a dagger and so have I: let us leave the King's house now and settle the matter. Or else be silent when I pass you because, as I have said, your words are those of a fool rather than those of a wise knight.'

Guillaume was furious, indeed he was raging with anger, and wanted to go outside with him; but the gentlemen who were around them held him back by force. Hearing the disturbance, the King came towards them and asked what was going on.

Guillaume knelt and entreated him to let the combat take place on the following day. The King looked at Curial. He said nothing, but kissed the King's hand as though he had already consented. The King was surprised and asked 'Why do you kiss my hand?' 'Because I think that you have given your consent.' 'Oh!' said the King, 'this Lombard is a knowing fellow!' All those who were standing round marvelled at the cleverness of Curial, although he spoke with soft words and not with the fierceness and vehemence of the Breton.

So by the wish of both parties the King cited them for the next day, and sent for the weapons, and having approved them returned them to the knights as fair and irreproachable. The King was young and very easily offended, and he had been angered by Curial's words because the bystanders had all said that he was insolent; and confident of the strength and valour of the Breton, he put his hand on his head and swore that he would let the battle take its course to the end. The knights heard this and showed that it pleased them.

The next day the knights were in the field early in the morning, and after the usual ceremonies they began to move towards one another. I tell you, the fool learns much when God sends a master to teach him, and thus Guillaume learnt to tremble as he had not known before. They closed, and gave each other tremendous blows with the axes. Although Curial was strong, indeed extremely strong, he also had knowledge, he was able to control his body and his breathing, and he knew how to recognise an advantage in fighting: and when he saw it, he never lost it. The other man, reckless and foolish, expended all his strength with incredible rashness, and the longer they fought the more he strove and the more he tired himself. Curial struck him on the arms and on the hands so that the Breton began to flag, and compelled by weariness he drew back four or five paces. Curial did not follow him but stood where he was.

Weary and harassed, the Breton began to take a rest, of which he certainly had great need, while the other knight waited for him to move. The Breton, who should have returned to the fray, retreated a little further, and raised the visor of his helmet: and by all these signs Curial could see that things were going badly for the Breton. The King was of the same opinion, and so were all those who were watching the fight. When Curial saw that the Breton made no move, he said 'Why are you here, Guillaume? You were bolder than this in the King's chamber; now you need no one to hold you back.' Shamed by this slight, Guillaume hurriedly lowered his visor, and, eager for death, he rushed at Curial with quick steps and began to fight fiercely. Curial, who was by no means asleep, struck the Breton a mighty blow with his axe on the right hand, so that the Breton's axe fell to the ground. He reached for his sword, but Curial had already given him another blow, on the head, so hard that it doubled him up. Letting go of the sword, the Breton tried to seize Curial and to clasp him round, but Curial struck him again on the head so that the Breton could hardly remain on his feet. Then Curial hit him once more, so hard that he fell stretched out on the ground. Perhaps he was already dead; but Curial struck him two more mighty blows as he lay on the ground, which made his brains come out of his head in many places. The Breton lay still, Curial ceased, and the officials approached to examine the knight, found that he was dead, and went to the King.

The King ordered that Guillaume should be taken from the field and placed in a church nearby, and holding Curial quit, without honouring him or congratulating him on his victory, sent word to him that he should return to his lodging. Those who had accompanied him to the field, however, escorted him back to his lodging.

Curial straightaway ordered a ship to take him away; and the next day, when he wished to take his leave of the King, the King sent a message to say that he did not feel well, that Curial should go with God. Curial saw that he was not in favour there; he travelled to the sea in secrecy, to put himself into safety, and setting sail, returned to France.

News of this combat became known in France and in the neighbouring regions, and Curial was held in greater esteem than ever. The King of France, who loved Curial and hated the Breton, showed that he was very pleased with the result, and told everyone so. He wanted Curial to be his vassal so that he could give him advancement and show him favour; but Curial considered himself so wealthy that he did not give it any thought.

★

The King of France wished to hold a general court of his kingdom in Le Puy-Sainte-Marie, following the ancient and laudable custom of the kings of France his illustrious predecessors. It occurred to him to contrive that the Marquis of Montferrat, his wife and his sister should attend, and that perhaps he could bring about the marriage of Curial with the Marquis's sister. As he thought this over, he determined to bring it to effect, and he decided to celebrate his court on the first day of the coming May. He wrote to the Marquis of Montferrat, begging him earnestly to come to the celebrations and to bring his wife and sister. When the Marquis received the letters he took counsel, and it was decided that he should certainly go, for three reasons: first, because it would give great satisfaction to the King; secondly, because he could settle the matter of Anthony, Monseigneur; thirdly, because it might be that the King would provide a husband for his sister. Accordingly, he replied to the King that to serve him, he was ready to attend the solemn celebration of his noble court. And the King was very pleased.

But he had to change the day, because he learnt that the Turks had invaded the Empire and were waging war, and that many of those whom he had summoned would be going to a battle which had been agreed between the Emperor and the Sultan for the twentieth day of April. So he wrote again to say that those who were to have come to his feast on the first day of May should come instead on the day of St Mary in the coming August. And he wrote this to all those who wished to honour him on the said day: and all replied that they would do so with pleasure.

★

When Curial heard of the battle or contest that was to take place

262

between the Emperor and the Sultan he quickly sent for some of the doubloons he had brought from Tunis and meanwhile invited many knights and gentlemen, asking them to take part in the battle in his company and at his expense. He had a good and joyous response, and as soon as the money arrived he paid his men and departed. The knights and gentlemen who were already prepared left also when they had received their pay, and made their way to the frontier where there were most Turks: and it is said that they were the first foreigners to arrive at that frontier. The Emperor learnt of the arrival of Curial with a thousand men-at-arms and was very glad, knowing that he was one of the best knights in the world, and he wrote to Curial praising his arrival, and made him many offers, as was reasonable.

Curial studied the manner of fighting of the Turks, who would engage every day in hand-to-hand combat whoever was prepared to bear arms . . . They also skirmished in bands, and sometimes many different nations joined in skirmishing, so that it was more like a fight to the death than a skirmish. Curial observed them for many days, and he saw a Turk named Kiriçi, a very strong man, large of stature and captain of all the Turks on that frontier. He was a bold and enterprising fighter, who had killed many Christians in duels and was also so feared in the skirmishes that he could not find anyone willing to stand and fight him, for all the Christians avoided him, much as if he were a tempest or a thunderbolt. Such was his strength that all the Turks called him Hercules the Mighty. After Curial had watched him many times on various days and seen that no Christian would come forward to fight him, he was very angry, and he swore by St George that if the Turk showed himself the next day, he would fight him.

That night St George appeared to Curial and said 'Ah, knight, my friend! Today you swore to fight the Turk named Kiriçi. Go into battle in safety, and wear this cross of mine on your breast, for you will be the victor not only in this battle but in all that you undertake at the request of others. I entreat you not to challenge any Christian to combat; but if you are challenged, you will be the victor.' And he disappeared. When St George had disappeared Curial awoke and found a little white shield on his breast, with a red cross as bright as spurting blood. At once he rose from his bed and had the shield sewn to his doublet so that he should never be without it. And from thenceforward he had such devotion and such confidence in St George that he did not think any man in the world could constrain him.

The next day, as our Lord God had ordained and by the agency of the Fates, the unfortunate Turk, with many others, came to a

263

skirmish which had already begun, and showed himself to be a wonderful leader, captain and lord. He was treated with such reverence by the others that they could not have done more if he had been the Sultan. Kiriçi, who was very eager to fight, dismounted in front of his men. Curial armed, and as soon as he was ready he saw the Turk in a place convenient for a combat on foot, and that there were a lance and a mace close by for him. He saw too that all the Christians were looking at him but that none was bold enough to fight. Curial was greatly ashamed that the Christians should hold back in such a way, and he went forward and sent word to Kiriçi to move away from his men, and that he would fight him. Kiriçi asked who he was, and was told that he was a great foreign captain who had come with a thousand men-at-arms, so he sent his men further away, and ordered that none of them should move.

When they had exchanged various pledges and assurances, Curial showed himself, and the Turk, brandishing his lance and with the mace in his left hand, advanced towards Curial. Seeing him come, Curial, with a lance in his right hand and a good axe in his left, went towards the Turk. They exchanged lance thrusts, and although each struck the other in the chest, their trusty armour kept them from harm. Then they took their second weapon, the axe and the mace, and each began to beat the dust from the other's cuirass with such might that all who were watching marvelled. The Turk wore a helmet without a visor, Curial a basinet with the visor down, and as they were exchanging hard, rapid blows, Curial noticed that Kiriçi had no face-piece, so he struck him in the face with the point of his axe. When he realised that he was wounded, the Turk buffetted Curial most cruelly, showing his great power, and Curial knew that this was the hardest and fiercest warrior he had ever fought: but he continued to strike him in the face. The Turk was dazed and was losing a great deal of blood, and not knowing what else to do he let go of the mace and tried to grapple with his enemy. But Curial gave him no chance, giving him such a great blow on the head that he stumbled, and followed that with another blow so hard that he fell dead to the ground. Seeing that he did not move, Curial drew back, thinking that his soul was already in the kingdom of Pluto. When the Turks saw that Kiriçi was dead, in whom had been all their hope, they felt great sorrow, and they sent to ask Curial to give them his body so that they could bury it. Curial said that he was very willing, but that he wished to have his arms and armour. The Turks disarmed the soulless body and sent the armour to Curial, and Kiriçi's body was sent to his own land and buried honourably amid the general sorrow of his people. The armour of this Kiriçi was all of leather, edged with gold, with many pearls and precious stones, and so it was of great value.

Within a few days the Sultan learnt of the death of Kiriçi, and this was a great loss to him. He would rather have lost many others than this single man, who was a close kinsman, a great captain, a lord over many people, a valiant and strong fighter, the one and only hope of the Turks. They gradually began to withdraw from that frontier after Kiriçi's death, fearing the forces of Curial. But the Sultan was a valiant and bold knight, and he went in person to that part, and reinforced his men so that all felt safe, and those who had left returned in shame. The Emperor too heard the news with the greatest pleasure in the world, and when he knew that Curial had taken part in the fight he was very happy and felt sure that the knight would be the destroyer of all the Turks. He sent him a large sum of money, to pay him and his men, and he made him his Grand Constable and asked him to undertake the command of that frontier, for soon, or at the latest by the day fixed for the battle, he would join him. And he ordered that everyone should obey Curial – which was already the case without the Emperor's order.

★

At the same time, or at least with little delay, the news reached Montferrat that Curial was made Constable of the Emperor and Captain General of all his army on the Turkish frontier. They knew already that he had slain Guillaume du Chastel, and now they learned that he had killed Kiriçi, a knight of great renown, very experienced and famous, and all were glad.

The Marquis, with much warmth, passed on the news to Guelfa, and she, to show herself other than she was, answered merely 'My lord brother, do not be surprised at that, for we have always seen and known that God loves him and makes him win all the battles in which he finds himself. Did you not see how after seven years of captivity he came out with honour and won in a moment greater honours and greater favour than he had had before? What can be said of that captivity but that God wished to send him a scourge so that he should not think more highly of himself than he ought? I have heard that a noble Moorish girl, the daughter of the man who bought him, refused the hand of the king who loved her, and killed herself because Curial would not love her. So he whom God wished to help is helped and others strive in vain. This man cannot fail to become a great lord in the world.'

'By my faith, sister,' replied the Marquis, 'I am inclined to go to him, in disguise.' Guelfa answered that it did not befit his dignity,

265

and that he would come in the course of time, and then he should see him. Then the Marquis said, without thinking further, 'Indeed, sister, I shall go, whatever befalls, and I shall do three things: serve God, see Curial, and also win the love of the Emperor, which is no small thing.' And at once, swiftly giving his men their money, he set off, and in a few days he had joined the Emperor, who welcomed him warmly and made much of him.

As the day for the battle approached, the Emperor assembled all his forces and ordered them to proceed to the place where it was to be fought. He himself mounted and set off, and by stages the army gathered together in the appointed place, and a convenient site was sought, and well found, for the tents. When all were lodged and the camp provided with an infinite store of provisions, he ordered, in writing, that all who were to take part in the battle should come there. Among these was Curial, the Emperor's Grand Constable, leader and captain of many soldiers who had guarded the frontier and held it marvellously well and were glad of his company, and they would not leave him for anything in the world.

The Marquis, who kept out of Curial's sight in order not to be recognised by him as yet, observed the men who came with Curial, and saw how they were all content, and how the Emperor made much of him, and the kings and princes, dukes, lords and great barons paid him honour. He was troubled, and saw that he was nothing compared with Curial, and he would be even less if he were to declare himself to him; and he did not know what to do.

But the gentleman whom the Marquis had sent to Curial at Angers went to Curial without the Marquis's knowledge, and told him that the Marquis had come in disguise but with a considerable and worthy company, and that he had made his presence known to the Emperor alone. 'Tell me, friend,' said Curial, 'does he want me to know him?' 'I do not know,' replied the squire, 'but it would seem no rather than yes.' 'Go to him, then,' said Curial, 'and tell him that I know he is here, and that I will come to him straightaway.' And he sent a gentleman of his company to go with the squire so that when he returned he could show Curial where the Marquis was lodged. When the Marquis received the message he asked the squire 'Do you know where he is?' 'Yes, I do', answered the squire. And so the Marquis, seeing that the visit could not be avoided, went to Curial's tents.

It is true that he only wished to see Curial and to speak with him, and that he had come only for that purpose, but he had not wanted to see him so soon. He found Curial already preparing to go to visit him, and there was much embracing and rejoicing. When the lords who accompanied Curial saw him making much of the Marquis,

266

they too showed him great honour – otherwise they would have paid little attention to him; and indeed the Marquis had never before found himself so highly considered nor treated so well as he was that day. Curial begged him not to leave his tents, and to consider them as his lodging. And the Marquis took Curial's request as a command and agreed, and Curial saw to it that he was splendidly served, and gave him freely and sufficiently all that he needed.

Curial was well served, always with minstrels and great ceremony. He invited many great lords and gave great gifts, and these and other similar acts won him great favour and honour. When the Emperor, who already knew of the matter of Guelfa, learnt that the Marquis of Montferrat was lodged in Curial's tents, although he had a high opinion of Curial because of his merits he thought even more highly of him on this account, and showed him greater favour and gave him great gifts. The Marquis was amazed, and troubled, and did not know what to say, and he too strove as best he could to do and say things that could and would please Curial. So numerous were the great lords who thronged around Curial that the Marquis hardly had the opportunity to speak to him: but Curial would call to him, and seek out his company, and the Marquis was better pleased with this than if the Emperor had fêted him.

★

All the councils of war took place in Curial's tent; thither came the Emperor and kings, dukes and princes and all those who were called to the council. With common accord all agreed that Curial, who, as you have heard, was so great a knight and also Grand Constable of the Emperor, should command all that was to be done, and everything was committed to his charge. For so numerous was the multitude of great personages that it would be impossible for them all to agree, and all would be content with what the Grand Constable decided. This was the resolution of them all, and the Emperor, an old and indeed ancient man, since this was the general will, called Curial to him. Curial knelt before his sacred majesty, and the Emperor raised his arms and put them on Curial's shoulders, and said 'Constable, you have heard what has been determined. I commit to you the service of God and of all Christendom, which depends on the outcome of this battle.' Without waiting for his reply, all the kings and lords present praised him and swore to obey him and to follow his ordinances without question. And then they left the council.

Curial thus found himself not only honoured but with a heavy charge. At once he sent for the Emperor's secretary and learnt the total number of soldiers, the number of lords and how many men each had; and he would have liked to see them in the field so that he would have a better knowledge of them, but fearing Turkish spies, he did not dare order a review.

The Turks did otherwise, for when all were assembled together, they held a review, so that the Sultan could see the whole of his army. Curial, who was not asleep, having obtained a safe-conduct from the Sultan, went in the capacity of ambassador, to reach agreement with him on some points relating to the battle. By lucky chance it was the day the Sultan was reviewing his army, and because he had no fear at all of the Emperor, he gave no thought to the ambassador but rather took him in his company and showed him all his soldiers, conveying to him through the interpreters that if he had not seen enough he could come back again, and as long as they were in the field he could watch them as much as he wished. Having agreed with the Sultan that on the third day from then, which was a Monday, they should join in battle, Curial took his leave and returned to his own men.

When all those who were members of the council had gathered together, Curial described to them what he had seen and how the Sultan had behaved. They were all troubled, and looked at one another. Curial saw this, and showing the greatness of his heart, he said to them in a strong voice 'O excellent lords, let us have no fear of the great number of our enemies, which you have heard from me, for you have so many men of such quality that you could fight not only these but the rest of the world, and defeat them in a single day! I swear to you that since your majesty has been pleased to entrust to me this battle I shall be the victor; and I am sure that neither now nor at any other time can I be defeated, such is my destiny. Accordingly, let every man take heart, for the Turks will be defeated, slain and destroyed, and I shall soon be sharing out all their spoils amongst you. There is no further need for words except to say do not take in vain the grace which God gives you, but go forward with it; and if today you feast to celebrate your victory, I swear on my honour as a knight that you may do so in the certainty that you will not be disappointed.'

They were all somewhat comforted by this, and rising from council they only awaited the moment when they would be ordered forth to battle, since Curial had charge of everything. Curial looked to his command with great diligence and solicitude. He drew up a list of all his battalions, and they amounted to twenty-four. To each he appointed a good captain, renowned and strong, and early on Monday morning, just before daybreak, he ordered them into the field by the light of the moon; and all the battalions having been drawn up in prescribed order, when the sun began to rise the Imperial banners were already resplendent in the field. The old Emperor was full of joy when he saw all the lords ready and drawn up in prudent order, and taking his place on a lofty eminence, with some fortifications around him and worthy knights to guard him, he began to await the enemy, who seemed already to be in the field.

The Turks were not asleep either, and when their thirty battalions were in order they began to move to the attack. Against them came two Christian battalions mounted on swift horses and with an incredible longing to fight. They strike each other in the chest with lances, they unseat and kill one another, some fall this way, some that, and a fierce and cruel battle is engaged. The Turks throw in another two battalions, and against these Curial sends only one of his, which he himself leads. He strikes with his lance the leader of the Turks, with such force that it pierces right through him. The Christians lay about them with such vigour that it seems to them that the Turks are unarmed – those barbarians without the law fall and die, and their spirits go to the house of Pluto. The Turks send forward another four battalions, against which Curial uses three of his: they fight hand to hand, and there you might see a grim and terrible conflict. The Turks send in another six, Curial five of his, who face the Turks with an incredible thirst for battle, and there is a cruel and grim fight. The Turks turn back and the Christians can hardly pursue them, so great is the multitude of dead; they advance with difficulty over the lifeless corpses which lie on the ground. The shouts, moans and clatter are such that no man can hear another. The Turks advance all their battalions and begin to strike the Christians again with great force. Curial too advances his battalions and regains the ground that the Christians were beginning to lose. He takes his place in the centre, and with his invincible sword performs deeds worthy of remembrance, he runs hither and thither among the battalions, soaked in Turkish blood so that the red cross on his white surcoat is hardly visible. He gives a loud shout to his men who, hearing the voice of their valiant and noble captain, recover their strength and renew the fighting, raise their arms and strike down those unbelievers, whose spirits without faith leave their bodies, and countless numbers die.

The heat increases. The knights are brave and daring and well-armed, and they strike without mercy, giving blows without quarter, and of those there was no scarcity because with great liberality each man distributed his strength among his enemies. The horses were wading in blood, trampling on dead bodies which lay so deep that their hoofs never touched the ground. The Christians, who were of many different nations, rivalled each other in deeds which cannot be told or written: and it was well that they did so, for the Turks fought so valiantly that if it had not been for the mighty efforts of the Christians for a time they might have been defeated.

When the scouts came to Curial and told him that all the Turkish forces were engaged and that there were no ambushes, Curial, who had eight thousand men-at-arms concealed in reserve, who had not yet taken part in the battle, went to them, and as a sign of victory sent them forward, admonishing them to do well. The battle was in the balance and no one could tell which way the scales would go, when our knight, the very light of chivalry, thrust into the midst of the enemy with the eight thousand fresh troops. Wherever he saw the Sultan's banners, there he attacked with swift heart, right amid the throng of soldiers; and crying 'Lord St George, now is the moment for your help!' they tore down the banners, trampling them underfoot, ripping them to shreds, breaking up and destroying the thronging multitude of Turks. There you might see severed hands and feet fly to the ground, heads burst open, lungs and livers cut to pieces, groans and cries and lifeless bodies, and the noise of the blows and weapons was such that neither heaven nor earth heard such before.

I have read in Titus Livy of the victory that Hannibal had over the Romans, and that of Scipio over the Africans, and that of Catiline, and no less of Julius Caesar and of Pompey, but I think that if he had known of this one he would not have written that the others were greater. Here they were not fighting for tyranny, but only for the faith of Jesus Christ, which burned in the hearts of the Christians. Here was not merely a matter of bodies, but of bodies and souls together, and each man fought in defence of his faith.

When they saw the fresh troops coming to their aid, the other Christian forces, who through weariness were fighting feebly, took new heart and recovered their strength, and it seemed to them that they had done nothing all day. They flung themselves forward and penetrated the broken ranks of the enemy, who were already in disorder, slaying them without mercy. The wretched Turks turned to flight, and as most of them were weaponless they were pierced and transfixed by the sharp and cutting lances and swords of the Christians. They had already lost their banners, their best captains, and almost all of them were already dead. They took to the shameful help of flight, which makes cowards bold, for he who flees does not lack a pursuer. What more can I say? Those who in all that day had not dared to strike a blow or enter into conflict began to give chase, and now were the bravest and cruellest in striking those who could not defend themselves, and in killing those who on their knees begged for mercy, so that they could not have been held back by chains. But all were of service, and if there had been more of them the feat would have been no less great.

The Sultan, seeing that the day was wholly lost and that there was nothing he could do, took to flight, sorrowful and weeping. Long was the pursuit, but Curial, like a wise and diligent captain, led the Christians, holding them back so that they did not go too far, fearing that the Turks might re-form and that the pursuers might come to grief through greed in following up the desired and most welcome victory. An infinite number of Turks were slain, and many were the prisoners taken. Every victor, however, returned to his tent on the command of the captain.

★

Because Curial could find no trace of the Marquis, he was greatly afraid that he might be dead, and sorrowed greatly in his heart and that night he could not eat or sleep. The next day he sent spies to find out what the enemy was doing. He learnt that the defeated forces had scattered, each going his own way and fleeing as fast as they could, and those who had been able to escape were returning, with great difficulty, to their own lands.

Curial had the battlefield searched with great diligence, but the Marquis was not to be found among the dead nor among the wounded, and so he thought that the Turks must have taken him off as a prisoner. And this was the case; and by due stages, by agreement with those Turks who returned to redeem others, the Marquis was set free. Curial exchanged two important Turkish lords for him, and thus rescued him.

Then the booty was surveyed and equally distributed, and each took his share, carrying it back to his lodging with great joy. Curial, who could not abate the singularity of his magnanimity but exercised it each day more, graciously assigned his own share to the Marquis of Montferrat together with the part that was his by right, and when he had come, gave it to him freely and liberally. The Marquis sold what was not durable, and rejoiced all his life in great wealth and the very great honour which all paid to him, and content beyond measure, praising Curial highly, said everywhere he went that Curial was the best and greatest knight in the world. With these tidings he returned home early, and he added to them, that greater men than the Marquis of Montferrat lived in Curial's house and did him honour.

Great was the general rejoicing in Montferrat when their lord returned home. And Guelfa listened willingly to all the deeds that

Curial had done, and although in public she praised him very little, she extolled them in her heart and afterwards went over them with the Abbess and with Melchior, and held them in great esteem.

★

After the Emperor had won his victory over the Sultan and the other Turks, he returned to his own land, and having made many gifts to those who had served him, he dismissed them, and each taking his leave returned joyfully home. Curial too went to the Emperor to take his leave, telling him that the King of France wished to celebrate a solemn court at Le Puy-Sainte-Marie. Before the Emperor let him go he spoke to him thus: 'Curial, I am not able nor do I know how to repay the honour that you have brought me in this battle, which you alone have won. You have served our Lord God and have done a great boon to me and to all Christendom. I pray that our Lord, who is the reward for all good things, will reward you for it, for I cannot do so sufficiently. Here is my house, it is at your service and pleasure more than for any other man in the world. Count on my help wherever you are, and write to me, for indeed I shall not fail you but aid you as much as is in my power.' And having said this, he bid him go in the name of God.

Curial went to his lodging, and that evening he put all his things in order so that he could depart in the morning. All his men were complaining that the Emperor had not given him anything and they were discontented, speaking ill of the Emperor, who was without doubt the most open-handed, most fair and most liberal lord in the world, and had determined to benefit him. Accordingly, early in the morning, long before Curial could have departed, there was the sound of many people and of many beasts of burden, or pack-animals, at the door of Curial's lodging; and this was reported to Curial. The Emperor's chamberlain and treasurer came before Curial and said to him 'Lord Curial: the Emperor, knowing that it is in no way possible to reward you for the labours you have undertaken or to repay the honour you have procured him, could not find words to convey this to you; but asking a thousand pardons, he begs you to accept patiently this little present, which is a poor thing both for him to give and for you to receive in respect to the cause which moves him, what the Emperor should do, and what you deserve. The Emperor means well towards you, and if God gives him life he will remember it every year.' Curial accepted with great reverence, giving many thanks to his most exalted lordship for this great and precious gift, offering him his service whenever he could be of use. And the truth is that the Emperor had not left in his own house nor in those of his vassals any money, vessels or jewels of gold, or precious stones or pearls of great price, for they were all sent to Curial.

So Curial departed, more pleased than can be expressed, and with good and notable horses slowly made his way towards France by easy stages, and by the fifteenth of June he was close to Le Puy-Sainte-Marie. There he began to take his pleasure in that region, now in one town, now in another, and occupying himself in seeing to the preparation of trappings and many other such things for the coming great celebration. As the time was already drawing near, everyone began to set up tents, to erect stands and all the other things necessary for the occasion. Curial, not wanting to be recognised, set up tents in four different places so that he could be now in one, now in another and would not always have to go to the same place. And so everyone, well prepared, awaited the appointed day.

The meeting place was very large, surrounded by many stands and well provided with all things necessary, and I think that if it could always remain as it was then no one could ask for another paradise in the world.

★

We have left Guelfa far away from the things we have been relating, and since this work is hers it is right that we should make some mention of her.

Fortune, not forgetting her intentions towards Curial, appeared to Guelfa one night in a dream, accompanied by many of her servants. The evening before, Guelfa and the Abbess had been talking of the Marquis, who was then in Germany, and they did not yet know anything about the battle nor whether it had taken place or not. Guelfa was very anxious on her brother's account, and still more on that of Curial even though through shame she did not say so, and she was having bad days and worse nights. So she and the Abbess were closeted in her chamber and after much talking, wearied by their long sleeplessness, they fell into bed: and as soon as they were lying down, a strange sleep fell upon them so that it seemed to them they had never slept before. As they slept, the following vision appeared to them.

They found themselves in a most delightful meadow surrounded by an infinite number of trees, some full of blossom, others bearing fruit of various kinds, all deliciously perfumed; and the green of the meadow was so fresh that it seemed to them that they had never seen such a delightful place. Freed from all the sufferings they had undergone, their spirits felt a refreshment and a pleasure so great that, as

273

it seemed to them, nowhere in the world could they find so much or greater. While they stood silently in this paradise, listening to the celestial birds (they thought) which were harmoniously singing angelic songs in different kinds of melody, they saw approaching a goddess with a radiant face, showing great joy in her smile, with shining eyes which for their splendour seemed two brilliant stars. She was accompanied by knights and gentlemen in great number, and a copious multitude of ladies and maidens. This lady wore a mantle of various colours, embroidered with stars of silver and gold. She went towards Guelfa, who knelt to await her, and said to her 'Friend, know that to please the false old woman I have beneath my mantle, I have persecuted and ill-treated your loyal and valorous Curial until he thought he was lost, and had I not feared that Atropos would snatch him from my hands, to please this wicked old woman I should not have pardoned him yet. Know that I am that Fortune of whom so much is told. I have resolved to return Curial to his former estate, favour and renown, and even to higher estate, as you will soon know. For I have prevailed with Mars, that he shall have victorious arms, and with them he will enter this battle which is to be done between the Emperor and the Sultan. Mars will be beside him on the day of battle and will give him the lance of Achilles and the sword of Hector. Know that from henceforward I shall attend him with honours and favour above all others of my servants, and I shall give him copiously and freely of my gifts. By my order and command Camar gave him so much money, which your Melchior holds for him, that I do not think so wealthy a knight, however great a prince he may be, exists in the world today.'

When Guelfa heard her speak it seemed to her to be a celestial voice, but she answered 'Lady, I beg you of your mercy to show me the false old woman whom you say you have beneath your skirts'. Then Fortune opened her mantle, and as though she were shaking out or sweeping away rubbish, she threw out an old woman, very long and thin, with a beard, long, bushy eyebrows, her eyes circled by coarse lines and reddened and watery with rheum; she was wrinkled and colourless, so lank and skinny, with a neck like a guitar, with no flesh between skin and bone. She wore an ash-coloured robe of rough cloth, very old and faded, torn and patched; she was barefoot, and her swollen feet were bleeding in some places with yellowish blood. Her head, her shoulders and her hands were all a-tremble, and there was not a tooth in her head; saliva dribbled from her mouth and mucus from her nose. Her ears were like dried-up or withered peaches, and her fingers and toes and knuckles like two- or three-year-old shoots pruned from the vine. Her skin was falling from her body in flakes so that she resembled a vine whose bark was falling away. In short, she could not even be compared with an old, mangy monkey, or with anything else however vile and despicable.

When Guelfa saw her she drew back to get further away from her, and began to curse her. 'Have no fear,' said the old woman, 'and be silent, for I have been in your house a long time, and been honourably kept, according to my estate.' Guelfa asked 'What is your name?' 'In faith, do you not know me?' said the old woman. 'I was long your companion against Lachesis, and my shadow still touches you a little. Know that I am a poor woman, and I serve without pay, and my name is Envy.' 'Poor you are,' answered Guelfa, 'and unfortunate, and I pray God you will never dwell in my house or in any other, through you come so many evils to all men.' 'Come, come,' said the old woman, 'while I have such friends in your house, your two old men, I do not doubt that I shall have lodging wherever you are. I live most often in the houses of great lords, and I am venerated by persons of high estate, no less than if I were adorned with precious raiment.' 'As far as I can,' replied Guelfa, 'I shall surely forbid you entrance to my doors, and I shall throw out those two inmates, your friends, so that neither you nor they can exercise their profitable office in anything that concerns me.'

Then Fortune, who had been listening to all that was said, said to Guelfa 'Let those two old men remain in your house, dear friend, for even if they go away those who prosper will not lack those who envy them. They could have no worse punishment than to die with their envious thoughts. Do you wish to do worse to them than the contrary of what they desire? So I commend you to God. I must give way to another goddess who will soon, at my request, come to visit you.' And turning away, she disappeared.

Guelfa and the Abbess were still so heavy with sleep that they could not wake, and in that same meadow, while they were still wondering and amazed at what they had seen, another vision appeared to them. As they looked towards the east it seemed to them that the heavens opened and the star Diana, which precedes the sun announcing the coming of day, began to send out arrows of light which struck the eyes of the two ladies; and turning their gaze in that direction, they saw the resplendent Venus, who by many is called Lucifer, bright and very luminous, climbing the sky through the arc of the third heaven. Sending down a ray which lit up the earth, it set gently and softly on the fresh green grass of the meadow a most excellent lady, with an infant wrapped in her robe. And as she moved forward into the meadow you might see knights and gentlemen helping ladies and maidens to alight from their steeds and then with amorous kisses do them pleasant honour. Each one, taking his lady by the arm, gathered as closely as they could around the goddess, with such merriment that no tongue can describe it. At once minstrels began to play with such melody that I think even Orpheus and Mercury might appear unskilled in comparison with such sweetness.

The goddess who won primacy and superiority over all others by her resplendent beauty came towards the two ladies. Her head was garlanded with the eyes of Argus, full of unbearable radiance. She wore a mantle of crimson gleaming with sparks of gold, which seemed to the ladies to burn with so pleasing a fire that they thought it the greatest glory of paradise. From the fire sprang sparks and spirals of bright fire which spread over all parts of the world, and those who were touched by the flame suffered most sweet, indeed the sweetest, anguish, and they longed to suffer it more than was possible; and some who suffered never wished to be cured of the pain.

With an angelic voice the goddess spoke to Guelfa thus: 'O beloved friend! O ungrateful and thankless one! How can you not wish to remember how I have preferred you above all those whom I have called to my service, and how I gave to you as your lot one of the best and most noble knights in the world, who has loved and served you loyally? Despising the gifts which I, kinder to you than you yourself, had graciously bestowed on you, led by the lying tongues of two envious old men, false and deceitful, whom you have in your household, you made vows and promises against all conscience and in contempt of my divine jurisdiction, thinking to appropriate to yourself what pertains to me, which I would not permit to you nor to anyone else who might choose to try to do so. If I wished to treat you in accordance with your resistance and your ingratitude, I should make you labour fruitlessly for as much time as you, through your proud cruelty, caused Curial to remain a captive. Remember the fair Camar, who killed herself for him, because he was faithful to you and was suffering infinite toil for your sake. I now command that from henceforward you love him for as long as you remain in this world.' And opening her mantle, Cupid, whom she had concealed beneath it, wounded Guelfa's left side with a golden arrow, so cruelly that the whole shaft was hidden in the lady's heart and left no sign or mark to show where it had entered. At once Guelfa fell to her knees, and repenting of her past cruelty, offered herself willingly to do all that she was commanded by the goddess.

This Cupid, the son of the said goddess, was a young lad, all shining, dressed in golden feathers with great wings and a cloth before his eyes. He was deaf; and his face, feet and hands were as red as fire. In his left hand he held a bow, and at his side was a quiver full of white and golden arrows, and he continually let fly, sending his shafts to all parts of the world without seeing whom he struck. And when he had wounded the said lady, you might see great rejoicing and dancing; and it was granted to Guelfa and the Abbess to know all whom they saw. There were Pyramus and Thisbe making much of one another, Flor and Blanchefleur, Tristan and Isolde, Lancelot and Guinevere, Frondino and Brisona, Amadis and Oriana, Phaedra and Hippolytus, Achilles alone, threatening his son Pyrrhus, Troilus and Cressida, Paris and Viana, and many others whose names I omit for brevity's sake.

Day was approaching, and a celestial dew moistened the earth; the dream and the goddess vanished together. The two ladies lay in their bed, troubled in mind and unable to do anything but think. Guelfa wondered whether she had indeed been wounded and put her hand to her side, but found no sign of any wound. So they waited for the day, and when it was come they rose from the bed, and neither one nor the other spoke or said anything of what they had seen.

So now let us return to the matter which we were writing of before, that is, of the tournament and great celebration that was to take place at Le Puy-Sainte-Marie.

★

The Marquis, his wife and sister, arrived at the appointed place, and when their tents had been set up in a very pleasant spot, they found within the city lodgings befitting their rank. Guelfa was accompanied as always by the Abbess, to whom she opened her heart, and she begged her to try to see Curial or one of his servants and to find out where he had his tents. Curial was not there however, but had kept away so that he would not be recognised. The King had already dealt with the business pertaining to his kingdom; and all things which concerned the tranquil and peaceful state of all his dominions being set in due order and all the legal statutes proclaimed and confirmed with the public and common assent of all the great lords of the realm, the rest of the time was entirely given up to the celebration of feasts and festivity.

Monday was the day of the August feast of St Mary, and so on the Sunday before the eve of tournament celebrations took place. All the ladies mounted into the stands, and the Queen, seeing the incredible beauty of Guelfa, began to make much of her, not only for her sake and that of Curial but also to spite Lachesis, who was also present. The two ladies looked at each other, and although Guelfa, being a widow, was dressed in black, nevertheless such was her grace that the honesty of her black apparel seemed to increase her beauty. Lachesis looked her full in the face and did not take her eyes off her. All the knights and gentlemen were gazing at her, and the more they looked the more each of them longed to look, and to all it seemed that since the coming of Guelfa Lachesis had lost half her beauty.

Meanwhile in the field many lances were being broken on either side. The Queen kept Guelfa beside her and never tired of looking at her. The Duke of Orleans, who was a very notable knight, took the field with a good company and broke many lances and performed marvellous feats; and other dukes, princes, counts and great noblemen, in large numbers, broke many lances and did marvellous things.

Curial arrived, suitably but not richly accoutred, and because of this he was not recognised, for everyone knew that extremely precious trappings had been made for him and for his horses, and that he was the best-apparelled knight in the world. And, moreover, they thought that since Guelfa was present, he would want to show himself and make himself known, so that his coming was universally awaited with great longing. However, the Duke of Orleans, who was a valiant knight with many accomplished and valiant knights in his company, set his heart on lowering Curial's pride during this tourney.

While matters stood thus, a knight, well-mounted but not very richly apparelled, came into the field. He stretched out his hand and took hold of a pole which had been set in the ground before the Queen's stand, from which hung a jewel of gold with many pearls and diamonds, which had been offered as the prize to whomever fared best in the eve of tourney combat: and he said 'This time you will come with me'. The many people who were close by began to laugh, and they said to him 'Friend, you do not seem to deserve the prize for what you have done so far'. So setting spurs to his horse, and with a very strong and thick lance in his hand, he rode against a knight and unhorsed him, then another, whom he made leave the saddle, he met another and sent him to the ground, and thus he did to six knights while his own lance remained unharmed. And he went back to the post, and said 'I think that the jewel will still be mine this evening'.

When he heard what the knight had done, the Duke of Orleans came to that part of the field and rode against the knight and struck him in the middle of the shield, breaking his lance on it. But the other knight met him with such might that he sent him flying to the ground, while his own lance remained unbroken. 'Ah, St Mary,' said the King, 'who is this proud knight?' Lachesis fainted to see the Duke fall, and the knights who accompanied the Duke, wishing to avenge his shame, began to joust with the knight; but all, one by one, he treated as he had the Duke. And the knight returned to the post and said 'It seems to me that the jewel must be mine'. The Queen answered 'Yes, it will be, unless another takes it from you.'

Everyone was longing for the arrival of Curial, thinking that he would defend the jewel, but they awaited him in vain. They were as deceived as are the Jews who await the Messiah, who had him among them and still waited for him, as they hope for him still today. In many parts of the field many lances were broken, and there was much merriment. Guelfa was sure that the knight who was doing these things was Curial, although he did not wish to reveal himself. Then, when the hour for supper had come, the King put an end to the eve of tourney combat, giving the prize to the proud knight who, fixing his lance upright in the ground, hung it on that, crying the King's mercy to guard it for him.

Having commended the prize to the King, the knight turned and rode away; and many people said 'This is surely the haughtiest knight in the world'. Others, wondering, said he might be Curial. 'No,' everyone said, 'for Curial is the most gracious and courteous knight in the world, and this one is just the opposite; and Curial is so distinguished that he always comes with the greatest pomp in the world, and this one has come very poorly accoutred, so that this cannot be Curial.'

The King and the Queen supped separately in the stands, the King inviting many lords and great nobles, and among them the Marquis of Montferrat, and the Queen invited Guelfa and Andrea. While they supped, since nothing was talked of save the haughty knight, the King asked the Marquis if he had any news of Curial. The Marquis answered no, and that he did not think that Curial had come to the tournament, adding that he believed that if he were there he would not for the world conceal it from him. 'Ah God!' said the King, 'how I long to see him! I believe for certain there is no more valiant knight in the world, and all those who have come from Germany tell marvellous things of him.' 'I too can tell you some', said the Marquis, and he told him many things which the King had not yet heard; and the more the Marquis talked, the more the King longed to see Curial. 'Well,' said the King, 'either he is ill or he will be at the tourney tomorrow.'

After supper the Queen, who loved Curial dearly, called the Abbess to her, knowing that she was close to Guelfa and knew all about her and Curial, and she begged her, as she loved her life, to tell her the truth about a matter she wished to know. The Abbess

279

promised, and so the Queen said 'I beseech you to tell me whether it is possible to mend the break between Guelfa and Curial'. The Abbess said yes, on one condition: that the King and the Queen and all the court assembled there should beg her to forgive him; and she told her about the vow. 'It is done!' said the Queen. 'Whether Curial comes or no, the request will be made, whatever happens.' The Queen told the King, and the King said that certainly it should be done.

Not long after, a gentleman, all masked, came to the King and told him, so that no one in the world could hear, that Curial was near and wished to speak to him without being recognised by anyone. The King withdrew to a small chamber, and Curial entered and bowed humbly before him, the King laid his arms on his shoulders. Curial begged to commend to his protection the Marquis of Montferrat, his wife and his sister. The King answered that he was willing, for his sake, adding that he had invited him for the love he bore him, and that if he pleased he would do his best to arrange a marriage between him and Guelfa. 'Sire, I have asked what I wish from you', answered Curial. 'Concerning the rest I say nothing. Do as your majesty pleases.' 'Curial,' said the King, 'why did you not take away the jewel you won?' Curial laughed and said 'Who gave you to understand that I won it? Do not believe it, sire.' The King answered 'Do not hide yourself from me any longer, Curial. I beg that tomorrow you come to the tournament in your best array.' And Curial said that he would.

As soon as Curial had turned his back the King called for the Marquis and told him in great secret that he had seen Curial and that it was he who had won the prize and that the next day he would come to the tourney in fine array. 'That he can well do,' said the Marquis, 'better than any knight in the world.' Then the Marquis took his leave of the King, and with his wife and sister returned to their tents; and he told his sister that it was Curial who had won the prize and that the next day he would come in fine array. Guelfa did not make much comment on the news, but neither she nor the Abbess slept all that night but with great joy they stayed awake talking of Curial all night. Guelfa was wounded in her left side, in the middle of her heart, and had no pleasure or repose save in talking of Curial. So passed that night, which was the longest in the world.

★

The night had fled away, and the star that forces and compels men to love showed its shining face, sending its luminous rays to announce the coming of day. Guelfa, who could not sleep, rose from her bed and went distractedly around the tent. The Abbess, who knew what ailed her, laughed for joy, and rising also, began to prepare herself, so that before anyone else was about, no adornment remained to be put in its place. Guelfa's face was shining, and joy added to her beauty which seemed to increase wonderfully.

The dallying sun was approaching, and his chariot seemed not to move, for the lead horse, whose name is Titan, which draws it in the morning, to Guelfa's mind moved lazily and tardily. However, when day was come everyone arose very merrily, and all went to look at the lance from which hung the prize jewel. It was in the form of a harrow such as is put on fortified walls for fear of scaling-ladders.

Curial, aware that Guelfa was at the field and that she had never seen him in a tourney, dressed and armed himself with such magnificence that it would be much for the greatest king in the world; and when the hour of the tourney came, he rode happily to the field with thirty knights of his household, valiant and accomplished. Curial bore a shield all black with a hooded falcon painted in the centre, as he had done on other occasions, and he and his followers wore trappings of black and russet, with shields of the same colour, except Curial alone whose shield, as we have said, was all black. Curial's horse had a bell at his neck which as the horse moved could be heard a long way off; and six horses, accoutred in the same way, with six pages all well-dressed and richly arrayed, went before him, with six lances carried before him, so stout that no knight was ever strong enough to bear them in a tourney.

The stands were full, and infinite numbers of people were met at the appointed place, with the sounds of many trumpets, the cries of a multitude of people, some singing, others making a great noise with drums, and then the melodious sounds of minstrels, as that light of chivalry approached the stands. The people crowded round him in such numbers that they gave him no room to go close to the stands.

However, with much difficulty Curial made his reverence to the King, who was holding the Marquis by the hand, and then he approached the Queen, close by. Making a deep and humble bow to her, he gave a loud shout, and manoeuvred his horse a little, and cried out to the King, the Queen and all the other lords and ladies 'I beseech you to win pardon for me from a lady who says that she is ill-pleased with me, by crying loud to beg her for mercy.' So first the King began: 'Whoever she may be, I pray that for my sake she will pardon you.' The Queen repeated the words of the King, adding 'And if I am she of whom you speak, I pardon you.' Then the Queen turned to Guelfa and asked her to repeat what she had said. With some confusion and embarrassment, Guelfa repeated the

281

self-same words. Then you might see lords and ladies in great numbers, and in short the whole court, call out to the unknown lady on behalf of the knight 'Mercy! Mercy! Mercy!' So loud were the cries that one man could not hear another, and four kings-of-arms and many heralds clad in Curial's livery went among the whole assembly calling 'Mercy', and inviting and encouraging people to join in the shouting.

Everyone gazed at Curial, who had come in such magnificent pomp that nothing else was spoken of. Worldly glory went with him, and that day he had all she could offer. Fortune nailed her wheel, and against her nature was keeping steady and unmoved. Then Curial unfurled a black standard, still bearing a falcon, but now it was unhooded, and there were letters of gold on the streamers which read 'Rather envy than pity'; and with all his men he carried the standard to the corner of the field to the left of the King, and there he rested.

★

The field began to fill with people come to bear arms, and soon lances were being broken on all sides, and many lords, with many good followers, began the tourney. So Curial, taking one of his lances, went into the middle of the field, met a very renowned knight and unhorsed him, then another whom he also unhorsed, then another, and so he did to all who came against him; and there was no knight he met in an encounter who did not desert his horse. Everyone said 'This is the same knight as yesterday, the honours of the day will surely be his.'

The Duke of Orleans was very confident of his ability, and intending to avenge his fall of the previous day he sallied out against the knight, who was then fighting in front of the Queen, and he struck him boldly with great force, so that his lance flew into pieces. But never did he perform a deed which so soon had its reward, for the other knight sent him flying out of his saddle as far as his lance was long, and so mighty was the blow that he received that he had to be helped to rise. Lachesis was watching, and cursed the knight, but Guelfa, in her heart, returned the compliment. Lachesis thought she would die of anger, and was afire with rage. The Duke's knights rode against those of Curial, lances were broken on both sides and then they put hand to sword and a very hard fight began.

The Duke was taken up into the stands where, sitting between the Queen and Guelfa, he watched the marvels of the tourney. Lachesis continued to speak ill of the knight of the falcon – not of his skill as a knight, which could not be faulted, but of his pride and vainglory. The Duke told her to be silent, for there had been a time when she

had said quite the contrary, at which Guelfa laughed; and the Duke
went on to say that he did not think, in faith, that there was another
knight in the world as noble and as valiant and that, in faith, he did
not wish him ill even if he had unseated him twice in two days.
'What can I say?' said the Duke. 'There is no knight in all the tournament who can stay safely in his saddle unless this one wishes it.'

Curial came towards the stands, and the King saw him and said to
the Duke 'Here comes the courteous knight who helps all to dismount.' 'So God help me,' replied the Duke, 'I am very grateful to
him, for he has helped me twice in two days in such a way that it was
more like flying than dismounting, so lightly does he do it.' As they
were talking thus, Curial rode up to the pole which bore the prize,
on which there was a very rich crown of gold, and said 'I think that
you will be mine.' 'Yes indeed, I grant you,' said the Duke, 'and
God give me no honour if I try to take it from you.' Guelfa could not
hold back from speaking and said 'You do well, sir, to leave to him
what you could not take from him.' The Duke, with a great laugh,
replied 'I am generous to him, lady, with what is his own.' The King
laughed and they all laughed.

Curial thrust his lance, which was still unbroken, into the ground
beside the pole and took his sword into his hands and began to strike
blows with it so unrestrainedly that his actions seemed to be more
miraculous than something human. He struck shields from necks,
helmets from heads, and those who approached him with a sword
did not feel any security. The King crossed himself; everyone
marvelled. Then the Marquis, who could not take his eyes from the
knight, entreated the King to order the knight to leave the tourney,
because his presence lessened the sport.

So the King sent a king-of-arms to ask the knight to come to him,
and at once the knight, who was very obedient, came. The King had
him mount into the stands, and asked the Queen, Guelfa and
Lachesis to take his helmet from his head; and they did so. The Duke
saw that it was Curial, and embraced him in a very friendly way,
and all past injuries were forgiven in that moment. When Lachesis
saw him she wanted to move a little further away, but the Duke said
'Come, wife, I'll make you friends. Now kiss him, for my sake.'
And so Lachesis kissed him, and the Queen made all the noble
maidens in her household kiss him. The tourney was seething no
less than fire, everywhere you might see lances, swords, staves
striking such a storm of blows that you would not have heard
thunder had there been any. Certainly Jupiter and Juno never sent
such noises to the earth. Any knight who had strength in his arms
had an opportunity to prove it then, I can tell you.

★

When Curial had taken off his armour and put on the King's best robe, he sat among the ladies, who would not allow any man in the world to come near him. Meanwhile the King took the Marquis aside, and with a great array of words besought him to give Guelfa to Curial as his wife; and the Marquis answered that there was nothing in the world he would so much like to do. Then the King and Queen, calling Guelfa and the Marquis and the Abbess aside, told Guelfa of the proposed marriage. Guelfa was silent, and for bashfulness did not and could not reply, so the Abbess broke the silence and said to the King 'Sire, what are you waiting for? I say yes for her and answer that it pleases her.' The Marquis said 'Sister, I beg you, I pray you, to do as the King commands.' Then Guelfa answered the King, not without a trembling voice and a face heavy with bashfulness, 'Not for any desire that I have for a husband, as I have never thought of marriage, but because I have no voice to oppose anything that your most high majesty commands, do with me whatever your pleasure is.' Well content, the King and Queen sent for the Archbishop of Rheims, who was the King's cousin, and Curial and Guelfa each mounted a palfrey and were led to the centre of the assembly; and amid general rejoicing the King had them betrothed.

Loud was the cheering; and then the knights resumed the tourney. Then Curial and Guelfa returned to the stands and there Guelfa, retiring to a private place, was marvellously attired and adorned with so many and such precious jewels that everyone was amazed. The beauty of the lady outshone all who were present. Ah, how Lachesis thought she would die of three envies – of her husband, of her beauty and of the attention paid to her! Look at her – her colour came and went a thousand times, and although she strove hard to conceal it, she said to herself 'Blessed art thou among women'.

The King ordered that the tournament should end that day, and so it happened. Oh magnanimous and magnificent King! Oh excellent and valorous heart! The King did not forget the singularity of his liberality: he took the herse jewel and the crown which were the prizes, and gave them to Guelfa: and to Curial he gave the principality of Orange.

And so he who was a knight born to a poor family, favoured by Fortune after infinite misfortunes, through his virtues, which never failed him, and also through love, who is a far more powerful goddess than Fortune and who never left him or deserted him but continually sustained him, striving against Fortune and the Misfortunes and overcoming them, in spite of the secret assaults of wicked and persistent Envy, was rewarded in such a way that this valiant and virtuous knight, by his own merits, won in a single day a wife and a principality. As the day was already declining and the sun, threatened by the darkness already preparing to come, hurried on his horses – three of which, that is Titan, Aethon and Lampos, were tired and had been unharnessed, and drawn only by Philogeus, having left behind more than three quarters of the day – with greater speed than can be told was speeding towards the realm of Hesperia, that excellent and most high King, accompanied by many nobles, taking Guelfa's reins, entered the city. Guelfa rode between the King and the Queen and Curial amidst dukes and great lords, with a mighty noise of trumpets and minstrels, the shouting and singing of many knights and gentlemen who, full of merriment, increased the pleasure and the celebration; and so they entered the city of Our Lady.

When they had been fittingly lodged, the King took supper; and seated at his table were only the Queen, Curial and Guelfa. At the other tables were dukes and duchesses, counts, nobles and other notable people. They were all served by great lords, so that the feast was a great one in many ways, and he who was best able to make merry added most to the rejoicing. You might see knights and gentlemen, many of them with black eyes, others with their arms in slings and bandages because of the knocks they had taken in the tourney, but they did not refrain from laughing and singing and dancing. Many were the dishes in that supper, and precious wines in great abundance, so that everyone was splendidly served.

And he who longed to see festivities must have been well employed in this one, for in living memory no one had seen so great a celebration, and all were certain that the King had held and solemnised that royal court solely to achieve this marriage.

A great part of the night had passed in this way before the King gave leave to everyone to return to their lodging. The Duke of Orleans took Guelfa's reins and so accompanied her to her lodging, with all the dukes and lords, and each one taking a friendly farewell went to his own place. The Marquis and Andrea, Curial and Guelfa, remained in their lodging and full of inestimable joy were hardly able to go to sleep; but after a long while, as the night was already departing, they went to bed, compelled by drowsiness.

But who slept? For sure, neither the Marquis nor his wife slept, nor was the night long enough for them to put an end to talking. Guelfa and the Abbess remained awake and hardly knew what to do with themselves for happiness. They recalled the skills and great deeds of Curial, and Guelfa, who had been almost mute until that day, now certainly recovered her voice and said such acute and subtle things of him that few minds could comprehend them, for

285

even if until that day the gates of her mouth had been tight shut, she had kept open those of her ears and of her understanding.

Nor did Curial sleep, for he was as if enchanted, thinking how he had obtained his desire with honour, and he spent all the night talking with Sir Galceran de Mediona. And not only these but an infinite number of others also who for weariness had more need to sleep than to wake, passed that night thinking or talking.

★

The King, who was a very far-seeing lord, appointed a day for the wedding, and wished there to be no more tourneying in that place. By stages, with all the other people, he came to his chief city, and allotted worthy and notable lodgings to the Marquis, his wife and his sister. Curial entered with splendour his own dwelling, which he had not lost in spite of the persecution of Fortune.

Many were the banquets, great the celebrations in Paris for that wedding. Every man and woman did their best to dress as well as they could, but Guelfa, who had her own jewels and those of Curial, far surpassed all the other ladies. Everyone gazed at her and admired her, and admired her many precious jewels, such that no lapidary in all the world would presume to give them a price. Curial was happy, everyone made much of him both by merit of his skill in chivalry and the other gifts of grace that our Lord God had copiously bestowed on him, and because they saw that he was a great lord and very rich. Fortune appeared to him among all those people, and smiled on him and made much of him, so that nothing was spoken of save him and Guelfa. Everyone said that Lachesis was of no account. The Duke, who was constantly with Curial, said 'You have stolen my wife, Curial, for not many days ago I had the most beautiful wife in the world, and now I see that you have her! But I swear that no one in the world should envy you, for if you have her, you have her truly and you have deserved her by many years of service and have bought her at a great price.' Many were the jesting words that were said on this side and on that, and everyone was talking of Curial and Guelfa so that gradually their whole story and glorious deeds became well known by all and were spread by many people in all directions.

Curial gave his damsel Festa as wife to Sir Galceran de Mediona and shared with him what he had, freely and liberally. After many days, very happy and rich, Galceran returned to Catalonia with his wife, with whom he was not a little pleased.

The King, who did not sleep all night long, had a great feast prepared and invited an infinite number of people to Curial's wedding, honouring him on a single day as bridegroom and as prince. Great were the banquets and feasts, the dancing and jousting, and in short the King omitted nothing that pertains to such a celebration. I shall not trouble to describe the dishes, the wines, the jousting or the dancing, for I have said enough about them in these books and I shall omit them for brevity's sake. Nor shall I describe the desire of the bridegroom and bride to go to bed. Those who wish to know should read Master Guido delle Colonne where he treats of the sleep of Jason and Medea, even if the comparison is unequal because that was the matter of a moment and this had been longed for for many years. But because Master Guido worked hard at such descriptions I recommend him to you.

The celebrations came to an end, as do all things. Everyone finally tired of long and heavy expenditure. So the Prince and the Princess, the Marquis and his wife and all the rest, taking their leave of the King and Queen and receiving precious gifts from them, returned happy and rejoicing to their lands. And weary old Melchior, when he saw the Prince, embraced him with tears of joy saying: 'Now lettest thou thy servant depart in peace, Lord, according to thy word.'

The end, thanks be to God.